between us

AMADA BEACH BOOK TWO

ASHTYN KIANA

to anyone who needs the reminder:

be gentle with yourself.
especially on the days when getting out of bed feels like lifting
a thousand-pound weight off your chest.

and to my best boy, Hurmen

I went to the shelter thinking I was saving you,
but it was the other way around.
I'll miss you forever.

Author's Note

Between Us is set approximately seven and a half years before *Always Been Yours*. As these are interconnected standalone novels, it is your choice where you'd like to start in the series. Going forward, the rest of the books will follow the same timeline as *Always Been Yours*.

My intentions are for this story to be one about healing, love, and finding our home. However, I understand some of the topics throughout the novel may be hard for some readers.

Content disclosures for *Between Us*:

- Multiple explicit open-door scenes between the main characters. These contain on-page sexual content in graphic detail. Turn the page to find out which chapters to be aware of.

- Multiple mentions of bullying during secondary school. There are in-depth conversations regarding what the FMC has faced, and the bullies are seen on page.

- Mental health, therapy, and medication are big parts of the story and the FMC's journey. However, these topics also touch on the veterinary field, and the specific struggles that are faced in the career.

Dicktionary

Please use the guide below to modify your reading experience at your discretion. Your mental health and comfortability are always the most important things while reading.

$$\mathscr{ÍÍÍ}$$

Blake & Adrian's Playlist

Everything Has Changed (feat. Ed Sheeran) (Taylor's Version) by Taylor Swift
Swing of Things (feat. Powfu) by MAY-A
Ribs by Lorde
Tiny Moves by Bleachers
Scared to Start by Michael Marcagi
ceilings by Lizzy Alpine
Feels Like by Gracie Abrams
CVS by Winnetka Bowling League
Can I Call You Tonight? by Dayglow
I'm in Love by Jelanie Aryeh
Hunting Season by Chelsea Cutler
I Hate It Here by Taylor Swift
Wish on an Eyelash by Mallrat
Slow Down (feat. H.E.R.) by Skip Marley
Lucky by Choker
Ultraviolet by Aidan Bissett
you! by LANY
Eighteen by beabadoobee
Stay by Rihanna, Mikky Ekko
Kissing In Swimming Pools by Holly Humberstone
sweet nothing by Taylor Swift
Skin by Rihanna
THAT'S MY GIRL by Frank Sativa
The Way You Love Me by Chelsea Cutler
Soul Mate by flora cash

Prologue

Blake

Two weeks ago...

Tilting my head, I stop in front of the new painting my therapist Catalina hung up in her office. Truthfully, I don't really understand abstract art but this...

Quickly twirling around to face her, I blurt out, "This looks like a..." I trail off, suddenly embarrassed.

I'm partly horrified but mostly not surprised. I've only been seeing Catalina for about four months, and she's different from the other three therapists my mom sent me to first. And from anything I would've expected a therapist to be like.

First, there was the one who seemed promising but started to insist that if I just dressed more 'feminine' and 'wore my hair down more,' that would *surely* fix all my problems. Like trying to 'fit in' never occurred to me in the years I was bullied.

Next, there was the old man who was strict and boring, but his biggest flaw was being a goddamn Los Angeles Outlaws fan. It doesn't matter that my brother might never it to the MLB after tearing his ACL and got his on-again-off-again girlfriend pregnant. I could never, and would *never*, be an Outlaws sympathizer to any degree—unless my brother had been drafted by them in another universe. But he wasn't, and I know he agrees.

And lastly, there was the sexist man who not only insulted my mother by blaming her for the years of bullying I faced, but also forced me to sit on his couch as still as possible—sometimes even with my hands under my legs—because "fidgeting is an *ugly* habit."

Obviously, none of those worked out. It's taken us about eight months to find a therapist who I'm happy with. And really, I *love* Catalina. She's about forty-five, if I had to guess. She's beautiful in a comforting way rather than intimidating. Her warm brown skin complements her dark chestnut hair, but it's her bright, inquisitive green eyes that are the most noticeable. They have this way of looking past your skin and bones to see deep into your soul. Not in a judgmental way, but to better understand you, your life, and your emotions.

The fact she's fluent in Spanish is a plus. It wouldn't be a deal-breaker, as I speak in English more often than not, but it just adds an extra layer of comfort, I guess.

More than anything, Catalina's warmth reminds me of my mom. And that's probably the main reason I feel so safe in this small office with her. Just like my mother, Catalina is quick to laugh and easy to joke with.

Her head tips back at my observation, letting a contradictory wicked laugh out. She sounds like a Disney villain even if it couldn't be further from the truth.

"Like what, Blake?" She doesn't comment on me wandering around her office. Catalina's never minded my restlessness and fidgeting. I'm well aware it's not appropriate in every situation—and we're working on other coping mechanisms—but it's nice to not feel judged by my habits here.

Making my way to the seat across from her leather armchair, I glance back at the large pink painting. There are four different shades layered together with lines curving and overlapping at different points.

"A vagina," I finally say, turning back to look at her. "You bought a *vagina* painting. For your office."

Catalina breaks out into a cackle. "It's not a vagina."

I just stare at her, waiting for her to go on. "It's a... blooming flower."

"You're horrible." I shake my head, both amused and embarrassed on her behalf. "Does your wife agree?"

The wedding ring was a dead giveaway from our first session, but it wasn't until her wife was walking out after lunch, and I was walking into Catalina's office, that we saw each other.

In their defense, I was a few minutes early. Catalina was clearly horrified that her personal and professional life were unintentionally mixing, but it got worse when she realized her wife, Lara Henderson, was my sophomore chemistry teacher. She's about ten years younger than Catalina, and they both kept their maiden names for professional reasons. I never would've guessed otherwise.

Lucky for all of us, I happened to love Ms. Henderson. It could've resulted in me needing to find another therapist, but I already really liked Catalina. So, I stayed, and I'm glad I did.

She points her finger at me. "We don't talk about her."

I roll my eyes. "Well then, what would you like to talk about?"

"Oh, I *don't know*," she sarcastically draws out the words. "How about you? The reason insurance is paying my bills?"

I can't help but laugh and shake my head as I plop down in the large egg chair. Catalina has the typical couch you'd expect in a therapist's office, but there's also this option and a variety of anxiety blankets she keeps stored for clients.

"I made *one* shitty comment—very early into our sessions, I'd like to add—and you'll never let it go."

It's true. During what was probably my second time seeing Catalina, I made a comment about how she doesn't *really* care. She's only here for the check my insurance sends her every month.

Rationally, I know that's not true—I even knew it back then. But I have a very small circle of people who are close to me. My parents, my mom's best friend, my brother, and my only two friends from high school. It's kind of a pathetic list, if I'm honest with myself. So, it's hard for me to believe someone would *want* to be here.

"It's good to keep you and that mouth in line sometimes," she teases.

She's not wrong. After years of feeling helpless and some days terrified to go to school, I started to act out more in situations where I felt safe. Lately, I have more of a handle on my emotions thanks to Catalina and the Lexapro prescription I got a couple weeks ago.

I'm sure it wasn't the *only* mean thing I've said to Catalina in our short time together, but it's the only one she chooses to pick on me for. Probably because it was a pretty mild snub.

"I'm spending the weekend with Margo and Meera. It's probably the last time I'll see them before they both leave in a week."

The three of us look like an unlikely group to say the least. Margo is tall, perfectly blonde, a total goth babe, and hopelessly in love with our best friend's oldest brother.

Said best friend, Meera, is petite with a deep golden complexion and dark brown hair, a musical genius, and the heart of a romantic, but the attention span of a rubber band.

I'm the athlete between us with an average height and, according to Margo, "the one with the best tits between the three of us, even if I refuse to show them off." And as far as their viewpoints on love go, I fall somewhere in the middle.

They've been a surprising duo since elementary school, and despite growing up in the private school system, were almost as much of social pariahs as I was.

The only reason I made it as long as I did at Serenity Prep Academy was because they took me under their wings and have loved me fiercely ever since. Even if I sometimes still feel like the odd man out.

"How are you feeling about them leaving?" Catalina probes.

Thinking it over, I pull one of the pillows onto my lap and pick at a loose thread. "I mean, I'm happy for them... of course, I'm so happy for them." Margo has wanted to join a fashion program for as long as I've known her, and every time she mentions Parsons School of Design there are stars in her eyes. Then there's Meera, who has worked her ass off her entire life and was accepted to fucking *Juilliard* on a full scholarship. In a few years, Margo and I'll be watching her perform in one of New York's top orchestras at this rate.

"You can be happy for them *and* miss them, Blake."

"I know." I nod, trying to convince myself. "They're my safety blanket, you know?"

"They are, and they've been a very loyal, supportive one at that. But you need to live your own life too."

Blinking back tears, I quietly admit, "I don't know how... They're doing such amazing things—together no less—and it's hard not to feel like I'm being left behind. Again."

Before I started at SPA, I already struggled with things like fitting in and feeling misunderstood. More so from being younger than my brother and our family friends. But sometimes the festering wound opens again.

She leans forward, waiting until I finally make eye contact with her. "You're so young, Blake. You're *eighteen.* You have no idea the amount of life you still have ahead of you. There's a passion out there for you, and it'll be just as fulfilling as Margo's and Meera's."

I take a deep breath, trying to let her words seep into my bones and soul, hoping I'll believe it one day too.

The rest of our session goes by quickly. We talk more about how I can prepare myself to say bye to my friends soon, and Catalina reminds me it's only until fall break.

By the time I'm walking back to my car, I feel better. Even if that never-ending hold on my heart is still present, I've learned to live with the little figurative storm cloud always hanging over me.

As I'm settling into my old black Jetta, I roll the windows down and pull my phone out of my small bag. A few texts are waiting for me in our group chat, *Island of Misfit Toys*. Margo named it, of course.

Wed, July 23 at 2:02 PM

Margo

> Blakeee babe

> Are you done yet? I need every second of your time possible

Meera

> You know she has therapy today

> Take your time. We'll meet you as soon as you're ready

Margo

> It's been an hour. She has to be done soon

Meera

> Omg go fix your eyeliner or something

I can't help but snort at Meera's response. We've had to wait on Margo's make-up more than a few times, especially when we were younger, and she was first learning how to apply it properly.

Margo

> It's already dark, sharp and perfect. Thx for your concern though!

Before they really start bickering, I type out my reply.

> I just finished

> Are we meeting at my house or the store?

Margo

> Your house

Meera

> K I'm grabbing my bag and keys now!

Closing my messages and pulling up my music app, a small flash of color catches my attention. When I look up, a smile immediately tugs at my lips.

I'm not surprised when I find a monarch butterfly on my dashboard. Maybe most people would be, but for as long as I can remember, butterflies—especially monarchs—have kind of been my thing.

My mom once told me that my late abuelo viewed monarchs as a sign of better days when he immigrated to the United States in his late teens. I never had a chance to meet him, but I like to believe they are his way of reaching out to me, wherever he is now.

And at this moment? It feels like he's smiling down on me, maybe trying to help convince me there's some truth to Catalina's words.

There's so much life to live.

Adrian

Later that evening...

"Can you stop, crazy lady?" I playfully swat my mom's hand away. Most adults would have a little more decorum in a grocery store but not her.

If anything, it motivates her further. She pretends to lick her thumb, then reaches up to rub off a smudge that's definitely not there. When she still doesn't stop, I place a hand on her forehead and push her away. She's only five-foot-two, and I take after my dad, meeting his height of six-foot-two, plus a couple of extra inches. So, this is my go-to move when she's being a little maternal pest.

She's become a helicopter parent for the first time in my life over the last two months. It's all in good fun, and I know she was soaking in the time we had together before I moved out again.

But *this*? Her only goal is to embarrass me because she's bored of waiting on my father. It's not an easy feat though.

We're both laughing—her almost hysterically. Even though I call her a crazy lady, we both probably look pretty maniacal right now. Especially considering my dad is sto-ically standing next to us, focused on his phone as he scrolls through another list of "Food All Young Adults Should Have in Their First Apartment." It doesn't even matter that this isn't technically my first apartment. But since it isn't on a university campus like my last one and I don't have any roommates now, they're treating it like a bigger deal than it is.

We got to Amada Beach yesterday so they could help me move into my studio apartment before my classes start in a few weeks. It's a small space so we're almost done, but my dad insisted on getting groceries for me before they leave tomorrow afternoon. I insisted I could shop for myself but he wasn't having it.

I'm not going to rain on their parade, especially when they're being gracious enough to help me pay rent while I'm in my Doctor of Veterinary Medicine program. It's another thing they insist on.

Truthfully, my mom can use her spit to wipe off any smudge, and my dad can scour the internet for every list ever made about the matter. I'm more grateful to them than they'll ever know.

As successful nurses, my parents have a better understanding than most about how important these next four years are for me.

San Diego *never* would've been my first choice. I don't care much for the beach, and I had enough of it while going to college in Florida. When I hypothetically think about my future, I've never been sure of where I'd like to end up, but I've always imagined more of an urban city vibe—like Chicago or San Francisco.

Growing up, we moved often for my parents' jobs as travel nurses, so I've been to more than half the states and never would've guessed I'd end up in Southern California.

Nothing is keeping me in Amada Beach forever but for the next few years, I'm stuck here.

At least the University of California, Aurora Hills has one of the best D.V.M. programs in the country.

As my mom and I settle down to listen to my dad while he turns down an aisle, a body slams into me from the side.

"Oof," I grunt at the same time a soft, raspy voice lets out a low, "Oh *fuck*," as her phone drops between my feet.

Grabbing her slender arm, I help balance her as she almost tips over trying to step back. It takes her a second to gather her bearings again.

I watch as she looks down at her feet.

As some of her black hair falls into her face despite the bun it's tied up into—even noticing the bright pink scrunchie holding it up.

Then as she looks over her shoulder, searching for whoever she must have come to the store with.

And *finally*, I watch as her head tips back toward me and her striking gray eyes meet my dark brown ones.

Her mouth slightly pops open as she processes her surroundings. "I'm sorry," she apologizes quickly, gently shaking my hand off her arm.

I let it fall to my side, almost in a trance as I blatantly stare at one of the prettiest women I've ever seen.

My smile slowly slides across my face as I quickly bend down to grab her phone. "No reason to be sorry. I wasn't paying attention either."

She nods her head, biting the inside of her cheek. Instead of saying anything, she takes her phone back and eyes me with open curiosity. Just as I'm about to offer my hand and introduce myself, my dad's deep voice calls from down the aisle.

"Adrian, hurry up. We need to find the cornmeal."

What the fuck?

I quickly turn around to find my mom watching me with a small, curious smile. My dad is looking down at his phone, engrossed in whatever reason I'd ever need fucking cornmeal, seemingly oblivious to the girl I almost body-slammed in the aisle.

But as I move back to face the beautiful stranger, she's already slipping away.

Slowly walking backwards, she watches the interaction between my parents and me. She doesn't say anything, nor does she stop when my attention is back on her. The tug on her lips is small and shy, but it's also kind of teasing—like she *knows* I'll be thinking about this moment for days.

That's when I notice the two girls waiting for her by the entrance. The petite one with long dark hair looks like the cat that caught the canary, and the tall blonde is watching with apt attention.

When the stranger is halfway between me and her friends, she turns on her heels and jogs toward them. I wait, hoping she'll glance back and give me one last look at her silver eyes.

But she doesn't. When she gets to her friends, she loops her arm through the blonde's and pulls her out of the building, with their other friend bouncing on her heels behind them.

A few seconds later, my mom walks up to me and bumps me with her hip. "Cute girl," she says, tipping her chin toward the exit with a knowing smirk.

"You could say that," I mutter, turning toward her.

She watches me in that assessing way only a mother can pull off. "That smile is going to get you in trouble one day."

I scoff and drop my arm around her shoulder. "You couldn't even see my face."

"I'm your mom—I don't need to be able to see your face to know when you pull out that no good grin of yours."

A laugh tips my head back. "Eyes in the back of your head *and* x-ray vision? Do all moms have that, or are you extra special?"

"Both," she retorts. With a pat to my upper back, she adds, "It's a small community, you know."

Yeah, I know... hopefully small enough that I run into the girl with lightning eyes again soon.

Chapter One

Adrian

The door to my apartment slams behind me at the same time I roll my eyes. My mom can't see me since we're on the phone, but the lack of traveling right now is making her lose her sanity.

She's going on about the silent feud her and the neighbors are having. Apparently, they changed their flowerpots the same day she and Dad did.

God forbid.

I know some people have horrible neighbors, and we definitely have had some bad ones throughout the years as we moved around for their jobs. But Mr. and Mrs. Lewis are among some of the best people we've lived next to.

Even if they tend to have a habit of subconsciously seeing it as a competition for the best kept yard. They're like eighty years old, retired, and bored as hell. Plus, Mrs. Lewis makes the best peanut brittle for Christmas.

And from the long, dramatic sigh my mom takes at the end of her rant, we both know she's just restless. This always happens when they've been in one place for too long. My dad has moved into the educational field now, but they've always loved travel nursing more than anything. Especially Mom.

I grew up moving around a lot, until high school. But even when we were at our house in Bakersfield, Mom would do flight nursing. She's always said she likes not getting too comfortable in one job—being thrown into a new environment and having to adapt to someone else's routine. It's thrilling to her.

Whereas I think Dad enjoyed the different learning opportunities and new facilities more than the adventure part of it.

I grew up seeing my parents as basically the closest thing to real-life superheroes, and I had a happy childhood. The *happiest*. But I've known since I was younger that when I grew up, I'd want the stability they never craved.

The three of us know the only reason they've stayed in California for the last few months is because I graduated with my bachelor's degree in May and they wanted to be with me when I moved here, to Amada Beach.

Which is exactly why I suggest, "Why don't you take an assignment for the rest of the year somewhere? I know you're itching to do something other than flight nursing right now." I shrug, even though she can't see it. "Plus, there are still a few states you haven't been to yet."

"Only nine," she mindlessly comments. But I can tell she's thinking about it. "Are you *sure* you'd be okay with that?"

That makes me pause and I fall down onto my couch. "Yeah, of course I'm sure, Mom. Why aren't you?"

She's quiet for a second before she finally admits what's been on her mind. "I've just been feeling guilty. This time you aren't across the country, but only a few hours from us. And before, my assignments were more than likely closer to you."

"So?" I probe, feigning confusion.

I'd never tell my mom this, especially now, but I was sad as fuck when they left. It does feel weirdly different this time than when I moved out for undergrad. There's this unspoken understanding that I'll probably never live in my parents' house again.

"You're out there in San Diego alone. And I want to make sure we're here if you need anything."

"Mom," I draw out, appreciating her concern, even if it isn't necessary. "This is a huge part of who you are—and one that's inspired who I am today. I've never wanted you to stop on my account."

"I know," she quickly confirms.

"I'm even closer to Grammy and Pop now, so I'll be with them as often as I can. And a three-hour plane ride is just as easy, if not easier, for me than a car ride."

She doesn't say anything for a long moment, and her resolve starting to crack.

Good.

"Maria will still be here if there is an emergency..." she reminds me, but it's for herself. My godmother, Maria, is my mom's oldest friend, practically family since their dads were also best friends. She's always treated me as more than her godson, and I've had my own room at her house since I was twelve.

"True," I agree, hoping to further encourage her. "Plus, if I get this job, I won't have a lot of time off between that and my courses. So *please*, do what you and Dad want, and don't worry about me."

"We'll always worry about you," Mom chastises affectionately.

"You know what I mean." Rolling my eyes, I kick off my shoes and grab the protein shake from the gym bag at my feet.

After a quiet moment she finally says, "I'll talk to your dad, but let's talk about this interview! It's a big step, Bub."

Nodding to myself I take another drink, buying time to figure out how I'm feeling. "I feel good about it. If it's meant to happen, then it will."

It's kind of cliché, sure, but it's been my motto throughout life, and it hasn't proven me wrong yet.

This interview feels different. I saw the veterinary assistant job posting the night before I moved to Amada Beach. I stayed up later than I planned, revising my resume and adding my new degree. Dr. Timothy Miller, the owner and lead veterinarian of the animal hospital, called me about thirty minutes after my parents left my new apartment.

Dr. Miller's call was a pleasant surprise and gave me something to look forward to. When he said he wanted to be transparent ahead of time about the hours he was expecting and the hourly pay, it was better than anything I expected.

"Good, you're going to do great. But just remember, your dad and I don't mind helping cover what the loans and grants don't. So *if* it doesn't work out—but it definitely will—don't pressure yourself to find another job."

"Thanks, Mom." She's not quiet about the fact she'd rather I didn't work while finishing my education. She understands having to balance work, school, and life. I know my parents have worked hard to make sure I don't have to worry about that. It's a conversation we've had multiple times, yet I can't put into words how grateful I am. Not that they've let me when I've tried.

But I *want* this job. It sounds like an amazing learning experience. Amada Beach Animal Clinic is a small hospital but it's highly respected, working with many of the facilities, zoos and sanctuaries in the area. Plus, it'd be nice to get out of my apartment for more than just the gym and when classes start next week.

"Call us first thing tomorrow to tell us how it goes?" Her voice is hopeful, as if I'd deny her such simple motherly pleasure.

"Will do. My first class is at eight a.m. tomorrow, though, so it will be *first* thing."

"Doesn't matter what time—we wanna hear all about it."

I smile as I stand and promise again to call. We say our goodbyes before I take a shower, collecting my thoughts and practicing the interview questions I read online again.

But as I'm walking to my car, I notice the dark clouds rolling in from the west. My lips tug up, feeling a little more confident than I was a few minutes ago.

Maybe most people would consider storms a bad omen, but not me. I've always found comfort in the chaos of thunderstorms, especially loving the refreshing feeling that lingers in its wake.

To me, this feels like the universe is giving me a pat on the back as I put my car in gear and pull out of the parking lot.

Fighting the urge to bounce my leg, I run my hands down my thighs. *Again.*

I'm pretty sure Dr. Miller can't see the fidgeting from his side of the desk. Or he's choosing to ignore it. Which is good, considering fidgeting isn't the best nervous habit for someone who wants to perform surgery as a career.

The interview seems to be going well, and the more he talks, the more I want this job.

He's willing to work with my school schedule since he's planning to hire more than one person for the position. On top of that, even though he's not a teaching facility, he's willing to mentor me during the time I'm working here, and he works closely with the Aurora Hills Animal Hospital—one of the most respected teaching facilities in California.

One of the veterinary surgeons who works with Dr. Miller specializes in exotic animals, partners with the San Diego

Zoo, as well as the big cat and exotic animal sanctuary nearby. Not to mention another doctor who specializes in equine health, or the number of aquatic animals the facility comes into contact with.

I'm still figuring out what my path in this career will be, but there's something about *this* place that feels promising. Like it has the potential to make whatever that decision is a reality.

"I can't promise anything," Dr. Miller starts, breaking the short silence. "I have a few other interviews to go through, but this feels like it could be a great match. Just a couple more questions—though I should warn you, they might be a bit more personal."

My eyebrows furrow but I give a slight shrug. "Go ahead and ask, sir."

He tilts his head back and forth, seeming to think over his words. "How would you describe your relationship with your mental health?"

Some of the new tension starts to dissolve as I piece together where this is going. "I've been lucky to never go through a hard time in that way. But that doesn't mean I underestimate how important it is."

He offers me a small smile, seeming to accept my answer, but is unsure. "I assume by this point, you've heard your instructors talk about it a time or two. So, I won't nag you, but I do like to get an idea of where someone's headspace is, especially when they're taking on a job in this field while still going to school."

As a vet student, I've learned about the mental health statistics in almost every course I've ever taken.

Initially, when I was just eighteen years old and taking my first introduction into animal sciences course, I fig-ured it would be similar to what I've seen my parents go through in their careers as nurses. It's a high stress job that often breeds compassion fatigue and burnout.

And that's true about being in the veterinary field as well. But according to the studies, all of that mixed with consistently having to perform euthanasia and the different types of expectations on veterinarians from the clients, results in one of the highest rates of suicide for a profession.

Working in the field before you've even gotten your license can cause burnout early on, even though it's great on a resume and offers hands-on experience.

"I understand. It's a huge reason why I'm thankful you're offering me three shifts a week—if I do get the job," I add with a wry smile. "But I hear you and your concerns, and regardless I know it's time to start thinking about that aspect of the career."

That seems to appease him. He nods and adds, "With this not being a teaching hospital, there are some limitations in what I can offer. However, for someone at your level and applying for a veterinary assistant position, there shouldn't be any hindrances. Aurora Hill's facility is fantastic, but it's much bigger. Eventually, that's what you'll need. Obviously I can't offer you a residency even if I wanted to—but right now, there's a lot more hands-on training, as well as one-on-one mentorship opportunities, than what you would find anywhere else."

It sounds like he's trying to sell *me* on the job, rather than the other way around.

"I'm not necessarily *looking* for jobs, sir. I happened to come across your posting and it sounded like a dream come true. Any extra experience and knowledge I can gain, I'll happily take."

He gives me an assessing look. It reminds me of the way my dad looks at me when we're talking about the big decisions in life. Like he sees something that I haven't quite figured out just yet.

"You're *choosing* to work while you go to school? May I ask why?" His tone is neutral but there's still that weirdly paternal expression on his face.

That's the first question I am slightly unprepared for. Not even my parents asked me that. Maybe they didn't have to—they just knew.

I pause, thinking it over for a second—trying to find the right words to articulate why I'd choose to add more responsibilities onto my hectic course load.

"There are a few reasons, actually. Like I said, this seems like too great of an opportunity to turn down. I'm new to town. And to be completely transparent, even through study groups and coursework, making friends in a strenuous program like animal medicine can be hard." Sitting up a little straighter, I add, "And my parents have never shied away from hard work and what it took for them to get to their positions as highly respected nurses across the country."

"Is that so?" It comes out curious, no sense of a double meaning.

"Yes, sir." I nod. "My dad went to nursing school while on a football scholarship at UCLA. My mom worked two jobs to put herself through school. They've worked hard to make sure I don't *have* to do that, but I want to. I'm excited to start my career and my priorities have shifted, even in the three months since I graduated with my bachelor's degree. I don't see why I should wait to start my career in this field."

Dr. Miller chuckles easily. "Fair enough. And as long as you can find a healthy balance, I completely agree."

After a few more minutes and questions—some routine, some more personal like how I'm adjusting to Amada Beach—Dr. Miller stands from his side of the desk. So, I follow suit.

"It was great to meet you, Adrian." He reaches across the table and shakes my hand.

Firmly, I return the gesture and tell him, "You as well, Dr. Miller. Hopefully, I'll talk to you soon."

With a warm smile, he nods once. "Good luck in your classes."

Accepting his dismissal, I walk out of his office and to the front doors. When I see the storm clouds have cracked open, letting a heavy rain pour down, I smile to myself.

Chapter Two

Blake

Leaning back in the chair with a furrowed brow, I try focusing on my knitting project in front of me. Technically, I should be focusing on my actual job—a receptionist at my dad's vet clinic.

Really, it's an animal hospital by this point. But when we moved to Amada Beach, it started as a much smaller facility and has grown exponentially over a decade and a half.

One of the perks of working for a parent is, he doesn't usually mind when I bring in things like this. Having something to focus on helps my anxiety stay at bay, so these quiet days can be hard if I don't have tasks or a form of distraction.

The only good piece of advice I got from one of my former therapists was finding hobbies that will help with restlessness and overthinking. It was my mom's suggestion to try crocheting. I picked up sewing in school quickly and she had learned from her mom, so she was able to teach me.

I have now surpassed her skills and there are more blankets, and other random items, than anyone knows what to do with.

With my brother's first child being born in about four months, I've been focusing my crafts on her. I've finished a baby blanket and a variety of peluches. So far, she has plushies of a dog, a cat, a rabbit and a cow.

For the last few days, I've been working on a onesie design I found on Pinterest. It's my first time knitting. Everything online said it's easier than crocheting, but I'm not picking it up nearly as quickly as I hoped.

And maybe I would if I hadn't chosen a pattern that switches colors and designs repeatedly. But it is freaking cute.

I'm determined by this point though, and I'm almost done with the back piece.

My goal was to finish the little leg sections by the end of the day, but I've gotten to the point where I have to be honest with myself—it's not happening.

Feeling frustrated, I pull on the yarn harder than necessary to undo the small mistake I just made. It's not only that, though. One of the worst parts of having anxiety is how little it makes sense.

Ever since I had to say bye to my friends before they jetted off to New York City together for college, I've felt *off*.

Like I've lost my security blanket, just as Catalina suspected.

From the moment I woke up today, the reality of my situation has weighed me down with insecurities and overthinking.

I have faith in my friendships, and I'm so excited for both of them. These are the goals they've had as long as I've known them, and I've learned to be inspired by them rather than envious.

Selfishly, I wish they could've stayed.

I wish I had a plan for my life, so I could've gone far away with them.

Except, I don't think I'd *want* to leave Amada Beach, or my family. Which brings me back to wishing they didn't have to leave for their dreams.

I'm adjusting to this new feeling of loneliness since I left them at the security gates. And as much as Catalina has insisted that this will be good for *all* of us, I'm just not seeing how when it comes to me.

But I've learned to trust her, and the signs from the universe—like the group of monarch butterflies that were flying over my car as I was leaving the airport.

I'm so absorbed in my project that I don't even notice my dad leaning against the front desk until he starts talking.

"Hello." I look up at the sound of his voice, wondering why he's greeting me so formally, when I realize he's making a call. A few calls, if the list of names and numbers he just set down means anything. "This is Dr. Timothy Miller, from Amada Beach Animal Clinic."

My gaze moves back to the pattern that's pulled up on the computer, but for some reason, I can't pull my attention away from my dad and whoever's on the other side of that call. He has an office only three feet away from us, although he hates "being locked in there," as he puts it. So, depending on the call and how busy the lobby is, he often takes them out here.

I've learned to tune him out, but there's just *something* about this particular call that holds my interest. I can't put my finger on it though.

"Adrian, great to talk to you again. Sorry to bother you on a Saturday afternoon," he continues. Assuming that this Adrian says something back, my dad easily responds, "I'm doing well, thanks for asking. How's the beginning of your semester going?"

They talk for a couple of minutes about Adrian's course-work. I pick up that he's a veterinary student at the University of California, Aurora Hills, and he's in a course taught by a good friend of my dad's.

"I know it's only been a couple of weeks since the semester started, but I wanted to check in and gauge how it's going?" From the corner of my eye, I watch him nod along to whatever the guy's saying. "Amazing to hear. That's actually why I'm calling a few weeks later than probably expected. I wanted to make sure you had time to get a realistic idea of what this semester is going to look like for you."

He's quiet again, listening intently as Adrian says something. There's a different level of interest my dad has with this person. It'd probably look normal to any of his other employees, but I'm his daughter. I recognized that faint furrow in his brows and that tiny hint of pride when he said, 'Amazing to hear.'

It's *almost* the same way he'd say he was proud of my brother and I after we aced a test or won in either of our respective sports.

But that's not what I can't figure out.

It's why he's taken this type of interest in, what I can only assume, is a virtual stranger.

"Well then," he says with his normal calm contentment, "I'd love to extend a formal job offer to you, Adrian. If you're intereste—" He's cut off, but rather than being put off by it, he chuckles and continues on. "In that case, if the same schedule works for you that was included in your application, you can come in for orientation on Tuesday night. Let's say four p.m.? That'll probably be your normal start time anyway, but it'll allow you some time to finish the paperwork before the lead vet assistant and I come in for the evening."

After a few more details and instructions, they say their goodbyes, and my dad turns to put the phone back on its stand.

"Who was that?" I ask when he's done making a few notes and leaning toward the phone for his next call.

He lets his hand drop to the desk and gives me an easy smile. When people meet the two of us at first, they assume I look like him out of my two parents. And I do have a lot of his features—raven black hair with a natural beach wave to it, porcelain skin, and the raspy note to both of our voices. But that's where the physical similarities end.

He has dark brown eyes like my brother, but I got my mom's light gray ones. And just about everything else from her. To be fair, it's the same for my brother. He looks more like our dad, even though he has my mom's golden tan skin and mocha brown hair.

"Adrian," my dad says as if it should be obvious.

I roll my eyes playfully. "No shit, Sherlock." Unlike my mom who scolds me for cursing, my dad just chuckles in that easy-going way of his. "Who is Adrian?"

"A new vet assistant. He interviewed a few weeks ago but he's currently earning his DVM, so I wanted to give him time to adjust before offering him the job."

"I would assume since you interviewed him, he *needs* the job? Especially if he's looking?"

"That's what you'd think," he replies as he starts to look for a chart. He's the best multitasker I've ever seen, so I'm sure he just remembered something about a patient without missing a beat in our conversation. "But he just wants to work here."

"Do you like, know him or something?"

Now he looks at me curiously, probably because of my own growing interest. "Other than when we met in the interview, no. Why, Blake?"

"I don't know. You just seemed like you knew him." I shrug and start to pack my yarn and knitting needles into my bag. Margo, Meera and I have a weekly call that was pushed back so I could cover this shift, and they'll be calling in ten minutes.

"Oh, no. I just... have a feeling about him," Dad says thoughtfully.

Now I can't help but huff out a dry laugh and actually roll my eyes. "I'd love to hear more about that," I sarcastically mutter.

He always has "feelings" about things—sometimes it's as simple as knowing what my mom will want for dinner that night or as extreme as declaring to know who his son's soulmate is when he's only like twelve. He's right about fifty percent of the time, and I'm sure it's obvious which way it goes with the given example.

"It's been a while since I've met someone this young who is this motivated for the career. Obviously, graduate programs and teaching hospitals are full of them, but I'm neither of those things." He's quiet for a second, always thinking through his words before vocalizing them. "There's not a lot of chances for me to share my experience and passion for this field with someone in a mentorship kind of way."

Not fighting the small smile that pulls at my lips, I tell my dad, "That makes sense."

And it does. My dad has never pressured my brother, Grady, or I to follow in his footsteps. And even though he's told us he wasn't a particularly athletic kid himself, he made it his mission to be the best baseball and swim dad out there.

To learn how much he'd enjoy having that mentor-mentee relationship with someone makes me want it for him, and weirdly appreciative for this Adrian person.

Before he goes back to grab the phone, he looks down at his watch. "You better get going, honey. I know you have your own phone call to make."

I jump up and give him a quick side hug. "Thanks, Dad. And I'm really happy that you're excited about this new employee."

With a kiss to my head and a smile, he gestures for me to head out at the same moment that the evening receptionist is walking inside.

Chapter Three

Blake

I jog to my car eagerly and hurry to connect my phone's Bluetooth. Margo is a stickler when it comes to time management, whereas Meera often gets lost in her art and her own head. So when we decide on a time, we all know to set an alarm.

And only seconds after the clock hits our agreed time does my phone start ringing.

"Hi," I greet as I finish getting settled in my car and turn the volume up. My plan is to swim a few laps since I didn't make it to the gym's pool this morning. We usually talk for about an hour and a half, so I decide to take a drive up Pacific Coast Highway and loop back down.

I've made the mistake of going home while on one of our calls, losing all motivation to go to the pool by the end of it. And even more so than knitting and crocheting, that is my biggest comfort and has been long before either of those hobbies.

"Oh my God, I miss you," Meera instantly blurts out.

Chuckling, I tell her, "I miss you guys too." It comes out more casual than it feels. Against Catalina's advice, I made a promise to myself that I wouldn't allow my friends to worry about me instead of living their new lives. They've spent enough time doing that.

"Obviously that goes without being said," Margo states. "Let's save the sappy shit until the end. Instead, tell Blake more about the hot TA."

Awkwardly giggling, Meera goes into a new story about the hot TA she's been flirting with for the last few weeks. She immediately called two nights after getting to New York City to tell me about the guy she just met at a random record shop she found with Margo. It was a total meet-cute moment, according to her. They both had shown up to the store and wanted the same album—a first pressing of *Elgar: Cello Concerto in E Minor, Op. 85* with cellist Jacqueline du Pré.

I can imagine that exact rendition sounds like, and what the album looks like, because Meera's been searching for it for years.

After a "heated but flirtatious argument," he agreed to let her have it as long as he could know her name. *Her name.* That's it—not her number or anything else. Obviously, she agreed, even though she would've been willing to give him a lot more than that. Her words, not mine.

The serendipitous meeting was ruined for her as soon as she walked into one of her introductory courses, and he was handing out the syllabi. According to Margo, it only adds to the romcom-esque vibes rather than deters it. Meera doesn't agree, but they've already run into each other three completely random times. So personally, I'm with Margo on this one.

Out of the three of us, Margo probably has the easiest time dating—keeping in mind she was still a teenage girl dating high school boys. So that's... subjective. She's had both casual flings and exclusive boyfriends. I say she's had the easiest time because she's tall, outgoing, and gorgeous. And all of her relationships have ended on her terms—usually a mix of boredom and a delusional belief she's meant to end up with Meera's oldest brother Jatin.

Meera, on the other hand, has had two long-term boyfriends. And even though they both ended, she'd be the first to admit that they were 'pretty epic' and definitely something you'd see on the CW. So the cards are totally in her favor for this to be her next star-crossed lover.

I fall on the opposite spectrum of Meera. I've never had a long-term relationship, and the closest thing I've had to an exclusive one was an agreement that we were physically intimate with only each other. Everything else has been a random hook-up or a short-lived fling. Sometimes it's what I wanted, sometimes it's all that was offered.

After her long-winded story, with every unimportant minute detail possible, Meera takes a loud, deep breath and pleads, "Someone else, *please* talk. I'm tired of hearing my voice. Let me hear yours."

Margo laughs and calls her dramatic, but she goes next. It's no surprise that Margo's fitting into the eccentricity of New York City perfectly. She's excited for most of her projects this semester, and there's a small venue she went to with some of her classmates that features local metal bands.

SPA wasn't as hard on Margo and Meera as it was on me, but that doesn't mean it was easy either. So, the ache in my chest isn't only from sadness. There's also a lot of happiness in hearing how well they're doing out there.

"Blake's turn," Meera singsongs. "What's new with you?"

Failing to fight my sarcastic snort, I flip down my sun visor and cheerfully say, "Oh, you know—absolutely nothing." I'm not trying to sound pitiful; it's just the truth.

"There has to be something. Anything. *One* thing," Margo insists, but it sounds like she's brushing her teeth as she's talking. They're a few hours ahead of me now, and she's probably getting ready to go out for the evening.

The only thing that comes to mind is how my dad's hiring a few new employees, although I still don't know why my thoughts linger on it. I consider asking them if we even know an Adrian, considering most of the boys our age I know are through their brothers, or my own, since we went to an all-girls school. But my dad said he's already finished with his bachelor's degree and in his first year of his program. So, the chances we know *that* Adrian are unlikely.

Choosing not to ask, I tell them about the painting class I've been attending with my mom and her best friend, Bonnie. All three of us are terrible, but there's wine for them and I'm the designated driver. And about how I've been reading at the library a couple weekends a month when they need someone to fill in for the kid's stories.

"The next Mother Theresa right in front of our eyes, but *way* more progressive," Margo teases with her smooth, sweet voice that contrasts her physical appearance. It's naturally silky in a way that makes boys think she's doing it just for them. But if you know her, the sarcasm is always present.

"Shut up," I laugh and check my mirror before switching lanes. "Someone has to help the youth, so they don't end up like you."

"Hey, I'll have you know—" she starts but is cut off by Meera's loud, theatrical sigh.

"Ladies, ladies. Let's get back to the important matter at hand—*Halloween*. It's on a Friday this year, and obviously, our baby Blake is going to die of boredom without us." All of our birthdays are within two months of each other, but I'm the youngest—hence, the stupid nickname. "And I'm not ready to lose our traditions. Maybe when I'm six feet under we can talk about it, but until then, not a chance."

"I'm sure I'll survive," I insist, but truthfully, I *am* bored without them. And going to the annual haunted house with her brothers has been our thing since seventh grade. I'm not ready to lose that either.

"Personally, I *will* die if we don't spend Halloween together," Margo insists.

"You wouldn't rather spend it at your colleges?" I ask, feeling a little insecure suddenly.

"No," Meera all but screeches.

Margo just scoffs and adds, "Don't ever offend us like that again."

Not able to fight the smile growing on my face, even though they can't see it, I just say, "Okay, sorry—I will never commit the sin again."

"Amen," Margo declares. "Because I have the perfect idea for a costume, and I've already started to look into fabrics."

As I head back toward Amada Beach and the gym, I ask, "So, that means, some of that fabric will be showing up at my door, huh?"

"Yes, it's a *tradition*," she mocks in Meera's voice. "Plus, it's my year to choose the theme."

"Fine," I draw out dramatically. "Let's hear them."

It shouldn't be a surprise, but Margo's idea is actually brilliant. It's sentimental to the three of us, and the modern spin on the outfits she's already started to sketch are cute, not losing any of the quirkiness of the characters.

And I might give her a hard time for being dragged into her bigger sewing projects, but I don't hate it either. I'm pretty good at it—though nowhere near her skill level—and it turns off my brain similar to swimming and knitting.

So, I told her to send the fabrics to me and I'll get started on the easier parts of it and leave the finer details for her during fall break.

I let all of those thoughts go now though.

As I step into the humid, chlorine-scented natatorium, I let the familiarity of it fall over my senses and I instantly feel calmer. That warm, contentedness only grows when I realize that I'm the only person using the pool right now. Since the gym was pretty empty on my way inside, I don't expect that I'll have to share the space with anyone else tonight.

Quickly, I slip out of my shorts near the edge, slide the nose plug on, and dive in. Sometimes, when I want a harder workout, I'll wear the cap. Today, it's more about the comfort of the water and stretching my body.

But when I come up for air, some of my hair has already started to fall out of my bun, and I curse myself for forgetting to put it into a braid.

Turning onto my back, I float like that for a few minutes and stare at the ceiling.

This is definitely a perk of having the pool to myself.

Not that I mind sharing it, and everyone's respectful to leave each other alone. There's just something different about knowing you're alone out here. Maybe that's scary to some people, but I've always found myself a lot more fearless here.

People feel far away, and my thoughts don't seem so daunting.

I don't just feel weightless, I actually start to believe I am sometimes.

At least until I have to drag myself out and into the real world again.

When that stupid phone call between my dad and his new employee pops up, I start my first lap.

I begin with a slow breaststroke, liking the way it stretches me out after a long day of sitting at the front desk. It's by no means my most graceful, or fastest style, but it's become my favorite since I stopped swimming competitively.

It's almost relaxing, and there's a certain level of focus that goes into the coordination that I don't need for freestyle or the backstroke. And it doesn't require nearly as much exertion as the butterfly—I only willingly choose to do that one when I want to make sure I'm sore for the next three days.

So, not often.

As my body gets into the smooth movements, I start to let my mind drift away from them. Over the next week, I'm watching the Paulson's boys, and I promised another older woman that I'd walk her dog while her husband was out of town. Mentally making a schedule for those tasks around my work schedule, I realize that I'll be working this Tuesday. The same day that the newest hire starts.

Shaking my head under the water, I focus back on my movements and try to ignore the feeling in my gut that is telling me this all means something.

And the single monarch butterfly I find waiting on my car's hood only hammers in the point further.

Chapter Four

Adrian

My peripheral catches on someone walking into the small office I've been set up in as I finish up my new employee paperwork. An easy smile spreads across my face when I see Dr. Miller standing in the doorway.

"Hey, didn't mean to disturb you," he greets and walks to sit across from me at the small table.

Straightening to look him in the eye, I shrug, letting him know I don't mind. "Hi, Dr. Miller. I'm almost done here."

He sits across from me and folds his arms over his chest. It's not in a closed off way, but more of a relaxed stance. "You don't always have to call me doctor. Tim will be fine, unless we're in any professional setting, whether it be the client or the patient."

I nod and set down my pen, wanting to give him my full attention. "Yes, sir."

He just smirks and shakes his head. "Once you're done, come find me up front and I'll give you a tour of the facility."

"Will do. Should be just a couple more minutes."

He walks back out, leaving me to finish. When I turn the page, I realize I only have three more questions on the tax form. Quickly filling in my information, I stack the papers and tentatively walk back out to the front.

I'm usually a pretty confident guy, but there's been this lingering nervousness all day. It was there when I woke up at six a.m., as I was driving to my courses, and stayed with me even through the short workout I was able to squeeze in during my break.

It's not that I feel unqualified to be a vet assistant, but I know this is a huge professional opportunity. I'm *lucky*.

Assuming that everything Dr. Miller said is accurate—and I do have a trustworthy feeling about him—he works *hard* to create a different environment within his business than what may be the standard. And, based on how much he seems to enjoy the opportunity to mentor, I'd guess that's part of the reason why he's never taken his facility to the next level and opened a teaching program. He'd lose a lot of the control he currently holds over the finer details of the business. Like offering part-time employees benefits and the amount of time he'd have with patients and staff.

The way he talks about working here, and the close relationships he encourages, makes me think that Tim Miller is in this career for reasons that don't involve money.

"All done?" his deep, warm voice asks from the front desk when he sees me standing nearby. He's talking to who I assume is one of the receptionists. Nodding, I walk up and hand him the paperwork. Before I have a chance to introduce myself, Tim does the honors. "Adrian, this is one of the morning receptionists, Olivia."

Sticking out my hand, I shake hers and state, "I'm Adrian. Nice to meet you."

She offers me a warm smile that peeks through the long chestnut brown hair falling along her cheeks. Her voice is deep and rich. Pulling her hand back, she says, "You too."

"Cool scrubs," I nod toward her. The *Avatar: the Last Airbender* design is somewhat subtle—a pattern of the four elements—but it was one of my favorites growing up.

This time, the tug on her lips feels more genuine and pulls across her strong jaw, reaching her brown eyes. "Thank you. There's this small online store that sells a lot of medical apparel for different fandoms."

"If it's the website I'm thinking of, my mom loves that one too." I think I'll take after my dad and his solid colors in this case, but the bright colors and patterns are an essential part of my mom's work attire.

She smiles and turns to Dr. Miller, promising to finish the morning tasks before the evening receptionist, Blake, gets here in thirty minutes.

Not paying too much attention to their conversation, I look around the lobby and take in my new job. It's a clinical area, much of what you'd expect from a medical waiting room. But there's a bulletin board on one wall. From here I can see a variety of announcements, photos of animals, and other little tidbits about the community.

"Adrian?" Dr. Miller pulls me out of my thoughts. There's a patient expression on his face when he tilts his head behind him. "How about a tour?"

Standing at my full height, I nod. "Yeah, sounds great. I'll see you around, Olivia."

"Nice to meet you," she calls after us.

As we make our way to the back, behind the secured double doors, Dr. Miller briefly describes each of the different rooms and anything specific to remember about each one. Mostly things like which operation rooms can administer anesthesia and which can't, or the kennels for patients who have an extended stay versus the ones here for a short period of time.

I meet a few of the employees along the way, and we stop so he can introduce me to each one. Including Julie, the head vet technician, who has been working with Dr. Miller since the clinic opened almost two decades ago. And Dr. Michael Fisher, the veterinarian who specializes in aquatic animals.

"It felt prophetic, you know?" he jokes easily, his smile is partly hidden under his thick, gray mustache.

Dr. Miller—er, Tim as he's continued to insist on—just rolls his eyes as if he's heard the same line a million times.

We continue walking, making our way through what seems to be a big loop. My suspicions are confirmed when we get to a different set of double doors and we come out in the lobby, but on the opposite side of where we started.

"That's about it. I know it can be overwhelming at first." That's to put it nicely. From my research, I knew it was a large facility, even if it's smaller than other vet hospitals. But it's set up in a way that makes it much bigger inside than it looks from out here. There are multiple exam rooms when you first walk in, as well as ORs, long-term and short-term kennels, bathing areas, an outdoor space, and even a small hydrotherapy station. "But you'll get the hang of it. And there's always people around to ask if you're looking for something."

"Okay," I agree. "I'm sure it'll be fine after some time..."

I trail off when my gaze moves back to the front desk. We were in the back for close to an hour and a half, so I didn't expect to see Olivia here anymore.

But I never expected to see a vaguely familiar face.

There's no recollection of *where* I know her from. I'd assume classes if Dr. Miller hadn't mentioned I was the only veterinary student working for him right now.

Her silky raven black hair is loose, falling around her shoulders. She keeps pushing one piece behind her ear as she stands and looks down at the computer. But once again, the same strand falls into her face, and I try—I *really* try—not to stare at her long, thin neck that's stretched taut with the phone between her other shoulder and ear.

"Oh good, you can meet my daughter." My head turns toward Dr. Miller, but he's already stepping toward the desk.

She's still on the phone, except when she notices her dad, a smile starts to tug on her full pink lips, bringing attention to the perfect cupid's bow. The smiling quickly stops when her eyes move to me.

That same mouth falls into a small, shocked O. She looks almost as confused as I feel. The way her eyes slightly widen, and the color that paints her cheeks, makes me wonder if she recognizes me too.

When my eyes move up her face, meeting her gray ones, it clicks.

Chapter Five

Adrian

The girl who ran into me at the grocery store.

I walk toward Dr. Miller and stop on the other side of the desk like I'm in a daze.

Her eyes bounce between her dad and me a couple of times before she turns her attention back to the computer and her call.

"Yes... Yes, *Polly*," she says a little more aggressively. Her dad laughs under his breath as he flips through a chart sitting next to Blake. "Okay... Yes, okay. See yo—ugh," she scoffs, pulling the phone away from her face to stare down at it. "See you in hell, you old hag," she mutters and drops the phone on the stand.

My eyes widen and move to her dad's expression. But he doesn't look the least bit concerned about her customer service skills, even though he lightly scolds, "Be nice, Blake."

"Me?" she asks incredulously. She opens her mouth to defend herself, but she seems to remember I'm standing here too. Her lips clamp together, and she stares at her dad.

Setting the chart down, his eyes shift to me and says, "This is my daughter, Blake. She's a lot nicer than you'd guess at this moment." My eyes slide to her, and she's giving me a look I can't quite explain. Her expression is blank, but she won't look away either. She *does* roll her eyes at her dad's words, and I'm not sure how true they are either... or that I mind the thought. So I don't fight the smile that breaks through.

"And I don't condone or accept rude behavior toward the patients. Blake and Polly just... have their own relationship," he concludes with a smile.

"It's an *enemyship*," she insists. We both look at her for a second in silence. With a quick side-eye thrown my way, she looks back to Dr. Miller and says, "It's a real word. I looked it up."

I laugh lightly and watch as her cheeks grow warmer just as they were starting to fade to her normal complexion. "What?" she asks, finally looking me in the eyes.

And *fuck*, they're even more captivating when she's looking right at me—almost like seeing straight into my soul.

"I love the commitment to the bit," I cheekily retort and slip my hands in my pockets.

She purses her lips, making me think she's fighting her own grin. "It's true hatred. So I scheduled her for a day I'm off," she says and swings her gaze back to her dad.

He doesn't look the least bit perturbed by it. Honestly, from first impression, he seems like one of the chillest men I've probably ever met.

"Mick's running late," Tim tells us. Turning toward me, he says, "His daughter has some health problems, so sometimes he may be a few minutes late if you're ever working the shift before him. Though, with your school schedule, that shouldn't be much of a problem."

"No problem if I do. And I'm pretty limited with my courses, so I'm happy to help out whenever I can if it's needed."

Tim offers me a grateful nod. From the corner of my eye, I see Blake assessing me again, but she still doesn't say anything.

"I need to meet with Julie before one of our next appointments. I had hoped to be here to introduce you to Mick, but

I'll have to leave you to your own devices for a little." I nod, feeling more comfortable being here.

"Honey"—he turns toward his daughter—"would you mind showing Adrian around the front? Show him the extra supply closets, employee lockers, and the weight stations. Those kinds of things."

She looks speechless, like a deer in headlights. After a second, she just nods and offers him an awkward smile. "Sure, I'll make sure he finds Mick too."

With a few more words and thanks to Blake, Tim takes the chart he's been half-focused on and goes to the back again.

She turns toward me, and we just stare at each other for a second.

"You're the gir—" I start but she cuts me off.

"Technically, everything other than the weight station is in the back, behind the doors," she says as if the tour really is the most important thing right now. I close my mouth and listen, even though I really want to talk about the grocery store. "But we—the receptionists—help the assistants with the upkeep a lot. So they're treated as the front. It's confusing."

It's really not, but she continues to ramble, and it doesn't stop. She spews out random, useless facts about why it's considered "the front" and even moves into the overall layout of the building.

Obviously she's nervous, and it's fucking adorable. I fight everything in me to not let my smile appear this time, afraid she'll get weird and close up again if she thinks I find her entertaining.

And she *is* entertaining. Not only that, I like the sound of her voice. It's soft and raspy, even more so than I remember from our brief run-in.

Over the last month, I've wondered about her a few times. Every trip to the grocery store is spent imagining her standing there when I turn the corner to another aisle. Preferably without my parents or her friends this time.

But now that I'm seeing her again, I take in her defined cheekbones, full lips and the striking eyes that captivated my attention that night. Blake really is one of the prettiest girls I've seen face to face—maybe even the prettiest I've ever seen.

"Anyway..." she trails off and wraps a loose strand of hair around her finger. Once she seems to catch onto her own chattering, she corrects, "We can go back there really quick."

Turning on her heel, she goes through one set of double doors, and I follow behind her. It's a more in-depth tour of the back area, providing details about what responsibilities fall on different departments and how the rooms are organized.

The last stop in the back area is the supply closet. She walks in front of me to open the door, and I let my eyes drop to her perky ass for a second. If I didn't have to worry about being caught by her, I'd let them linger. It's hard not to when she has a perfect bubble butt in well-fitting scrubs. But my gaze is back on her face by the time she turns around and holds the door open.

I step inside the dark room, turning around when the light flicks on and I hear the soft click of the door closing. She stands in front of it for a long moment before walking to her right, pointing out things like extra scalpels and needles, and where the door to the small stock room of cleaning supplies is. I don't move from the middle of the space where I've been since we walked inside. I twist my body to follow her as she gives more explanation than necessary and points at things.

As she makes her way past me and toward the door, I stop her with a question. "You're the girl from the grocery store, right? The one I bumped into?"

Moving to look at me, we're only about two feet from each other, even though it feels closer—more intimate. She doesn't step back but seems nervous with the way she starts to gather her hair on top of her head. It's basically the same messy hairstyle she had that night.

"I don't know what you're talking about," she quietly insists.

Laughing, I lean forward, slipping my hands in my pockets so I don't do something stupid like brush my thumb along her cheek. "Your eyes are a dead giveaway."

"Excuse me?"

"They're a unique color—maybe I'm crazy, but I don't think I'd forget them."

"Yeah," she says slowly, a light pink spreading across her cheeks. "You're crazy."

Nodding, I lean back and tilt my head. A small part of me feels rejected, the other part is growing more interested in Blake. Maybe she doesn't remember running into each other.

"My bad then," I shrug and play off the insult. She scoffs, opens her mouth like she's going to say something but chooses to close it instead.

When she doesn't say anything else, I step around her and hold the door open.

With a guarded but curious glance, she exits the small room and takes the lead back to the front lobby. I let her finish the rest of the short tour without any more teasing, my interest only piquing more and more.

Soon after, Mick comes in for his shift, and I spend the rest of the evening shadowing him. He's easy-going and the entire shift feels educational, however none of it's anywhere near as interesting as Blake.

Chapter Six

Adrian

Reading over the same line in my textbook for the third time, I'm not really paying attention as I walk into work. At least not until I get to the front desk and drop my book down.

I expect to see Olivia behind the desk, since she was here last week and in the few days since starting, I've come to realize she works strictly mornings. As far as friends at the clinic go, she's the closest to one I have so far. Everyone's nice enough and welcoming, and I've met almost the entire staff by now.

Olivia is a trans woman, about ten years older than me. She's one of those people who can have a conversation with anyone and always makes sure to check on me any time we cross paths. The new friendship has been a key component for making me feel more comfortable over the last two weeks.

Though I'm happily surprised to see that it isn't Olivia smirking up at me, it's Blake.

She looks shocked to see me, but from the knitting project splayed across her lap, I figure she was just engrossed in her newest project. It's not the first time I've seen her working on something during a shift.

Her silver eyes are wide, but it quickly morphs to what I've started to call her 'pretend to be bored' face. She wears it often, at least when I'm around.

I haven't found a way to ask Olivia about her without being obvious. If she wasn't my boss's daughter, I might care less about that fact, but I digress.

"Brain shriveling up yet?" she teasingly asks.

Placing both hands on the desk, I lean forward, closer to her height. She's sitting on the other side, so even hunched over, I tower over her. "Don't tell your dad, but I was having my first course-related meltdown when he called and offered me the job."

For the first time since I met her, Blake *laughs*. Not a quiet chuckle or a teasing snicker under her breath—a full breathtaking laugh.

A pretty smile pulls across her lips and playfulness sparkles in her eyes, making the silver come alive like lightning hitting the ocean. It's the delicate rhythm of her laugh that draws me in, reminding me of the rainstick I grew up playing with at my godmother's house. Just like the instrument, her laugh starts as a sudden rush—unexpectedly whooshing right out of her—before evening out to a soft, warm trickle that fills the space between us.

Suddenly, I'm thinking back to those ships kept in the bottles my Pop loves so much, and I wonder how I can do just that but with the sound of her laugh instead.

Not seeming to realize the all-consuming effect she has on me, she retorts, "Knowing his perfect student is in fact *not* perfect, would crush his soul at this point." She rolls her eyes at the joke about our mentorship, but there's no animosity in her expression.

"I mean," I chuckle and start putting the textbook in my backpack, "even as a first-year undergrad, I'm sure you know the struggle of a new school year by now."

She's quiet for a long moment—long enough that I finish and zip my bag. When I look back at her, she's busying herself with the yarn, pulling apart a row of stitches and avoiding eye contact.

"Uhm. No, I wouldn't know." Her response is abrupt, and she seems upset by my words.

"I didn't mean anything by it, Blake. I just assum—"

"I get it." She throws me a quick side-eye. "I'm just taking some time off, okay? I don't really know what I want to do yet."

Tilting my head until I'm in her field of vision and gaining her attention, I say, "Hey, there's nothing wrong with that. Universities are expensive, and they'll always be there whenever you're ready." She just eyes me. It's a little suspicious, like she doesn't fully believe my words. "Not to mention, millions of people live successful lives without a college education too. Plus, there's trade schools and different certifications, depending on what you want to do. And some peopl—"

"Okay." She holds up her hand to stop me, but there's a small, amused smile gracing her lips. "Stop. I get it. Thank you."

With a rueful grin, I tell her, "I'm sorry. Really."

She rolls her eyes and holds up three fingers. "I believe you, Scout's honor."

I study her and cheekily retort, "You don't look like a Girl Scout."

"No, I definitely wasn't one. But you *do* look like a Boy Scout—probably had every badge and even invented new ones."

"Nah, I wasn't too into all the outdoor shit. Plus, we moved around a lot for my parents' jobs. I was in the chess club for most of my childhood though."

She squints but there's amusement back in her features. *Mission accomplished.* "That actually seems very fitting."

"Because I'm smart?" I puff out my chest.

She shakes her head and gives me a wry smile. "Because you look like a pretty boy who's too scared to get your hands dirty."

Staring down at her as offense takes over, I have to fight the tug on my own lips to not mimic hers. "What is that supposed to mean? I'm going to school to be a veterinarian."

She tilts her head, giving me a long once over. "Is that supposed to mean something to me?"

"Uh. *Yeah*. It means that I'm obviously willing to do what I need to get the job done."

A slow, saccharine smile spreads across her lips. "Is that so?"

Cautiously, I nod but I feel like I've stepped right into the trap she placed perfectly for me.

"Well, if that's the case, there's something I could *really* use help with."

"I should probably find Mic—"

"He's going to be about fifteen minutes late, so just enough time for you to do this one, *little* favor for me."

"Fine," I answer slowly. "What is it?"

"Great, you've already agreed. No givebacks." She points and squints at me.

I'm ready to run in the other direction until her expression morphs into pouty lips and innocent doe eyes that I just know mean trouble from her. But she is damn gorgeous. I think I'd follow her through the gates of Hell if she looked at me like that again.

"There's a mess in room four. Benji the Beagle had diarrhea. *Again*. Poor thing just can't stay out of Terry the Tabby's litter box."

"That sounds... disgusting," I shudder. "And do you always refer to the patients by their name and breed?"

"No," she snorts derisively. "But if Polly the Pain in My Ass comes in and you don't use the 'proper names' for her 'fur babies' she'll leave a one-star review on Google."

I pick up on the nickname from the woman she was on the phone with last week and shake my head. "Are you speaking from experience?"

A soft pink paints her cheeks, but she doesn't answer. Instead, she offers me a keychain and a smug reply, "That unlocks the supply closet."

I grab the keys and cross my arms, looking down at her in the desk chair. "Let me get this straight. You don't want to clean the dog crap off the floor—"

"And exam table," she grimaces.

"Awesome. So instead of doing what your dad probably asked you to, you're pawning it off on me?"

As soon as I'm done talking, the bell over the door rings, and we turn to see a woman walking in two large greyhounds. "Oh, would you look at that?" she notes. "Not only did you *already* agree, but I have to help this owner."

Turning back to her, I shake my head again and push off the desk chuckling. "You're going to pay for that, Miller." I walk back to the lockers and supply closet, finishing the cleanup right as Mick arrives.

He apologizes for being late again, but I cut him off before he can feel too guilty about it. He told me last week that his daughter isn't only sick, but she's currently going through a second round of chemo.

I understand priorities, and that's clearly the top one.

And if I'm being honest, there's a selfish part of me that loves getting a few minutes to talk to Blake. We've been too busy the last two days we worked together, and her job doesn't bring her to the back very often.

That ten minutes we just shared will most likely have to hold me over for another week before I get more of her snarky attitude.

Chapter Seven

Blake

Trying to use the computer screen as a shield, I discreetly peek over the top to watch as Mary—the woman with the two greyhounds that came in about an hour ago—leans forward and squeezes Adrian's forearm. *Again.* It's the third time she's done that since I introduced them.

It's no secret around here that a *lot* of the PTA moms from the ritzier neighborhood, Aurora Hills, are suddenly in need of a new pool boy. In the roughly six or seven shifts he's worked, this isn't the first time that one of them has stayed after their appointment just to *chat.* And I'm sure it won't be the last.

He's been working here for exactly two weeks and this is the second time I've watched this scenario play out. Olivia—our workplace gossip queen—told me that the other receptionists have mentioned it too.

And both times I've sat here, sneakily watching it happen, there's been this... dark, inky feeling that spreads through my body. It's as if I have no choice but to watch as he talks to the woman, like I need to know every little detail of their interaction, while at the same time I'd rather rinse my eyes out with salt than have to watch *this.*

I'm sure there's a name for that feeling, but I'd rather not identify it. Nor the one that flutters in my chest when he shows little interest in those women.

He doesn't offer her a second glance as he strides confidently toward me, that goddamn grin easily plastered to his face. Unlike me, he's quick to laugh and offers easy smiles to anyone he comes in contact with. But ever since that day at the grocery store, it's felt like the one he offers me is different. Softer, more genuine somehow.

Anyone with two working eyes can see how handsome Adrian is. He has a clean fade with short, natural curls and dark brown eyes that are almost a perfect match to his deep mahogany skin. Somehow, his round face and deep dimples give him a cute boyish charm, but don't negate from the fact he's a few years older than me—four at least.

Twisting my lips to hide my smile, I don't say anything, just watch him. Most of our interactions start because he initiates them, unless it's work related. It's not that I don't want to talk to him. Sometimes it just feels like I've lost all of my social skills outside of my family and friends. Before I can even open my mouth, my anxieties have already played through a hundred ways I could ruin this somewhat easy banter he keeps alive. And that's the last thing I want.

It sparks something in my chest that he never seems to mind my awkward reluctance though.

Right as he's about to speak, the phone rings. I try to hide my small smirk at his slight disappointment as I grab it.

"Hi, Amada Beach Animal Clinic. This is Bl—" I'm cut off by the familiar voice of one of our clients, Lela. If the Spanish she speaks wasn't enough of a clue, then the hoarseness of someone that used to smoke a pack a day is a dead giveaway. If she hadn't recognized my voice, she would've used English herself, but it's not her first language nor preferred one.

"Ah, hola. ¿Cómo estás, Lela?" I listen as she tells me about why she's calling. She's a talker though, so it's never a quick story. This time, it starts with how her daughter came to visit with her kids, and one of those kids found a lump on her cat, Chispa.

"Claro que podemos revisar eso," I tell her, promising that we'll get Chispa checked out. Doing my best to ignore the way Adrian tilts his head and watches me with a curious expression, I continue our conversation in Spanish. "Let me see what our earliest availability is right now."

I can practically feel the hesitancy from her before she asks in a low voice, "Will this be expensive? I'm sure we can figure something out if it is..."

My hands freeze over the keyboard as she trails off, lost in her stressful thoughts. Without trying to chide her, I ask, "Lela, did you go over those pet insurance brochures my dad sent you a few weeks ago?" Her silence is my answer, and I tsk as if I'm the seventy-five-year-old woman, not her.

She chuckles, and I can almost imagine her swatting me away. "She's just so young. I thought we had time."

"It's best to get it for her now, while she's young and it can help with any preventative care. But it's not too late. Let me get an updated list of the ones we accept here, and we can go over the options together."

It takes a bit of convincing for Lela to accept the help—multiple promises that it's not at all an inconvenience, *and* I will do the talking if she has to call anyone while setting it up. Finally, she agrees once I emphasize that this is her best option if it's something serious with Chispa. Before we get off the phone, I make plans to visit her tomorrow morning so we can get the appointment booked as soon as possible.

When I swirl to my right to put the phone away, I'm startled by Adrian's presence. I got kind of distracted while talking to Lela and assumed he would've walked away by now. But he's still standing there with that curiosity gracing his face.

"You know Spanish?"

I nod. "It's my mom's first language, but I'm the only one other than her who is fluent. My dad and brother understand almost everything, but speaking it is another thing altogether."

"Makes sense. I've taken a few classes, but it's never really stuck."

Looking up through my lashes, I tell him, "You should reconsider how hard you tried. I know most of the clinics and hospitals in the area would pay close to fifteen percent more if you were bilingual."

His mouth practically unhinges. "Shut up. *Fifteen?*" Slowly, I nod again. "How do you know that?"

"You overhear a lot when you're easily forgettable and the boss's daughter," I joke.

He's quiet for a second before he speaks in a low voice, "Trust me, I've never considered *that* word to describe you." My mouth pops up in a small, surprised O.

Since the grocery store? I mentally ask, not able to form the actual words. It feels too vulnerable somehow. Especially after I pretended that I didn't remember him. I definitely did—so did Margo and Meera, who both screamed when I told them he's one of my dad's new employees. I still haven't admitted that I wondered about him almost every day, eventually assuming he was just a tourist taking a late summer trip.

Never missing a beat at my badly timed silence, he effortlessly returns to a much safer topic. "Anyway, what was the client saying? Lela, I think?"

Nodding, I swallow and glance around, breaking eye contact. Looking back at him, I explain our conversation and her worries about the financial costs if the lumps aren't benign. "So, I told her I'd help her choose between a few plans and make some calls if she has questions."

"Really?" His brows scrunch in what looks like surprise. I can feel my face fall into a scowl at his response, and he quickly backtracks. "No, *no.* I didn't mean it like that—like you aren't someone who would help in a time of need. It's just that not every person would offer up their free morning to help an elderly woman sign up for pet insurance either."

I can still feel my hackles rising, but I try to be receptive to what he's saying. To *listen* to him, rather than let my own deafening insecurities start to take over.

After a second, trying to gather my thoughts, I slowly reply, "I can understand that. Kind of. I mean, I *know* that's how a lot of people are. But it's not how I was raised. I don't even think my parents really had to *teach* my brother and I what it means to be a part of a community—especially one like Amada Beach. They just lived their lives, and we followed by example, you know?" I can feel myself starting to ramble, so I take a breath. "So, yeah. I guess it's not really something I'd even think twice about."

Plus, Lela's basically like a surrogate grandmother. But even if she wasn't, even if she was the Pain in My Ass herself, I'd still help if it was within my capabilities.

"I like that." He stands up straight and nods, more to himself.

"What?" I ask incredulously.

"I like that that's how you see the world. More people should have that outlook."

I offer him a shy but genuine smile. "You're in the right place if that's what you're looking for."

He doesn't look convinced, but he doesn't argue with me either. Instead, he just shrugs and says he should get to the back before the next wave of appointments. I don't stop him, even though I want to. We've talked more today than we've gotten to in a single shift so far.

Adrian never makes me feel embarrassed or uncomfortable, and for me... that's rare.

Chapter Eight

Blake

Some days, it doesn't feel like there's much to talk about in therapy. Over the last few weeks, I've been talking to Catalina about my medication and the symptoms I'm still facing—like insomnia—but I tend to downplay how bad it is some nights.

My anxiety attacks are fewer and fewer, as the weeks go on. I only had one last week. It was the morning of my brother's birthday, and another year we didn't get to spend it with him. I've experienced loss in different forms—relatives who pass away, friends that move on from you, lovers that forget about you, and the insurmountable grief that comes with realizing that your childhood was spent surviving rather than living.

But the further Grady drifts from our home in Amada Beach, and worse our *family*, the more I realize that this is a pain that only goes away with a resolution. And when you have a brother who would do just about anything to avoid putting his problems onto someone else's shoulders, it feels like a hopeless battle.

And sure, I could talk about that with Catalina, but it's an old topic between us now. I know she'll ask, *again*, if I'm planning on talking to him about my feelings. About how the distance hurts, and how I didn't expect things to change between us so drastically when he left for college. My answer would still be a quiet, yet firm, *no*.

Because, sometimes, I'm still a coward when it comes to my own feelings. No matter how much progress I feel like I've made.

So instead, I vent about work. About the clients, like Polly, who I can't seem to avoid at any cost. I tell her that I've decided birds of any kind are my least favorite animals and patients. And before I know it, I'm telling Catalina about beautiful stay-at-home-mom Mary, and the other women who Olivia has caught lingering for *him*.

A second before one of her eyebrows ticks up in interest, I know I fucked up by mindlessly mentioning Adrian one too many times. Probably more than that because I've somehow worked his name into every story I've told so far.

I'm constantly on high alert to make sure no one suspects I have a very small, unimportant crush on him, but this is one of my safe places. And I let that guard down with the woman who's literally paid to make it her business.

"You've mentioned that name a few times... *Adrian*. He's a new employee?"

"Uhm..." I slowly start. "Yes, he is. Anyway—"

She shakes her head and leans forward. "We should talk about him."

"That's okay."

"Fine." She crosses her arms over her legs and gives me a knowing smile. "What else is going on at work then?"

I squint at her and twist my lips, making a silent vow to not fall into her very obvious trap. "I'm meeting with Lela today. I don't know if you remember her—"

"The woman whose daughter recently moved away. You check on her and her husband, Jorge, often."

My cheeks warm but I try to ignore the hint of pride in Catalina's voice. It's similar to when Adrian was asking me about the phone call, but it's not quite that same. That felt almost reverent.

"That's her," I nod in confirmation, and explain the large lumps they found on Chispa and how Lela doesn't understand how insurance works. Especially for an animal.

"And I thought he walked away," I ramble and pick at the fuzz on the pillow. "But he didn't." I'm not even sure I'm really talking to Catalina at this point, or if I'm still trying to make sense of Adrian's attention.

"He as in...? This Adrian?"

I roll my eyes but continue to avoid her gaze. "Obviously."

She lets out one of her signature cackles and argues, "With how closed off you are sometimes, *no*, it's not obvious."

I shrug. "There isn't really anything to talk about."

"But you'd like there to be? Based on you wanting to bring him up anyway."

"He's the hot guy I bumped into at the grocery store," I blurt out.

She lets out a shocked laugh. "Really?"

She knows about my little accident at the store that night. Not because he kept popping into my mind—I left that information out—but because I was actually embarrassed as hell. He's objectively gorgeous. Like the type of attractive that could model if this vet thing doesn't work out.

Nodding, I tell her about overhearing my dad's call and officially meeting him on his first day. By the end of it I even admit, "There might be a teeny tiny crush, but it's like a shooting star. It'll pass. Quickly."

"Maybe so," she muses but doesn't push the topic anymore.

"It's not important."

She nods, not looking convinced. "If you say so... Back to Lela then. Is Adrian going to help too?"

I roll my eyes and stare at her blankly. "I thought we were moving on?"

"Sorry, sorry," she amends, but I know she isn't in the slightest.

Choosing to ignore my own desire to talk about Adrian, we finish our appointment discussing my plans for the weekend, and how the long distance is going with Margo and Meera. The distance is hard, but I haven't felt any great shifts in our friendships either, even if the loneliness is daunting sometimes.

Chapter Nine

Blake

I'm never *dreading* work—if anything, it's one of the few places I feel completely comfortable—but there's definitely a heaviness today.

After my therapy session last week, I went over to Lela's house as promised. It didn't take as long as she expected. My dad had helped me narrow it down ahead of time, so she wasn't overwhelmed.

We went through the three companies my dad suggested looking into and called an agent with the best fitting option. It was a pleasant surprise that he knew Spanish, so Lela was comfortable knowing she didn't accidentally miss anything if I had translated.

From there, the rest of the process was smooth. With the help of the agent, we got Chispa signed up and submitted. It was processed within twenty-four hours, so getting her an exam and appointment for blood work happened within the week as well.

My dad expected to get the results back yesterday, but when he got home, he admitted the lab hadn't called yet. I've worked here long enough to know how fast and reliable the one he works with is, so I know the information is coming today—if not already.

Pushing through the front doors, I smile at Olivia when her head pops up.

"Hey, girl," she greets me, but there's already a sly tug to her lips as I get closer.

Shaking my head, I ask, "What's going on?"

"You'll never believe this. It's a new record."

With a confused tilt to my head, I round the desk and drop my bag on the floor. "The amount of times Dr. Fisher made the name joke?"

She snorts and twirls the pen in her fingers. "No, but I think he did hit that the other day. I mean our new resident pool boy."

It's my turn to chuckle. At times, I tend to ramble uncontrollably, and I mentioned that joke to her. She thought it was way funnier than I ever did though.

But considering Olivia's happily married, I know she doesn't have a crush on our newest employee. Despite what I told Catalina, my crush doesn't feel fleeting. I'm not saying I'm ready to get down on one knee and propose to the guy, *but* the small spark of interest has grown into those pesky butterflies everyone goes on about.

We don't have a lot of time to talk on our shifts but when we do, he makes sure to find me. Our conversations have stayed more superficial since the college debacle.

Usually, we talk about his classes and what workouts he has planned when he leaves a shift in gym clothes. Or he'll ask me about my craft projects or about the town. He swears he's not interested in staying in Amada Beach for longer than it takes to finish his degree and gain some experience. However, he *loves* knowing about some of our residents.

Without me having to ask, Olivia continues, "You remember that woman Quinn? She has the parrots?"

I shudder, knowing exactly which client she's talking about. Birds aren't uncommon patients, and some of them are fine. But I didn't bring them up in therapy for no reason, and Quinn's three are the exact reason why.

I hold up my hand and show her the small cut on my palm. "Yeah, I know those little fuckers."

She grimaces. "I heard they bit you, I didn't know it broke the skin."

Dropping my hand, I lean on the desk and shrug. Sometimes I handle the animals, but that day Quinn wanted to introduce her parrot Jellybean to one of the kids in the waiting room. It was a busy afternoon, and he got spooked.

Thankfully, he somehow flew toward the desk rather than the kid's head.

Needless to say, my dad has to emphasize the importance of keeping animals restrained on the premises now.

"Well, she took her shot."

My mouth and stomach drop. Picking up the former, I ask, "What do you mean?" It's a stupid question, but I never thought one of the clients would show actual interest in him.

Is that even allowed?

She watches me with a curious expression for a second before confirming what I know. "Quinn asked Adrian if she could have his number."

To be fair, Quinn is probably about three years older than Adrian and gorgeous. She's also insanely nice—flying nightmares aside.

"Uhm." Rolling my lips between my teeth, I think through my words before accidentally word-vomiting. "What is the record he broke?"

Slower this time, almost cautiously, she answers, "How soon into a shift a client asked for his number, or a date."

"He gets *hit on*?" I mean, I know he does. I've watched it happen. But none of the women I've seen him interact with have taken it that far before.

There's a gentle lilt to her voice now. "He's never said yes. It's not technically forbidden, but it wouldn't be a good look for a young, new employee either."

Nodding, I twist my lips but don't say anything. Outside of a professional setting, I know Adrian wouldn't be doing anything wrong if he had taken any of those women up on their offers. But it still leaves me feeling...

Well, to be honest, it leaves me feeling jealous.

I hate the idea of him showing interest in another woman before I've figured out what this crush means.

Not that he's shown any in me necessarily, but he's *never* shown any during the encounters I've witnessed.

"To be honest," Olivia turns toward the computer screen and adds in a nonchalant voice, "I don't think his reputation at work is the only reason he didn't say yes. I think he really wasn't interested in *them*."

I've known Olivia for nearly a decade now—though our friendship has grown exponentially since I started to work here last spring. Which means she knows me well enough to read beyond my faux aloofness.

So, even if I want to believe her, I can't overcome the voice in my head saying she was only placating me.

In response, I offer her a pathetic attempt at a smile when she glances at me from the corner of her eye. Before the conversation goes any further, my dad comes through the double doors and slows when he spots me.

"Hi, honey." It's his normal greeting, but today his words feel weighted.

Pushing off the desk, I wave a little awkwardly. "Hey, Dad."

He nods toward his office. "Let's talk for a minute."

"Oh. Uhm. Okay..." I start following him but make the mistake of glancing toward Olivia on my way.

Her sad smile tells me everything I need to know about this conversation.

He settles in his chair, and I plop down across from him.

"What's going on, Dad?" My thumb starts to tap across my fingers. Usually, I try harder to fight off the habit, but I can feel the looming dread in the room.

He lets out a sigh and leans forward on the desk. "Have you talked to Lela today?"

Biting my lip, I blink back the growing tears and shake my head. "I called her this morning, but she hadn't heard anything yet. She never called me back... You got Chispa's results, didn't you?"

Nodding sadly, he tells me, "We did. I went to tell Lela and Jorge in person on my lunch break. Chispa has four mast cell tumors—all of them malignant."

"Wow, okay," I murmur and stare at the wall behind him. "So, obviously that means they're cancerous. But what *else* does it mean?"

"Take a breath, Blake. I have high hopes for Chispa. We caught it early. Three of the lumps were small, and the fourth one is due to an almost overnight growth. It isn't uncommon in these cases. More often than not, surgery is enough. But we're ordering more tests to make sure it hasn't spread to any internal organs."

I let out a long breath and finally meet his eye. "You feel good about her chances though?"

His brows quirk up. "So *now* you're interested in my instincts, huh?"

With a small tug to my lips, I shrug. "When it comes to work, *always*."

There's amusement in his eyes as he nods firmly, "I can't make any promises, honey, but I have a *really* good feeling about Chispa's diagnosis."

Nodding emphatically, I push off the chair. He follows me toward the door this time. "I believe you, Dad. It's just... that cat means *everything* to Lela since her daughter moved. She's lonely without her grandkids."

His expression softens, and he squeezes my shoulder. "I know, Blake. Trust me, I *know*. And that's why I'm going to do everything I can to make sure she's healthier than ever."

Looking up at him, I read a novel's worth of unspoken words on his face.

Finding the balance between professional and personal relationships hasn't been the easiest feat for my dad. He's gotten to a great place within the last few years, but that's after facing a minor scandal a few years ago.

When you live in a small town, it's not as simple as quietly doing a favor for a friend under the table... because before you know it, everyone in Amada Beach knows, and a lot of people have pets and their own troubles—financially or otherwise.

My parents are beloved in this town, so the backlash didn't last long. Soon after, people understood that it wasn't feasible to offer free medical care to every single animal, no matter how badly he wished he could.

The mental impact of that time had a lingering effect on my dad. He's a happy, albeit quiet man, so I'm sure most people couldn't tell. But it was a dark time for him—and unfortunately, not the first that I remember in my life.

So, I fight my instincts to push about Chispa and try my best to believe his words as reality, not just a promise.

"You okay?" he asks, his tone more serious now.

Nodding I take a breath, trying as best I can to ease my features. "I'm not surprised, just..."

"Disappointed," he finishes for me. "I understand that well."

"That's exactly it."

Gently, he grabs my hand and stops the tapping. This time, I hadn't noticed I started again, but my mind feels disconnected from my body right now. "You know, honey, this could've had a different outcome if you hadn't taken the time to really listen to Lela that day. Focus on that for now."

I scrunch my nose when my eyes burn again. It's a path my brain hadn't explored yet, and I'm not sure it ever would have. But even my anxiety can't tell me he's wrong.

In the short time I've worked here, I have learned a few things. Like the fact most insurances won't cover a person, or animal, who is already diagnosed with a life-threatening illness.

Lela and Jorge's options would've been a lot more limited had she not signed up for the plan last week.

"Okay," I agree, nodding more confidently now. "Yeah, that's a good point."

He offers me a proud smile and turns toward the hallway before stopping abruptly. Leaning around him, I spot Adrian standing just around the corner. It's obvious he didn't want to interrupt, and he looks more awkward than I've ever seen.

The sight has me biting back a grin.

"Sorry—I was waiting."

"We're finished. What do you need help with, Adrian?"

"Olivia checked in the hedgehog—Willow—and she's ready to see you." He grimaces. "It looks like mites—if I were to guess," he quickly adds.

My dad chuckles easily. "I wouldn't be surprised if it was. Is that her chart?"

Adrian nods and hands it to my dad. He takes it, walking away as he begins reading the notes.

Instead of following, Adrian hesitates. I don't move toward the chair a couple feet away, choosing to watch him back. When my fingers start tapping again, I bend my arm and hide the movement, rather than even attempting to stop it.

His expression is observant where I'm sure mine is confused. When I'm about to break the silence, he reluctantly asks, "You okay?"

Oh.

He definitely overheard part of our conversation then. "Yeah, I will be."

I can tell he wants to push the subject, but he just motions his head in understanding and starts to turn toward the back. It's on the tip of my tongue to stop him, to carry on our conversation a little bit longer. Even if the actual words are beyond me.

Chapter Ten

Adrian

Walking out of the gym's locker room after my workout, I'm not paying attention as I slip my earbuds back in and click back into the podcast I was listening to. I've only recently started to get into them, since I don't have as much time for TV and need something other than music to break up the silence at times.

Right as I'm about to slide my phone into my pocket, a shorter, lithe body bumps into my side and something clatters on the ground.

"Oh, fuck," she murmurs, I think. I can't hear her properly with my earbuds in. I'm still gathering my bearings when she steps back, and I pull out one of the earpieces. "Sorry." It's quiet, but this time I recognize the soft, raspy voice before I process the dark, messy bun that's become familiar over the last few weeks.

"Do you think we'll ever stop running into each other like this?" I tease. At the sound of my voice, her head snaps up, and she stares at me in surprise. Clearly, she hadn't put it all together yet either.

"Adrian?" she gasps like I'm an alien, bending down to get her phone and water bottle. "What are you doing here?"

Letting my eyes do a quick once over—hoping I'm discreet but probably not. Knowing she mostly only uses the gym for the pool, I assume she also finished her workout, based on the outfit.

I take in her long, toned legs in the short tennis skirt. Underneath her unzipped ASU hoodie, she's wearing a cropped tank top that leaves just a sliver of smooth, fair skin along her waist.

Yeah, she definitely has the body of a swimmer.

The only time I've seen Blake out of her scrubs was that first night at the grocery store, and truthfully, I didn't even pay that much attention. I was too focused on the striking gray of her eyes and the soft blush that often makes an appearance.

She looks good in anything, I'd guess, but seeing her like this is different. Better, because it's just *Blake* and how she exists in the world. I've thought about what she might dress like, and I never really considered skirts. It adds a layer of quiet softness to her overall demeanor, which is similar to her personality.

I can't help my cheeky grin as I say, "The same as most other people—working out."

"Oh, right... duh." She looks away and grimaces at herself. "I just meant I haven't seen you at *this* gym."

Eyeing her, I notice she's doing that nervous tick where she taps her thumb against each of her fingers. It starts with her index finger to her pinky and repeats.

Over the last month, I've only seen her do it a few times. Usually on the days she's extra quiet and aloof, rather than her normally reserved yet sarcastic personality. So it's clear those were bad days for her, though I don't know what the reason behind them was.

I have a feeling this one has to do with the woman Lela and her cat. I haven't met them yet, but Blake's seemed down since I overheard her talking to Dr. Miller last week.

I know this client has a special place in Blake's heart, but from what I've seen, she *cares* a lot. Probably too much, which is why she's always trying to make it seem like she's cold and uninterested.

"It depends," I shrug and slip my hands in the pockets of my sweats. "I like it better than the campus gym, but that's more convenient sometimes."

"Makes sense," she nods still avoiding eye contact, but I don't miss the sadness subtly etched into her features.

"You were leaving, right?" I ask, a thought suddenly brewing.

"Yeah, I am." She starts to move around me. I take a step to the side, giving her more room to walk down the hallway, while I fall into sync with her. She gives me a curious glance but doesn't say anything.

"Do you have plans tonight?"

The question comes out right as she's taking a drink from her water bottle. She chokes from surprise, sputtering some droplets down her chin and onto her chest. Her awkward nature's one of the most endearing things about her, especially because it seems heightened when she's talking to me.

Wiping her face and side-eyeing me, she shakes her head.

"Want to get dinner? There are those food trucks I've been wanting to check out."

"Oh, The Loop. Yeah, the food's really good."

"Great, I'll drive," I chime in.

"Wait. What? No. I didn't mean 'yeah' like that. Just in like, confirmation of where you were talking about."

Opening the exit door for her, I ask with faux hurt, "So, you don't want to have dinner with me?"

"I—what? No—"

I cut her off, playfully clutching my heart and attempting puppy dog eyes for the first time in my life. I wouldn't consider myself a particularly 'girl crazy' person, despite what my mother might say. But since I turned sixteen and started lifting weights, I've never had to really *try* when I liked someone either.

Blake, though? She doesn't make it easy on me. It's rare she holds a full conversation with me, and I have to initiate *all* of them. Sometimes when she sees me, a light blush graces her cheeks, and she will avoid me when possible.

I've considered maybe leaving her alone and taking her alleged disinterest at face value, but then I see her watching me over the computer screen or eavesdropping when I'm talking to the clients—specifically the women. And it gives me a new surge of hope.

And this is a prime opportunity.

"I guess I'll just eat alone... again."

She scoffs, but her expression falls in either remorse or guilt. I'm not above using it to my advantage at this moment, though it doesn't make me feel *good*.

"You're manipulating me," she accuses when we stop next to her old black Jetta.

Shrugging, I lean one arm on the hood of her car. "Is it working? I'm hungry."

Her mouth falls in indignation. I can almost see the word 'no' forming on her tongue, but she surprises me. "You're buying, I assume?"

A big, dopey smile forms, and I probably look like a love-struck fool. *I feel like one.*

"Of course."

She nods once and unlocks her car. "I'll meet you there?"

I wouldn't mind driving her, so it could feel like a real date. But I can see her fighting her instinct to run for the hills so it's a small compromise on my part.

Plus, I can save that for our first *official* date.

Chapter Eleven

Adrian

"This place is cool," I muse as Blake, and I walk into The Loop. It's my first time coming here, even though I pass it while driving multiple times a week.

It's more or less a large lot that's been renovated into a seating area with tables and lanes for the food trucks to park in. There are about four right now, sometimes more depending on the day. It's in between the local businesses and the beach, which makes it convenient despite where you're spending your day in Amada Beach.

"It is," Blake easily agrees, seeming more at ease than when we first ran into each other. "These four trucks"—she points in front of us—"are always here. They opened The Loop about two years ago and rent out the other spots to different trucks throughout the week. It can be hard to catch the others sometimes, but these are the best ones in my opinion."

I take in the four trucks as Blake fondly describes each one. There's a pizza one that seems to be an extension of the local parlor Tossin' Tomatoes. The truck's name is Slice of Tomato. There's also a waffle truck named Stacks, a barbeque truck named Finger Lickin' Good BBQ, and one named Gringo's Tacos that made me laugh, but Blake swears that it's one of the most popular trucks in the city.

"What are you getting?" I ask, leaning toward the barbeque myself.

Typically, I'd go home, and either make something or warm-up one of my prepped meals for the week. My dad turned me into a bit of a foodie when I was growing up, and I love to cook. It's one of my favorite hobbies outside of weightlifting. I don't have as much time for it as I wish. Even most of my pre-cooked meals are more or less the same, rotating between about six different options.

I can't say I hate where my night has ended up—not at all. The half-written paper due next week, and the study guides for my upcoming exams, can all wait a couple more hours if it means I can spend that time with Blake.

"Waffles," she says with a surefire decisiveness. I like seeing her so confident, but I'm amused at how serious she is about this. She gives me a little smirk over her shoulder, already walking in that direction. "You can laugh all you want, but you already promised to pay."

"Fair enough," I tease and stride forward, catching up with her quickly.

I wait with Blake while she orders her ridiculously curated waffles and pay, but after making a plan for her to find a table when her food's ready, I head over to *Finger Lickin' Good BBQ*.

Immediately, I'm impressed with how customizable the menu is, making me assume that it could be tailored for diets and working out. Personally, exercise and lifting became an outlet. It's helped me to break up the academia and move my body during the day. I was a pretty scrawny kid though, so the weights and large appetite have only worked in my favor as I've gotten older.

So, I decide to splurge on the brisket plate with sweet potato fries and coleslaw.

While I wait for food, I look around, trying to find Blake in the crowd. It isn't too busy—probably because it's a Monday—so it only takes me a few seconds to find her. When I do, I chuckle under my breath at the sight of her waffles. I'm sure it'll be even more absurd up close.

Thankfully, my food comes out soon after so I can get back to the table and watch Blake devour the sweet concoction. I drop down in the seat across from her and nod toward her plate. "You could've started to eat."

She shakes her head and looks up from her phone, laying it on the table. She leaves the screen up, seeming to not even think about it, and I like that. It's such a small gesture. But it feels like even if she's guarded, she isn't trying to hide anything either.

"I didn't mind waiting for you. Plus, you need to see it in all its glory." She waves a hand out and we both laugh, though hers is a little more shy.

"I'm all for dessert and sweets, but *that*... that's a bit much."

Mostly, I'm giving her a hard time. She did basically make it an ice cream sundae—vanilla soft serve, chocolate sauce, peanuts, with bananas and cherries included—but it's the extra sprinkles and whipped cream that really takes it to that next level.

I like that Blake has a sweet tooth, and doesn't feel any unneeded embarrassment from eating what she wants—even if that's a waffle sundae at eight p.m.

Shrugging timidly, she cuts into her food. "I *love* the carne asada tacos, but I beat a personal record today."

Watching with a small tug to my lips, I ask, "What was your record?"

"About two years ago, I swam the 100 meter in a minute and three seconds. But today, I did it in a minute and a second." She smiles to herself, taking her first bite.

"Congratulations," I praise. Despite leaning more toward mental activities than physical ones, I was still competitive.

This is obviously a big accomplishment for her, and she's celebrating it over waffles with *me*. "Do you still swim competitively?"

"No," she replies after she swallows. "I stopped during my junior year. But I love it. For me, not anyone else."

There's so many questions forming in my brain, starting with *why* did she stop competing. Something in the back of my mind tells me that's too personal of a question though. I don't get the impression Blake wouldn't have quit what she's passionate about without a damn good reason.

I end up going with, "I think it says a lot about how much it means to you then."

She seems to appreciate the deflection, her shoulders visibly relaxing. We carry on in easy conversation like that for a while. She avoids any topics surrounding the years she was in secondary school, outside of her two best friends and swimming.

She doesn't seem to have any problems talking about either of those. I learn about the reserved, but secretly lively, Meera and the protective gothic one, Margo. But I also find out that Blake didn't *just* swim competitively. She's really fucking good. Great, apparently, since her record is nearly pushing collegiate levels.

"Why didn't you go to college for it?" It's the first time I've brought that subject up since I made the assumption she was already attending a university.

"For swimming?" she asks, genuinely surprised by the question. I guess it's the same thing as asking why she quit but it just blurted out. "Honestly? By the time I was old enough to seriously start considering being scouted for anything higher, I had learned my lesson about... a lot of things."

That stands out to me, particularly that pause. Blake's younger than me, but she carries herself like she's lived a hundred years sometimes.

"One of them being that swimming is *my* thing, *my* comfort," she continues. "Sometimes I miss the races and adrenaline, but when something as big as your education depends on it, it's not fun anymore. There wasn't an ounce of enjoyment for it once I got the scholarship to the private school. And even if I wanted to be an Olympian, I'm not *that* good. Plus, I don't even know what I want to do for a career. College seems pointless to me. At least right now," she adds.

"That's fair. Even undergrad was a lot of work."

She looks at me for a long moment. "Have you always wanted to be a veterinarian?"

I nod, finishing my bite. The food is freaking delicious, so I'll definitely be stopping here on my way home from work now and then. "At least since I was a sophomore in high school, I'd say. My parents are nurses. I've always admired them—even seeing them as real-life superheroes while I was a kid—but I've never been drawn to the healthcare field.

"My best friend's younger sister has epilepsy, and her service dog got cancer. It was a really hard time for her. He'd been with her since she was just a toddler. He was pretty young and retired after that. I don't know. It's hard to explain, but that changed something for me."

There's a soft expression I've never seen on her before. "That's beautiful, Adrian. And it makes sense." She offers me a small smile that morphs into a grimace. "No I mean, what prompted it isn't beautiful, but you know... the outcome?"

It ends on a question like she isn't sure what she meant anymore. I can't help but laugh. Blake's inability to shut up is quickly becoming one of my favorite things.

"Nah, I knew what you meant. I underestimated how taxing the job would be though, and I'm not even technically working *the job* yet either."

She doesn't say anything for a long moment. I start to wonder if this is too deep of a conversation for her, grasping for another deflection, when she says quietly, "I overheard my dad once. He was saying that they teach you about the less desirable aspects of the job, but there's no way to *know* how it'll affect you until you're there, doing it... I wish I had more advice to offer you, but talking to someone, like my dad or a therapist might help. Especially if you're feeling that way."

My brows furrow in surprise. Blake's openness to seeking mental health doesn't necessarily match her closed off personality. At the same time, I've seen the way she's emotionally receptive to patients and clients. So, it makes me believe Blake's advice is coming from a place that not only respects the benefits of therapy but understands it.

"I've never really considered that," I admit. It's not that I have negative feelings toward it or that I think I'm above it. I just don't have any deep seeded traumas. "Truthfully, I never thought it could be a preventative sort of thing, I guess."

Looking at me through her lashes, she quietly says, "You'd be surprised by the emotional tools someone could provide you, and it would only help you in the long run." She gives me a smug, knowing look as she takes a huge bite of her waffles.

The tug of my lips that never loosens when she's around pulls even wider. Nodding slowly and watching her, I realize Blake's right. Being proactive about my future is what has gotten me into one of the best DVM programs in the country, as well as the job at Amada Beach Animal Clinic. There's no reason that shouldn't include my mental health as well.

I like that Blake feels comfortable enough to push me to be better, and I plan on listening to her about this.

Chapter Twelve

Blake

Shoving everything into my bag, I don't stop to wrap my yarn better. It just gets thrown haphazardly into the tote like everything else.

Well, with the exception of the mango and chili lollipop I found waiting for me on the desk this morning—and a sticky note with a smiley face on it. That's safely in my hand because it's pretty much the only thing that's gotten me through the day.

I don't even know what's wrong. It's just one of those days. From the moment I woke up, it felt like my own brain was assaulting me with insecurities and 'what if' scenarios.

Like, *what if Margo decides her new fashion school friends are way cooler than I am, and she moves on from my friendship? What if Meera makes it so big in the classical music world that I never see her again? What if she doesn't make it at all because of my selfish thoughts?*

And so on... and on... and on...

If my dad wasn't my boss, I would've called into work today. But I didn't want to talk to him, or my mom, about how I'm feeling.

Sometimes it's hard to talk to them. Especially when nothing is really *wrong*, I just feel... desolate. It could be because I miss my friends, or that my brother never answers his goddamn phone anymore. Honestly, there's always been this part of myself that feels lonely even when I'm surrounded by the people I love, and who I know love me. It didn't take my high school bullies to create that crater in my heart. It's been there for as long as I can remember.

Even if it's counterintuitive, all I want is to crawl into my bed and be alone for a few hours.

Practically jogging to my car, wanting to avoid having to talk to anyone else, I don't notice the two completely flat tires until I'm about to step in.

"*Why*? Why, why, why?" I ask no one while I drop my head on the roof of my car.

I mean, could the day get any worse?

The day started off bad due to my own brain, but it only went downhill from there. I was stuck on a forty-five-minute call with Polly as she lectured me about the prescription *my dad* wrote for her cat, and something I have absolutely no say in. After that, Lela came in with her husband and Chispa for a pre-op appointment. She started crying when she told me that the operation is scheduled for five days from now. Then the system crashed, and we lost almost all of the appointments scheduled today. And it was just one thing after another.

So, even though it may seem like an easy answer, I pull out my phone, thinking about my options...

Tears build in my eyes, but I bite my lip, fighting them off as much as I can.

I will not cry until I'm in the comfort of my own bed, I mentally repeat for the hundredth time today.

I could call either of my parents, *of course*, and they'd be here in ten minutes, but they were really excited about cooking tonight. My dad got a new Blackstone, and he's been thinking about fajitas all week. It's kind of adorable when he gets in these moods. Plus, I need all the time I can get to pull myself together before I have to face them. They'll know I had a shitty day before even seeing my face.

The towing company is only about five minutes away, and Mr. Bennett wouldn't charge me full price, though still more than I'm willing to pay right now.

I'm about to say *fuck it* and call for a tow when I hear Adrian and one of today's mid-shift veterinarians walking out. I turn around to find them both looking at me with concern. Adrian turns to say something to her but motions in my direction, then he's walking to me while she reluctantly goes to her car. I cross my arms and wait, not having any other choice.

"That sucks," he observes.

"No shit," I mutter under my breath.

He chuckles easily and sticks his hands in his pockets. "Is your dad on his way?" I shake my head. "Your mom?" I roll my eyes and shake my head again. His features grow worried and a little frustrated—something I've never seen before. "What are you going to do?"

"I was just about to call a tow truck." Pulling out my phone again, I watch from the corner of my eye as he timidly leans forward on his toes and looks around.

"I'll take you home."

I snort, but there's more and more butterflies taking flight, by the second, in my stomach. "No, thanks."

He snatches my phone and holds it away from me. Not far enough that I couldn't reach it if I tried, nonetheless it gets my attention as he wanted. "You're *not* going to pay a hundred bucks just to get a ride home. It's like ten minutes, I'm sure."

Just about everything is within twenty-five minutes, at most, if it's within Amada Beach's limits.

"Your car will be fine overnight," he pushes on.

"I'll call an Uber then." It's nothing personal against him. I have a hard time accepting help from people, especially ones I barely know.

He lets out an exasperated sigh that finally brings my gaze to his. He's shaking his head at me, but it looks more helpless than anything else. He takes a small—almost minuscule—step toward me. It somehow feels like everything and not enough.

"You'll have dinner with me, but you can't let me help you?"

I have to fight my expression from cracking open. "I'm just... not having a good day, Adrian." I twirl the chili lollipop between my fingers. "You don't want to spend time with me right now."

With two strides, he closes a foot of space between us. It's close enough that he reaches forward and gently tilts my chin up, but not enough that we're touching anywhere else.

"I get to decide how I want to spend my time. And if you'd just pay attention, you'd know I want to spend more of it with you, Storm Cloud." I'm surprised by the nickname. He's never called me anything other than my name before. But before I can comment on it, he adds, "Your feelings don't scare me."

I roll my lips between my teeth, feeling closer and closer to breaking down by the second in Adrian's presence. And the scariest part is I kind of want to.

I shut my car door without saying anything. It's a silent answer, and he smiles in understanding and victory. "Are the doors locked?" he nods toward my old black Jetta.

I click the key fob and hold out my hand. "Can I have my phone?"

He hands it over and waves me toward his green Durango. It looks a bit older but still in good condition. We don't say anything as we walk toward his vehicle, and I don't know if I could talk even if I tried.

Underneath those emotions I'm a little scared. There's a tension between us that I've never felt before. It isn't uncomfortable but it's... new—electrifying even—and feels a hell of a lot more than just a lift home.

He holds the door open for me then walks to the driver's side. I watch from my seat and try to steady my breathing.

Glancing at him as I buckle myself, his gaze is focused as he rounds the hood, a satisfied tug playing on his lips. The way his muscles move when he opens the door doesn't help my heart rate.

He's still quiet as he starts the car and shuffles through his Spotify. The music is set to a low volume, and he doesn't push me to talk, so I don't either. It's not what I expected but I appreciate it. It grants me a moment to gather my bearings, and in a way, I guess it does feel something like what I assume companionship would.

Chapter Thirteen

Adrian

Tim has mentioned the neighborhood he lives in a couple of times, so I drive in silence until I'm at the light to turn into it. "I'll need directions from here," I glance over at Blake.

She's doing that anxious thing where she taps her fingers to her thumb, and this isn't the first time I've noticed it today. The few days we're both scheduled, we almost always end up working the same shifts. So, I've seen her a few times since we got dinner about a week and a half ago. Unfortunately I can't say I've made as much progress as I would've hoped.

But today was different. Blake wasn't her usual guarded, aloof self or her normally awkward, quirky one. It's the first time I've ever seen Blake truly have a *bad* day. I assume it started before we got to work, and from what I saw, it only progressively got worse as the day went on.

"It's the eighth right," her quiet voice pulls me out of my thoughts. "Apricot Lane."

I haven't wanted to test my luck. It feels like that's all I do with this girl—push for more without pushing for *too much.*

Plus, I'm not someone who is uncomfortable with silence.

The tapping grows faster as she stares out of the passenger window. "Are you okay?" I ask quietly, not wanting to startle or upset her.

She nods, staying silent until I'm turning onto her street. Without looking at me she says, "It's the one with the orange tree." I recognize her dad's car outside, but I don't say anything. "And I'm fine. It just feels... I don't know. Embarrassing? I live with my parents." She gestures toward the house.

I'm not convinced that's all that's wrong, but it's a lot more vulnerable than I would've expected from her.

It doesn't matter to me whether she lives with her parents, or that she's not in college, or that she doesn't know what she wants to do with her life. Because I agree, it's totally okay and understandable to take a few years off if you aren't sure what's next.

It makes me feel protective of her. Not totally in a *friendly* way either.

"I know that. I knew that before I offered you a ride. It's not a surprise, Blake. And it's nothing to be embarrassed about." She shrugs and looks out the windshield with a blank expression. "Before I moved out here, I was living with my parents. I moved back in with them immediately after graduation. You're eighteen—"

"Almost nineteen," she quickly cuts in with a coy glance my way.

Trying to rein in my grin, I continue, "You're working, plus I know you do shit on the side too." Blake picks up random shifts at the flower shop when they need extra help, and in the last two weeks, I've seen four different moms ask if she'd be willing to babysit for them. She always says yes. "And you live with your parents." I shrug. "I'm twenty-two, have a college degree, and not only did I move back in with my parents for a while, but they help pay my rent. Like, all of it."

Slowly, she nods and gives me an unsure look.

We sit in silence again, this time looking at each other, shamelessly taking in the other's features. Her brows stay a little furrowed, and there's the ever-present downturn to her lips I'd give anything to lift. But right now, all I can do is offer her a small smile that I hope gives her at least a little bit of comfort.

She has a cute heart shaped face with full cheekbones and a permanent pout that only highlights the deep pink of her lips. Her raven black hair contrasts her smooth pale complexion beautifully, especially under the sunset.

I love her eyes the most. It's so cliche, I know. And that's exactly why I've never allowed myself to tell her that—she'd never let me live it down. It's true though.

They're light gray and moody. Her gaze is sharp but when she looks at you, it feels like she's really *looking at you.*

They've reminded me of a summer thunderstorm since the night at the grocery store. It's why the nickname slipped out earlier. It'd been on the tip of my tongue since The Loop. The more I get to know her, the more I realize that the imagery is perfect for her in more ways than just physical.

After a minute, a pair of headlights pull us from the moment we're sharing. Chuckling at Blake's groan of misery, I assume it's her mom getting home. And when the car stops and the woman with the same eyes and heart-shaped face walks out, I know I'm right.

If it weren't for the mocha brown hair and her light golden brown skin, Blake would be almost a mirror image of her mom. Selena is effortlessly and agelessly beautiful. But the way Selena's eyes and Tim's dark hair mixed is *flawless.* Maybe that has more to do with the actual human they created and raised, but even a month later, I know I've never seen someone prettier than Blake.

Selena looks momentarily confused before it morphs into the joy you only see on a meddling mother's face.

She leaves her car door open and walks to the passenger window of mine.

With a warm smile, she knocks on the window.

Blake turns to look at her but doesn't roll it down. Selena's eyes flick toward me, and I shift in my seat.

She knocks again, saying something to Blake in Spanish. I remember enough from my beginner courses to pick up the word *window* and based on her tone, I think she's telling Blake to lower it.

My eyes move to Blake, waiting to see what she does. I've only heard Blake speak Spanish a few times, but I'd be lying if I said it doesn't turn me on every time. Who cares if she's talking about a dog's bowel movements if she sounds like a fucking angel doing it?

She says something back to her mom. It's quick and a little snarky from her tone, though I don't exactly know what. My guess would be something along the lines of 'go away.'

Selena talks too quickly and scolds Blake. I'm immediately lost but I understand *Blake Carmen.*

Oof, the dreaded middle name. I understand *that* tone too. It's the universal sound of a mother telling you she's done with your shit.

This time Blake rolls her eyes and presses the *down* button.

"Hi, Blake." Tilting her head to look around Blake, she adds, "Hi, Adrian."

"Hey, Mrs. Miller." I give her a wave.

Blake snorts and Selena looks amused. "I've already told you that Selena will do fine." Turning back to Blake, her face grows concerned. "Where's your car?"

"Two flat tires," Blake mumbles.

An expression I don't know how to read crosses Selena's face, and she asks quietly, "What happened? Is everything okay?"

Blake glances at me, then down at her lap. "Yes, Mom," she quietly mutters before adding what I assume is a quick explanation in Spanish. "I think it's just from driving through that pothole by the clinic."

"You're sure? It wasn't—" But she's cut off before finishing the question. Confused, I glance at the girl in my passenger seat.

Blake gives her a sharp look and shakes her head once. "No, Mom."

Selena watches her daughter for a second before conceding. "Oh, I'm sorry, morrita. Your dad will go to the next council meeting. It needs to get fixed." Blake just nods but won't make eye contact with anyone. "Did we miss your call?"

She scoots down further in her seat. "No, I got a ride." She gestures toward me. "And, Adrian, thanks for that. I'll just..." She points her thumb over her shoulder toward the house, and I can't stop the grin that spreads across my face "...be going."

"Don't be silly," Selena immediately jumps in. "Adrian, come have dinner with us. Do you like fajitas?"

Blake turns toward me with wide eyes, a clear sign she's silently begging me to say 'fuck no.' But I *do* like fajitas. And thankfully, her parents like me.

"I do," I nod and ignore Blake's death glare, "and I'd love to stay."

I swear to God her eye twitches while I just keep grinning politely at her mom.

"Great," Selena beams. "Would you mind helping with the groceries?" She drops the keys in Blake's lap and walks away without a single bag in her hands.

I follow Blake to the car and grab a majority of the reusable bags before she can. Trudging up the porch steps, I follow her inside and take in their warm, inviting home for the first time. There's a lot of boxes out with a variety of holiday labels, but it doesn't detract from the natural comfort of it.

Blake drops the grocery bags onto the kitchen island and whips toward me. "You don't have to stay," she whispers. "You can sneak out. I'll cover for you."

"Cover for me?" I ask in a normal voice. "What would you say?"

Still whispering, she says, "I don't know... that your girl-friend called—"

"Don't have one," I grin.

"*They* don't know that," she hisses. "Fine. You actually hate fajitas and didn't want to be rude."

"I love them, and I don't want to back myself into that corner in the future." Selena's always bringing food to the clinic, who knows when she'll stop in with fajitas? And like hell will I miss out on that because Blake wants to kick me out of her house.

"You... pulled a Benji then," she smirks.

"*Blake*," my voice is firm which only makes her lips turn up more. It's such a rare sight that I'd let her tease me endlessly just to see it again. "I'm not going to tell your parents that I fucking *shit* myself."

She sucks her lips between her teeth but within seconds she's laughing. Really laughing. It overtakes her whole body until she actually clutches her stomach. It's that low rumble that's distinctly Blake.

"It was worth a shot," she shrugs.

"What if I had agreed to that?"

She just continues to laugh, not offering me an answer. It's such a soothing sound, so I just stand there and watch her like an idiot.

"Is Grady coming home this year?" Blake asks hopefully from beside me. A few minutes after she accepted I wasn't going anywhere, her dad came in to ask me for help at the Blackstone.

I suspect that there were some ulterior motives. I haven't even found a time to ask Olivia for intel on Blake, but last week she informed me I'm not exactly subtle when it comes to my crush.

However he wasn't interrogating me like Blake's father, or interviewing me like Dr. Timothy Miller, DVM. He was just Tim Miller, getting to know me, Adrian Jones. Selena has been pretty much the same.

Even if Blake wasn't here, I would still want to be. It's the first time I've felt a semblance of *home* in months. Even if it's not my home, it's enough.

Selena shakes her head. "Arielle will be having the baby soon and she'll need to rest. Your dad and I are getting on a plane as soon as she goes into labor, and we'll visit again after New Year's, if you want to go with us."

Blake scrunches up her nose. I had a feeling she was a homebody—nothing wrong with that—but the way she blanches at the thought gains her a warning look from her mom that says *be nice*.

"He'll be visiting toward the end of January," Tim amends with a soft smile. Blake just nods.

As if on cue, Blake lights up and gives Tim a sweet smile. "I forgot to mention earlier, thanks for the candy." She's already looking at her plate again, so she misses the way I stiffen *and* the look of confusion on her dad's face.

"What candy?"

I can feel them the second Selena's knowing eyes land on me. It took her only seconds to put it together—I was the one who left the gift for Blake.

"The lollipop you left on the desk for me this morning." She's still looking down at her plate, completely oblivious to the growing tension in the room.

"Oh, uh," Tim starts, clearly unsure about what to do. He doesn't want to take the credit for it, but he doesn't want to throw me under the bus either.

"What?" She finally looks up, glancing around. I clear my throat, and her attention falls on me. She doesn't say anything for a moment then finally, she breaks the silence. "Adrian, did you get that for me?"

"Yeah," I shrug, trying my best to act casual. I didn't think about *this* when I agreed to stay. I was totally cool with leaving the lollipop for her and moving on. I didn't need the recognition. Hell, I didn't *want* it.

I don't even know why I stopped at the small market she's always talking about. When I was driving past it this morning before classes, I thought to myself, *I just want to brighten up her Friday a little.* But not even I have the balls to say all that in front of her parents. "The little *mercado* down the road from me sells them. I've seen you eat them a few times."

"The one on 4th and Meadows?" I nod, knowing it's the only one in Amada Beach that sells the exact brand she loves. I've overheard her talking about it with Olivia, but it really is a coincidence that I live on 4th and Palms, only one street up. "Wow," she blinks. "Thanks, Adrian."

"You're welcome. I'm sorry you had a bad day."

"It's okay," she nonchalantly lifts her shoulders. "It wasn't all bad, in the end." She grabs her plate from the table and walks to the sink. All I can do is follow and hope for another minute of time with her, even if that means spending my evening cleaning my boss's kitchen after a day of classes and work.

Chapter Fourteen

Blake

"Well, look at that," my dad mumbles. I lift my gaze from my phone to him, but he's staring out the windshield with a small, surprised smile. Turning to see what he's looking at, my breath catches when I find Adrian leaning against his car that's parked next to mine. It's his day off but that's not what has my mouth going dry at the sight of him. I've never seen him out of scrubs or sweatpants, like when we ran into each other at the gym, but this is different.

He's wearing a pair of gray jeans and a dark blue button down. His deep mahogany skin seems to glow under the morning sun. When he notices us pulling into the parking lot, he pushes up, giving us an adorably shy smile and runs a hand over the back of his neck, avoiding the soft curls on top.

Before my dad can turn the car off, I'm out and walking toward him. "What are you doing here?" I ask quietly, looking around like we might get caught doing something illicit.

"I thought I could help out today. You need a ride to the tire shop, right?"

"No," I say as my dad's walking up. "I'm going to borrow my dad's car. He'll help me get the tires off and put them back on."

"I've got it," he pushes. "I'll get you coffee and if it takes a while, lunch too. I just don't want to sit in my apartment all day." He pouts a little and it's pathetic, but somehow, he *still* looks happy.

I look at my dad, and to his credit he has a blank, yet friendly expression. I don't get the feeling he was in on this, but it still feels slightly like an attack, and I'm on the defensive. I cross my arms. "I don't *need* help, Adrian."

"Let me help anyway," he practically begs.

Defeated but not necessarily disappointed, I quietly ask, "Why?"

At that, my dad gives me a side hug and places a kiss on my temple. "Let me know if you need the keys." I nod, and we watch as he walks into the clinic.

Once the door shuts behind him, Adrian answers, "I need a break from studying and thought I'd spend the day with a friend." My brows furrow at his openness and his choice of words. With a smooth smile, he stuffs his hands in his pockets, leans back on his heels and adds, "Unless you want to be *more* than friends... You wouldn't find me complaining."

"Oh my God," I mutter and look away, hoping that he can't see the blood rushing to my cheeks from this angle.

His laugh tells me otherwise.

It's been a while since I've kissed a boy and trust me, I've spent a lot of time over the last few weeks thinking about kissing *this* boy. I just don't know if Adrian's serious or not. I've never had a *bad* experience hooking up or dating, but none of them have been anything to write home about either. More than anything, I'm not interested in being another good time for someone.

Even if I'm *positive* that even a peck would be anything but mediocre when it came to Adrian.

"Please spend this beautiful Saturday with me. It's not every day that I'm free from school *and* work," he argues.

"You're right. It's not every day... just every Saturday."

He chuckles and pushes forward without missing a beat. "Please, Blake, *please*." With a quick once over and a mischievous glint in his eye he adds, "I'm not afraid to get on my knees and beg, if that's what you want."

Slightly more prepared for his flirting, I just roll my eyes and lightly shove his shoulder. "I guess I can write it off as charity."

Chuckling, he gestures for my keys and opens the trunk. I watch as he takes one tire off and trades it for the spare, then he takes the other off but leaves it on the jack. He squats down and lifts both tires at the same time, one under each arm, and turns toward me with a content expression.

He's been talking this entire time, and I couldn't tell you a single thing he said. I mean the few seconds that his muscular forearms are flexing under the weight as he walks from my car to his SUV, has me so hot and bothered, I momentarily forget we're supposed to be going somewhere.

Which means getting into his car.

And I have to move to do that.

Shaking myself out of my stupor, I pull my eyes off of his body only to find him smirking at me. He looks all too pleased, and that simply won't do.

With a saccharine smile, I tilt my head and say, "Sorry, I just wasn't sure if a *flaco* like you could carry a tire—much less two."

Walking to where I'm leaning against his car, he stops in front of me and looks down at me with unadulterated amusement shining through his dark eyes. "You can stare as much as you want, but don't be a liar about it."

With that, he opens the passenger door and watches as I climb in.

The mechanic shop is packed. They did say they could probably get my tires fixed in between appointments. It isn't ideal, but it's better than having to come back before work tomorrow.

That's one of the beauties of living in a small town—your dad saves the mechanic's dog after he got a tennis ball lodged in his throat, and you're given special treatment for years after.

But still, it'll be at least three hours until they have a long enough lull to even glance at my tires... and that means I'm stuck with Adrian.

Okay, maybe *stuck* isn't the right word. It's not *really* a hardship.

Especially not when he stopped at Morning Drip, one of the food trucks at The Loop.

Or when we cross the street, and he puts his hand on the small of my back.

And the way he stretches his arms after laughing really hard is kinda cute too, like he lets the happiness completely overtake his entire being anytime he gets the chance to.

I wonder what that's like. To be so comfortable in the good moments, never worrying about when the rug's going to get pulled out from under you.

Even now, as I sit across from him in this little sandwich shop, he looks so content. We've barely spoken in the last ten minutes but it's nice. The quiet's always nice with Adrian.

Every few minutes I'll catch him staring at me or he'll find my gaze on him, but neither of us have called each other out yet. We just look away and fall into another round of this little game we've created.

It's new, but spending time with Adrian has made that ever present ache in my chest lessen. I miss Margo and Meera more than I can explain, but I wouldn't want them to be all alone in another state, and I know they don't want that for me.

"What's brewing in that head of yours, Storm Cloud?"

My head snaps in his direction, but instead of letting me chase his gaze, he holds mine. Choosing my usual tactic, deflection, I muse, "That nickname again."

He smirks, already seeing past my walls. "You like it?"

Biting down on my lip, I try to ignore the flutter in my stomach because goddamnit, I *do* like it.

"You mean do I like being called chaotic and temperamental?" I tease.

He laughs and shakes his head. "No. Well, maybe *sometimes*." I jokingly scoff. "But more like strong, alluring... refreshing."

Refreshing. That word sticks out to me for some reason. I've never been described as the breath of fresh air for someone.

My face warms and there's no stopping the butterflies now. "It's typically '*Sunshine*.'"

"I like rain better." Speechless, my mouth drops open. "And it matches your eyes."

Before I have to even think of a response our server drops off our sandwiches, thus putting me out of my awkward misery.

For like half a minute.

"That looks good," Adrian leans forward looking at my Chef's Club. His Monte Cristo sits untouched in front of him.

"Uh, thanks. Yours looks..." I grimace at the side of jelly. "Interesting."

Leaning across to grab one of the halves of my sandwich, he takes a bite and nods appreciatively. I'm too stunned to say anything, but he's lucky I come from a family that regularly picks off of each other's plates. "Do you want to try mine?"

I snort. "No, thanks."

"Come onnn," he drags out. "It's good." He dips a corner into the jam and holds it out for me. "My whole day is riding on this moment."

Rolling my eyes, I grab for the sandwich but he tsks and pulls it out of reach. "Try again," he taunts.

He leans in closer and watches my mouth, waiting. I reach for it a second time, as he shakes his head. Dropping my hand, I wearily lean forward, and his smirk grows. My heart feels like it's about to beat out of my chest, but I can play along in this game.

At least I *want* to play along.

Resting my elbows on the table, I place my chin into my hands and open my mouth. Taking a bite, I lean back, watching him watch me.

Doing my best to not have any reaction, I finish chewing as he takes a bite. "What did you think?" The glint in his eye makes me think he doesn't mean the sandwich.

It doesn't stop me from saying, "Disgusting." Because the savory and sweet sandwich *is* disgusting. And for one second I feel real, gut wrenching dread at my quick response.

But Adrian just laughs and shakes his head. "I'll pretend to believe you."

Yeah, he was not talking about the food.

Chapter Fifteen

Adrian

After lunch, Blake and I are walking around the small shopping area, still waiting for the mechanic to call her back.

Not that I'm complaining. Not at all.

Today has been the best day I've had since moving out here. Months before that even. Everything we're doing is mundane and an inconvenience to her I'm sure, but I've enjoyed every minute of it. I wish I could take Blake with me on all of my errands. It doesn't matter that she tries to hide her smiles or responds mostly with snark and sarcasm—fuck, I *love* those things. It's all just more fun with her.

Even though we're just outside of Amada Beach, closer to the upper-class neighborhood Aurora Hills, she knows the area and a few of the locals so we stop in at some of the shops. It's a surprise if we don't leave with something that one of the shop owners insists she takes, no charge. Homemade sea salt and lavender soap. Popcorn with chocolate drizzled on top—her favorite I learned. Fresh fruit cups with *chamoy* and *tajin*. A pair of clay earrings, and a matching set for her mom. We each got an iced tea plus a small batch of leaves in the mixture her dad loves. Even the owner of *Wearing Sunsets*, a middle-aged Black woman with waist-length braids and a warm smile that reminds me of my mom, insists that Blake take a cute octopus onesie for her brother's baby that's due in just a few weeks.

I knew Blake's family was popular around Amada Beach. It's obvious from the interactions I've caught between her and some of the pet owners. Hell, even Polly loves Blake, but they have their own... *thing* going on. Who am I to interfere between two grumpy ladies? My mom definitely taught me better than that. But *this* goes so much further than just growing up in a small community or having outgoing parents. This is Blake not only spending her life here, but her putting herself out there and being an essential part of so many people's lives.

I've seen this side of her every day we work together, but I get the impression it's another part of Blake that she underestimates about herself.

Part of me thinks that Blake's naturally introverted and isn't interested in meaningless socializing. Although that doesn't feel quite accurate. She clings to conversations and key details about a person, but she never initiates those moments either. She just waits for them to find her.

It feels wrong to say for someone as resolute as Blake, except I think she's *scared*.

More than anything, it was the look on Selena's face last night when Blake said she had two flats. I didn't understand it at first, I just couldn't let it go either. It was fierce and protective in a way only a mom can be, even if it seemed like a bigger reaction than necessary, especially after learning how easy-going Selena is. She doesn't take much seriously it seems, except for *that*.

I consider asking Blake more about it, when I glance down, and any thoughts other than 'pretty girl' leave my head immediately.

She's walking next to me with a small smile on her lips as she ties her long, raven hair up in a messy bun. I watch as she gathers the strands, trying to catch all of them with a sweep of her hands along her neck. And I can't help but wish that it were *my* hands running up her neck, tangling into her hair. How easy it would be to fist the silky locks and pull her into the perfect position to take her plump pink lips with my own.

That's another thought that has been plaguing me over the last few weeks. One that makes a naughty appearance at the most inappropriate times... like this morning in the shower.

She ties her hair into a knot, and I notice that the scrunchie she's using is bright pink—a total contradiction to her baby blue and white outfit—but it's a cute quirk I've noticed of hers over the last few weeks. Her hair tie *never* matches her outfit, almost like it's intentional on her part.

When she catches me staring, her skin flushes and she pulls on the sleeves of her crewneck. "What are you looking at?"

And suddenly I decide today is not the day I want to bring up any of those questions about her past, and why her mom was so worried yesterday. I just want to enjoy today with her. Maybe I can worm my way so far into her life that she opens up to me without me having to ask. I just have to show Blake that I'm here for her, in whatever way she wants.

"You," I tease.

"Well, stop," she mutters looking aside, and I don't miss the way her lips curve up just the slightest bit more. "I didn't think it'd be so hot today." It is warm for this time of the year, and she's wearing a thick Nike crewneck but otherwise, she's in a short fucking tennis skirt and sneakers. It's somehow sexy and innocent at the same time, which is extremely fitting for her. She notices me staring at her smooth pale legs and squirms under the attention. "I get warm easily, especially when I'm nervous." Her head flies up and she gapes at me for a second, trying to recover. I do my best not to smile but I'm sure it isn't a great attempt.

"Or when my feet are covered," she adds quickly. I scrunch my eyebrows and let her word-vomit all over us—another quirk I've picked up on *quickly*.

"I'm serious. I can't sleep with my feet covered, and I hate the winter if only because I can't wear sandals. I also kinda hate working at the vet clinic because of that. That's not the only reason, as you know," she nods in my direction but won't look up. I do know. There's a lot of aspects of the job that aren't easy for Blake, like everything going on with Lela and Chispa.

There are parts of the job she's great at though. I've heard her talk to her dad a few times about different scheduling and filing software he should look into. Apparently, it's been damn near a decade since he made any changes to those things. For all of Tim's best traits, I could definitely see the middle-aged man getting stuck where he's comfortable. Not only that, according to Olivia, Lela's situation wasn't the first time Blake's offered to help a family understand things like pet insurance and which brands of foods are the best.

Blake has one of the biggest hearts I've ever seen in a person, even though she tries to hide it from the world. I don't know if it's even possible to keep such an integral part of oneself a secret—especially when it brings so much light to people's lives.

So Blake might not want to work around animals, but she was *made* to help people. She's resourceful, organized, and innovative. However, that's something Blake needs to come to on her own, and there are so many paths it could manifest. Sometimes I have to remind myself she's only eighteen. In some aspects, she's wise beyond her years and tolerant in a way that isn't always born into someone—rather, one that suggests she had to learn how to be. Other times, she's so much of the young woman that is her age.

I remember that contradictory feeling of having all the time in the world and needing to figure out your entire life right at that moment. I see that in Blake a lot.

Pulling me from my thoughts, her rambling continues. "Sometimes even just the thought of putting socks on is abhorrent. Especially in a humid environment like this? Ew." She waves one hand in the air next to her head. She's still going, spewing out whatever thought works into her mind next. Usually, she goes for teasing when she feels flustered, but this is almost like she's trying to put as many words as possible between 'when I'm nervous' and whatever I say next. She's not getting off that easily today, though.

"Are you nervous?" I ask as I take another step toward her. She takes one back and I follow, crowding her against the brick wall of the little candy shop we're standing outside of.

"Uh, no," she murmurs, her eyes wide and glued on mine. I move one of my hands to lay on the wall near her hips and lean down toward her. I've never been this bold with Blake before. Not because I haven't wanted to, but I know that the animal clinic isn't the right place either. With more confidence, she doubles down and says, "It's the sneakers."

I laugh. "The socks, too, right?"

She swallows and nods. "Right. The socks." Then she gives her head a little shake, like she can't believe she said that.

Chuckling, I brush my cheek against hers, whispering in her ear. "You make me nervous too, Storm Cloud."

She lets out an almost inaudible scoff and shoves my shoulder, without enough force to push me further away. "Don't make fun of me," she says quietly. When I lean back she's looking at me with an uncertain expression, like she doesn't believe what I'm saying.

"I would never," I promise her. She shrugs and tries to look away, but I gently grab her jaw, pulling her captivating gray eyes back to me. "Blake, I swear, I would *never* make fun of you. I may like teasing you a bit," I add with a smile, "but not like *that*." Not wanting to overwhelm her, I take a step back, catching the flash of disappointment that flits across her face when my hand drops.

We stand there staring at each other for a long moment, only inches apart. Blake is leaning against the wall, with her ankles crossed and hands twisting in front of her skirt, her eyes assessing me the entire time. I stand in front of her, my hands in my pockets now, mostly to stop me from grabbing for her, and I look back at her. I try to wear all of my emotions for her, not wanting to hide anything from Blake.

I want her to trust me. Yeah, with her secrets and quirks, but with more than that. I want Blake to trust me with *her*. I want her to be comfortable and sure in my presence. For her to hear my words and trust that I always mean everything that I'm saying. I'd never lie to her or try to deceive her.

I don't get the impression Blake is very forgiving, or that people in her past gave her any reasons to learn to be.

So, I let Blake take me in and make a silent oath to prove to her that everything will be different with me. I'm not sure how, since I don't know *what* has happened to her, but I know that it will be.

As I'm about to say something—anything to break the tension—a Monarch butterfly flits through the air between us. They're common in the area, but I can't think of a time when one got so close to me.

On the other hand, Blake doesn't look surprised by our fleeting guest. If anything, her expression softens, and she looks up at me with more surety than a few seconds ago.

Giving me a small nod, she straightens up in front of me and takes a deep breath. I don't say anything, just letting her come back to the day together when she's ready.

Pretty girl, always so stuck in that head of yours.

Shyly, she looks away and breaks the silence first. "Let's go into the candy shop. It's my second favorite in town."

I jerk my chin toward the entrance and place my hand on the small of her back, like I've done a few times today.

Except this time, she leans into me. Not a lot—just enough for our hips to brush with each step and the wispy stray hairs to tickle my upper arm—but it's enough. More than that, it's *progress*.

"Are you sure?"

I hand the cashier my card and give her a questioning look. "What?"

The candy store Gumdrops & Giggles is like something out of Willy Wonka. There are rows and rows of jars full of gummies, licorice, taffies, suckers, and anything else you can think of. There's a small 'Build Your Own Brownie' station that reminds me of a giant Easy Bake Oven. On another wall there are hundreds of options of lollipops. Not to mention the small counter in the back that looks like it's set up for different pop-ups to come through. Today, there's an ice cream stand.

As soon as we made our way to the back of the store and Blake saw it, she grabbed my hand and pulled me toward it. Apparently, it's '*exactly* what she needed.' You know, after the coffee, lunch, and five other things that have been fed to us since we started to walk around.

I'm really just impressed that she can put down so much food in only a few hours. It's weirdly endearing to watch too.

"Are you sure that's what you want?" She licks her spoon clean then uses it to point to my cup of butter pecan with caramel and green apple slices. "That's for old people," Blake teases.

"You got pistachio. How is that any better?"

"Yeah, with chocolate chips, whipped cream, and *sprinkles*. That's fun, dude."

"And I got salted caramel," I shrug and take another bite.

"Yeah, with *green* apples." She subconsciously reaches up and brushes her thumb along my lower lip. If that wasn't enough to make my brain shut down, she follows up by slowly sucking the caramel off of her thumb, making my dick twitch in response. Without missing a beat, she continues, "Objectively the worst fruit in the world."

When I don't respond after a few seconds, she turns around to find me frozen in place. My brain is still trying to catch up with my body.

Considering that most of the blood instantly moved south, that might be why I'm mentally lagging.

As if she realizes what she just did, her mouth falls open and she stares at me with those sweet doe eyes. "Oh—I—I didn't..." She shakes her head. "I'm s*orry*," she blurts out.

Cocking my head, I take a step toward her and gently slip my hand around her waist. "Was it good?" My voice is huskier than I mean for it to be, but I don't *want* to hide what she's doing to me either. I think it's important that Blake realizes the effect she has on people... on men... on *me*. I only care that she sees what she does to me. And how fucking badly I want more.

"It was good." It's a breathless whisper, pink tinting her cheeks and her stormy eyes growing darker but also more uncertain. "I like caramel well enough."

"At least it wasn't a waste then," I smirk. Glancing down to her cup, I take a slow step forward, seeing if she's going to run. When she doesn't, I lean down. "You tried mine, now I wanna try yours." She sucks in a sharp breath.

"I think the saying is 'you *showed* me yours.'" I raise my eyebrow and give her an irreverent shrug that says something along the lines of, *if you insist.* "Oh shut up," she mutters. Refusing to look me in the eye, she lifts her spoon and holds it out for me. Keeping one hand firmly on her waist and the other in my pocket, I ignore the handle and wrap my lips around the curved end. Slowly, she pulls the spoon from my mouth, and I can feel her chest rising and falling in a shallow rhythm as she watches me clean the spoon then my lips.

"Mmmm," I nod in acknowledgment. "Not bad."

"Um, you liked it?" She's flustered and I'm half hard.

"Yeah, Storm Cloud, I liked it." Slipping my arm from her waist to her shoulders, I tuck her under my arm and whisper in her ear, "I like everything you give me."

Her lean tilts back as she looks up at me, falling into step beside me. "Oh."

"Yeah, *oh.*" I grab her spoon and lift it to my mouth again, stealing another bite. "Now let's go check on your tires."

Chapter Sixteen

Blake

Of everything I've learned about Adrian, the thing that surprises me the most is he listens to a *lot* of Rihanna. I'm not judging nor am I complaining. It's just endearing to see this gorgeous, always-cool-always-collected man sing along to *Only Girl (In The World)*. I'm talking about choreographed hand movements here.

We're heading back to the clinic after we finished our ice cream and picked up my tires, making it my third car ride with him. Yesterday, when he took me home, I noticed a few classics playing quietly. I mean, I may not be as big of a fan as him, but no one can just skip over the intro to *Take Care* without at least subtle lip-syncing along. It wasn't until this afternoon that we got stuck in traffic that I noticed he might be *really* into her.

Umbrella played, followed by *Rude Boy* and *Birthday Cake*. That's when the lightbulb went off. I mean, he knows *every* word. It's impressive. We're listening to the sensual words of *Skin* as we turn down the street of the clinic. He's quietly singing along, bobbing his head as we roll to a stop. I'm watching from the corner of my eye, hoping he doesn't notice how hard I'm blushing just from the lyrics of this fucking song.

I mean, obviously I've heard it before. But I'm usually alone.

No, I'm *always* alone. So I can't think of a single time that I've been in a situation where I had to sit through a dirty song or graphic movie scene with anyone. Well, other than Margo and Meera; they hardly count in this case.

It's just a song. Adrian clearly knows that. Rationally, I know that. So I'm trying to pretend like I've spent the last couple minutes thinking about *anything* other than what *his* skin would feel like on mine. All I have to imagine from real-life experience is mediocre hook-ups at best. And I can only hope—no, scratch that, I *know*—Adrian would be better than that.

No hate for the few boys I've been with. We were just teenagers. None of us knew what we were doing. But I can truthfully say there was effort on their parts. What more can a teenager hope for?

It's not like I've never orgasmed, just not with someone else. I know enough about my body to know how I can get myself off with my own hands, and sometimes the help of a small bullet vibrator. I don't love full length romance novels—or books in general—and porn almost always grosses me out. *But* some of the erotic short stories that female-centered sites have get the job done well enough. There are even some 'series' I follow.

I wonder what my librarian mother would think. *I mean, it's not a book, but it is reading.*

I accidentally let out a quiet laugh, and Adrian gives me a curious glance. Yet he doesn't push, somehow always knowing the right moments to leave me be. Instead, he just settles back into our comfortable silence.

Either way, my point is, even though I haven't experienced an orgasm with a partner yet, I don't feel totally helpless either. I feel like with the right person, we could figure it out together.

And now my thoughts have spiraled out of control all because of a song and the steady, somehow erotic bob of his head. I'm not saying *Adrian* is that person. Not that he couldn't be either...

Only that I've had a lot of experiences tainted or taken from me in general. And yet, somehow, even though I went to an all-girls school and haven't ever had a *real* boyfriend, all of my sexual experiences have been pleasant. Not earth-shattering, stars-bursting euphoria, but learning experiences that I never left feeling hollow. I can't say the same thing about how I felt going home from school every day.

So, I feel hopeful that one day I'll experience a mind-blowing moment like that.

But no matter how great of a day it was, or how much he flirted with me, today is *not* that day. Turning into the parking lot and finding my dad standing against my car, phone to his ear most likely talking to my mother, is a stark reminder.

Adrian pulls into a spot near my car, leaving enough room to put the new tires on.

"She's here," I hear my dad mutter into the phone. *Yup, my mom.* "I'll call you back, sweetheart. I'm going to help Adria—yes, of course. I'll stop. I love you too." His screen goes dark, and he pushes off the car. "Hi, honey. Adrian." He wraps an arm around my shoulders and nods toward the guy carrying one of my tires over.

"Hey, Tim," Adrian answers before I can. He drops the tire and crouches to start lining it up. "How wa—"

"You don't have to do that."

Grinning over his shoulder at me, he just shakes his head. "I don't mind at all, Blake." I'm equally relieved and disappointed that he didn't use his new nickname for me. I bite back my response and shrug shyly out of my dad's hold. "How was the clinic today?" he continues without missing a beat.

And with that, they fall into a comfortable conversation as Adrian replaces my tires, and I stand to the side, shocked and watching.

It's interesting watching my dad and Adrian interact outside of work. Last night, I had the same thought. It's so easy for them.

My dad's not as social as my mom or brother, but he's not awkward like me, either. Adrian, on the other hand, could have a full conversation with a taxidermied cat if he was left to his own devices. Yet there is an underlying comfort between them, and they have more interests in common than just animal medicine. Like cooking—or in my dad's case, grilling—and chess.

I'm embarrassed to say I never knew my dad was in his high school's chess club until he mentioned it to Adrian last night. When I texted Grady and he said he didn't know either, I felt slightly better.

But *still.*

After about twenty minutes, they're finished and putting the spare back in the trunk of my car.

Slowly closing the small distance between me and them, I grab my keys from Adrian. "Thank you for doing that. And thanks for today, Adrian."

"It was a good day," he promises.

Clearing his throat, my dad turns to shake Adrian's hand. "Thanks for all your help today. It made Selena feel better knowing Blake had someone to go with." I scoff and roll my eyes but don't say anything. "Anyway, I'm running to the store, so I'll see you at home, honey."

"Bye Dad," I call after him before facing Adrian again.

"So," he draws out and sways a little awkwardly. "I was wondering if I could have your number?"

"I—oh," I start to answer before his question is fully processed. "You want my *number?*"

"Uh, yeah," he chuckles and looks away, running a hand down the back of his neck. "We've had dinner and spent the afternoon hanging out. I'd say that makes us at least friends. Right?"

Twirling my keys in my hands, my stomach sours at the prospect of being friend-zoned by him. And it confuses me a little bit after the day we spent together.

Against my better judgement, I nod and hold my hand out. Quickly, he unlocks the device and hands me it with his contact list open.

"There you go," I mumble and hand him his phone back. Without saying anything, he takes it and types something in. Watching for a few seconds, I can't tell what he's doing exactly so I say, "Okay, well, I sh—"

Suddenly, my phone vibrates, and I have a message from an unknown number. Before I open it, I know who it is. And the short message that reads, 'Adrian :),' is confirmation.

When I look back up at him, he's slipping his phone into his pocket and taking a step toward me. "In case you ever need a ride or anything else, you have my number now."

"Oh, okay," I agree with a quick nod.

He smirks down at me and shakes his head. Gently lifting my chin with his thumb, he meets my gaze and says, "I hope you use it. Bye, Storm Cloud."

Blinking up at him, I watch him pull his hand back and walk backward toward his car a couple spots away. He doesn't break eye contact until he's almost there.

As he's about to turn, I call out, "Bye, Adrian."

The last thing I see before getting in my own car is his bright smile and the appreciative look he throws my way over his shoulder.

Chapter Seventeen

Blake

I make it home before my dad, who had to stop at the hardware store for a new paint swatch my mom wants for the kitchen. We all know she's not going to change a damn thing, but we let her have her fun anyway. Selena Lucia Miller may be a fun-loving, take-life-by-the-horns, and all those other idioms type of woman, but she despises change in her home. She likes the comfortable and the predictable where that's concerned.

And who am I to judge? That comfortable and predictable have always been my saving grace.

After I drop off the multitude of gifts for my family on the counter, I make my way upstairs, only to find the devil herself waiting for me in my room.

"Hello, mother," I say dryly but with a tender smile.

"Oh good, just the daughter I was looking for," she says as if she had any others, and pats the spot on my bed next to her. I roll my eyes but plop down in the spot anyway. "¿Qué ha estado en tu mente últimamente, morrita?"

What's going on in that head of yours, little girl?

It's her favorite way to start one of her maternal conversations. Unfortunately though, I know what this one is about—the same thing that had her worrying when someone else dropped me off after work.

Rolling my eyes, I retort, "¿Esto de nuevo?"

I knew she wasn't fully convinced last night, but it doesn't mean I want to have this conversation. And I didn't think she'd bring it up this soon.

"Yes, '*this again*,'" she repeats but in English now. "Blake, what happened to your tires? Was it those gir—"

I shake my head earnestly, cutting her off. My parents and insurance pay Catalina very good money so I can talk about my past there. Not here. In my home, in my room. I refuse to let *them* taint everything.

"No, no. It wasn't anyone, Mom. Lo prometo," I emphasize the promise to her. She takes a breath, not looking wholly convinced.

She does her best, still it always comes back to *the incidents*. Plural. I know she means well, but I don't want to talk about it—about the fear, the shame, the way it all mixed into anger before fading into a hollow, exhausted numbness.

And from the look on my mom's face, I know she's replaying that day we all ended up in the head mistress's office, rather than the swim trials that were happening in the gym—the last day I ever stepped into that god-awful building.

Trying to shake off the memories and lingering dread, I link our hands together. "I really think it's just because of that stupid pothole by the clinic. Even the Pain in My Ass was complaining about it when she brought Benji last." Giving her a wry look, I add, "It might be the *only* thing that we've agreed on."

"Blake Carmen, don't be mean. You know she's just... eccentric."

"O loca," I mutter under my breath.

Her airy laugh fills the room as she leans back on the pillows, pulling me down and wrapping an arm around my shoulders. We lay like that for a while, staring up at the glow-in-the-dark stars she helped me put up when I was younger. I remember being so jealous when I walked into Grady's room and found him with the girl from next door, Vivi, jumping on his bed and sticking them on the ceiling.

The next day, my mom came home with all different packs—different sizes, colors, and a variety of space shapes—and spent hours helping me place each one meticulously and filling me up on homemade pan de dulce until my stomach hurt.

Grady never cared that I had more or *better* stars. For him, it was about the little redhead girl he got to spend those hours with. For me, it was about not wanting to feel left out. Again.

"How was your day with Adrian?"

Finally she brings up the topic I know is the other reason she was waiting for me.

"My day was fine. There's a bunch of shit on the counter from everyone."

"Don't cuss," she reprimands. "He's quite handsome, isn't he?"

I don't have to look at her to know she's smirking. It isn't the first time she's commented on how attractive he is—like anyone with two semi-working eyes could miss it. Even now, in the dim light of my room, I can't help but remember how the sun made his dark skin glow, like he just absorbs the light and radiates it back out. Don't get me started on the way his biceps flexed under the soft button-up when he caged me against the wall and took up all of the air. Or the way his eyes soften every time he knows I'm starting to feel flustered, though he never lets me off the hook, either. I weirdly enjoy it.

Handsome doesn't do Adrian justice. I don't think I know of a word that really encompasses it.

Instead of telling her any of *that*, I just shrug and ask in a teasing tone, "You know you're married, right? Unless you're looking for a new pool boy like all the other moms that come into the clinic."

She just throws her head back in a laugh and swats at my elbow. "We don't even have a pool."

"*Mom*," I scoff, even if I'm chuckling along with her. "I don't think most of those women do either."

After her laugh dies off she quietly adds, "You know, your dad said he had a feeling about him."

I roll my eyes. "What? Like he'll be a good vet?" I mean, he's an amazing vet assistant, and will be an even better veterinarian, but my dad's always going on about his *feelings*. Like how he had a feeling about—

"Hmm, I'm sure there was that. It was more like he had a feeling about you two. Quite similar to what he used to say about your brother." *And Vivi*, goes left unsaid.

Aaand there it is.

"Yeah, because that was sooo spot on," I mock. "They only haven't spoken in what? Four years?"

"I think they talked at our vow renewal a few months ago."

Yup, my parents have been married for twenty-five years. Crazy to think about, even if I've only been alive for eighteen and a half of those years. Last spring, they had a small event in our backyard to celebrate. It was simple and beautiful. But...

"Vivi was drunk as a skunk." I tilt my head in thought. "In fact, all of the Davies were."

Vivi and her three siblings grew up in the house behind us and moved to Amada Beach about a month before we did. After she and Grady met at a Fourth of July party, their mom Bonnie and my parents became best friends. Eventually, we spent holidays together and a gate between our backyards was installed.

While our parents are still close, Grady and I don't talk to the four siblings much anymore.

She waves her hand dismissively. "Either way, I think they talked."

I snort. *If only you knew how that conversation went.*

"And now another woman is having Grady's baby. Dad should turn in the vet coat and open a tarot stand on the pier," I say dryly.

"You're right, Grady *is* having a baby with another woman. But a baby doesn't make a couple fall in love, Blake."

"You don't like her." It's not a question. Despite wondering for a while, her statement only confirms it.

She shakes her head and sighs. It's deep and tired, like everything going on with Grady is really taking a toll on her. I mean, it's been a hell of a year for him between tearing his ACL and finding out he's having a baby with his ex-girlfriend. Not to mention the years before that were centered on me and my wellness.

My ever-present, ever-dedicated mother must be exhausted.

"It's not that I don't like Arielle. She's a nice enough girl. She's ambitious and polite. And she sure is a gorgeous little thing, isn't she?" Tall, slim, and elegant with dark hair and bright blue eyes. She's gorgeous. And aloof and stuffy. "I just don't see her or Grady being a good fit. He's my son, but he's not perfect. None of us are. And I just worry that their flaws will start to pick the other apart rather than balance each other out."

"Do you think he picked Arielle because she's the opposite of Vivi?" I startle myself by letting the question fly out. Call me an annoying little sister, but Grady's relationships are fascinating to me. He is definitely not the most emotionally vulnerable person you'll ever meet. Yet he's charismatic like our mother and a go-getter like our father, so all of his relationships are complex and messy in a way I don't understand. And I'm not sure I ever want to.

"Sometimes, yeah. I'm sure similar thoughts went into Vivi's previous relationship, too." She shrugs again, and I know that's all she'll say about that. She gossips like a hairdresser on a Saturday morning, still there are some things she refuses to talk about out of respect.

"However, that's not the point. The point is... a relationship is about balance. Your hard edges need to smooth out theirs, and vice versa. Does that make sense?" I shrug, not really understanding but not sure I wanna have this conversation either. She carries on regardless. "I've never had any sort of *feeling*, but as your mom, I've always seen you with someone... less jaded," she says gently.

"Even from a young age, I could see that this life was going to take a toll on your soft spirit. And despite what anyone might try to tell you, that is your biggest strength. You still love so much after what you've been through. You just don't give it away to anyone." I can hear the emotion behind her words, and it makes a knot grow in my throat. "I won't tell you who to be with or try to persuade you. It's *your* life, morrita. But I hope you find someone who's captivated by life and the unknown, someone to smooth those hard edges."

We don't say anything for a few minutes. And I appreciate the silence because I'm starting to understand what she means. Or as much as someone with my amount of experience in life can.

There's no denying that what she says sounds refreshing. Invigorating, even. I *am* jaded. I've felt beaten down and exhausted by life for as long as I can remember. And for the second time today I'm thinking, there's no guarantee that it is Adrian, but maybe it could be him.

Chapter Eighteen

Blake

It's almost midnight and I'm lying in bed, wide awake. I wouldn't say I have sleep problems *anymore* because they are rare and random. But it still happens often enough that I find myself wishing, that my anti-anxiety medication made me drowsy. Instead, I take my pill every morning; any later and it'll be impossible to sleep. About a month ago my therapist and the psychiatrist she works with decided it would be a good idea to up my dosage a bit. I didn't disagree since I was starting to show symptoms that made my mom worry again.

Margo and Meera leaving for college didn't help, but it's not their fault that I'm naturally an anxious mess. And I didn't want them to be worried about me while they should be out, living their lives.

So even though I was reluctant to go through the initial adjustment period again, I'm proud of myself for recognizing the signs. Especially the quiet symptoms that are so easy to ignore—like not going to the pool for days on end, or the frustrating combination of fatigue and restlessness that always finds me. There's also the signs like not eating because I'm constantly nauseous, or zoning out when my mom's talking to me, that are harder to hide, even from myself.

Truthfully, I did it as much for them as I did for myself. And Catalina had to remind me, again, that it's okay to hold onto the hope of other people if I can't find it in myself sometimes.

So even though the higher dosage has fucked up my sleep the last couple of weeks, I can't bring myself to complain about it when my head feels quiet most of the time, and I'm not sick to my stomach just from existing.

It's been pretty loud up there since I woke up yesterday, but it's not just my anxiety playing on a loop. It's also Adrian.

My mind has been replaying the last forty-eight hours and everything my mom said since I laid down. I haven't tried to stop it necessarily, since one thing I've learned in therapy is fighting the thoughts is sometimes worse than giving them space. Sometimes we just need to let ourselves feel and think without shame.

But *fuck*, for someone who can't sleep worth crap tonight, I'm fucking tired.

It was a long day. A good day—no, a *great* day if I feel like being honest with myself.

I know my friendship with Adrian is still new, but I've never felt like this before. So seen and understood. And that seems crazy because how could this impossibly perfect man understand *me*?

My phone lights up on my nightstand, pulling me from my obsessive thoughts.

Sat, October 4 at 11:47 PM

Adrian

Thanks for today 🚬

I feel like I should probably be thanking you dude

Nah I was the lucky one

We could maybe do it again sometime?

"Oh my God," I mutter to myself before shoving my face in my pillow. I don't know whether it'd be worse for him to leave me on read, or reply and say no.

Definitely being ghosted. Although being rejected by him would hurt horribly, I think.

Storm cloud

Are you asking me on a date?

"*Fuck me.* Who just calls someone out like out?" I quietly seethe.

Oh no

No no no

That'd be ridiculous right?

If I asked you out? HA

Decent joke though

I meant we could just like… hang out again?

Hang out?

Is that what it's called when a guy *chooses* to spend his entire day off helping me get my tires fixed? When he doesn't complain about carrying the bags that the shop owners keep shoving at me? Or when he was comforting me with his hand on my back?

I'm new to all of this but it feels like more than that.

> Too bad

> I would've said yes

I stare at the screen for at least three minutes, not sure what to say. There's no way to save face after saying that and I don't know how to flirt. I know I can do it sometimes when I'm not thinking about it, and when I don't feel the pressure to perform. And that's what this feels like.

There's a simple comfort that comes from his soft eye contact and amused smirks. It fills me with this sense of calm fortitude I've never felt before.

When my phone buzzes again, I look down. When it *keeps* buzzing, I just stare. And stare. And stare.

Adrian is FaceTiming... slides across my screen over and over.

When I wait too long, the call ends.

"Oops..." I mutter.

> I know you're awake

> And looking at your phone

My phone starts buzzing again, but this time, I answer on the second ring. His easy smile lights up my screen. "Hi."

"Hey, storm cloud," he says quietly.

"You don't have to whisper," I laugh.

"You are."

"Yeah, but I live with my parents." I watch my face turn pink in the little rectangle, and I have to consciously stop myself from tapping my thumb along my fingers—my most stubborn, nervous tick.

"It kinda feels like we're in on a secret, you know?" He shrugs.

I scoff with an eye roll. "I don't know what kind of secret that could be."

"Well, I wouldn't mind being your *dirtiest* secret," he says smoothly. My eyes pop up to meet his gaze, and he winks back at me. When I let out a little gasp, he tips his head back and laughs. It's easily become one of my favorite sights but getting to watch it happen when he's in bed—one arm crooked behind his head as the other holds the phone in front of him—it feels intimate and... yeah, quite secretive somehow.

He shakes his head and gives me a long, assessing look. "Nah, I'm playing, Blake. You don't deserve to be a secret, and I'd never let anyone treat you as one."

With a small smile, I admit, "I don't know what to say when you say things like that. And it makes me feel bad..."

"Why do you feel bad? Because you can't wax poetic about how much you like me?" I just roll my eyes even though we both know that, *yes*, that is exactly what I meant. "Don't worry, I have a huge ego. I can be patient while I work you open."

My eyebrows flick up and my mouth drops open at his innuendo. *He's on a roll today.*

After a second, he chuckles and rubs the back of his neck. I've learned his tells—he bites the left corner of his bottom lip and scrunches his nose almost unnoticeably when he's embarrassed. It doesn't happen often, but it makes him look cute and boyish when it does. Right now, he's grimacing hardcore and refusing to make eye contact with me.

Seeing Adrian so flustered makes me absolutely giddy.

To the point a *giggle* pops out of me. I slap a hand over my mouth, which only makes us both laugh even more. I don't think I've ever made the squealing noise that just burst out of me.

Plus, Adrian *accidentally* saying something totally filthy to me makes me laugh harder than I have in a long, long time.

The fact that it was an honest to God accident somehow makes it the perfect cherry on top of the day with him.

After a couple minutes, I realize that he's stopped, and now he's just watching me. It almost looks like adoration in his expression but let's not be ridiculous.

Right? Right...

When I finally calm down, we just watch each other for a few more seconds. Finally, he breaks the silence, "I didn't mean it like *that*. I meant like, emotionally, you know?"

"Yeah, sure thing," I nod emphatically, trying to keep my smile at bay. I fail. Miserably.

"Whatever." His tone is still playful and easy-going.

"That was the dirtiest thing anyone has ever said to me," I chuckle. I don't know why I admit it. Then again, everything feels safe with him.

"Blake," he says, suddenly very serious, causing me to sober right up, "that was an accident." Before my heart can crack in half, he continues, "The next time, it won't be. And I promise, I can make it a hell of a lot filthier if that's what you want." His eyes rove my shocked face before he adds with a smirk, "What you *need*."

"Oh," I squeak out. A smug look slides over him at my dumbstruck expression, and we can't have that. *Absolutely not.* "Are you going to stutter like a schoolboy after that time too?" I retort with a small victory shimmy into my pillows.

His snort makes my eyes snap to his. "Says the girl who could audition to be a tomato."

"That's not true," I grumble, as my cheeks turn impossibly red. Yup, they skipped pink this time and went right for a perfect impersonation.

"Yeah, sure thing," he parrots back to me.

I start to roll my eyes, a huge yawn breaking out of me instead. I stretch my free arm up and slip my hand further into my sleeve. "You should get some sleep."

"You're the one that works tomorrow," I say as I snuggle further into my duvet.

"I work at the *clinic* tomorrow, sure. But you're babysitting those boys you're always complaining about, right?"

I love that he remembers my schedule.

"Ugh, yes. The Paulson boys—those little shits are going to give me a coronary one day." Typically, I work Sunday mornings with Adrian, but Kevin and Erika Paulson are good people who often need cheap, if not free, help with the kids. And I'm one of the last people willing to put up with their antics.

Laughing, he shakes his head looking through the screen with affection. "Good night, Storm Cloud."

"Good night, *flaco*." He smiles at the endearment, but I wonder if he knows it literally translates to *skinny*. He's thin in the sense that he's tall, lean and cut except that's not why I used it. It reminds me of my mom calling my dad *gordo*. It technically means *fat* but is often used in a loving way.

When I see him moving toward the red button, I sit up suddenly. "Hey, wait—"

He jerks the phone back. "Everything okay?"

"Yeah," I swallow, and his eyes track the movement. "Um, well, it's kinda silly really. Never mind."

"Nope." He settles back into his pillows. "You can't get rid of me until you tell me."

In that case...

"I was just, um—I was wondering if I could text you to-morrow. If you won't be too busy, you know, after work? I don't think we'll work together again for a few days..." I trail off in embarrassment.

"I was already planning on texting you first thing in the morning, but you never have to ask. Texts, calls, carrier pigeons, they're all welcome."

"This is San Diego, dude. We use seagulls here."

"Oh"—he lifts one hand in a fake placating gesture—"excuse me, I'd hate to offend the wicked creatures."

I fall back in laughter, thinking back to the story he told me recently. He'd only been in Amada Beach for a couple of weeks at this point, so he didn't know how determined, and fearless, the local seagulls were until they'd already knocked the entire plate out of his hands. "You're still mad about the cheese fries, I see."

"It was a horrible welcome to the town."

"And yet, you've forgiven Benji for the bowel movements."

He rolls his eyes. "I'm a professional, Blake. You can say shit like an adult. And *he* wasn't the siren who took advantage of a desperate man."

"You're delusional," I shake my head. "Get some sleep. It'll help."

"I'll talk to you in the morning." The last thing I see before I click end is his playful smirk.

Sun, October 5 at 6:23 AM

Good morning storm cloud

I hope you slept well

I slept like a baby just so you know

So now I can confirm that…

You're still a siren and I'm still just a desperate man stuck in the lure of your heart's song

Don't EVER free me I beg you

Chapter Nineteen

Blake

Stepping out of my car, I stretch my arms above me and let my head fall back for a moment. It's colder today than it's been all week, but the sun is bright and still feels warm on my skin. It makes me feel hopeful for a quiet Sunday morning.

I crack one eye open as a car door slams a few spots away. When I see his lazy smirk, I can't help but smile in return. While my head is still tipped back, I let it fall to the side. "Good morning, Storm Cloud," he says smoothly as he makes his way toward me. I watch his long, languid strides—letting myself get lost in his presence for a moment.

I've become accustomed to the nickname over the last week, except it still sends a spark of electricity through me every time I hear it.

Adrian stops in front of me and doesn't hesitate for a second as he pulls me into him.

His muscular arms wrap around my shoulders, letting one fall to my back while the other lightly curls around my neck, holding me to him. I'm certain it's the best type of hug to ever exist. And I really hope he was planning to make this a normal thing now.

When I step further into the hug and wrap my arms around his waist, he whispers, "That's better." His lips are right by my ear, and his chuckle feels like what I'd imagine his knuckles would, brushing down the side of my neck.

I'm probably holding him a little too tightly, but I really don't want to stop. He doesn't seem like he's in much of a rush either.

My suspicions are confirmed when he keeps one arm around my shoulders, tucking me into his side and walks us toward the door.

"I thought you were opening this morning?"

"My dad let me sleep in since we don't have anything scheduled for another hour or so," I tell him. My eyes are fixed on his handsome face as he opens the door and leads me inside, without ever losing contact.

"That was ni—Polly?" Adrian asks cautiously, dropping his arm. I peek around his large frame and can see the old woman sitting by herself, twisting her hands in her lap.

Slowly, she turns to face us as tears silently slide down her cheeks. Adrian walks toward her, falling into the seat across. I follow, suddenly feeling guilty that I agreed to my dad's offer.

"Hey, wanna talk about what's going on?"

Polly takes a deep breath and sits up straighter. "Benji the Beagle is in surgery with Dr. Miller. I didn't know what was wrong when—" her voice cracks and even my bitter heart does too in response. "When he was trying to cough something up and could barely move this morning, so I brought him right here."

"Does Dr. Miller know what's going on now?" Adrian glances toward the hall to the back operating rooms. As a vet assistant, he can't perform surgery, but I know he's itching more and more to be able to help in a bigger way. It was one of the first and few similarities between us I noticed.

She sighs and rolls her eyes. "Yes, we know. The land-scapers were over yesterday and left a pile of branches in the corner. They're coming back today to finish, so I didn't think much of it." She shrugs and bats the tears away. "He ate them. Not all of them but enough to puncture his salivary glands and fill his stomach. I don't know much else than that right now."

"Oh, Polly. I'm so sorry," he comforts. "You'd be sur-prised how many times a month someone brings a pet in for eating something they shouldn't have."

"Yes, well, that little shit has really done it now, hasn't he?"

Gaping, I glance at Adrian. I have never heard this woman swear, and the thought of her saying anything bad about her dog is even crazier. He bites his lip, trying his best to stifle his laugh.

"Listen, why don't I go check on Benji the Beagle and Dr. Miller, then I can come back and sit with you for a while?"

She starts to nod but I cut her off. "I can wait with Polly." She and I share an unsure glance; her husband passed away a few years ago and I doubt her daughter can be here unless it's an emergency. No one, not even the biggest pain in my ass, deserves to be alone in a moment like this. "We don't have a lot of appointments today, so I can come sit with her when I'm not at the desk." I tilt my head toward the back hallway. "They'll need more help than I will."

Polly and Adrian look like I've grown a second head. "Hey, it's called compassion," I snap.

"Oh, honey, we know what it's called"—Polly absent-mindedly pats my leg—"we just didn't think you had any."

I turn my head back toward Adrian and find him biting back another laugh. "See? We will be fine."

"I don't know about that..." He plants his hands on his thighs and pushes up to a standing position. "But I'll go check on Benji an—

"The Beagle," Polly and I add in unison. I don't miss Adrian's amused smirk.

"My apologies, Polly. Benji *the Beagle* and I'll report right back."

Three hours later, Polly and I haven't moved much. About forty-five minutes ago, after Adrian's last check-in to let us know that surgery is still going as expected, she grabbed my hand in a death vice and hasn't let it go unless someone goes to the desk. I can't say I'd be any different if it were my dog, though.

Only three people have come in with their pets, so I've had a lot of time to spend with her. I know that she was sitting alone for about thirty minutes before we showed up. She won't talk much about the time between finding him sick and when I walked in, which is okay. I don't think I want to hear the details anyway.

Thankfully, it's not often that someone comes into the clinic alone or in an emergency, but it does happen. And whenever my workload allows it, I always find myself in the same position—sitting with them and offering a hand to hold when needed.

Most of my life, I've felt like I'm just wandering through the days aimlessly. There are some things I'm certain of—like how I want a big family, and I never want to lose my love of swimming again. But neither of those things feel like my purpose in life either. I want to dedicate my life to something *good*, something fulfilling. I've grown up watching my parents make an impact on our small community without even trying. While my mom's best friend, Bonnie Davies, and her four children have been treated as Amada

Beach's sweethearts since moving in, my parents took on a different role when we arrived in town a month later. Tim and Selena Miller are the caretakers of those who need it and the backbone of everything they're a part of.

They're who I aspire to be and always have been.

But I've never felt even a spark of desire to work in any sort of medical field, nor in childhood education. Yet, in these moments, when I can offer quiet fortitude, it feels like maybe I do have a purpose. There are other times when this job ignites a small flame in my soul—like helping Lela when Chispa first got sick, or when I volunteered with my parents at the local shelter a few times.

Placing my other hand on top of our interlaced ones, I give her a little pat, a sign of support between us, even if I'm still lost in my own thoughts. I'm not very good with words, and I can't say Polly is much better herself, so I hope it's enough.

Finally, almost four hours after my dad took Benji the Beagle back, he comes around the corner. His shock of seeing me with Polly quickly morphs into fatherly pride. She doesn't notice, so I stand, gently pulling her with me.

"Everything went great." The old woman slumps against my side and starts crying in earnest now. "Liane's with him in the room, and he should start waking up soon enough. How about you walk back with me?"

Making my way back to the front desk, I feel Adrian following close behind me. Before I can plop down in the chair, his large hand snakes around my waist as he gently turns me toward him. He assesses me for a few seconds, before asking, "You okay, pretty girl?"

My heart melts into a puddle at his shameless concern and *another* sweet nickname. Placing my hand over the one he still has on my waist, I offer him a squeeze in reassurance. "I'm okay. But mostly I'm glad Benji is." Nodding in understanding, he releases his hold on me and rolls the extra chair closer to where mine is. We sit quietly, both trying to make our mundane busy work seem like it takes more focus than it does. I'm organizing pre-appointment paperwork and confirming the appointments made online, while Adrian scrolls through a few of the afternoon patients' charts.

I glance up at him, just watching the way his eyes squint when he's concentrating on something he may need to know about the animal, and how he double taps his finger on information, like pointing it out will help him remember it later.

He looks up at me with his signature lazy smile right as one of the exam room doors opens to my dad leading only Polly out. There's a burning sensation behind my eyes as I remind myself that my dad and Adrian said things went as great as anyone could've hoped for. As my worry for the dog starts to fade, I realize that he's probably just staying for long-term care. It's not abnormal for animals to require extended medical supervision after a big surgery.

"Thank you so much, Tim," Polly says in a raspy voice, still raw with emotions.

Placing his hand on her shoulder with a soft squeeze, he just nods. "Of course, Polly. You don't need to thank me. Benji the Beagle is a staple around the clinic. We wouldn't want anything to happen to our little friend."

I choke down another wave of emotions and try my best to offer Polly a friendly smile, feeling like we may be turning over a new leaf today.

She clearly has other plans.

"Blake, sweetheart," she pauses, one hand on the counter, and I stupidly think she's going to thank me for being with her today. Nope. "It's not professional to leave the desk so often during your shift. What if someone else had needed something?" she tsks and turns to offer Adrian a smile on her way out.

I sit there, jaw on the ground and eyes glued to the old woman's back, completely shocked. My dad just chuckles and stands on the other side of the desk. Adrian leans forward with an amused smirk of his own and gently closes my mouth with his pointer finger.

My death look swings toward him. "Have I ever told you that woman is a pain in my fucking ass?" My dad doesn't even bother to correct me. He knows my relationship with Polly well.

"You have, Storm Cloud." His use of my nickname in front of my dad for the first time freezes me in place but simultaneously sends a warmth through my entire body. "You know that's just Polly's way of thanking you. It's been a hard day for her. She can't rock the boat too much, okay?"

I roll my eyes and lean back with crossed arms, but nod anyway.

My dad leans across the desk and affectionately squeezes my shoulder. "I'm very proud of you, honey. She may not know how to show it, but I know it meant a lot to Polly that she didn't have to be alone today."

I know he's right, and I like the confirmation that I was able to help in a significant way today.

Adrian just watches me with a growing smile, his eyes taking in every detail of my face, and I can tell he's contemplating something, I just don't know what.

"What?" I finally snap. My dad chuckles again, and for the first time in my life, that sound is getting a little annoying.

Okay, no. Not annoying. Just overwhelming.

"Do you have plans tonight?" Adrian asks. I glance at my dad, feeling my cheeks warm. I shake my head, not trusting my voice to come out strong. "Will you go to dinner with me?" His smile is shy and tentative, but he doesn't cower from either of our gazes.

"Oh, um." I glance around, feeling a million pairs of eyes on me even though we're the only three people in the room right now. Clearing my throat, I add, "Yeah, dinner sounds great."

"Can't wait." He taps the arm of the chair and starts to push off. "I'll pick you up at seven."

Before I can process what just happened, he's pushing through the double doors to the back hallway. And maybe I'm imagining it, but there's a small swagger to his step that wasn't there before.

Chapter Twenty

Adrian

I shove my hands into the pocket of my *Space Jam* hoodie and hop up the stairs leading to the Millers' front door. I'm a little worried that Blake's going to put a lot of effort into her appearance when I'm taking her to the smallest hole in the wall in all of California. And truthfully, I'd be happiest if she just wore one of her little tennis skirts and crewneck combos, like she did when we got her tires fixed last week. But the evenings have started to get cooler recently, so I doubt it.

Taking a deep breath, I quickly knock three times and take a small step backwards.

Blake has this idea of me in her head—always calm, always collected, always confident. I love that she sees me as a solid force because that's what I want to be for her, but I'm only human.

She makes me nervous—that good, butterflies in the stomach, heart stops when I see her type of nervousness.

All I want is to impress Blake, get her attention, and never lose it. It's only been a few weeks, yet I can confidently say that I want her around me all the time. Not only is she cute as fuck and has the snarkiest mouth I've ever heard, those rare vulnerable moments that I have to gently pull out of her, always feel like a victory.

The door pulls open, revealing a pair of lightning gray eyes that are the twins to the ones that have been taking up residence in my mind. Selena.

"Adrian. *Pasa pasa*," she waves me forward with a warm smile. As I step through the threshold of the Miller home, she closes the door before patting my back in greeting. "It's so nice to see you."

"You too, Selena." As I follow her further into the house, I ask how the school year is going—she's a librarian—and take in their house for the second time.

Their home is warm and quaint. Even though I have a pretty good idea that Tim makes much more than what his lifestyle would suggest, and Blake has shyly mumbled the word inheritance once or twice, there's just so much love. It's like a comforting hug as soon as you step within the threshold. A variety of knitted blankets—most likely made by Blake—are spread across the couch and tucked into baskets. There's likely enough for more people than could actually fit in the house. Just like the last time I was here, I can smell a variety of spices in the air and the low tunes of a Mexican folk song in the background.

"Blake should be down soon," Selena tells me. "She stayed late to help Tim at the clinic. I think she feels bad about sleeping in this morning."

"She said Tim offered to let her come in later though."

She nods and points toward the stool on the other side of the island. "He did but..." seeming at a loss for words, she shrugs and says, "that's just Blake. Should I go check on her?"

I quickly shake my head. "No, that's okay. I don't want to rush her." I rub the back of my neck as I feel the blood rush to my cheeks. "I'm a few minutes early actually."

Selena looks up from the bread she's kneading and assesses me for a few seconds before a small smile of approval pulls on her lips. "Blake doesn't like to be kept waiting. She gets her impatience from me."

Chuckling, I drum my fingers on my thighs and bob my head. "Yeah, yeah. I've definitely noticed, but I don't mind. I'd shift my whole day around if it meant spending time with her."

This time, her hands pause in the dough when she looks up with an appreciative smile. "I'm happy you moved to town, Adrian."

"I am too." Surprisingly, it's the truth. I've been to almost every state, and a few different countries, although I hadn't spent a lot of time in San Diego growing up. We only ever stopped here when we drove from my hometown, Bakersfield, down to a small town where my mom and godmother are from.

I hadn't been sure how I felt going into the school year. And I can't explain it, but it feels like I'm right where I'm supposed to be.

Selena slides a plate of sweet, shredded coconut balls toward me; she calls it *cocada*. Falling into silence for a couple of minutes, it's neither uncomfortable nor inconvenient, just feels normal. In some ways, it offers the same comfort as sitting in the kitchen with my mom and godmother growing up.

The sound of socks shuffling across the wood floor has me perking up like a sad puppy left at home.

Blake.

Turning in my seat, I watch as she makes her way over, unaware of my presence. Her long black hair is tied up in a messy bun—more strands falling out than not. She's not wearing a tennis skirt, but the black leggings tucked into fuzzy socks and her *Rocket Power* crewneck are just as good. Better, in fact, because the top is so big it looks like it could even fit me, and that was my favorite show growing up.

"Hey, Storm Cloud," I call from across the room, grabbing her attention. Now that she's noticed me, I watch the pink color slowly creep up her neck. "I like your sweater."

She glances down, uncertain, and gently shrugs. "It was one of mine and Grady's favorites," she says quietly.

A huge grin pulls across my cheeks. "Mine too."

She just rolls her eyes and slips on her Vans. "Well, I'm glad to see I didn't overdress." She nods toward my hoodie and jeans. "Where are we going?"

"It's a surprise, but I'll let you pick the music."

"Deal." She quickly places a kiss on her mom's cheek then leads us toward the door.

Chapter Twenty-One

Adrian

Sliding out of my SUV, the gravel crunches below me and the cool air blows around me. It's a little drier here since we're further from the coast, but only about an hour and a half from Amada Beach.

Walking around the hood to her door, I give myself the same pep talk I've been trying to drill into my brain since I asked her to dinner. Since I made up my mind that I was going to bring her to this small hole in the wall, out in the middle of nowhere, and just hope she doesn't think I'm planning to kidnap her or something crazy.

And considering I stopped at a rundown little diner in an almost ghost town, I know the picture it might be painting. Except this place is special to me.

When I stop outside of Blake's door, she doesn't look skeptical though. Just curious, like she knows I wouldn't waste her time by driving her all the way out here.

I swing the door open and watch as she steps down. She's taking in every detail of the area, from the three-quarters moon to the dirt parking lot to the colorful lights shining in from the small diner.

Our movements fall into step with each other, and after only a second of hesitation, I sling my arm around her shoulders and tuck her into me. The way she sways from unsure and doubtful to confident and at ease in a second, makes me want to get to know her better. It makes me want to find out what could make a naturally confident person like her feel as if she has to constantly question herself. It makes me want to spend the rest of my life making sure she never feels she has to again.

"Why here?" I look down at her, how small she looks against me, the way the moonlight illuminates her milky skin.

"It's important to me," I answer simply. She tilts her head in interest, not prying for more information yet.

The diner looks like it's from the fifties, not in a *Grease* way or something similar, but like it was actually built over half a century ago and hasn't been renovated once. Some of it—the kitchen and systems—has been, just not everything. The wear and tear of the booths, and the scratches on the tables, are from years of patrons coming in and out daily, not from lack of care. I've seen firsthand how well loved SunRay's is.

As we scoot into a booth, I tell her, "My parents are nurses, and travel nursing was something they'd always wanted to do. But my mom got pregnant with me when she was only starting her career." I ruefully shrug, not actually feeling guilty about it.

I'm really close with both of my parents, and I know they feel fulfilled in their careers despite having a child sooner than they expected. It doesn't mean that we don't tease each other about their accident, also known as myself.

Tilting her head, she asks, "You moved around a lot?"

I nod. "For a while, yeah. It was mostly when I was younger. My mom's ten years younger than my dad, so she was *really* just starting her career when she found out she was pregnant. Travel nursing had been one of her goals, and he helped her make sure she could have it all."

Her lips softly tug up the more I tell her, so I decide to just continue on my long winded explanation of why this place is one of my favorites in the world.

"Usually, both of my parents would get a contract somewhere and we'd all go for the summer or a half of a school year. If not, my dad usually stayed in Bakersfield with me and my mom left for a few weeks. But there were a few times when it was too great of an opportunity, like the more competitive hospitals, and it didn't work with my schedule. So, I stayed with my godmother."

She never married and doesn't have any kids of her own, so I've always been treated as her surrogate son. Her three sisters have children of their own, and I know she spoils the hell out of them too. 'It's her responsibility as the fun aunt,' she'd insist with a wink.

And honestly, I loved my childhood. Of course, I missed my parents when they were gone, but Maria would always take me to visit them if they were gone longer than two weeks, and they never missed a holiday or a birthday. I never felt unloved, not for a second.

"Her family owns this place. They opened it in 1958."

When I get to the point, suddenly understanding her need to over explain out of nerves, a new light reaches her eyes and she sits up a little straighter, taking the space in with a new perspective. I sit back and glance out the window, letting her eyes trail along the walls of photos and knick-knacks, wondering how long it'll take her to realize...

She turns in her seat to look at the wall behind her and does a double take of the framed picture. Of me. As a senior in high school.

Yup, my godmother's mother put my senior photo up on the wall in her diner. It's embarrassing, but she's done it for each of her grandkids and I love the hell out of her.

With the biggest smile I've ever seen on her, Blake looks back to me. "That's you!" She points to the photo.

Chuckling, I rub my hand down the back of my neck. "Yup, that's me. Seventeen, a cocky little asshole, and counting down the days until graduation."

Her eyes stay trained on seventeen-year-old me as she gently shakes her head. "No, I don't believe you were an asshole for a second."

I just shrug. I was a cocky little shit in the way most young boys are—even the ones that were kind of nerdy in the chess club and only found his physical strength when he turned sixteen. But I like to think that I was kind and tolerant, that I never picked on anyone. Never had a girlfriend that I wasn't faithful to, but when I was single, I was single.

I wasn't the worst kid, though I don't think anyone would call me the best, either.

Breaking up our conversation, an older woman with dark olive skin and silver hair sets two milkshakes on the table. "Adrian Ray, it's been too damn long. Do you hear me?"

I look up at my grammy. Sunny Klein. Technically she's my godmother's mom but she's always loved me harder than that. And I freaking adore her in return. I catch Blake's head whipping back toward me, catching my middle name, the second half of the diner's name.

Grammy's tone is stern, but her gaze is affectionate. I learned a long time ago there's not much this woman would get mad at me for. Sliding out of the booth, I tower almost a foot over her at six foot four, but don't get it twisted on who is in charge here. It sure as hell isn't me.

"Come here, you old bat." My tone is full of love, and she laughs as she half-heartedly swats at my arms that wrap around her. "I didn't think you'd be here so late. That's all."

"You know this is my favorite time of the year."

She means Halloween, and from a single glance around, you might guess it's her favorite holiday. There are fake spiderwebs tacked up alongside plastic jack-o-lanterns and floating bats. She has tablecloths with a variety of patterns on almost every surface and different shaped lights hung around. One of her regulars does window murals, and this one is a coven of witches around a cauldron in a graveyard.

Christmas is my favorite time to visit, but you can count on a monthly theme despite what time of year it is.

Grammy's wearing an apron with black cats printed all over and little candy corn clips throughout her wavy, gray hair. She's getting to that point in life where it seems like there's new indications of her age every time I see her—deeper lines around her eyes and fresh sunspots from her free time spent in her garden. In spite of that, she's had one of the most youthful, loving souls for as long as I've been born.

"Yeah, I should've figured," I smile down at her. "Is Pop here too?" My pop, Ray Klein, is where my mom got my middle name from. My mom's dad and Ray have been best friends since they were five years old.

Snorting, she shakes her head and tries to push me back into my seat. "You know he can't miss his evening shows."

Looking at Blake, I explain, "Pop loves *The Real Housewives*. He watches the reruns almost every night." She snorts and glances back toward Grammy, who is currently smiling like the cat that caught the canary.

"Hello, dear," she interjects before I get the chance to introduce them. "Who are you?" The question is blunt but it's just how she is, not her being rude.

Unsurprisingly, Blake just smiles wider. She doesn't care about niceties—that's why she loves Polly even if neither of them ever admits it.

"Hi, ma'am, I'm Blake. Adrian's... uh..." She trails off, eyes flashing to me. I don't try to fight the grin that pulls at my lips, even as Grammy's eyes assess her then flit to me. She could've said friend, it wouldn't have hurt my feelings even if I wish we were more. And as much as I like watching Blake flustered, I throw her a rope.

"My date," I declare confidently. Blake's eyes grow in surprise but she's still smiling. And blushing. I'd never really been a fan of pink before she came along.

I just shrug implying, *I gave you the chance first.*

"Adrian Ray," Grammy starts, "how long have you had a girlfriend? Do Cami and Maria know?"

"My mother and godmother," I clarify to Blake. "And no"—looking back at my grandma—"because this is only our first *real* date. I'm in the process of courting."

Blake snorts, loud. "Courting? What is this, a Jane Austen novel?"

Grammy cackles next to her. "Oh, I like you, girl. Don't make it too easy on him." She winks and Blake preens at the attention.

"Oh great, a mutiny is forming," I mutter playfully.

"Just wait until your momma and Maria get their hands on her, then we can talk about a real mutiny." She sets a hand on Blake's shoulder. "Any allergies?" Blake shakes her head. "Picky eater?"

"I don't like mustard or turkey alternatives. Pig bacon and ground beef only."

Grammy laughs and pats her head. "You are perfect. I'll bring out some food for you two, trust me." Blake nods, and I do too, liking the way that Blake trusts the old woman simply because she's connected to me. Maybe Blake trusts me more than either of us have even realized.

Looking at me for a long time, with a small, smug smile that looks delicious—like something I'd love to get my own mouth on—I can see the wheels turning in her head. Finally, in a low voice, she leans forward on the table and asks, "Courting, huh?"

Pushing one of the milkshakes toward her, I scoot forward in the booth and , "You're not a dumb girl, Blake. So don't act like it."

Her face flames and she nibbles on her bottom lip. The one that isn't smirking anymore. Yet there's still a soft vulnerability that rarely comes out when she says, "I'm not a glass half full type of person, Adrian."

"I know that. But I'm willing to prove I'm someone you can put your trust into. I wouldn't spend time with your family or bring you to meet *my* family if I was messing with you. If anything, please believe I have more respect for you than that."

For some reason, that statement makes Blake speechless. She looks like she'd believe that a starved great white shark wouldn't bite her before she believing my statement. So it leaves a sour taste in my mouth when she impassively replies, "I believe you."

I don't push it, though. I'll show Blake what I think of her, and what I think we could be together if she gave us a chance.

Both God and I know that she's been the only thing on my mind recently, especially during those private moments late at night or during my morning showers. Except I don't want only that with her.

Blake is so much more than a fling. Not to get ahead of myself, but she is easily wife material, and I've never met another woman I thought that about. And we're both young. So I'm not in a rush to tie her down but I don't want to wait too long for someone else to catch her attention either.

To my surprise, she's the one to break the silence. "So, that's your grammy," Blake muses with a small smile. She's looking at me again as if she's seeing me in a whole new light. One she likes, I hope.

"That's her," I nod.

"I like her."

"She likes you."

With a smile, she takes a big slurp of her milkshake. "So, you're not only close with your godmother—Maria—but her entire family."

Taking a sip of my drink, I nod and tell her, "Yeah, I am. Even before I started staying with Maria while my parents were working, I'd always been treated the same as Grammy's biological grandchildren. And that goes for her kids and my mom's parents as well."

"That's how I feel about Bonnie, my mom's best friend. She lives in the house behind us. I'm not very close with her kids anymore. They're all older than me. So, you know how that goes..." She trails off with a sad shrug but doesn't pause long enough for me to ask her about it. "Bonnie's basically my second mom though, and her kids probably feel similarly about my parents."

"I get that," I tell her in comfort. "I'm not really *close* with my cousins either—Maria's nieces and nephews, I mean. We're close in age but we grew up all across California and Arizona, so we didn't spend a lot of time together."

Seeming to think through something, she takes another drink and looks out the window. A few seconds later, she asks, "Do you ever regret it?"

My brows furrow in confusion. "Regret what?" I ask with a shrug.

"Not trying harder, to be close with them. Now that you're older."

"Oh." I'm a little taken back by her question. "I've never really thought about it like that. Maybe it was just the circumstances, but even if we had lived in the same city, there's no real guarantee that we all would've been best friends. And I don't think it would be too late to bridge that gap if any of us wanted to."

"You... don't want to?"

"I've just never thought about it," I repeat with a shrug. "Not being close with someone doesn't mean you're on bad terms with them."

"That's a good way to look at it," she mutters before focusing on her shake again.

"Do you regret it?" I ask, my tone gentle. "Not trying hard enough with Bonnie's kids?"

She has a sad, helpless expression when her eyes find mine again. "Honestly? I think about it *all* the time, and I have no idea how I feel about it. It depends on the day, usually."

As I take a second to find the right words for her, Grammy comes back with our food, setting a cheeseburger down in front of both of us and a basket full of chicken tenders and fries in the middle. There's ranch, ketchup, barbecue, buffalo, and honey but no mustard. There's no doubt Grammy will mark down which ones were used, in case Blake visits again.

I really hope she does.

"Thank you..." Blake trails off, realizing she doesn't know what to call her. She looks at me, but I helplessly raise and drop my shoulders, knowing exactly what she's going to tell Blake.

"Just Grammy, dear." She leans over and pats her cheek. "Enjoy."

Blake smiles as she watches her walk away, stopping at another table of regulars along the way. She picks up a chicken tender and dips it in the buffalo then the ranch before taking a bite. With a quiet hum of approval, she takes another bigger bite and does exactly what my Grammy told her to do.

After a few seconds of silence, I finally break it. "Hey, Blake?"

Pausing as she dips a tender into sauce, she looks up at me through her lashes and I'm momentarily struck by her lightening eyes, not for the first time. There are times, like now, when Blake looks at me like I could be exactly what she's been in need of her whole life. I know because sometimes I catch myself feeling the same about her.

"Yeah?" It's so quiet, I don't know if I would've caught it without reading her lips.

"It's good to be accountable, but not *everything* in life is your fault nor responsibility. So, maybe the real question isn't 'do you regret it?' but do you have anything to regret in that situation?"

She looks at me with scrunched brows and a cute tilt to her head, and as the seconds tick by, I can see as she processes my words. Her shoulders straighten, eyes staring off in thought.

"I've never thought about it like that," she whispers. Without looking up from the tray of food, she admits, "I guess I just always assume I did something wrong..."

There's a voice in the back of my mind telling me that this is more than just her estranged childhood friends, but I can't fit the puzzle pieces together fully. "No one's perfect, Storm Cloud, but you've got to be nicer to yourself."

With a wry smile, she shrugs. "I'll try."

Biting my tongue—knowing better than to push this too far—I silently make a promise to myself to not be another person in Blake's life that makes her feel as if she's somehow forgettable, or worse, unwanted.

Chapter Twenty-Two

Adrian

Blake hops out of the car as I pull the gas pump out. I let my eyes take in her black leggings and '90s crewneck for the millionth time tonight. "Where'd you get that?" I finally ask. It's clear that it's a well-loved, but taken care of, piece of clothing. It's not something you'd get at Forever 21.

Dropping her eyes down for half a second, she leans into the passenger seat. Probably looking for something I assume, but at this angle, her cute bubble butt is jutting out. And yeah, I let myself look at that for the millionth time tonight too.

"My brother left it when he went to college, so I kept it."

"I like it. I'm going to borrow it sometime," I tease.

She shrugs and closes the car door. "Do I get to borrow yours?" She tips her chin toward my *Space Jam* hoodie. The thought of her small frame drowning in my anything lights my entire body on fire.

What I want to say is, *you could have everything I own.*

What I actually say is, "Do you even like the movie?"

She scoffs, and in a high-pitched voice that I assume is supposed to be Bugs Bunny, she quotes, "Why Michael, I thought you'd never ask!" She blushes at her own goofiness, and fuck, it's cute. Everything about Blake teeters on the line between adorable and sexy as hell. And yet, she somehow doesn't realize the allure she has. At least on me.

She holds up her wallet like it's a trophy. Must've been what she was looking for. "Want anything?"

"Just a water." She nods and gives me a quick 'cool,' before turning on her toes and walking inside. I wish I could just watch her the entire time, forever, always. But to avoid looking like a total creep, I turn back to the gas pump.

When I'm climbing into the driver seat, I look to find Blake standing in one of the aisles except she's not alone. There's a group of about five girls, all around her age. Everyone looks happy and giggly except for Blake. I open my door right as her eyes meet mine.

The reminder I'm here doesn't seem to bring her any sort of comfort. Instead, she just shakes her head slightly before dropping her gaze and backing down the aisle. I watch as she drops the water bottles on a random shelf, falling further into herself with each step.

Every instinct in me is screaming to get out. To go to her. To grab her, hold her, protect her. But she's speed-walking to the passenger seat and locks the door before it even closes.

"Sorry about the waters," she mumbles. No other explanation.

"It's okay." I slowly raise my hand, hesitating for only a second before wrapping it gently around the nape of her neck. She finally looks at me, and even though she's trying to hide them, I can see the tears in her eyes. "Do you want to go home?"

She nods, avoiding eye contact again. I put the car in drive before immediately placing my hand back on her body. I grab her hand, interlacing our fingers and drop them in her lap. She doesn't say anything for the rest of the ride, clutching my hand with both of hers and not fidgeting even a little the entire way. And in my core, I know to not push about whatever happened inside with those five girls. I also know that I can't leave her when she's this upset either.

It's a silent ride home. She's holding on to my hand the entire time, as if it's the only thing grounding her to this moment with me. And for now, that's enough. At least until we get to her house.

Rolling to a stop next to the curb, I try not to let my avalanching concern overwhelm her more than she already is.

She doesn't wait for me before opening her door and practically crawls out of my car. Glancing over her shoulder, she offers me a small smile that quickly morphs into unadulterated anger at the sight of me stepping out of the vehicle.

Good.

Be mad. Fight with me. Just feel something.

"I don't want to talk about it, Adrian," she snaps. "Just go back to your car."

She's about halfway to the front steps, and I've only made it to the curb when I stop. I don't turn around though.

"Just," her voice cracks, and her hands fly up to cover her eyes, "just leave me alone. Please. I thought I could do thi—" Her sobs overtake her, and maybe it's from the entire day, but this morning didn't trigger such strong emotions. This is different. This anguish is coming from her fucking *soul*.

With a few quick strides, I'm standing in front of her. I'm too afraid to touch her right now, so I just stand with her. I try to be a force of strength and comfort, and whatever else she needs, at the moment.

"Blake," I say in a low voice, "I'm not going anywhere. We don't have to talk about it, I just need you to know that we can. Not tonight. Not even tomorrow. You're safe with me."

"You don't understand," she hiccups.

"You're right. I don't understand, but I want to. I want to know everything about you. And I'll give you all the same."

"You say—" She tries to take a deep breath, except she can't through the tears. "You say that now, but if you knew everything..." Still covering her eyes, she starts to frantically shake her head as her breathing grows more labored.

Closing the small space, but still keeping my arms at my side, I let out a pained sigh. "There's nothing that would change my mind about you. I'm here for you in any way you'll have me. This thing between us? It's not so easily broken. I promise. I know you don't trust easily, Blake, but I'm begging you to try with me."

Leaning her head on my chest, I finally have the go ahead to wrap my arms around her—going for the hold that I've quickly realized I love for her—an arm tightly around her back and one hand tangled into her silky black hair. We stay like this for a bit. After a few minutes, in the smallest voice I've ever heard, she whispers quietly into my chest, "They made my life hell for years."

I pull her in tighter, and sigh with relief when her arms finally lock around my waist. I don't want to jump to any conclusions, but it's starting to make sense why Blake is so skittish around new people, and why she treats herself like some unimportant afterthought. I have a pretty good idea who those girls are, or at least what they were to Blake.

Nodding against the top of her head, I try my best to comfort her. "I was hoping it wasn't anything like that," I admit. "But you survived. You're here." So fucking gently, I slide my hands to her jaw and cradle her face like it's the most precious treasure in the world. And I'm starting to think she may very well be. "I'm here now. You don't have to survive anymore... you can live. You're safe, Blake."

"It doesn't feel like it," she whimpers and rubs a hand over her chest.

Placing my own over hers, I murmur against her hair, "I know. But it is. You're home now. You're here with me, and I'd never fucking hurt you. You're *safe* now."

Her face crumples as tears slide down her cheeks while she softly nods. She doesn't believe the words yet, I just hope she trusts me enough to want to.

I drop my forehead to hers and whisper one last time, "You're safe."

Chapter Twenty-Three

Blake

island of misfit toys
Mon, Oct. 13 at 9:29 AM

I miss you

Meera

I always miss you

Margo

Miss you so much, baby B. We'll see you in ten days though!

It's not soon enough

Meera

Is everything okay?

Biting my lip, I think over my next response. I'll tell my friends about the run-in I had last night soon—it's inevitable. But I still haven't told them about how Adrian and I are closer than coworkers, especially after last night. And I haven't fully processed the last twenty-four hours myself.

It's too overwhelming and embarrassing. So, I vow to tell them when I'm with them in person and have their physical comfort.

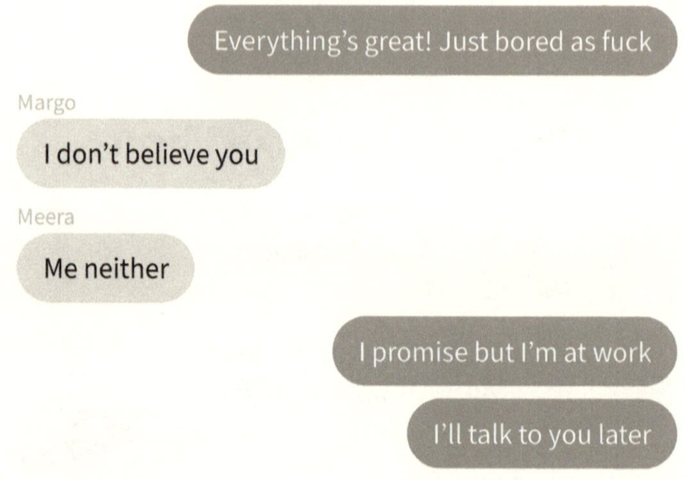

Slipping my phone in my bag, I ignore the churning in my gut from lying to them and make my way across the parking lot.

The little bell over the door sends a sharp pain through my head. Usually, I'm one of the few who doesn't find the sound a small annoyance, but I'm still feeling emotionally drained after yesterday, resulting in a lingering headache. It's been a while since I've gone through that many highs and lows in such a short period of time.

I guess there aren't a lot of reasons for it to happen when you spend a majority of your time alone, now that my best friends have left for college. Even then, I don't think I'd give back even a second with Adrian to avoid the bad.

When I went to grab our waters, I never expected to run into five of my old teammates from Serenity Prep. Not that anyone on my team was necessarily nice to me, but three of these five were particularly terrible. I don't know why they chose me, or if there was even a reason, and Catalina has spent a lot of time reminding me that it always had more to do with them than with me.

I don't know how I was able to hold it together for the hour and half drive home. When I turned around and saw him standing there, I knew every wall I had built up was about to crumble. All I wanted was to crawl into my bed and not return for a very long time.

During the entire drive home, I was trying to form the words to tell Adrian how I know them, except they tasted like vomit every time I tried to open my mouth. I think he's the one person in my life that I couldn't lie to, and that is fucking terrifying. But after last night, I find myself wanting to tell him more.

I drop into the chair behind the front desk and my head falls backward. I've been doing my best to avoid my parents, because with one look, they will know something's going on. So, when my dad called me earlier to ask if I could cover a few extra hours since Olivia's getting sick, I jumped on the excuse to get out of the house, knowing it was only a matter of time before he and my mom got home. However, now that my four hour shift has turned into eight, I feel *exhausted.*

Taking a moment to myself before someone comes in, I think back to last night.

To the feeling of his strong hands cradling my face.

To the moment he pulled me back into his chest and held me until I stopped crying.

'You're safe.'

Even just remembering his words has me blinking back tears. Being with Adrian is the safest I've ever felt outside of my family. I don't know how long we stayed out there but at least half an hour.

I didn't want my bed anymore. I just wanted him. And like always, he seemed to have wanted to be there as much as I needed him to be.

At some point, we naturally detangled from each other, and he silently walked me to the door. He pulled me into his chest one more time, holding me tighter like he really didn't want to leave me, and whispered a promise that he's only a call away, even though he's working tonight too.

"Hey, Blake," one of the vets, Dr. Evie Lemmings, calls as she walks around the corner. I give her my best effort at a smile, but she doesn't seem to mind. She's been working here for almost a decade, so I've known her far too long to feel pressured to put on an upbeat act. I'll save that for the pet owners.

She doesn't stop on her way to the employee's storage closet, but she tells me with a small smirk, "There's something in the break room for you."

My eyebrows furrow, pushing off the chair to stand anyway. As soon as I step inside though, my expression quickly turns to a scowl.

Fucking Polly. That pain in my ass.

I see the container sitting on the counter, and for whatever godforsaken reason, my legs keep walking closer, even though I know exactly what it is. She uses the same type of aluminum container every time she brings her stupid oatmeal raisin cookies in for the office. Like, seriously, who doesn't just make chocolate chip or any other flavor?

I stop right in front of it and stare down at my name. The lid is clear so I can see right through it and... yup, that's oatmeal. My eyes roll before I can stop them. For half a second, I actually consider throwing them in the trash, but even I know that'd be mean.

As I'm turning away, Evie pops her head in and looks down at my hands, confused. "You're not going to eat any?"

"No," I shake my head. "I don't like raisins."

Smiling, she just nods. "I know. They don't have any." With that, she turns back to the exam room she came from. Now I'm confused.

Peeking over my shoulder, I take another look. Almost instantly, I realize that she's right. There is oatmeal but no raisins. It actually looks like... chocolate chips and walnuts? My favorite?

"Goddammit, Polly," I mutter with a watery laugh. I quickly bat the fresh tears away, then I pile three onto a napkin and take my place at the front desk again, feeling just a little bit better than five minutes ago.

And who would've thought that would ever be thanks to the Pain in My Ass herself?

Chapter Twenty-Four

Adrian

It's been a long week, and it's only Monday. So, I had no plans do anything other than go straight home, maybe order a pizza, and spend another few hours studying for this fucking histology exam in a week. It's the topic I've been struggling with the most this semester. It's the least hands on right now, so that's probably why.

The thought of extra pepperonis and microscopic structures left my brain when I saw Blake's car still in the parking lot. An *hour* after she got off.

After last night, I started to go into panic mode, ready to call the special forces in to find her. After taking a deep breath, I opted for trying her number instead. Thankfully, she answered on the second ring—even though I could tell all evening that she'd rather be anywhere than back at the clinic today.

That's how I ended up here... standing in Benji the Beagle's kennel while Blake sits on the floor in front of me.

When I asked where she was, in a small voice she admitted, "I'm not ready to go home... and he just looked so lonely, Adrian."

Immediately, my feet took me inside and to the back of the building, where all the hospitalized animals stay.

Polly was here for most of the day, sitting with him while we were in and out to monitor his vitals and administer antibacterial medications. Now, he's out for the night with the amount of pain medications he's being given.

So, if I had to guess, *no*, Benji probably wasn't too lonely when Blake found him.

She looks up at me, and from her red eyes and the faint tear streaks on her cheeks, I also don't think it was him that needed the company.

I'm proud of Blake for not avoiding me today. I expected it after she was practically forced into a show of raw, unwanted vulnerability. And I'm getting to know her well enough, so I was prepared to be patient with her. I would give her a few days to regroup or offer silent support if necessary.

But when I got to work and caught Blake alone in the small kitchen area, picking up chocolate chip cookies, she surprised me. Without a word, she walked right up to me and tentatively opened her arms for a hug. Without a fucking second of hesitation, I closed the gap between us and held her for a couple of minutes. It didn't feel like nearly enough time, but the gesture itself felt like I won the lottery.

"Hey, pretty girl," I quietly greet her.

With the saddest eyes I've ever seen—with the exception of last night—she whispers, "Hey, Adrian."

"Mind if I sit?"

She shakes her head and scoots over on the towel she must have laid on the floor. The kennel workers are great at keeping it tidy around here, but I don't blame her for the precaution.

Benji's lying next to her, so she can only offer me so much room unless half my butt hangs over the small ledge. It's a tight squeeze but I don't mind. Our sides are pressed against each other, and I can smell that fresh, melon scent I've started to associate with her.

After a second of hesitation, I watch from the corner of my eyes as Blake leans her head on my shoulder. I feel the same hesitation in my body as I reach out and let my hand settle on her thigh.

We're both still in our scrubs, but it doesn't matter. This still feels like an incredibly intimate moment with Blake. Actually, there have been a couple of times where we felt so close even the act of sex couldn't connect us in the way those small moments have. Like when we quietly share tidbits about our lives up until now, or when she let me hold her while she broke down.

Until Blake, I only understood intimacy to be something physical. And it's certainly not that I don't want her in that way—because I sure as hell do—but I'm not in a rush.

Hell, I'm still waiting for the right opening to finally kiss her.

Everything else will come in time. And I'm realizing that this emotional intimacy may be just as new to Blake, and ten times as important.

I'm so lost in my own head that I only notice Blake slipping her arm under mine. She's loosely holding onto my forearm while her other hand rests on Benji. Seeming lost in her own thoughts, I wonder if she's realized that she's slowly moving further and further into my space. Any more, and I'll have to decide between slipping off the side or wrapping an arm around her.

As if it's any choice at all.

After about fifteen minutes of sitting quietly together, I finally ask, "Do you want to talk about it?"

It's a lame question but it feels like I've just dropped a bomb in our silent sanctuary. All evening, I caught myself wanting to ask if she's okay, but it felt more like insincere filler. Because even with only a crumb of information, it's obvious that Blake wouldn't have had that strong of a reaction to running into some girls if she was okay.

And asking who those girls are feels too forward. Blake needs to guide the conversation here, even though there's a protective voice in my mind screaming at me to find out what's wrong and immediately make it better.

She looks down at Benji and twists her lips to the side. There's a large part of me that expects her to ignore the question. And even if it kills me a little, I'd do it if that's what she feels she needs.

But *fuck*, I want her to just take that last leap of trust toward me. It's easy to assume who those girls are, or what they were to Blake in school. Except I don't want to do that. It isn't fair to start creating my own ideas of her, or her life, even if my intentions are good.

As I try to get myself to accept her silence, she finally starts talking. "Those girls in the gas station, they're... I know the—they... they made my life hell, if you want the truth," she finally spits out.

"I do," I murmur close to her ear. "I want to know everything you're willing to share."

Turning to look up at me, her bottom lip trembles, but after a long moment, she nods.

She fucking nods.

And I know, even if it was made out of sheer desperation, Blake just made a decision about our blossoming relationship. It's one that changes *everything*, and one that I know there won't be any second chances if I fuck it up.

Chapter Twenty-Five

Blake

"I don't really know where to start... I guess it's easier to go back to the beginning?" I look at Adrian, feeling unsure about opening this wound, but not sure I could stop if I wanted to. He nods once and it fills me with enough courage to go on. "When I was in the sixth grade, I was offered a swim scholarship to the local all-girls private school. I was younger than my brother and our friends, so I didn't really see why I shouldn't take it. And my parents were so proud of me, you know?"

Looking back, I didn't really *want* to go to Serenity Prep Academy. But—not for the first time either—it felt like everyone close to me was moving on without me. Of Bonnie's children, Vivi's the closest to my age, only two years older. From there, the age gaps just continue to grow. It never felt as noticeable when I was younger, except as we all moved into middle school and high school, two years started to feel like decades. And anything more than that, a century.

And when my parents, coach, and I got the news that the prestigious school wanted me, they were all so *excited*. It felt like, if I wasn't working toward something greater through swimming, then why was I even doing it?

Part of me felt like I didn't have the choice to say no, and the other part of me didn't want to lose the attention I was getting from everyone for once—my brother, the Davies siblings, everyone.

He nods again, giving me the silence and space to take this at my own pace.

"Anyway, I started in the second half of the year, and it just was... miserable. From the beginning. And three of those five girls from the gas station? They were the ringleaders." I shrug helplessly. I wish I understood what I did—why the hell I was so unlikable from the moment I stepped into that school.

"What happened, Blake?" Adrian asks. His voice is rougher, rawer.

"What didn't happen?" I laugh without humor. "The swim coach arranged a sleepover with one of the girl's moms. They were just trying to help me in a new school, but Morgan, Marissa, and Becky had much different ideas for that night." I'm too embarrassed to tell him the details. Like when I woke up to discover they were trying to do the old hand in warm water prank to make me pee myself, only to discover they'd already drawn all over my face with permanent markers. Though all of that's *nothing* compared to the rumors they started about me the following week—like how I allegedly did piss myself while I was fully awake and how I ate a moldy slice of cheese, ignoring the fact we were playing truth or dare. Instead they told everyone I was "poor and used to it."

A small, watery smile plays at my lips. "The only good thing to come from it all was Margo and Meera—my best friends."

Meera has her own torrid history with some of the girls on my team from when they were in elementary school. Margo, on the other hand, moved to Aurora Hills when she was ten. From the stories I've heard, she had no interest in being friends with the 'mean girls,' and after one school project together, she never let Meera go back to such horrible treatment.

I don't think they ever questioned whether or not to take me under their wing when the rumors started. The two of them sat down next to me that same day at lunch and never left my side after that.

"Some things got worse, but they made it bearable, making sure I wasn't ever alone."

He squeezes my thigh gently. "I like those girls then."

Chuckling under my breath, I nod in agreement. "Yeah, me too. A lot."

"I—Blake," he slowly starts, clearly thinking through his approach. "I don't want to belittle what they did to you at that sleepover; it was malicious and wrong, and just plain *cruel*, but what do you mean that it got worse?"

Taking a deep breath, I try to sum it up the best I can. "There were more rumors. Then came taunting—just stupid nicknames like *Blake the Flake* or *Snake* or *Rake* or something stupid along those lines. Then I..." I shrug, awkwardly, hating that I feel so embarrassed about something I have no control over. "I was an *early bloomer*, if you get what I'm saying. And things *bloomed* well into high school.

"After that, everything... escalated. Like Morgan 'accidentally' hip checking me over the pool's ledge while walking into practice, or Marissa 'accidentally' shoving my phone and goggles through the cracks in the bleacher. And let's not forget, when Becky thought it'd be funny to try to catfish me as a new boy from the all-boys school."

"No one did anything?" He sounds affronted, as if he'd go yell at the head mistress even two years later.

"I hid a lot of what was going on from my parents. And the only time they were brave enough to push the boundaries more was whenever Margo wasn't around." Meera's a lover but Margo? She's a fighter—especially when it's to protect her friends. I tried arguing and fighting back a few times, but it's a losing battle when it's three against one, and a whole team that turns a blind eye in fear of being the next target.

"And I guess you could call it luck that Meera's two older brothers went to Astoria Academy, the sibling private school, and were stereotypical popular jocks. Not that any of the boys ever really tried, but Jatin and Dev never let any of them fuck with Meera, Margo, or I."

"But you graduated from an online program. You've mentioned that a few times. So... what happened?"

My eyes start to fill with tears as I get to the *big* incident—the one that almost broke me.

"When I was in the locker room, changing and mentally preparing for our semi-finals, Margo burst in, walked right up to Morgan, and sucker punched her." I glance up at Adrian and laugh at the shocked wide-eyed expression. It's overall not a humorous situation, but as I was watching this play out in real time, I felt exactly how Adrian looks.

"I had no idea what was going on. I always turned my phone off leading up to a race or meet, so I didn't get any of their messages. Even Dev was trying to call me. But as Marissa and Becky tried to pull the two of them apart, Meera came to my side and told me... or I guess I should say she *showed* me."

Adrian's entire body tenses next to mine and I wish I could read his mind. Sometimes it still doesn't even feel real, like I'm just sharing a horrible story I heard from a friend of a friend or something. We like to tell ourselves that things like this don't actually happen—but all of this is my real life.

"Morgan must have been bored that day because she decided it'd be funny to snap a few pictures of me changing into my suit. And even funnier to send them to her boyfriend's friends at Astoria." I shake my head, looking back down at Benji. It's one of those situations where, rationally, I *know* I have no reason to be embarrassed, or ashamed, but my brain doesn't typically live by rationality.

"What?" Adrian asks after a stunned second. His voice dipping even lower and dripping with unfamiliar anger. It doesn't scare me though—I recognize his anger as the same protectiveness of Margo and my parents. It feels different coming from Adrian though. It's stronger, more potent, but it's also comforting in a different way than anyone else.

"I mean, you couldn't really see anything. One was just my back and panties—boy shorts that day thankfully." I lift my hand in a fake hooray. He offers me a small smile and I know it's more for my benefit than anything. "But the other three... like I said, I was *growing* well into my teenage years. So, even with all of this"—I gesture to the front of my chest with my hands—"covered, there's still quite a bit of side boob.

"And no matter how generally nice they were, I can't exactly blame them for how almost an entire school of teenage boys reacted to a topless photo." I transferred out of the school only a couple of days after this, so I'm not sure exactly what happened or what was said. And there's not a single part of me that desires to.

"Yes, you can," Adrian quietly seethes next to me.

I shrug, not really wanting to argue about the maturity level of sixteen year olds. "I didn't swim that day. Neither did Morgan, Marissa or Becky. We spent the entire evening in the office of the headmistress, Mrs. Trainor, with our parents. Margo and Meera's too."

Skipping over the details, I tell him about how Mrs. Trainor said *all* six of us girls have put her in a hard situation—as if my friends and I were as responsible for this as the other three. He looks slightly less disgusted when I tell him how my mom went the fuck off on Mrs. Trainor and the three girls, threatening everything from child neglect to the distribution of child porn. The scowl that doesn't fit his handsome, normally happy face returns when I get to the part about how Morgan's dad turned around and threatened my mom for defamation.

That was quickly settled once the police got there and looked through their phones, so her dad shut up very quickly. Regardless, it was a long, horrible night.

"Blake... I—" He trails off, at a loss for words. There really aren't any in these situations though.

So, I tell him exactly that. "It's not your responsibility to fix it. And my parents forced me to press charges."

It's not that I didn't want to, necessarily. I was just so fucking *tired* by that point. I wanted it to be over, and at the time, it felt like another few months of dragging out my misery and humiliation.

"*Good,*" he vehemently declares.

I shrug again, suddenly reminded of the helplessness I spent so long feeling during those months. "The lawyers came to a deal before we had to go to court. They had to pay for emotional damage and got a few hours of community service that summer. Maybe, according to the judicial system, I received justice, but it doesn't feel like it. I was just so... *tired.*"

I mean, how can it? They lost a state championship and only a few hours of their summer break after everything they did to me. I feel like I lost *years* because of them. And the fact that those were supposed to be 'the best ones of my life' only pushes the knife in deeper.

Adrian lifts his hand from my thigh, slips out of my hold, wraps that arm around my shoulder, and pulls me in close. The gesture brings fresh tears, but I don't try to hold them back. It doesn't feel necessary when I'm in Adrian's presence.

Truthfully, I didn't really question it when Adrian said I was safe with him. As scary as it is to trust someone new, he's proven, more than once, that he deserves it—the last twenty-four hours only confirming that for me.

It probably started around the first time we ran into each other at the gym, but slowly I've started to let myself accept that he's showing obvious interest in me. It's more than friendship he wants, but it's not only a physical attraction either.

"I know I'm not at fault," he quietly tells me as he turns my chin up to him, using his other hand, "but that doesn't mean I shouldn't care. And I do—because they *hurt* you and that really pisses me off. You're right though, I'm not going to apologize on their behalf."

I nod once, relieved. A large reason why I shy away from talking about this is because of the fake niceties people respond with. It doesn't ever do anything for me, and I think it's more to make the other person feel better. Like apologizing on behalf of my bullies cements the fact that they themselves are a good, caring person.

It doesn't and at this point, I'm just *too tired* to fight about it.

Still holding eye contact, he leans his forehead against mine. "I won't hurt you. I *promise* you, Blake. If you give me a chance, I'll do everything in my power to make sure you only know happiness from here on out."

The hand that's been restlessly petting a sleeping Benji tentatively grabs onto his scrub top when I turn further into his embrace. His free hand drops down to my thigh, except this time he pulls my bent knees toward him. I'm as close to being in his lap as I can be without lifting my butt off the floor.

With only a couple of inches between our lips, I quietly murmur into the space, "You... you could start now."

His brows furrow and the hold he has on the back of my neck tightens. It isn't painful, but the gesture itself is possessive. "What do you need right now? Just tell me, pretty girl, I'll make it happen."

"You," I breathe, surprised by my own courage. After the baggage I threw at him, and the way he willfully took off some of the weight, I feel like I can do anything if he's with me. "I just... I need to know you mean it."

He pulls away just enough to look at me. It's an assessing gaze, and I get the feeling he's looking for something. I don't know *what* exactly, but I find myself nodding anyway. It's a silent acknowledgment that I *trust* him, and permission for him to do whatever it is he's thinking about.

It honestly feels a little bit like a quiet plea too. Because I just *need* something. I need to feel anything other than this sickly familiar burn in my chest. But more than that, *I want to feel him.*

As if he read my mind, he lets out a soft sigh before pulling me to him by the nape of my neck. It starts tentative, with just a few brushes of his full lips against mine.

When he moves to pull away, I grab on tighter to his shirt and tug forward. There's no hesitation on his part this time. He slips his hand further up my neck, tangling into the long strands that are free from a hair tie, for once. His grip is tight, as he holds me where he needs to take the kiss deeper.

He bites on my bottom lip but I'm already opening for him. The anticipation of his tongue tangling with mine makes me feel a lightheaded sense of euphoria but it's nothing compared to the actuality of it.

The kiss is slow as we explore each other in this new way. It's not tender by any means though. It's sensual and rawer than anything I've experienced. Some of that may be due to the heaviness of the last few days, but it mostly has to do with the way he continues to savor the taste of me, pulling me further out of my own head the longer he kisses me.

We don't take it any further than this, not wanting to rush it either. I get lost in his affection for what feels like hours. Even after that, another half hour passes before he stands and reaches a hand out to me.

Taking in the gesture for a second, I tentatively place mine in his—this is also a first for me.

I've never been walked to my car and held a guy's hand in public like this.

And I realize that for the first time, I feel possessive of someone. Even though it's almost ten o'clock at night and everyone else has left, I like the idea of holding onto Adrian in such a simple but claiming way.

And I'd probably like it even more during the day, when all those freaking Aurora Hills moms are around to see it.

Following in stride with Adrian, I can't help but look up and softly smile at him.

There's a heaviness in my heart that I haven't felt in months, but there's a new light in my *soul* that's never been there before.

Chapter Twenty-Six

Blake

Tilting my head, I take in the new painting in Catalina's office. It's an abstract blob of colors that reminds me of that rainbow fish book we used to read in elementary school.

"I see you finally replaced the vulva," I snark as my head rolls back in her direction, catching her playful smirk. "Did your wife make you do it?"

She points her finger at me. "We don't talk about her."

I roll my eyes but expect that response when I try to deflect attention off of me. "I guess we're done for the day then," I joke and turn on my heel to face her.

She narrows her eyes at me, trying to hide another smirk. "Not so fast. Let's talk about your love life."

I scoff in derision, but the way I anxiously shift in my seat clues her into the fact that there's actually some-thing to talk about.

"Something did happen then," she states more gently.

"The last few days have been... a lot."

Nodding, she asks, "How so?"

I give her a dry look. "Adrian and I went on a date."

She audibly gasps and looks as excited as a schoolgirl at the news. "Wait, what h—"

"Then we ran into Morgan, Becky and Marissa on the way home."

I watch her face fall into sympathy and concern. "Oh, Blake."

"Then I told Adrian about who they were and the *big incident*. And we kissed."

Her mouth pops open, yet even through her surprise, I sense a small spark of pride. She's always encouraging me to be more open about my experiences and reminding me that I have no reason to be embarrassed by other people's actions toward me.

I haven't told anyone about the events of my life since Sunday morning, so it feels good to get it off my chest.

"Why don't we start from the beginning?" she slowly asks.

With a long, drawn-out breath, I unpack the events of that weekend. I tell her about walking into the clinic to find Polly sitting alone. Benji's surgery and how we may have turned over a new leaf. "Okay, maybe not a leaf? More like a single blade of grass," I insist, making Catalina laugh. She knows all about my feud with Polly—it might even be one of her favorite things to talk about.

I surprise myself by telling Catalina every detail of the evening. From Adrian asking me to dinner and the moment I found Adrian in my kitchen talking to my mom, to meeting his grammy and how we slowly began to open up to each other.

"It wasn't until we were on the way home that it all imploded. He stopped to get gas, and I stupidly went inside for a water." I shake my head. "I didn't even notice them until I practically ran right into Morgan. And I just... froze."

"That's understandable, Blake." She leans forward, trying to catch my gaze, but I can't make myself look. "Was Adrian with you?"

"No." I shake my head again. "He waited outside and didn't push the subject, which I appreciated. Except when we got back to my house, I broke down on the front lawn."

Her brows scrunch in concern, and before she has to ask, I tell her about that too. I wasn't even mad at Adrian. He clearly hadn't done anything other than try to be there for me. It's just that everything was bubbling inside me like a pressure cooker. I needed to get it out, and had planned to do that in my room, alone.

But even just those extra two seconds of shock were two seconds too many. I couldn't hold it back anymore, and Adrian put himself in the wake of it.

"It was an already stressful day, Blake. And I can only imagine how it felt to run into your old classmates, especially in such a random setting. It's okay to give yourself some grace."

"I mean..." I shrug, kind of unsure. "I know that, but he didn't deserve it."

"You're right," she agrees, "he didn't. It's good you realize that, *and* that you're sitting here reflecting on your reaction. Sometimes, we take out our hurt and fears on the people we feel the closest to because we trust them not to leave. So, I'm not condoning your actions, but hopefully I'm putting them into perspective for you."

"I hear you, I really do. And he's been great. More than great, or anything I could have ever expected. He held me while I cried on my lawn and told me I was safe. And what's even crazier? I believe him, Catalina."

She smiles, and it's so genuine it actually hurts my heart. "That's a huge step for you, Blake."

I nod as tears brim my eyes. "I know. And then he held me while I told him about everything—from the stupid sleepover to the pictures."

"Then he kissed you?" she offers in a gentle tone, but the curiosity is clear.

Suddenly, the tears turn into sobs. "Yes, *then he kissed me.*"

The last hint of playfulness has left her features as she leans forward and asks in a somber voice, "What's going on, Blake?"

"I just suddenly feel so... *lonely.* I don't have anyone to talk about this stuff with."

"You don't?" she questions in a way that alludes to it being a trick. Instead of answering, I cautiously try to catch my breath and see where she's going with this. "Because I can think of three people who would love that phone call."

Scrunching my face, I turn away.

"Margo and Meera would love to hear about who the guy from the grocery store has turned out to be. And I know it's hard to believe sometimes, but your brother *loves* you, Blake."

I roll my eyes—snarkier than I mean for—but it's a genuinely touchy subject for me.

"I know he objectively loves me. I mean, obviously, I'm his sister. Yet he never tells me things. He hasn't wanted to be closer ever since he moved."

She tilts her head back and forth, seeming to think through her words. "I think Grady's problem is that he doesn't want his baby sister to fix his problems or see him as *less than.*"

I scoff in offense. "I'd never."

"I believe you, but *maybe* that's how *he* feels."

I purse my lips, understanding what she's saying. Maybe my brother's brain lacks rationality too, just in different ways.

"I think your big brother, who *cried* with you when you were going through all of that, would want to know that *you* still know you can come to him. Maybe that's the middle ground with Grady right now."

"I want to be there for him though," I argue, lip trembling. I can hear the petulance in my voice, I just can't help it.

"But maybe what Grady needs is for you to let him be there for you."

It's not fair, I want to whine, however a part of me knows she's right. Grady's always been my protector, and I think a part of him feels like he failed me, even though it was so far out of his orbit while we were in secondary school. He couldn't have ever known how bad it was because I didn't want him to.

"He's such a fucking martyr," I mutter and bat at my tears.

She laughs, not denying it. "Give him a call. I think it'll make you feel better." I cross my arms and nod, still feeling a bit childish but holding firm with all my stubborn strength. "Then call your friends. They'd want to know about the gas station. And you can save the big kiss news for when you need an out from the conversation."

Now it's my turn to tilt my head and assess her for a long moment. "That's actually the best advice you've ever given me."

"Glad to know you're finally getting your money's worth," she retorts. With a warm smile, she redirects the conversation to something a bit lighter before our session ends. "What are your plans for the rest of the week?"

"Ugh," I dramatically spat. "I'm babysitting the Paulson boys this weekend."

"Oh, good luck with that one." Her voice is teasing but I know she means it. The Paulson boys always have something up their sleeves. I'm their favorite babysitter, and they've made it known to every single person who's been hired. Part of that is only because I can keep up with the little shits... which also means they see it as a challenge to get one past me.

Not this time.

Chapter Twenty-Seven

Blake

"Hey, kid," my brother's deep, familiar voice greets me on the third ring.

I startle at the sound of his voice and almost drop my phone, having already prepared to talk to his voicemail. "Hi, how are you?" I quickly ask, almost worried he'll hang up if there's too much of a lull.

"Oh, you know," he answers nonchalantly.

No, *Grady! I don't know!* I want to scream.

Instead, I offer an easy, "Sure."

"What about you? How's everything?"

"Things are good... different, you know, big changes this year." I cringe at my rambling as I pick at the baja blanket lying across my lap.

"Oh yeah, I'm sure it's been hard since your friends left. How are Margo and Meera doing?"

"They're good," I amend. I fill him in on their lives, giving more details than he probably cares to have on my two best friends. But he's patient and quiet as I talk for close to ten minutes.

"I'm glad they're adjusting to college. It can be weird, for sure." I hear traffic in the background, so I assume he's sitting out on the balcony. He lives with his on-again-off-again girlfriend, now soon-to-be mother of his child, Arielle. And he won't talk about why, but he never includes her in conversations or Facetime calls unless it has to do with the baby they're expecting.

"Yeah... Yeah, me too..." We're quiet for close to two minutes before he clears his throat. Not wanting him to hang up, I blurt out, "I actually called you for a reason."

"Oh? Okay. What's going on, Blake?"

"I'm kind of seeing someone... I think?"

He lets out a quiet chuckle. "You *think*? And who? It better not be Cody again."

Cody's the guy on his baseball team I used to *hang out* with sometimes.

"No," I scrunch my nose. Overall, Cody's fine. He's nice enough. But now that I know Adrian? He doesn't even compare to the six-foot-four Greek God of a man that is Adrian. Any guy I've been with up until this point looks like Plankton in comparison.

"Good. He was an idiot."

"He was," I agree, "but he was nice."

"Yeah, that's why I never gave him too hard of a time."

"His name is Adrian... He works at the vet clinic."

There's a pause. "The vet clinic? As in our father's animal hospital?"

"Yeah, he's like, Dad's new prodigy, dude."

Grady laughs—it's loud, and real, and so rare these days that I soak it in like the sun. "Okay, so Dad obviously is planning the wedding then."

My dad's a bit of a romantic and very superstitious. "According to Mom, 'he had a *feeling*.'"

"That man and his *feelings*," he says in a way that makes me imagine him rolling his eyes.

"So... not to be rude, or cross a boundary or anything, but do you not agree with his intuition?"

Grady scoffs, but he gives me the respect to actually think about the question. We've always made fun of our dad for his gut instincts, sometimes as small as us acing a test, or larger like who he thinks our soulmates in life are.

"I think," he starts slowly, "Dad's the biggest romantic in the family, and we love him for that. But when Dad said he had a feeling about who I'd marry one day, I was probably twelve. What was I supposed to do with that?"

He doesn't have to say Vivi's name. We both know he's talking about the redheaded girl who we grew up with. Even though they've created the Grand Canyon's worth of space between them, they'll never fully be out of each other's lives since our moms are best friends.

While I ended up on Grady's side of that distance—unlike our parents and her siblings who were able to navigate their complex relationship better than I could—it was just another thing *wrong* in my life at that time.

Yet, I can't deny it feels wrong that I basically have a sister-in-law and it's not Genevieve Davies.

"I don't know," I sarcastically drawl. "You could've not," I fake gasp, "*kissed another girl at homecoming, Grady Miller.*"

"Shut up. I was like, fourteen, and that's exactly what I mean. I wasn't nearly old enough to even understand the difference between a crush and having feelings for someone. *You,* Blake Miller, are not a little girl anymore."

There's a mix of awe and disbelief hidden under his amusement. The words I can't say get lodged in my throat, and after a second, Grady must realize that.

He continues, "You're becoming a woman. And I don't mean that in the sappy, *Chicken Noodle Soup for the Soul* way that Mom does."

Appreciating him lightening the mood, I add, "You mean this isn't *the talk* about my choice between pads and tampons?"

"No," he deadpans, "though, I better buckle up for that within the next ten years." I laugh, and so does he, but it's short-lived. "You're growing into a young adult—one that's experienced more than anyone your age should. No one can tell you what you want or what's good for you. Not even Mom or Dad, or Catalina, or me. So, tell me, Blake. Do you want to explore things with this Adrian guy? Do you think he'd be *good* for you?"

With no hesitation, I quietly breathe out, "Yeah, I do. To both. Want that and think he'd be good, I mean."

I can hear the smile in his voice when he says, "You didn't need me at all, but I'm glad you called me to talk it through anyway."

Biting back tears, I whisper, "Me too. I really miss you sometimes, Grady."

"Only sometimes?" he teases.

"You know what I mean." I laugh but it's sad and watery.

I can hear him let out a large breath. "I know, I really miss you too... *sometimes*."

"Just call more, okay?"

"Okay, Blake. I'll try."

There's an undertone of reservation there that I can't place but choose not to push it. Instead, I use the last few minutes of our call to talk to him about anything I can think of before he actually does have to go to bed. It's the longest we've talked in a while, and even though I don't believe him, I'm really hoping he keeps his word.

Chapter Twenty-Eight

Blake

"What do you mean Zippy is missing?" I slowly ask the three young boys who are all grinning from ear to ear.

Mikey—the oldest and the mastermind behind every prank—shrugs, but the challenging glint in his eye tells me everything I need to know...

These little shits hid the dog.

I'm sure that they wouldn't have purposefully put Zippy in danger, however Mikey's only eleven. So I can't say he, or his younger brothers, make the most informed decisions either. Not to mention, their dear, sweet mother Erica loves this dog more than anything. Arguably more than her own children, but that's just my own assumption based on the fact that they're terrible.

"We don't know where he is," Mikey states, his voice dripping with faux innocence. "We were looking for something in the shed and he must have followed us out there."

Narrowing my eyes at them, I do my best to hide the sense of satisfaction I feel when his younger brothers, Shawn and Luke, take a step behind him. "What were you looking for in the shed, Mikey?"

That makes the boy show actual fear for the first time, because we both know exactly what they were looking for.

Christmas presents.

It doesn't matter that we're still about two weeks out from Halloween. He knows his parents start buying the presents as early as July, even if he doesn't fully understand the financial situation, or why they start so early. And I know as well as he does that Erica is going to be pissed if he finds their hiding spot for the third year in a row.

"Uh…" He scrunches his face, trying to think of any possible excuse. "We were… looking for… Zippy!" Rolling his eyes at me, as if I'm the idiot here, he adds, "Obviously."

Bending down to look him straight in the eye, I switch to my 'stern voice,' as the youngest, Luke, likes to call it. It's the only way they know I mean fucking business. "If Zippy slipped past you out the door, why would you have been out there looking for him?"

His mouth slams shut for a long second before he lets out an exasperated sigh. "Can you please just go find him? *In the shed?*"

"I swear to God, Mik—"

"You shouldn't use God's name in vain," Mikey scolds, shaking his head at me like a disappointed Sunday school teacher.

Taking a deep breath and closing my eyes, I count to ten. My family isn't particularly religious, outside of my maternal grandmother, but the Paulson family are active members of their church. I do my best to be respectful when I'm in their home, but it's hard when you're dealing with little gremlins.

Looking at the three of them, I offer an apologetic smile. "You're right, Mikey. I shouldn't have said that, and I'm sorry. If you have something planned in the shed—something sticky, or dangerous, or just plain stupid—you're going to be in a lot of trouble. I've always had a lot of patience with you three, but including an animal in your pranks is not okay."

With another eye roll, Mikey just demands again, "Go to the shed."

"Fine," I snap, catching the youngest child Luke's guilty smile before I turn toward the door that leads to the back-yard. I'm suddenly concerned about what these little shits planned this time.

As soon as I step into the dark space, Mikey slams the door shut behind me. I whip around but can't see anything in the pitch black. I only know it's him because he's at the age where his voice is starting to crack—or in this case, his laugh. *Poor kid.*

That sympathy is short lived though. It dies a fiery death in my soul as soon as I jiggle the knob only to find that the door is jammed by something on the other side and Mikey yells, "Find Zippy!"

"I'm going to kill him," I mutter and twirl around.

Using the flashlight on my phone, I tentatively begin to look around. It goes without saying that Zippy is more than likely not in here, but Mikey's a tenacious kid. He's not going to let me out of here. I could call their parents. Though it's been a few months since Kevin and Erica have been able to afford a date night, so I don't want to ruin that for them.

And it can't be that bad, right?

Without really thinking about it, I take a step forward and call out, "Zippy?" Immediately, I regret my choice to just play along when my foot lands on something. "What the fu—ahhh!"

Someone jumps up from behind me and grabs onto my shoulders. A high-pitched scream rips out of me as I try to untangle myself. "Let! Me! Go!" I helplessly scream, before I trip over myself and crash to the ground. Reaching for my phone that slid across the floor, I wince in pain when I try to scoot myself closer.

The pain is bad enough that I temporarily forget about being attacked. Using my other leg, I push myself close enough to grab my phone. As soon as I do, I shine the light at my ankle, and tears fill my eyes when I see the golf ball sized lump already growing on the side. As the first tear slips over and the pain starts to throb, I raise my camera light to the giant skeleton standing at about seven feet tall.

I recognize that damn thing instantly. Anyone who's ever been to the haunted house the construction company hosts every October would recognize that decoration. Kevin's worked there as long as I can remember, and I guess he's also the keeper of haunted props.

"Oh my God," I quietly seethe.

Swallowing down the tears, I start to dial before I think about what I'm doing. "Mikey! Get your ass in here now!"

The door flies open, presenting three startled boyish faces. "Blake, are you okay?" Shawn starts walking toward me. He's easily the sweetest of the three, but as the middle child, he's usually outvoted.

As he kneels next to me with tears in his eyes another voice pulls me back to what I'm doing.

"Hey, Storm Cloud," Adrian easily greets. "How's babysitting? I'm just getting home from the gym, but I thought you'd be busy for a wh—"

"Blake?" Shawn asks again, this time his voice is watery.

I run my hand down the side of his head and do my best to not let my own tears be heard in my voice. "It's okay, buddy," I whisper. "Adrian—"

Not doing a very good job of composing my emotions, Adrian cuts me off, "Blake? What's wrong? Are you okay?"

"I'm sorry, Blake." Mikey drops next to me. "It was supposed to be funny. I didn't mean for you to get hurt." He hiccups, growing more emotional by the second too.

"You're hurt? Where are you?" Adrian demands.

"I'm okay," I tell Mikey then I add in a louder voice to Adrian, "I'm okay. I fell down and I twisted my ankle... really bad." More tears slip down my cheeks as the pain grows, but it makes all three of the boys start to cry in earnest too. "I need your help. *Please.*"

"Send me the address, and don't move."

By the time Adrian finds the four of us in the shed, it's probably one of the most pathetic sights he's ever seen.

After we all sobbed for about five minutes, Mikey pulled himself together well enough to run into the house to grab a bag of ice, and a couple of water bottles. Shawn is across from me, doing his best to sit still while my ankle rests on his knee and he holds the ice for me. Luke is still crying hard enough to warrant him sitting in my lap, even though it fucking hurts every time he moves. And as a five-year-old, that's about every twenty seconds.

But it's the helpless look I give Adrian as his eyes find mine, that really completes the scene. I'm sure my face is puffy and pink from crying, and I haven't even attempted to fix my hair. I felt it snag on the skeleton's fingers on my tumble down, but it's been the least of my worries. Until now.

"Hi," I quietly squeak.

"Hey, pretty girl." My heart melts, not truly realizing how comforting his endearments are until now. Crouching down, he quickly introduces himself to the kids and gently extracts Luke from my lap. "What happened?"

My eyes cut to Mikey, who visibly gulps and shrinks down. "It doesn't matter how, but I fell down." I watch his gaze move to the giant skeleton still lunging forward behind me. His eyebrows tick up and a small smile plays at his lips.

Apparently that's all the encouragement Mikey needs, because he leans forward and adds, "I pranked her."

"*Mikey*," I scold. "And what had I said just a minute before I walked into this shed?"

"You said I better not have anything 'sticky, or danger-ous, or just plain stupid' planned. You didn't say anything about something *scary*."

Adrian snorts. Throwing a quick scowl his way, I turn back to Mikey and gesture toward my ankle. "What do you call that?"

He looks me up and down with a judgmental expression. "Being clumsy."

Adrian doesn't try to stop the laugh that falls from his lips. He's fully and shamelessly enjoying the show between me and the little pain in my ass. Which reminds me...

"Did I ever mention who the Paulson boys' grandma is?" I ask Adrian dryly.

Luke perks up at the mention of the woman who spoils them rotten. "Grandma Polly! Let's call her."

"No." I shut that down as soon as possible and ignore his bottom lip sticking out.

"Polly?" Adrian asks slowly. "As in..."

He trails off as I nod slowly. This time, he actually falls back on his butt from laughing so hard. It's that deep, rumbly sound that sends a rush of warmth through me every time. "The one and only."

"*Polly Paulson?*" he laughs.

Shaking my head, I tell him, "Polly Livingston. Their maternal grandmother."

"I'm starting to understand why people love the whole small-town thing." The ever-present hint of amusement twinkles in his eyes adding another layer of comfort to this moment. "What do you say we get you out of here?"

Nodding, I gently pull my foot from Shawn's knee and offer him an appreciative smile.

"Can you stand?" Adrian asks gently. The three boys peering over his shoulder look hopeful, but Adrian's ex-pression says he knows the answer. He is only asking to be polite.

I know the answer too.

Though I attempt anyway. Offering him a hand, I brace the other on the ground and try to keep my right foot in the air as I pull myself up. Hissing out a pained breath, I drop back to the ground and rub at my wet cheeks.

"This will be quick, but it might still hurt a little," Adrian warns, a second before he slips an arm around me, the other under my knees, and lifts me in the air. I gasp in surprise and throw my arms around his neck. The sudden movement does cause a sharp pain to burst in my ankle, but it numbs to something more bearable by the time he's standing at his full height. "You good?"

The low, concerned note to his voice sends a rush of heat through me. It's not the safe, comforting warmth of his laugh. No, this is burning hot and settles right between my legs. Looking up at him, with an expression equivalent to a lovestruck fool, I slowly nod and, not so subtly, nuzzle closer into his chest.

Chapter Twenty-Nine

Adrian

Following the three boys inside, I pull Blake close to my chest, doing my best to not knock her foot around too much. She seems to think I don't notice her staring at me since I scooped her off the ground, but she's not exactly subtle either.

Trying to hide my smirk, I bite my lip and glance down at her. I think she's in shock because she doesn't even try to look away. "Blake?"

"Hm?" she murmurs.

"You good?" I gently ask for the second time and set her down on the couch.

"Yeah, I really am okay now," she rasps. There's a soft pink hue to her face, which is still slightly swollen from crying.

As a boy, I can appreciate a well thought out prank—especially one that goes horribly wrong. But as a man who feels desperately devoted to Blake, it sends a mix of emotions through me. Anger, frustration, concern, sympathy. I'd break my own ankle right now if it meant she'd stop wincing in pain every time she tries to get comfortable.

Without thinking about it, I lean forward and place a kiss on her temple. "It's going to be okay."

"*Ew*," one of the young boys—the middle one, Shawn—yells. "Did you just *kiss* her?"

Laughing under my breath, I feel relieved when Blake offers a small, genuine smile. "Hey, Mikey?" I call out.

His head pops between us from behind the coach. "Yeah?" he squeaks.

Poor kid.

"We need more ice." He nods seriously and shoves his youngest brother toward the kitchen. I chuckle as the five-year-old almost trips as he scuttles around the corner.

"What else?" Mikey asks, seeming to know he's in deep shit.

"Go get a big stack of pillows for her foot. And do you have one of those stretchy Ace wraps by chance?"

Quickly nodding, he grabs his other brother's hand and runs down the hallway.

Watching the interaction with a rueful smile, Blake whispers, "I'm so sorry."

"No, you have nothing to apologize for." She opens her mouth to argue, but I run a hand down the back of her neck and continue first, "I would've been pissed if you called someone else—or worse, *didn't* call anyone. So don't you dare be sorry. Although," I add with a lighter tone, "maybe we should be concerned about how easily the three of them have accepted a strange man into their house."

Laughing quietly, Blake's smile turns more genuine. "You're not a strange man. Besides, they were really worried. Mikey's been a little prankster since he was old enough to walk, but he's not a *mean* kid. I think I'm the first person who's ever been hurt in the crossfire."

We hold eye contact as I reach to gently pull out the neon yellow scrunchie that's barely holding any of her hair up. It cascades in dark waves down her shoulders, and I can't help running my fingers through it. Relaxing further into the couch, she watches me quietly while we wait for the boys to get back with the materials.

A few minutes later, as we're both starting to worry about Luke in the kitchen alone, he comes running out with a grocery bag full of ice. "Sorry," he calls as he lugs it over with both arms wrapped wide to hold it. His little teeth are chattering from how cold it is. "I ha-had to get en-enough."

Blake quietly snorts but covers it with a fake sneeze. I wink. "Don't worry, buddy. You got plenty."

He perks up and eagerly asks, "Buddy? Does that mean we're friends?"

Grinning wide—both at how adorable he is and how Blake practically melts into the couch as she waits for my answer—I lean forward and ruffle his hair. "Yeah, I think we've all bonded after tonight."

He nods sagely, making both of us chuckle again. "I think so."

"Go get me a Ziplock bag and some paper towels, though." He's quicker this time and is back after only a minute.

Mikey and Shawn finally come barreling down the stairs. Neither of them stops in time so their sock clad feet slide straight by Blake. Scrambling like two cartoon characters, they pull themselves back and plop on the coffee table across from us.

"Pillows!" Shawn shouts and throws the stack at me.

"Here, Blake, let me wra—"

Grabbing the wrap out of Mikey's hands, I cut him off. "I'll do that, my man. You go make some popcorn and choose a movie to watch with your brothers. You're on lockdown for the rest of the night."

"*Lockdown?*" he spits back at me. His entire body flinches, and he grimaces like he's never heard of a punishment before. Which you can hardly call a movie night.

"Mikey," Blake scolds. "I can call your parents and ruin their night out, but you'll probably only get in more trouble."

He makes a bratty face in her direction as he turns on his heel to the kitchen. Shawn reluctantly follows him, but Luke climbs into the spot I vacate next to Blake. Sitting across from them while I wrap Blake's ankle, I'm mesmerized by the sight in front of me. Luke doesn't hesitate for a second before he nuzzles his way under her arm and looks up at her as if this is a normal occurrence.

We're both silent as he recaps the earlier events that lead to Mikey's grand idea. I'm not really paying attention as I get toward the end of the fabric, but Blake's low, worried question instantly pulls me back.

"Wait... Luke... you guys *hid* Zippy?"

"Yeah, of course we did. If you saw him, it would've ruined the prank." He shrugs, unconcerned. "I guess *you* kinda did that anyway though."

Her sharp eyes cut down to him quickly as I snort in amusement. Except once her eyes meet mine, I know something's really wrong. All the color has drained from her face, even the pink tint from her pain and embarrassment earlier. "I forgot about the G.D. dog, Adrian."

Sitting up straight, I ask the kid, "You have a dog?"

"Yeah! Zippy! Mom *loves* him."

Nodding, more so to keep myself calm rather than because anything's actually okay. "Where is Zippy?"

"In the attic."

"What?" Blake screeches, eyes wide in panic. She moves to get up, but I place a hand on her thigh before she can. "Mikey!" she screams at the same moment he runs back into the room.

"Wha—oh *shit!*" The memory of his family pet must dawn on him because he runs past us. Blake's body twists to watch him sprint up the stairs chanting 'oh shit, oh shit, oh shit' repeatedly. When she whips back to me, she's stunned into silence but frantically gestures to the stairs.

"Okay I've got it. You three stay here." Jogging toward the stairs, I call back, "Help Blake elevate her foot!"

"You're *positive* he's okay?" Mrs. Paulson asks for the fourth time. She's clearly upset about Zippy's injury, and I was warned how much she loves this dog.

Blake doesn't seem to mind Erika as much as she does her mom Polly, but I definitely see some similarities between the two women.

Blake and I tried our best to come up with a story for both of their injuries without getting the boys in trouble. Proving that he's a lot better of a kid than the town seems to give him credit for, Mikey admitted everything to his parents. From hiding Zippy, setting up the skeleton, and how the prank caused Blake to twist her ankle.

He's grounded for a week, but he scored a few brownie points with me. And from the way Blake smoothed his hair while he was telling his mom about our evening, I'd guess he did with her as well.

"We're pretty sure we located the spider that bit Zippy while he was in the attic. And there are no signs that it was venomous. He's just having an allergic reaction. The Benadryl will help, and he'll be able to get some rest. But if you notice *anything*, call the vet clinic."

Blake scrunches her nose but doesn't say anything. She doesn't have to though.

That's exactly what she was trying to avoid.

Looking down at the dog in Mrs. Paulson's arms before moving her gaze to her husband, she nods toward the kitchen.

"Okay, boys," Mr. Paulson says as he tries to round-up the three boys. "Tell Blake and Adrian good night, and we'll wait for your mom with a snack."

Each of the boys stop at Blake's side and give her a big hug, offering another apology as they go. To my surprise, each one pauses for a quick second to give me a squeeze before running after their dad.

We look back at Erika at the same time. "I assume this would cost a couple hundred dollars at least if I take him to get it checked."

Blake opens her mouth, seeming at a loss for words. It's clear that Erika would feel the most comfortable with taking him in. And there's a churning of guilt in my stomach at the realization that we made a somewhat big medical decision about her pet without her consent.

I glance down at Blake, trying to hide the avalanching feelings from her. I don't want her to feel guilty for a decision we both made. She didn't force me into anything. I *wanted* to help this family if I could. Though maybe it was short-sighted.

"It's hard to say exactly how much it could cost you. For liability reasons, Dr. Miller or whoever examines Zippy will need to run labs before they prescribe anything. That's where it starts to add up."

She sniffles and moves her gaze to Blake. With a quiet voice she says, "We can't afford that... especially with the holidays coming up..."

"I know," Blake cuts in. "That's the only reason I told Adrian to give him the allergy medicine. It was *me*, not hi—"

"Nah," I say as I take a small step forward, so we're in line with each other. "If I felt like there was *anything* more serious going on, I would've called Dr. Miller or whoever is on call. No matter what Blake said about it. This was *our* decision."

From the corner of my eye, I can see the stunned expression on Blake's face. It doesn't surprise me that she tried to take all of the blame. It does unsettle me that she still seems so surprised by me watching out for *her*.

Erika gives both of us a small, reassuring smile. "I appreciate you both taking into consideration our... situation. And I don't want to get you in trouble. I think," she sighs out, "this is the best choice for now. If we can avoid any sort of vet bill, it would be helpful right now."

"Of course. It's whatever *you* feel comfortable with. And if there's any problems at all, I can leave you with my number, but you have all of the Millers' and the clinic's contact information as well."

She nods and glances at the floor, wincing when she catches sight of Blake's wrapped ankle. "I'm so sorry, dear. I know I don't have to tell you how rambunctious they are, but this is another level."

Blake grabs onto my arm so she can hop closer to Erika. With only a second of hesitation, Blake pulls the woman into her arms, careful not to disturb the sleeping dog.

"It's okay. I promise I'll be fine." Blake pulls away and even though I can't see her, the smirk in her voice is evident. "They *will be* writing to Santa for a new babysitter after how strict I'm going to be going forward."

Erika laughs and looks visibly relieved that Blake isn't quitting on them. She offers Blake a hand while she hops back to me. "I don't think you should be driving on that."

She opens her mouth, probably to argue that it's only a couple streets away from her house, but I answer before she can. "I'll drive her. As long as it's okay if her car gets picked up tomorrow."

"Oh, of course!" Erika quickly nods. "I'd insist on taking her myself, if it was any sort of problem."

Glancing down at Blake from the corner of my eye, I bite down a grin before I add, "It's not at all."

Blake's hand flexes around my forearm, and I'd bet just about anything that if I looked down at her, that soft pink flush would be painting her cheeks again.

Chapter Thirty

Blake

Adrian tried to insist on carrying me to his car, but I assured him that I could make it there myself; with the help of him holding my waist. At least my foot was on the ground. Truthfully, I would've loved for him to fireman-carry me again.

Just not in front of the mother I babysit for.

It's been an embarrassing enough night at that house.

Though without an audience, I don't fight him when he gently lifts me off the ground by my waist and sets me into the passenger seat. For the fifth time since he found me on the shed floor, he leans over and places a kiss on my temple. "You good?"

I nod, kind of in a trance as he towers over me while carefully tucking my legs into the car. One of his hands slides up my calf before settling on the seat next to me. The position pulls him even closer to me.

"What do you want, Blake? Do you want me to take you home?" There's a shadow that crosses his gaze when he offers that. I know he would. He's always going out of his way to make sure I'm as comfortable as possible.

But I get the feeling he doesn't want to go our separate ways yet. And neither do I.

Slowly, I shake my head and whisper, "No. For once, I really don't want to go to *my* house."

I bite my lip, hoping he picks up my unspoken meaning here. From the way his eyes are glued to my lower lip as it flicks out from my teeth, I'd say he understands.

"How about we pick up dinner from The Loop and we can watch a movie at my place?"

Nodding, I gather my waning courage as the nerves kick in and lean forward. My lips brush his in a soft promise of what's to come.

Not only tonight—but for *us*.

As Adrian sets me down on his couch—I let him carry me this time—I slowly take in his studio apartment. I'm also silently cursing myself for being too hurt to snoop around while he runs out to get my bag and our food.

It's more or less what I would've expected, I think. There doesn't seem to be a thought-out aesthetic, but much like Adrian's entire personality, it feels naturally put together. He really doesn't have to think twice about it.

The couch I was placed on is dark brown leather. It isn't stiff and uncomfortable like I often feel the fabric can be. There's even a light gray blanket hanging over the side.

Without thinking, I pull it across my lap and continue taking in the small space. It's tidy, with only a few textbooks thrown around and a coffee cup left on his coffee table. That's not surprising though. It would actually be alarming if Adrian was a messy person. It doesn't fit the personality I've gotten to know so far.

The door opening pulls me out of my curiosity just in time to catch the small, smug grin on Adrian's lips when he sees me sitting here. It's gone in two seconds at most, but it lights a fire in me. One that settles low in my stomach.

He walks over and hands me the remote. "I'll get our food."

"Um," I blurt out, trying to stop him and buy a couple seconds of time. He turns back, concern quickly morphing into intrigue. "Or we could eat later. I'm okay right now if you are."

He tilts his head, assessing me for a moment. With an easy shrug, he moves toward the freezer. "I'm good for now." I quickly realize he's getting ice for my ankle, but he doesn't come back to the couch until he has a stack of pillows.

I can't fight the smile, especially when he grins at me like there is nothing else he'd rather be doing.

When he moves to set the pillows on the coffee table, allowing me to stretch out better, I pull my ankle away, trying to hide my wince of pain.

"*Blake*," he chastises, yet when I look back at him, all I see is pain on his face.

"I'm okay," I promise. "I just know I'll be uncomfortable sitting like that."

It's not a lie. This isn't my first twisted ankle. Even as a swimmer, I had a lot of conditioning out of the water. Except I would be lying if I said I didn't have ulterior motives.

He doesn't say anything, just watches, as I twist my body, so my feet are at one end of the couch. Moving the pillows for me, he sits back and watches me.

"What are you doing?" he finally asks when I don't lean back.

Per usual, I lose my bravado. Gesturing behind me, I hope he gets the point. I'm almost positive he does but is playing dumb when he lifts one eyebrow in response.

"Sit with me?" My voice is small and vulnerable, even to my own ears. Anytime I'm with Adrian, my walls fall inch by inch.

Without any more hesitation, he moves behind me. The couch isn't very long. Fortunately the seating cushions are wide enough that with some awkward twisting and stretching—mostly on my part—he leans back so I'm between his legs and gently pulls me into his chest.

Taken by surprise, I relax against him after a moment. "How's this?"

"Better," I agree.

He scrolls through Netflix, and I fix the small blanket across our laps. It doesn't take long before we agree on something, though I'm not paying much attention anyway.

It's basically impossible when all I can focus on is the strong arms, warm musk, and the steady beat of his heart against my cheek.

At some point, I must have dozed off because I wake up sprawled on my side, with my bad foot still propped up. Adrian's hand is gripping my thigh. It's not hard, but the way his knee is also bent underneath holding it up, I'd bet it's his doing that it's still where it needs to be.

The other clue that I fell asleep is that Adrian's now watching football highlights from the college games earlier today.

"I didn't know you liked sports," I murmur against his chest, rubbing the sleep out of my eye.

He laughs quietly. "Just because I never played sports, doesn't mean I don't like them. My dad went to college on a football scholarship."

"And he went to nursing school?" I ask, tone thick with genuine admiration.

"I know. I don't think I've fully wrapped my mind around what that must have been like."

I shrug, noticing the small drool stain on his chest. "Oh... ew. Sorry."

"What?" He must look down because he just laughs it off, like he seems to do for most of life. "Don't apologize. Your drooling and snoring were cute."

I scrunch my face and turn more onto my back. I don't argue with him. My snoring isn't bad, but it isn't non-existent either. And the drool... well, the evidence clearly speaks for itself.

"*Anyway*," I continue, changing the subject. "I mean, I think you shouldn't be surprised by your dad's work ethic. You clearly got all of it—plus your mom's I'm guessing."

"What makes you say that?"

"I don't know. It's just obvious. Clearly my dad sees it. I remember the way he was talking to you on the phone when he offered you the job." I snicker at the memory of how excited my dad was on that call. "He sounded almost as proud as he ever has for Grady and I."

Adrian's quiet for a second, so I glance up at him. Just in time to catch the end of that nose scrunch, and corner lip bite, that he does every time he's a little embarrassed.

"And from what you've said, you don't *need* this job. I also know you'll be required to meet certain milestones and gain specific experience, while you finish your degree. So, it says a lot that you're choosing to work here, on top of everything else you have going on."

His brows furrow, but there's a slight smile gracing his lips. "Your dad said something similar to that in my interview."

My mouth drops open, appalled. Though, in Adrian's defense, he probably has no idea about my dad's 'feelings' or the fact that this is tiptoeing too close to me having a similar one.

"What's wrong?" He's more amused than concerned.

"I—I don't even know how to explain it honestly."

He just nods and shrugs. "Okay."

"You're like, the easiest-going person I've ever met."

"I don't want you to put me on a pedestal or something." His tone isn't irritated, but more serious. "I'm only human—and I'm sure I'll mess up at some point. Hopefully not in a way that breaks what's happening between us. Just know I'll do anything I can to fix it." His eyes rove over my features, and he drops his head a few more inches toward me. "But it doesn't feel like I have to try around you, Blake. You make me feel like a..."

He trails off, unsure of his words.

After a few seconds, I impatiently urge, "Feel like what?"

"A *man*." He shakes his head. "I don't know how to explain that better. I haven't felt like a kid in a long time, but the feelings you've brought out of me... they're nothing I've ever felt before."

All I can do is nod because I *get it*.

The way Adrian simply looks at me is a heady thing, and it sends my nerve endings on high alert every time. I know that it's the mix of deep feelings I'm quickly developing for him that takes his smallest touches from a welcome gesture to a moment I'm quietly craving, every second I'm in his presence. Then I spend most of the night thinking about it in bed.

Lifting up my chin until it's aligned to his, I breathe shallowly as we watch each other. Our lips are only a few inches from one another, but without moving my foot, I can't reach any further.

I know we should talk about what happened tonight, with Zippy and the position I put him in. But selfishly, I don't want to. At least not right now.

Instead, I just want to get lost in Adrian's orbit—to feel a billion miles away from all of my anxieties and insecurities. I want to know what happens next.

But the ball's in his court—I wasn't scared he'd turn me down until about two seconds ago.

"I don't want to hurt you, Blake," he quietly murmurs, closing an inch of distance despite his words.

The hand that's been resting on his knee moves up to the middle of his thigh and I give it a light squeeze. "A kiss won't hurt me."

Chapter Thirty-One

Blake

His fingers started lightly tracing up my side at some point but at my words, those same hands grip onto my hips and hold me in place. It isn't hard enough to hurt, and even with my injured ankle, I know I could easily push him off—but his mix of newfound possessiveness, and endless consideration for me, makes it so much hotter.

He hasn't even touched me—hell, he hasn't even really *kissed* me tonight—yet my body is on fire in a way it's never been before. There have been glimpses of these feelings, smaller flickers of flames whenever he's near, but this is overwhelming.

Addicting, even, because I just want more before I've had any.

"Fuck me," he murmurs as his lips crash down on mine. He wastes no time pulling my bottom lip down with his teeth and slipping his tongue into my mouth.

And it's a good thing, or else I would've said something stupid like 'okay.' That's how far out the window my inhibitions feel right now as I'm wrapped in his earthy, cedar cologne.

It's hard not to move when all I want is to crawl onto his lap and get as close to him as possible. However, I know his care for me will win out over his apparent lust if he thinks I'm in pain.

So I do my best to sit still, but when one of his hands slips from my hip down to where my thigh creases, I can't fight it. My hips buck up and I let out a low moan in his mouth.

"Sit still, pretty girl," he quietly commands.

Nodding, I turn to watch the slow journey his hand makes across my body. With a gentle nudge of his head, he pushes mine to the side and kisses along my neck, even pulling the collar of my crewneck to get more access to my skin.

The sensation threatens to roll my eyes to the back of my head, though I don't allow it. Instead, I focus on the way his hand slips under the crew neck and skims my lower stomach. Just as I'm getting used to that, he moves back to that spot at the top of my thigh.

My breathing picks up even more when one of his fingers slips under the built-in spandex of my skirt. It's short enough that his long, thick finger easily skims the edge of my panties underneath. He groans behind me, and it's the sexiest thing I know I'll ever hear in this lifetime.

It's then that I realize his lips left my skin at some point, and I look up to find him watching the same show.

His Adam's apple bobs as he swallows before looking down at me with dark eyes. It's hard to tell with his deep brown irises in this light, but the way he's looking at me feels visceral, more primal.

"If you want to sto—"

"I don't want to stop." Almost desperately, I shake my head and grab onto his wrist, holding his hand to my center. On a breath, I quietly demand, "Keep going."

That possessive glint in his eye I sometimes catch is in full force for the first time at my words.

He removes his hand and tugs on the hem of my skirt. "Can I take this off?"

Nodding, I bite my lip, feeling a little nervous suddenly. From the way Adrian stiffens behind me, I know he can read the emotions on my face. Before he can switch into worry mode, I twist around as much as I can and grab onto his t-shirt.

"This too," I softly demand.

It's clearly an effort to even the playing field right now because there's no way I could comfortably do anything for him in this position. Without hesitation, he sits up, pushing me with him, and swiftly slides his shirt off.

Even with a partial view, I can tell he's perfect. He really is a Greek God reincarnated.

"Holy fuck," I blurt out before I can think to stop myself.

Adrian laughs, and the sound is so soothing, it breaks down any embarrassment I might have felt.

Slipping his thumbs into the waistline of my skirt, he whispers in my ear, "How's that saying go again? 'I'll show you mine, if you show me yours'?"

It's a teasing callback to the afternoon in the candy shop, and I like knowing he remembers the little moments we share.

With my hands braced on his thighs, I lift my butt off the couch so he can push the skirt down. Knowing it's the easiest choice, I only remove one foot and let the skirt hang around my other calf.

It feels ridiculous, but Adrian doesn't offer it a second glance. Instead, his gaze is fully honed in on the soft pink cotton thong I'm wearing. It's nothing special really, but from the way he's looking at it, you'd think I was handing him his first Playboy magazine.

Moving to push the scrap of fabric down next, his hand engulfs mine as he pulls it up to his lips.

"Keep that on." His other hand skims the edge of my panties, and I instinctively open my legs further, urging him to give me more. "I've spent a lot of time wondering what you wear under those scrub pants."

Typically, I don't wear this under my scrubs, but it's like a higher power was in my room while I was changing earlier tonight. I don't bother correcting him though, not wanting to break the spell that he seems to be under as he stares at my covered pussy.

When his hand moves further underneath the fabric, I stop watching his expression and let my gaze fall to the space between my legs.

"You've had a hard night, pretty girl. I can make it better."

"Yes, Adrian," I breathe.

Letting his fingers skim over my already wet slit, he muses, "The first time I see your pussy, it's going to be when you aren't hurt, and I can have both of your legs thrown over my shoulders."

"Oh my God," I whimper. The desperate need claws through my veins the longer he drags this out.

"But this pink here?" He snaps the fabric against my sensitive skin. "It looks so fucking pretty on you, baby."

Internally, I fucking *melt*. I've never been called that by anyone. And I'm more thankful now for that than ever—knowing it can't get better than the gravelly way it falls from Adrian's lips.

Before I've processed that one word, he goes on, "I know it'll be even prettier when you've soaked right through it."

Panting, I look up at him as he starts to push one finger into me at the same moment. It takes me by surprise—the good kind of surprise. The kind I've started to remember since meeting him.

He holds my eye contact as he slowly pushes into me, using his thumb to slowly work my clit when I tense around him.

"Shh, relax." He kisses my neck and settles on the nape, under my hairline, and gently sucks.

Whether it's his words, or all the different ways he's touching me, I let my body give into his control. It's not that I didn't want to from the start, but it's been a while since I was with anyone—and none of those boys were Adrian.

"That's my girl," he praises against my skin once he's pushed inside me fully. Moaning, I brace my good foot on the cushion and gently buck against his hand.

"Impatient, little thing," he teases.

I *am*, I want to scream, although it comes out as an unintelligible whine.

After a few, slow strokes he asks, "Think you can handle another one?"

"Yes," I breathe out.

A low groan falls from his throat as he pulls all the way out, only to line a second finger up and pushes both inside me. This time he doesn't let me adjust. He pushes into me in one, deliciously tortuous pump of his hand.

"Ah, *Adrian*," I cry. "Fuck." There's a little bit of pain, but it's gone in an instant. Morphing into pleasure.

Clumsily, I grab onto his forearm with one hand and push his other hand up my top. His knuckles lightly move up my chest until he makes contact with my simple, cotton bra. He pauses for half a second when he gets to the swell of my breast.

I don't show off my chest that much, despite how often my friends insist I should. So, even though I don't necessarily *try* to hide everything that's going on under there, I think there's a difference between seeing my silhouette in clothes and actually holding the full weight in your hand.

Adrian seems to agree as his hand gently cups me, seeming to test how I fit there.

"You're fucking perfect," he confirms, his low voice like a prayer.

His exploring touch turns into something more possessive and firmer as he grasps my breast harder, giving it small, pulsing squeezes. It feels good—more than good, *amazing*.

It's better than any other time I've been with anyone else. But I know my body well enough to know that the slow, languid strokes aren't going to get me where I need to be.

Turning my face into his bare chest, I whisper, "Faster."

He does what I say but surprises me by removing his hand from my breast and grabbing one of my wrists off his leg. "Show me." I watch as he slides my hand under my panties, but he doesn't let go.

With one hand, he continues pumping into my wet heat as the fingers on his other hand entangle with mine and he pushes us against my clit.

"Show me what you need, Blake, and I'll give it to you."

Nodding, I turn back to lay my head on his chest—reveling in the feel of his skin against mine. Pushing down harder than he was before, I guide our fingers in tight circles. As we fall into a rhythm, his other hand moves faster inside me, matching the speed I've set.

After a couple of seconds, he seems confident to take over again. Brushing my hand aside, he settles his palm against the sensitive bundle of nerves, and continues the tight, firm pattern as he pushes into me again and again.

His now free hand moves back up my crew neck and grabs the full weight of my breast again, flicking the peaked bud with his thumb. And the fact that I can feel myself on his fingers still, only adds to the sensations burning through me.

His other hand works my core faster, as do his movements to my pinched nipple over my bra. I'm lost in the sensation of having Adrian's full, lustful attention on me that I don't see my orgasm coming.

But that doesn't stop it—if anything, it hits me even harder because I wasn't expecting it. Crying out, partly because I try to push my hips up using both feet as leverage, forgetting my ankle, and twisting around to search for some form of contact with Adrian.

Seeming to know what I need, his lips drop to mine. It's an awkward angle, but that doesn't stop him from nibbling on my bottom lip and slipping his tongue into my mouth as I ride out my orgasm.

As my body unwinds and I come down from the high, he gently removes his fingers from inside of me. For a second, we both just look at his hand that I made a complete mess of.

I can feel my cheeks starting to burn and am about to offer to get him a napkin—even if I have to limp over there—when he does the last thing I had expected.

With a dark, glazed expression he brings his fingers to his lips and *sucks* them into his mouth. I'm already squirming in my seat, suddenly ready for a second round, when he groans in pleasure.

Catching me staring, he pops them out and smirks, using that same hand to gently grab me around the throat and kiss me again.

He pulls away enough to break the kiss but we're still stealing each other's air. "You're so hot," I blurt out against his lips.

A shocked chuckle falls out of him, as he tips my head back by my chin and murmurs against my lips, "That's exactly what I was just thinking about you."

Without any hesitation, I grab the back of his neck and pull his lips the last couple of inches down to mine. He holds me to him with an arm around my waist and we stay like that for a few minutes longer.

When it gets to around one a.m. I know it's time to go, not ready to take the leap of staying the night with him just yet.

Untangling from his embrace, he helps me pull my skirt back up and guides me to the bathroom to clean up. He offered to get a towel for me, but I'm still reeling from the level of intimacy we just reached. And from the small reassuring smile he offered me, I knew he could sense that.

I didn't, however, fight him on carrying me to his car and my front door.

Chapter Thirty-Two

Blake

A few uneventful days have passed since Adrian showed up at the Paulson's to save me and... other things. I've seen Adrian twice since Saturday night, and both times started with me doing my 'tomato impression,' as he puts it.

It's not that I'm embarrassed about what we did. Not at all. But it's all I can think about. And when I see him, the memory suddenly feels even headier.

We still haven't talked about what happened with Zippy. I did call Erika on Sunday to check in, and she said the bump was half the size as the night before already. That was good news, which I quickly passed onto Adrian hoping to put his mind at ease too. I figure there isn't much else to say since everything is okay with us.

If anything, the hardest part was hiding the truth from my dad. I have this pit in my stomach that's been there since I left the Paulson's. I'm positive he doesn't suspect anything, but I worry how Adrian's feeling, especially with how much time they spent together with some cases on Sunday.

Thankfully, my dad's probably too preoccupied with his newfound anxiety about how much interest I've taken in Benji the Beagle's recovery, as well as Chispa's surgery today. I know it comes from a good place, but it's frustrating to have him slightly hovering over me again.

He's worried about how involved I am with Chispa's case. Even though he doesn't realize the connection to that topic, the wrapped ankle I'm sporting only added to his concern, and argument, against me coming to the clinic on my day off.

Except I couldn't *not* be here for Lela and Jorge. Not that she had to ask, but her daughter called the clinic a couple of days ago asking if there was someone who could be there with her parents since she wouldn't be; I knew I had to.

And I know my dad has a vet tech, and an assistant, who speak Spanish and will be in surgery with him, but very few employees know more than the common greetings.

Even though he asked me to take an emotional step back, I want to believe he knows me better than that. And it was always going to be a big fat no.

Either way, he should be glad I didn't listen considering the evening receptionist called out, so I've been helping up here for the last hour. I'd rather be sitting with Lela and Jorge, but they're close enough I can keep an eye out if they need anything. And really, it's slow. I'm just up here so the vet assistants and kennel workers can focus on their jobs in the back.

The bell over the front door tells me that one of the last pet owners of the evening is here. Except when I look up, I am *not* looking at Diane Moore. Standing in front of me, looking equally surprised, is Cody Howard. As in the same Cody who played baseball with my brother, and one of the boys I had a long on-again-off-again fling with.

He looks just as surprised to see me, except he recovers quickly with an easy smile. "Hey, Blake."

It makes me feel weird and small sitting with him standing there. It doesn't feel like that with Adrian, I think. I always feel comfortable when he's around.

Clearing my throat, I slowly stand up, grimacing at the pain shooting up my ankle. I ignore the crutches leaning against the desk and lean my hands down to hold some of my weight.

"Hey, Cody. I wasn't expecting to see you."

"I'm just helping my mom by bringing Licorice in. Oh, and she got remarried. That's probably why you didn't recognize her last name." I just nod and try to smile. Makes sense. "How have you been?"

He's always been friendly, which is partly why I liked him well enough. I even used to feel like he was easy to talk to. But not anymore. It's not even embarrassment like I once assumed it might be. I feel kind of guilty for ignoring him, despite the fact that he's never shown interest in more than clandestine meetings—and even that sounds too appetitive for what we did. Which was met up in the backseat of one of our cars. And sometimes at the beach. And at one of our houses, though that was rare.

"I've been good. Just helping out here," I shrug. "How about you?"

"Yeah, I'm doing good. I'm actually going to Stanford." His grin overtakes his face, and I can't help but return it now. That was always his first choice, and he had been worried that he wouldn't get in.

"Wow, Cody, that's awesome. I'm really happy that worked out for you."

He gives me a small nod. "Yeah, thanks. I'm just home early for fall break. Are you going to UCAH?" He means one of the local colleges—University of California, Aurora Hills where Adrian goes. I shake my head. "The University of Southern California?" he asks, hope thick in his voice.

And I hate that.

It doesn't affect anyone else if I'm enrolled in a university or not, but this is the response I get from almost everyone. As if school isn't always going to be there. Or that it's somehow wrong to not want to spend my young adult years putting all of my time, energy, and money into a career I'm not sure I'll like in two years.

"No," I mutter with another small shake of my head.

He looks slightly confused as he opens his mouth, probably to ask about another college or swimming.

Before he gets the chance to let a sound out, another voice pulls both of our attention to the back hallway. "Is the patient ready to go back?" Adrian asks, his eyes glued on mine. He usually has Wednesdays off like me, but he's picked up shifts to help Mickey when he can.

How much of that did he hear?

There's not much of a reason to assume that I know Cody, yet I still feel like I got caught doing something wrong. The longer I look at Adrian though, I don't see any sort of accusation. But there is something sparked in his gaze. Something I've never seen from anyone before, at least not directed at me.

"Oh crap," Cody laughs easily, "I was so distracted from running into you I totally forgot why I was even here." I know he's talking to me—I can even feel his eyes on me—but I'm caught up in Adrian's orbit now, refusing to break our contact until he does.

With languid steps—the movements far too captivating—he closes the distance. I glance down at the small space between us. His chest brushes my shoulder as he leans around me to grab the pre-appointment paperwork and hands it to Cody.

Finally looking away, he adds, "You can finish that over there." He points to one of the chairs on the other side of the lobby. I try to bite back my smile. "And I'll take you back when you're done."

"Thanks, man," Cody says with a smile, not noticing the tension rolling off of Adrian in waves. I guess if you didn't know him, he somehow still looks friendly and approachable, except I do know him.

And the glint in his eyes gives me the impression he wants to regress back into a caveman and throw me over his shoulder, before running away from any man that's ever looked at me.

I don't think I should like that thought as much as I do.

Once Cody is sitting about twenty feet away with a black cat meowing in the carrier next to him, Adrian looks back at me, not saying anything. He just leans his butt against the desk in front of me, so I lower myself back into my seat, feeling much more comfortable with him there. He has at least four inches of height to Cody, but it isn't stifling. It feels almost like an invincible force protecting me.

"That's... Cody," I lamely try to explain. "I knew him in high school."

"You went to an all-girls school, right?" He playfully lifts a brow.

Rolling my eyes, I nod. "You already know I did. Don't be a dick," I snap.

He offers me a sweet grin, and my insides instantly melt like an ice cream cone on a summer day at the beach. "Okay, sorry, sorry. I'm just feeling..." He grimaces at himself, tilting his head back and forth. "Weird," he settles on.

I stare at him, trying to keep a straight face. "Weird," I repeat.

"Yeah," he breathes and looks at me almost apologetically. "I shouldn't have interrup—"

"No," I whisper, "You definitely should have."

He lets out a breath. "I wasn't planning to. That isn't really my place..." He trails off, like he's unsure about that statement.

I shrug, feeling a little helpless, but quietly admit, "It could be."

There's a heavy moment of eye contact before he breathes out, "Yeah?"

"Yeah," I nod.

"So you aren't *hanging out* with anyone else?" he teases, the easy energy we've come to know returns. Shaking my head, I think back to the first time we FaceTimed, and the slight panic I went into when I asked him to 'hang out' again.

"No, I'm definitely not *hanging out* with anyone else." This time my cheeks flame from the double meaning.

Leaning forward, only close enough for me to quietly hear him say, "Good. I'm starting to think you're the only person I ever want to hang out with ever again."

And just like that, I'm mentally turning into a puddle at his feet.

With his body still bent toward mine, he says in a more serious tone, "But I heard him asking about colleges, and I didn't want you to get in your head over something so stupid."

"I didn't plan on even having a second thought about him, actually."

That possessive expression greets me again, this time it's mixed with satisfaction.

Grabbing a pad of sticky notes, Adrian scribbles something down. I squint but wait quietly. Ever since he left the lollipop for me, I've found candy and notes waiting for me a couple of times.

A chair softly skids backwards, and we both look up to see Cody returning with the paperwork. Before he gets to the desk, Adrian leans forward, sticking the note to the computer screen in front of me. He smiles down at me and steps out from behind the desk redirecting Cody to the exam room to get the appointment going. Adrian gives me a quick wink over his shoulder before closing the door behind him.

Turning back to the computer, the note only says 'pretty girl' with a messy cloud drawn around it. Pulling it toward me, I rub my finger over it—feeling giddy like a schoolgirl—then fold it and slip it into my bag.

Chapter Thirty-Three

Blake

Holding my hand in hers, Lela tells me for the hundredth time tonight, "Gracias, Blake. Muchas gracias..."

"Lela," I squeeze her frail hands back and try to comfort her in Spanish, "you don't have to thank me. And everything is going to be okay."

"Si, si," she agrees while wiping her eyes. "Gracias a ti."

Because of you, she continues to insist.

Finally, after letting her fuss over my dad, the employees who helped in surgery, and me, Jorge leads his wife outside with a promise to pick Chispa up tomorrow after a night of observation.

And once that front lobby door closes, the last time for the night, the silent tears I've been holding onto slip out.

I have full faith in my dad to keep any promise he makes, but when it comes to things like this, you just never know.

Wiping a finger under my eyes, I'm about to turn back to finish the nightly duties when an arm wraps around my shoulders.

Even before I look up, I know it's my dad. With my arm around his waist and my head on his chest, I let the nostalgic feeling of being a girl in her dad's arms settle around me for a long minute.

"I told you not to come tonight," he lightly scolds.

Sniffing, I nod and say, "I know. Thank you for helping Chispa."

Looking down at me, he gives me a soft paternal smile. "I did my job, honey. You helped Lela and Jorge, in more ways than financially. I'm very proud of you."

My eyes water again, but it's partly because of the lingering guilt in my stomach that doubles at hearing his words.

Instead of meeting his eye, I offer him a small smile and tell him I'm going to finish cleaning up the front area.

As I'm closing out of the computer and double checking the appointments for Olivia in the morning, the last two names I expect to see pop up on my phone.

Margo and Meera calling... flashes by.

"Hello?" I answer confused, and slightly concerned, since it's almost midnight for them.

"You weren't texting us back," Margo demands. Rolling my eyes, I sit back and catch the sight of Adrian coming around the corner. A happy expression settles across his face as he walks toward me and plops his butt on the edge of the desk, like he always does when he comes to talk to me.

Looking at him but talking to my friends, I explain why I came to the clinic and ended up working the evening shift.

"See," Meera insists. "I told you she was busy. We saw her location." I laugh, but I check theirs just as often out of boredom.

"She doesn't work Wednesdays. Excuse me for being worried," Margo argues.

"Of me being at my dad's vet clinic?" I teasingly ask.

"I don't know," she dramatically states. "I don't like being ignored."

"Don't we know it," Meera mutters. But before Margo can snark back, she reminds our friend, "We called for a reason, and Blake probably hasn't read our texts yet."

"I have not," I agree.

Back on track, Margo asks, "I know it's kind of last minute, but how do you feel about getting an Airbnb this weekend?"

My brows furrow as I ask, "I thought we were just going to stay at one of our houses?"

"We can, if that's what you want," Meera insists.

"And we obviously vote yours." Mine is either the least crowded, or the least strict between us three.

"It's just so nice having privacy, and as excited as I am to be home for a week, I'm not ready to be around my entire family." Margo is the oldest of five, so her house can be a bit crazy at times.

"Yeah," Meera agrees. "We were just thinking that it would be nice to have some actual alone time together. I have some... things to catch you up on." Her voice squeaks at the end which has my mouth dropping.

"Bitch," Margo practically groans.

Meera laughs but continues, "Things I definitely don't want my parents, or brothers, ever finding out." She's the youngest of three, and her entire family acts as if she's basically the first daughter of the country.

I see where they're coming from—and it makes sense. Maybe I'd even feel the same if I were in their places. Yet it's one of those times when I have a stark reminder that I'm not in the same place in my life as them.

They talk over each other for a few minutes until Meera cuts in. "What do you think, Blake? I can look right now."

Shaking my head, even though the only person who can see me is Adrian. "I can look. You should be asleep. I'm fine getting an Airbnb, if that's what you guys want."

"It is," Margo insists.

As she and Meera continue making plans for the week they're home, Adrian taps on my shoulder. Looking up at him, he gestures to my phone. I mute it, looking up at him expectantly.

"Are you going somewhere?"

"What? Oh, the Airbnb. No. They just want somewhere to have a sleepover this weekend."

He nods before scrunching his nose and biting his lip for a quick second. "You can use my apartment."

"What?" I ask, stunned and certain I didn't hear him correctly.

"Don't waste the money on a bunch of bullshit fees." His sudden—and random—hostility toward Airbnb makes me laugh. It's always the most random things that irk him. "I'm going to visit my parents this weekend and make up the hours next week."

He mentioned that when he drove me home the other day.

"I... I can't stay at your apartment...?"

"But you'll stay in some random person's apartment? What if it's some weirdo who puts cameras up in the bathroom?"

It takes everything in me not to burst out laughing at this ridiculous conversation.

"What if *you* are the weirdo with cameras in the bathroom?" I argue because what do I even say to him right now?

With a cheeky grin, he says, "At least you don't have to worry about me spying on your friends."

My eyes narrow on him, and my lips purse to hold the smile at bay. "You... are something else."

He just shrugs and chuckles under his breath. With a shake of my head, I take my phone off mute, interrupting whatever they're talking about now. "I have an idea of somewhere we can stay."

"Where?" Margo asks, excitement clear in her voice.

Glancing at Adrian one more time, he just nods in confirmation. "Uhm. My friend is going out of town this weekend and said we can use his place."

It's quiet on the line for one second too long, so I know the bomb is dropping before it explodes. "Your *friend*?"

Margo demands, and I'm positive Adrian can hear her clearly now.

"By friend..." Meera softly prompts.

"You mean the hot guy from the grocery store?" Margo finishes.

Closing my eyes to actually avoid seeing the smug look on Adrian's face, I don't answer the question. "Do you want to stay there for free or not?"

"Obviously. And we will talk about it there."

"Sounds horrible," I chime in and finally look at Adrian. He quietly laughs, looking immensely satisfied by the fact I'll be staying at his place, safe from being stalked by anyone but him.

After working out a few more things, like how Meera is flying in early tomorrow to celebrate Diwali with her family, we hang up. I took the evening off to spend it with them; something I've done more than once since we became friends. Unfortunately, Margo has a midterm she can't miss on Friday morning, so we plan to pick her up from the airport.

Before he can say anything, I ask, "What is your problem with Airbnb?"

That makes him laugh as he stands at his full height. We're both done for the evening, and my dad's in the back, probably going over Chispa's overnight care.

"I'm saving you money, and possibly your life."

"I'll agree with the first half," I tease and shake my head.

He reaches down to grab the tote bag I brought with me and waits for me to stand with my crutches before striding toward the door. Still smirking and shaking my head, I follow him to my car, feeling almost giddy at getting to see my friends, and the change of events for the weekend.

Chapter Thirty-Four

Blake

Using the spare key that Adrian gave me yesterday, I unlock the front door for Margo, Meera, and I.

"How many times have you been here?" Margo asks, dropping her bag on the floor as soon as we walk in.

"Only once," I admit. Not wanting to elaborate, I walk further inside and drop my bag on the bed. It's been about a week and a half since my injury, and I've switched to only one crutch. It allows me more freedom, though not enough to go to the pool for another couple of weeks.

"It's like, really clean." Meera looks around.

Laughing, I nod and sit on the edge of the bed. Quickly, I realize that this is the first time I've been on Adrian's bed, and I have to fight the urge to jump off like I've been burned.

"That's a good sign," she continues.

"A good sign?" I ask.

Margo rolls her eyes, but Meera just looks at me over her shoulder with a small smile. "I mean... obviously something is going on here, right?"

Twisting my lips to the side, I make a decision to just be honest with them. I've always been private about whatever happened between me and Cody, or any other boy.

But this is the moment I had told Catalina I was looking for. I want to tell them about Adrian.

As soon as I open my mouth, the doorknob turns, and all of our heads move in that direction.

Without opening it all the way, Adrian's head gingerly pops in. "Hey, Storm Cloud."

"*Oh my God*," Meera quietly squeals, but it's still loud enough for him to hear.

"I tried calling..." he goes on, "I forgot to grab my laptop, and I have that paper I'm working on."

"Oh," I grab the crutch and awkwardly lift off his bed. "You can come in. I mean, *obviously*. It's your apartment."

He smiles easily and takes a step inside before shutting the door behind him. Ignoring the looks I know I'm garnering from Margo and Meera, I walk closer to Adrian leaving a few feet separating us.

"Thanks again. For letting us stay here," I awkwardly tumble over my words. Gesturing behind me, I tell him, "These are my friends, Margo and Meera."

Without seeming to think about it, he quickly squeezes my waist and smiles down at me as he makes his way to introduce himself.

Turning to watch, I silently thank my friends for reining in their craziness. I know it'll end the second he leaves again.

"Hey, I'm Adrian." He shakes Margo's hand. Somehow knowing she was the loud one on the phone last night, he adds, "Nice to see you again."

I can imagine the flick of his eyebrows as he jokes about the 'hot guy from the grocery store' comment.

Except he underestimates my best friend. Firmly shaking his hand, she agrees with a nod, "It *is* good to see you again. Especially in this new"—slipping her hand from his, she gestures around his living room—"setting."

Adrian just snorts and turns to Meera, who's watching their interaction quietly. "Adrian," he says and holds his hand out again.

She takes it and tells him, "Lovely home. *Very* clean, especially for a guy."

It's such a weird thing to say, but of course, Adrian just looks around—taking in his own apartment with a new eye—and says, "Thanks. I'm going to tell my mom you said that."

Stepping forward, I ask, "You're going to tell your mom I'm staying here?"

Turning toward me, he looks confused. "Did you tell your mom you're staying here?"

"I mean, yeah. Obviously. She knows you though."

"And mine know of you."

"What?" It comes out like a squeak.

"They were at the grocery store," he simply states. Through this entire conversation, I'm extremely aware of my friends who are watching it play out. "I've told them things about you," he continues.

And because in times of the slightest panic, I have no filter, I ask, "Like, *everything*?"

He tilts his head in confusion, looking at me for the first time like I've lost my mind. Then realization dawns on him, and he looks both amused and kind of embarrassed. "No, Blake. Not everything."

Behind him, Meera grabs onto Margo's arm, and both of their mouths are hanging open.

Recovering just as quickly, he demands through a laugh, "Please tell me you don't tell *your* parents everything."

That makes both of my friends burst out in giggles behind him. "Can you imagine?" Margo practically howls.

I'm honestly fucking embarrassed right now only it's different than feeling humiliated. I've made a complete fool of myself, except in front of these three people, that's okay.

I can laugh at myself and not want to cry in bed about it later.

"No, I promise," I tell him.

"Good." He nods. "Tell your friends whatever you want about what happened on the couch, but let's leave the parents out of it."

"Yes, agreed!" Margo claps in support of his idea, and of course, Meera follows right along.

Turning back to Adrian, I ask in a snarky tone, "Can I kick you out of your own home?"

With a giant grin, he steps toward his coffee table and picks up the laptop. He's walking back when Margo asks, "What are you doing on Halloween?"

Over his shoulder he says, "Not sure. Why?"

Instead of answering, she gives me an expectant look.

"Want to go to a haunted house?" I pose cautiously.

Immediately, he spouts, "*You* want to go to a haunted house?" Then he gestures toward my ankle.

"It's a tradition," Meera chimes in. "What does that have to do with your twisted ankle though?"

"The Paulson boys," I say.

"Ohhh," both of my friends slowly utter. Not needing more of an explanation than that at the moment.

"I'll go, sure," Adrian easily agrees.

"My brother Dev always tries to sneak something inside, like last year he lit some smoke bombs. You'd think he was eleven, not twenty-one. My oldest brother Jatin plays the chaperone."

Adrian nods and looks down at me with a sly grin. "I think I'm over pranks for the time being."

"Me too," I agree. "But you should still come."

With a final goodbye toward my friends, he stops next to me and looks down with affection. He doesn't make a move, and I realize he's waiting to see what I'm going to do.

And I figure my friends have already gotten some of the details I hadn't planned on sharing, so what the hell?

Putting the weight on my good foot, I lean up and wrap my hand around the back of his neck, pulling him down until I can reach his lips. It's soft and sweet, a small farewell before he leaves for the weekend.

Pulling away, I quietly murmur against his lips, "Bye, Adrian."

In a low voice, he says, "Bye, pretty girl."

I turn and watch as he walks out. As soon as I hear the click, the sounds of my friends behind me take over.

"*Blake Carmen Miller*," Margo practically screams.

At the same time, Meera asks in a lovestruck tone, "Storm Cloud? *Pretty girl?*"

"There's so much that you need to explain. Tonight."

"Now," Meera insists.

Shaking my head, I decide to give into the demands. "Well, buckle in because there are some stops along the way that you aren't expecting."

In a silent agreement, we each take over a task. Meera asks what we can move to make room for the sewing machines I brought. Margo starts to unpack the Halloween costumes she and I have been working on for the last couple of months. And I know my worth is in sitting out of the way and ordering our food.

Once that's all finished, and Margo has explained what needs to be done, I take a deep breath and give my friends what they want—the story of everything from the moment we left the grocery store up until tonight.

After my own interrogation, they take time filling me in on all the details we can't fit into a phone call. Like how Meera has the attention of her hot TA, and the quarterback of Columbia University's football team, Zane. And about the problems Margo is having with one of her professors.

By the end of the weekend, I feel more at peace, and caught up, with my best friends than I have in months.

Chapter Thirty-Five

Adrian

All week, Blake was tight-lipped about her and her friends' Halloween costume. Even though I don't mind a silly surprise that seems important to her, I teased her about it anyway. Only because the sight of Blake around her friends—so much more open and happier than I've ever seen—makes me feel some type of way.

And every time I ask again for a hint, she just smiles and says, 'You'll have to see in person.'

A lot of Blake's time this last week has been with her friends, which doesn't bother me. Somewhere along the way, my happiness has started to feel mixed up in hers. Seeing Blake's genuine smiles can turn any day around in a second.

I've tagged along with them to see a new scary movie in theaters one night and to dinner at The Loop twice. I feel bad to intrude, but I also can't bring myself to say no to Blake. I don't want to reject her from something that's within my power to give her—my time.

It helps that both Margo and Meera seem okay with having me around. If anything, I get the feeling they're trying to incorporate Blake's life into theirs, now that they're across the country. And even if we haven't had any of *those* talks—the ones about what this is and where it's going—it brings me an immense amount of satisfaction to feel like I have the approval of her two best friends.

That's a win. Especially because I know her older brother's opinion of me will be just as important, and I haven't met him yet. I already know her parents like me, at least as an employee, and a friend to their daughter. But I haven't been hiding my *intentions*, as my own father put them.

Also yes, of course I told my parents about Blake. We're just as close as she is with her own mom and dad. Plus, when I told my mom that my boss's daughter is the same girl that ran into me at the grocery store, she wasn't surprised in the slightest. She's real big on fate and that shit. And according to her, she could 'see the way I was looking at her as she walked away.'

I'm not trying to scare Blake away by asking her to meet my parents already—despite spending a lot of time with hers—but I know they're going to love Blake. They already like her from what I've told them.

When I get to her parents' house, Blake opens the door before I have the chance to knock. Taking them in, I'm surprised and *impressed* with the three girls' costumes.

Together, they made a modern, misfit version of the Sanderson Sisters. Margo is Sarah with her natural blonde hair styled in tight, ringlet curls. Meera is Winifred, opting for a burgundy red wig that she somehow styled into a bird's nest looking bun on the top of her head.

Blake is looking at me with part giddiness, part embarrassment. Probably because she let her friends put her long, silky black hair up in a twisted style that's almost identical to Mary Sanderson's.

And maybe she feels a little uncomfortable or silly, but *fuck it*, it's Halloween. I'd take this version of her over the closed off, aloof one she uses to protect herself.

"Hey, girls," I greet them with a smile and lean down to kiss Blake on the cheek. Careful not to poke my eye out. "You guys look great."

Gesturing toward the outfits, I mean it. Margo's designs somehow made the costumes feel authentic to the original movie, while giving them a modern twist with short, steam-punk inspired skirts and corsets over linen tops.

Mentally, I am on my hands and knees thanking Margo for putting Blake in that. Even with the extra shirt underneath, there's no hiding Blake's full chest when she's tied into the corset.

"Thanks," Blake smiles at me, some of her embarrassment fading away. After her friends quickly greet me, they run back to Blake's room to get their bags and whatever else they need. But Blake just stands in the foyer of her parents' house, giving me a long, almost affectionate look. "Are you supposed to be Bugs Bunny in *Space Jam?*"

I look down at my costume, even though I know that's exactly what I'm supposed to be. She does too—I think the question is more out of surprise.

"Of course," I answer with a cheeky grin. While I don't typically get into Halloween at the same level Blake seems to, I'm not so full of myself that I can't put on a costume and go to an event for one night.

This is the first time since I was a kid that I bought a costume rather than just throwing together a pirate or something at the last minute. But when I went to Wal-Mart with my mom last weekend, there was one more Bugs Bunny jersey costume just hanging there, *in my size.* I knew it would make Blake smile, since we've both talked about our childhood love of the movie multiple times.

Sometimes my mom's fate bullshit doesn't feel so phony, if I'm honest.

"You're cute," she teases, leaning toward me on her toes.

Taking a step forward, I take advantage of what will probably be one of the few moments we have alone tonight.

"And you," I slowly tell her, wrapping my arm around her waist, "you are so fucking *pretty*."

"Usually, I'd actually believe you, it's just hard when I have hair out of Whoville." There's a wide smile on her face that makes me think she does believe me, despite the costume. *As she should.*

"Doesn't matter what you wear. Still the prettiest girl I've ever seen."

With that, I drop my lips to hers and taste the mouth I haven't stopped thinking about. Not wanting to get too lost in our stolen moment—or caught by her mom—I pull away much faster than I would've liked. The soft sigh and pout to her bottom lip is all I need to know that it was too quick for her liking as well.

She never hides from my affection and even opens the door for it more than I would've initially expected. But with each little caress, and swipe of her skin, I realize that it should've been obvious from the start.

It took some time to prove to Blake that I cared about her—whether it was little things like the lollipop or helping her with her tires. Words hadn't gotten me anywhere with her at first. I'm positive she likes the compliments in the same way most people enjoy being told they are attractive, or smart. But I would bet that just about anything else *means* more to Blake than any words I can say.

And on the flip side, it's not always easy for Blake to express herself, or her emotions, verbally. There are the rare moments of vulnerability when we're completely alone, where she'll find the courage that's hidden under years of bullying and insecurities.

So, the soft kisses she easily offers in certain settings, and the way her hand always finds its way to my body when we're next to each other, is enough for now.

I'm a pretty patient man, so I can give Blake the time to work through her feelings about me. At some point, I'll need to have the 'what are we?' conversation with her, because even if she isn't seeing anyone else, this isn't a short-lived fling to me.

The more time I spend with Blake, the more I start to think about how I want her next to me every second of every day. And the friendly attraction I felt toward her has grown into so much more over the last two months. Affection, companionship, possessiveness, *need.*

I realize I was lost in my thoughts, mindlessly watching her as she moves around the room—gathering her keys and small purse. The soft shuffle of Margo and Meera coming down the hallway is what ultimately pulls me out of my trance.

Blake turns around, and suddenly, I have three pairs of eyes looking at me with an expectant expression.

"You guys ready?"

As one, they bound toward the door, guessing what they'll find at the event this year, and buzzing with excitement for the evening.

As soon as Margo and Blake step out of the car, a six-foot guy with dark brown skin and a Ghostface mask drops his arm around each of their shoulders.

Immediately, my hackles rise. Even more than when I saw her talking to that guy Cody, who's clearly some dude she used to hook up with.

I'm not mad at her for having a past. That would make me a huge hypocrite. But, considering I grew up three hours north from here and went to college in Florida, the chances of running into any of those girls are slim to none.

What really has me feeling like a caveman is the comfortability Blake's showing with this guy, compared to Cody at the vet clinic. The feeling burning through me does settle a little bit when she slips out of his hold, and turns her head, smiling when her gaze finds me standing on the other side of my Durango hood.

The backseat's door slams next to me as a petite, but clearly pissed off, Meera stomps around and stands in front of the guy.

Margo doesn't look perturbed, but she's not impressed by him either.

"Can you *not*?" Meera gripes. She pushes his hand off of her friend's shoulder and grabs the mask off of his head—which she has to get on her tiptoes to do. "Never going to happen, Dev." She smacks his chest with the costume piece.

Slowly, it clicks that he's one of Meera's brothers. Blake moves to the space next to me, brushing our arms against each other.

"That's Meera's brother, Dev," she confirms my silent assumption. "He's the middle sibling and thinks he's a real ladies man."

Looking down at her with a quirked eyebrow, I ask, "*Thinks* he is?"

She scrunches her nose and admits, "Depends on who you asked at my high school."

Laughing, I reply with, "Margo?" I tip my chin in her direction.

"Oh, no," Blake murmurs quietly, and shakes her head. Looking down at her and back to Margo, I notice she's not looking at Dev anymore. She's watching another, slightly taller and older version of Dev walk up. It's clearly their third sibling, although that's not the reason he looks familiar. I just can't place it though.

"Margo's had her eye on one of Meera's brothers for as long as I've known her, and it isn't the younger one." Blake takes a step toward me, clearly not wanting her friends to know she's filling me in about their lives.

"That one?" I ask, subtly nodding toward the guy who stopped next to them, rolling his eyes at his siblings bickering.

"Jatin, yeah," Blake chuckles, clearly amused by the situation.

It starts to click where I know him from when Meera walks over with her brothers. "Hey, Adrian. This is Dev and Jatin." She gestures over her shoulder at them.

"Hey, man," Dev easily greets, and my earlier hostility melts away.

Nodding in his direction, I look back to Jatin as recognition sparks in his eye too. "We have some classes together, right? I think the Bio lab is one of them."

"Yeah, I thought I recognized you from somewhere." We shake hands, both of our gazes catching on the three girls standing dumbstruck next to us. Each of their mouths are hanging open and their heads tilted in the same direction.

"Wow..." Meera mumbles when Jatin shakes his head impatiently at her. "*Of course* they have classes together. How did we not think about that?"

"I feel stupid," Blake simply says.

"Hey, neither one is my brother or boyfriend," Margo argues, holding her hands up in surrender.

Blake just snorts, and now having more of the big picture, it doesn't surprise me when Margo elbows her in the side. *Hard.* And for the first time since I met Margo last week, she's actually blushing as she tries to not look at Jatin.

To his credit, he tries to play it off like he doesn't notice what's going on either. He just tilts his head, giving the three of them an impatient look. "The single brain cell you three share doesn't seem to be doing so well with the long distance, huh?"

Chapter Thirty-Six

Blake

Apparently, Adrian has a penchant for grumpy personality types because he and Jatin have fallen into an easy friendship. I'm sure it helps that they're in the same program, though when I overheard them talking, it wasn't about classes or animal medicine.

Margo, Meera, and I are standing in line, waiting to order apple cider. We only come for the haunted house, but every year the event seems to get better. Stanley Maddon—the owner of the construction company and hardware store—has started to include concession stands and extra displays. Like a makeshift pumpkin patch during the day, and a few showings of Halloween classics throughout the month of October.

The Maddon's are nice, but I don't know them as well as other people in town. So since I was little, I've always associated this time of the year with Stanley and his company.

"I don't love the idea of a maze," I admit. The line moves at a snail's pace, but it's typical for Halloween night.

Looking up at me from her phone, Meera nods and says, "Buddy system."

"It's not all a maze," Margo insists.

That's true, but a section of the large warehouse is a fake corn maze that requires a warning about how people have gotten stuck in there for up to thirty minutes and requires a waiver.

And sure, *maybe*, the thing requires a waiver every year; I've never given it much thought. Stanley's good at what he does, but even I can handle walking from point A to point B with props jumping out.

The thought of being stuck somewhere? Alone and lost? That's a big fucking no from me.

"I'll wait with you, if you want," Meera insists. Margo doesn't say anything, but she's looking at me over our friend's head with soft, assessing eyes. I know she would skip the whole thing if I wanted to leave now.

There's a big part of me that would love nothing more, but I'm also aware that we're lucky to be able to continue some of our traditions this year. And it won't always be like this. Tonight could be the last time things are really the same.

So, I pretend to pull on my big girl panties—which makes Margo fucking cackle—and demand, "*Buddy system.*"

They nod emphatically, looking relieved and excited, but I squint at them in disbelief. They're the best friends I could ever ask for, but sometimes they're like trying to hold onto two ferrets in a public place.

In true typical fashion, as soon as we moved into the corn maze section, the two of them were off in different directions. *Neither* with a fucking buddy.

Though, that could be because Jatin and Dev went their own ways without a look back too.

Once we got back in line, I was feeling more anxious after committing to the haunted house. Adrian didn't ask, but he tucked me into his arm while we waited for our turns. And as expected, I was doing fine up until now.

Too nervous to take the first step in, I feel Adrian's strong chest meet my back. "You good?" he murmurs behind me. Thankfully, they let the groups in at a staggered pace, so I have a couple of minutes before someone runs into us.

I start to nod and say yes when I hear someone scream, the noise echoing in the warehouse. I'm pretty sure it's Margo, but it's not even the sound that makes me flinch.

Looking up at Adrian in the low-lit room, I admit, "The idea of being stuck in here is making me panic."

It's a quiet confession, one I'm not even sure he can hear over the noise surrounding us. Before the last word leaves my lips, his hand slips around my waist and he pulls me into him.

"I'll turn around right now and say I'm too scared to go through there," Adrian insists, bending down to rest his chin on to my shoulder. "Or I'll hold your hand the entire way and swear not to let go until we're out of this room."

His offer makes my heart melt, but all I say is, "This is important to them... me too."

"Ready when you are, brave girl." The variation on my nickname sends a new spark of resolution through me.

"Okay. I think I'd rather follow you though."

Without a word, Adrian moves in front of me. One of his hands reaches behind and grabs one of mine. My other one tangles into the back of his shirt. "It can't be that difficult."

He sounds confident, and I hate to burst his bubble, blurting out, "You weren't even in Boy Scout's."

With one final look over his shoulder, he teases, "It's a good thing we aren't really outside then, huh?"

Even though I want to chuckle, the best I can do is let out a huff of breath. We make a plan to walk straight, but either the room's bigger than even I expected, or the actors are really good at their jobs. Probably both.

My emotions have been extremely turbulent since we walked into this portion. First, I was panicking at having to enter the maze, then for about ten minutes I actually had fun. Now it's been about fifteen minutes since we were turned around by someone in a mask. I can hear people all around us, but I don't see anyone.

About five minutes ago, it occurred to me that is probably exactly what the actors are told to do.

"The haunted house is always massive, but I don't understand how they can build *this*."

"Yeah, I've started to wonder that too," Adrian admits. Turning around, he grabs my waist and pulls me into him. "Are you okay?"

"I'm better than I thought," I admit. "But this isn't my ideal situation at all."

"I hear that." He looks around only the fake corn stocks are taller than him, and my stupid hair. "We're going straight, and I'll shove a clown if I have to."

With a grateful smile, I grab onto his shirt and hand again, nodding. "*Please.*"

We do come across another actor except this time, Adrian tells the guys that he's about to have a panic attack. I'm partially hidden behind his back, but with the calm tone he uses, the employee definitely knows I'm the one they should be worried about.

He doesn't say anything, just moves to the side and points behind him. We only walk about ten more feet when there's a small clearing and a door.

With his hand on the doorknob, he throws it open and pulls us through.

I take a deep breath and look up at him with a grateful smile.

One that quickly slips off my face when I realize I'm still in the haunted house and the three high-pitched giggles coming from behind Adrian are all too familiar.

Dipping my head to look around his back, I can't help laughing at the sight of Mikey dressed as a mini-mad scientist pretending to saw off his brother's head. Luke is strapped to the table with fake blood spewing out of him. And Shawn is giggling manically from his place on the right of them, set-up to look like a floating head in a jar.

Adrian turns around, instantly recognizing the boys too. Their performance seems to get even more exaggerated once they realize we're their current audience. Grabbing his hand, I move toward the next door when something that's taller than Adrian pops up in front of us.

Screaming, I fly backward into Adrian's chest. He catches me before I twist my ankle again, not doing anything to protect me. Actually, when I look up, he's *laughing*.

Turning, I catch all three of the boys as they break character and laugh at my expense too. But it's Kevin Paulson's deep chuckle that pulls my attention to the stupid fucking skeleton that he's using as a jump scare.

"Oh my *God*," I mutter and clutch my chest.

"Got you! *Again*!" Mikey calls out from behind us. I just shake my head and try to catch my breath.

"I'm so sorry, Blake," Kevin grins. He's casual enough to make me assume we're some of the last people in here. "The boys were just so excited to surprise you tonight."

I huff out a dry laugh. "You guys succeeded," I tell them and lean into Adrian as he wraps his arms around my waist. "This is the worst year *ever*." That's directed at Kevin.

Laughing, he claps his hands once. "Stanley will be so happy to hear that."

"Bye now," I step forward, giving the skeleton a wide berth.

Adrian shakes Kevin's hand quickly and tells the boys, "See you guys later."

After two more, slightly less scary rooms, we finally step out of the back. Immediately, two bodies crash around me.

"I'm so sorry," Meera cries out around me. "You know I have the attention span of a chihuahua when I get excited."

Laughing, I wrap my arms around them and move them out of the way. "I do know that. And I'm fine."

Margo looks at me. "You're sure? I didn't think it would be that bad. It's like a hundred square feet at most."

"It wasn't as bad as I imagined." I'm not saying that just to make them feel better, but it's not on my bucket list of things to give another try either. "How long were you in the corn maze?"

"Like ten minutes," Meera admits with a triumphant grin.

"What?" I laugh.

"I just followed one of the actors until they got freaked out and led me to the door."

Stunned for a second, I finally sigh, "You're so weird."

Looking at Margo, she rolls her eyes and says, "I think twenty-ish."

"That makes me feel better, I guess."

Dev walks up and wraps an arm around Margo's shoulder. Jatin flicks it right off, before standing next to his sister.

"No luck this year," Dev admits. Stanley confiscated his firecrackers before he was allowed into the event. Though I figured there was more chaos he could've come up with.

Meera rolls her eyes and turns toward us. "We better get going. My parents have a whole day planned for us tomorrow."

Leaning down, I give her a hug, reveling in the mundane gesture.

"I'll get a ride with them since it's on the way."

With a nod, I wrap my arms around Margo too. We have plans to spend one more night together tomorrow, so I'm not hurt by them heading off on their own.

Plus, I have a pretty good idea of what their true intentions are when they give me mischievous grins over their shoulders, as they follow Meera's brothers.

Shaking my head at them, I turn around and look up at Adrian. He watches me for a second, then asks, "Want to get something to eat and watch a movie?"

Slipping my hand into his, I pull him forward with me. "That sounds good. I'm actually hungry tonight though."

With a downright wicked smirk, he agrees, "Me too."

Chapter Thirty-Seven

Blake

By the time we get to Adrian's apartment, we have two bags of tacos with sides, and I've almost detangled my hair from the crafty way Meera got it to do what it needed for my costume. The amount of hair spray and gel it took makes it feel knotted and disgusting though.

It's weird how comfortable I feel here, but after our evening and the weekend I spent with my friends, I've passed that awkward stage. It goes without saying that a big part of that's because of who this space belongs to.

Setting down one of the bags on the counter, I turn toward him as he carries the other, as well as my purse.

He pauses for a moment, seeming to consider asking what's on his mind or not, before finally going for it. "Did you snoop when you stayed?"

His voice is curious in a teasing way. So I admit, "I did not, no."

Tipping his head, he guesses, "Margo?"

"Yes," I confirm. "I feel bad for whoever she marries—they won't be able to hide anything from her."

"Don't you mean Jatin?"

The tone of his voice is so serious that a laugh flies out of me. When he gives me a confused look over his shoulder as he grabs us drinks, I add, "I love Margo; unfortunately, it's never going to happen for her."

Squinting at me, he slides a Gatorade my way. "You don't think so?"

Shocked, I ask, "You *do*?"

He just shrugs, "Maybe one day." I must look as skeptical as I feel because he continues, "I know you said he and Dev had your back in high school, but he doesn't look at you like a sister. Margo neither. He looks at you like you're *his* friends, not *his sister's*. Isn't that half the battle for her?"

Tilting my head, I open the bottle and take a drink. "I guess so," I finally admit. "But I'm not giving her that kind of hope, and neither are you."

He mimes zipping his lips. "Wanna go eat?"

Sliding my hand through my hair—or trying until it gets snagged—I shyly ask, "Can I take a shower? Is that weird?"

His smile is soft and affectionate. "No, it's not weird. I want you to be comfortable."

"This"—I gesture to my costume—"isn't comfortable." To Margo's credit, the themes usually go with our personalities, and we alternate each year. One year, we were different versions of Barbie from the movies for Meera. Another year, we were *Monsters, Inc.* characters for me.

And even though I'd never wear this on a normal day, I don't feel embarrassed about what I'm wearing or uncomfortable with my body. It's just not my style.

And it's not something I want to sit and watch a movie in either.

"Let me get you something to wear."

Without really thinking about it, I walk into Adrian's bathroom and pull my hair into a bun. Doing my best, I struggle a bit to unlace the corset, but it's an awkward angle.

When Adrian steps into the doorway with a pile of clothes, he silently comes up behind me and helps me untie the rest of the garment. My arms are bent to my chest holding it up, though for one crazy second, I consider dropping it. Even with the loose linen top underneath, it doesn't leave much to the imagination.

The way his eyes slowly move up my back until they meet mine through the glass, suggests he's thinking about the same situation. His knuckles gently skim against the bare skin of my shoulders.

"Do you need anything else?" he asks in that low, gravelly voice I've been blessed enough to hear a few times now.

Swallowing, I shake my head. "What about you? Aren't you going to shower?"

His eyes darken as he tilts his head. He looks at me with a predatory gaze I never would've expected from him. Thinking back to the joke he made when we were leaving the haunted house, he looks like he'd really love nothing more than to devour me right now.

"Do you want me to wait?" he quietly offers behind me.

"No," I breathe out and find the courage to let my hands drop to my sides. The corset top easily falls from around me, landing at my feet.

The light orange linen top is cropped to my belly button, leaving a few inches of bare skin between the hem and the skirt I'm still wearing. Through the thin fabric, my puckered nipples are visible.

Adrian's quick to notice, letting his eyes stray there unabashedly. "Blake..."

His voice is cautious, and a sudden wave of anxiety rushes through me. I'm practically throwing myself at him right now, and if he turns me away, I don't think I would recover.

Losing the battle of keeping my arms at my side, I start moving to cover myself and stutter, "I—I... just..."

Taking a step, pushing his chest to my back, Adrian lightly grabs my forearms and holds them at my sides. "*You* are fucking beautiful, Blake. I'm just making sure this is what you want. But believe me when I say I want you. So fucking bad."

Turning my head to look up at him through my lashes, I quietly whisper, "I want you, Adrian. *So fucking bad.*"

Groaning, he drops his head and grabs me around the throat, kissing me rough and possessively. Twisting around in his embrace, I meet him chest to chest and kiss him back just as desperately. Finding the hem of his jersey, I don't waste any time pushing it up and off his body.

When his arms come back down, they deftly move to slip my top off. It happens too quickly for me to second guess it, and the deep groan that comes out of his throat pushes any insecurities from my mind.

I know in a lot of women's opinions, I'm blessed in this department. And I don't mean to complain about my breasts because I love my body—more so for everything it's done for me, especially athletically, rather than how it looks. I'd be lying if I said there wasn't a small, vain part of me that loves them.

But with breasts the size of mine, comes things like stretch marks and larger areolas. No amount of exercise has made my boobs smaller over the years—if anything, my chest muscles have made me appear larger. And the stretch marks are mostly light along my shoulders—from years of swimming, and weightlifting when I was younger—but darker on my breasts.

I knew the chances were small—minuscule even—that Adrian would have found such shallow flaws in me, but I feel more vulnerable at this moment than maybe ever before.

Starting at my waist, both of his hands slowly move up until he's cupping each of my breasts. Even in his large hands, they don't quite fit without spilling over. Something Adrian seems to *really* appreciate.

The act of undressing someone has never been an intimate experience until tonight. Usually, it's a means to an end. Now, watching as Adrian finds the small buttons attached on my hip and begins unclasping them, feels like the closest thing to a religious experience I've ever had.

When it slides to the ground, he smiles down at my lower half—now in nothing but my bikini style panties and fishnets. Laughing in shy amusement, I quickly take the tights off and stand in front of him.

It takes everything in me not to cover myself from him, yet when he moves toward the waistline of his pants, a new type of nervousness takes flight.

I watch as he pulls on the fabric, freeing his already growing length and lets the shorts fall around his ankle. It's no surprise that even half-mast, he's thick and long. The evidence that he goes to the gym multiple times a week is written in every hard line and slope of his body. Running a hand over his short curls and down to the nape of his neck, he stands there—naked and extremely confident in his own body.

With nothing more than a smile, he turns toward the shower, slides the doors open, and turns the water on. My skin's already pebbling—whether from the cold air or his eyes on me—so I appreciate the gesture.

It's a small bathroom so he's back in front of me in a couple of steps. Leaning onto the counter, I watch as he quickly pumps out some oil into his palm and works it through his hair before washing his hands. Pulling me into his warm body by my hips, he leans down and kisses me—it's languid and tender and seems to be a silent promise of some kind. Letting him take the lead, I relax against him and for once try not to rush through the moment.

When the waters warm, he slips his fingers into the waistline of my panties and asks, "Ready?"

Nodding, I step out as he pushes them down and climb into the spray of water.

Chapter Thirty-Eight

Blake

Maybe it's a coincidence, but it's not a surprise that Adrian set the water to the exact temperature I like. He wordlessly follows me into the stall and presses his body against mine.

Between him and the water, I feel like I'm on fire. Leaning on my toes to kiss him, he slides his hand into the hair at the nape of my neck and pulls my head to the side—giving him access to nibble along my neck, but not for me to kiss him.

As if he can read my thoughts, he says against my skin, "Let's get your hair washed."

That's when I notice he didn't throw out the hair products I accidentally left here.

"I wasn't sure who this belonged to," he admits, and pops open the lid of the shampoo. "But it smells like you, so..."

A soft, gooey smile splits across my face. I'm not keen on overwhelming or strong fragrances, so I've used fresh melon scents for as long as I can remember. And a silly, possessive part of my soul loves that Adrian knowingly associates that with me now.

"It's mine," I confirm. With that, he squeezes a dollop into his hand and continues to wash my hair. As he does, I tell him about all the things Margo found in his apartment.

"Honestly, it wasn't a lot. Meera was right, '*lovely apartment*,'" I teasingly mock her. "There were barely any dirty clothes to complain about, your note-taking is impressive, and there's nothing questionable on your Netflix account." Closing my eyes and mouth while he rinses the suds out for a second time, they pop back open as soon as he's done. "The most talked about finding was the *un*-open box of condoms in your bedside table."

"That's scandalous?" he asks while gently working the conditioner through the knots.

"Not scandalous," I tell him. "Kind of disappointing to my friends, I guess." That makes him laugh—making my body pebble and warm at the same time. Tracing a pattern across one of his pecs with my finger, I confess, "It was a green flag in my opinion."

Looking down at me, his expression is a mix of curiosity and amusement. "Yeah?"

"I mean, I'm glad you think about those things. I'm not, uh, on birth control. I didn't like the pill, and unless it's a big deal, I'd rather no—"

"Blake," he quickly cuts me off. "I've never not used a condom with someone. So I appreciate you telling me that, but it's the type of decision you make on your own. I'll respect it."

Smiling, I let out a small sigh of relief. "Okay. Thank you." As he ties my hair on the top of my head, he just smiles and rolls his eyes at me. Probably for thanking him for that.

"*Anyway*, the box was closed," I continue, "does that mean it's fair to assume it's been a couple of months? Since you've... you know, been with someone?" I grimace, more at my own awkwardness than the question.

I'd be an idiot if I thought for a second Adrian gained this level of confidence with his body without *some* sexual experiences. And I'm not exactly a blushing virgin either. At the same time, I want to put some things into perspective for myself before we go any further.

He smiles at me as he wipes a glob of conditioner from landing in my eye. It's not pitiful or patronizing—just pure affection. "No, Blake. I haven't been with anyone in months. Closer to a year," he clarifies.

"Oh, okay," I breathe out with a nod. "It's been a long time for me as well."

His eyes rove over me before grabbing onto my waist and pulling me flush against his very hard, very naked body. A small moan falls from my lips as his thick cock brushes against my stomach.

"There's a lot we could do in here without a condom," he muses and drops a kiss to my shoulder.

"I mean, I should let the conditioner sit for a while," I whisper and tilt my head back, giving him access to the front of my neck and collarbone.

Chuckling against my skin, he slowly pushes me until my back is against the wall and he's towering over me. There aren't any more words between us; his actions are slow—giving me the time to stop him or object if I want to—as he drops a hand between us and slides his fingers through my wet heat.

"Adrian" I whine, needier than I've ever felt before.

"I'm going to take care of you," he murmurs against my skin as he moves his lips to meet mine. "I'm *always* going to take care of you, Blake."

And I believe him. God, do I.

And that realization is the most liberating sensation of them all.

"Remember when I made that joke about working you open?" My eyes pop open to find him smirking down at me. Nodding and remembering the first time he FaceTimed me, the laugh quickly dies in my throat as he pushes two fingers into me all in one go. Crying out, I almost miss him say, "I don't think I was kidding at all."

"Adrian," I plead, not sure what I'm begging for. Just knowing he's the only person who can give it to me.

"Mmm," he hums against my lips before dropping to his knees in front of me. Gripping one thigh—my still slightly injured leg—he throws it over his shoulder. Before he's even fully settled my weight on him, his tongue darts out and licks my clit.

"*Ahh*," I cry out and buck my hips, pushing myself further into his face.

Again, he hums in approval and pulls me closer. One hand on the thigh curled around him, the other now gripping my ass cheek, as he wastes no time getting fully acquainted with my pussy.

"Fuck, Blake," he groans. Seeming to gain some control over himself, he pulls away far enough to look up at me. With the way I'm angled—hips pulled toward him, back pushed against the wall—and each panting breath, my tits rise and fall, blocking my view of him for short seconds.

With his thumb, he spreads me open and takes in the sight of me before him. With a cheeky grin, he looks up at me and muses, "Such a pretty pussy for an even prettier girl."

I can feel my face flush, stunned by his words, yet feeling more alive than I *ever* have. Sex has always been more about quick pleasure, but with Adrian, it's about every little experience and sensation.

He takes his time learning my body—licking, sucking, nibbling along my heated, sensitive skin. One of my hands slaps the tiles over my head while the other continues to hold the nape of his neck, pulling him closer as I thrust my hips against his face.

"Clit—my clit, Adrian," I demand. Sliding his hand up to rub tight firm circles, he hums in approval and pushes me closer to the precipice.

"That's my girl," he murmurs in between licks. "Use your words, baby."

"God, *yes*," I moan when his tongue moves inside me in tandem with his fingers running along the sensitive bundle of nerves.

And with every swipe, I'm closer... and closer... and closer...

Until I'm thrown over the edge and gasping out Adrian's name, still holding him close to my center. As overwhelming as it is, the last thing I want is for him to go anywhere.

To his credit, he doesn't pull away or move. Even once the pleasure has subsided and my arms fall limply to my sides. His fingers move from my over-sensitive clit, but his tongue continues lapping at my lingering arousal.

I'm so lost in the way he's worshipping my body, I don't notice he moved his hand from around my thigh until I hear the wet slide of skin against skin.

He's fucking his hand while fucking me *with his tongue.*

The visual alone sends a new spark of need through my body. And from the look of tortured concentration on his face, I know he's close.

Slipping one hand down to touch my clit while the other grips my own breast, I begin teasing the nipple in a similar way to how Adrian does.

Noticing that my pleasure's building back up right alongside his, those eyes I could drown in drag open, and he looks at me with a dark, lustful gaze. I hold his eye contact while touching myself in rhythm with the way he's touching both of us, we slowly bring ourselves to orgasm—mine seeming to be the catalyst that brings his own pleasure.

Panting, I slip my thigh from his shoulder and lean against the wall. My legs feel like Jell-O, and I consider dropping to the shower floor right now. Before I can, Adrian slides closer and rests his head against my lower stomach, right above my pelvis.

"Fuck, Blake," he murmurs, placing soft kisses against my skin.

Taking a moment to catch my breath, I'm not sure what comes over me. But I find myself reaching for his shampoo. While I was staying here last week, I noted that it's specific for his hair type and smells like cedar wood.

When he hears the lid flip open, his eyes find mine. The smile he offers me is tender and endearing. Allowing me to take care of him—in the same way he did for me a few minutes ago—he sits back on his heels as I work the suds into his hair, scratching my nails down the trimmed sides and back up. The gesture makes him groan in pleasure.

It's different from the sounds he was making while between my legs, but it's just as consuming. Letting me spend more time than needed to shampoo his hair, he stands and rinses it out.

At his full height, it would be too uncomfortable for both of us for me to finish the task. Instead, I hand him the accompanying conditioner and move to rinse my own hair.

Once I tie it up and out of the way again, I gasp when Adrian suddenly presses behind me and moves the washcloth along my stomach. It doesn't take me more than a second to relax into his hold and let him do as he pleases.

The longer we're in our own little bubble—surrounded by the building steam and only the sound of running water—I get the feeling that Adrian somehow needs this moment with me too. Like he's getting just as much out of this newfound intimacy as I am. So, neither of us rushes as he finishes washing both of us and rinsing the lingering soap off.

I could stay here forever, I think to myself.

Until the water suddenly drops to a lukewarm temperature, and I yelp, trying to hide behind Adrian's large body to protect myself.

Laughing, he leans forward, turns the tap off, and twists around to me. Swiftly, he lifts me around the waist.

Letting out a startled squeal, I naturally wrap my body around him, so I don't fall.

"You'd just sacrifice me like that? After I made you come *twice*?"

After setting a towel on the counter, he plops me down and wraps another one around my shoulders. "If we were ever in a real situation where one of us had to sacrifice ourselves, I'd argue you'd never let me be the one to do it."

"Fair and true assumption," he agrees with a nod and wraps a towel around his own waist. Grabbing a small cotton towel for himself, he starts to gently pat his hair dry. "I know we're just hanging out, but I have to do something with my hair, or I'll regret it in the morning."

Adjusting the towel that he wrapped around my shoulders and moving it to tie around my chest, I hop off the counter and grab one of the spare combs he has. "I'll go change. Can I borrow this?"

"Go for it," he nods in my direction.

Without second guessing myself, I lean on my toes and place a kiss on his cheek. "I'll find us something to watch."

With that, I swipe the clothes he left for me off the counter, leaving him to his hair routine. Once I've combed out my own hair and left it to air dry, I contemplate the outfit Adrian picked for me. It's an old Nike tee and a pair of large sweats. Not only are they way too long for me, considering our height difference, but they look thick and *hot*. Temperature hot, not attractiveness—I don't find myself caring about that after what Adrian and I just shared together.

I'm only in the oversized T-shirt when he walks out of the bathroom a few minutes later, still contemplating the pants.

"What's wrong?" he asks.

Feeling silly, I shake my head and decide just to wear the stupid sweats. "Nothing, it's okay."

Tilting his head and contemplating if he should push the subject, he snaps into motion when an idea. With only one leg in the garment, I watch as he walks to his dresser and pulls out a pair of boxer-briefs.

Holding them in my direction, he teases, "Wouldn't want you getting too hot—covered feet and all."

Rolling my eyes, I snatch the underwear from his hand and pull them up my legs. Twisting around a little bit, I look up and tell him, "These are really comfy. I might keep them."

"Go for it," he offers easily. "You look cute."

He moves to pull on the abandoned sweatpants as I sit crisscross in his bed. "Sooo..." I trail off.

"So?"

"I just don't want the food to go to waste again, and I don't want you to have to drive in the middle of the night."

His eyes glance to the clock by his bed. Twelve fifty-three a.m. "I'd say it's already the middle of the night," he cheekily states.

"Oh," I flush at the realization of how much time has passed since we left the haunted house. "Do you want me to g—"

"No, I want you here. Unless you want me to take you home," he adds. Kneeling in front of me on the floor, he gently runs a hand up my neck and tangles it into my hair. "I want you to stay with me tonight, but only if that's what *you* want, Storm Cloud."

"I don't want to leave," I whisper. "I just... didn't want to overstay my welcome."

Shaking his head, he presses a kiss to my lips and promises, "You're not. I want you with me all the time now—it's becoming a problem I don't actually want a solution to. I don't think I could handle the idea of sleeping in my bed alone after tonight."

Not knowing what to say to that—or at least, not having the courage to scream the words that have been growing in my heart—I grab him by the cheeks and pull him into me. I know words will be a necessity at some point. Though right now, tonight, sharing our bodies feels more important than any words we could give each other.

Pulling away, Adrian tells me to get under the covers and hands me the remote to the TV. As I start to scroll through the movie options, he brings our food with extra plates and napkins before crawling into bed next to me.

As we get settled—me choosing what to watch and him fixing my plate of tacos—we spend the next couple of hours in a state of intimacy and comfort. One I know I'll never be able to replicate with someone other than Adrian.

Chapter Thirty-Nine

Blake

Sitting behind the desk, I silently watch as my dad goes over Benji the Beagle's care since he's going home today. Adrian is bringing the dog from the back kennel.

I've been too distracted to really focus on what my dad's saying for the last ten minutes.

I'm *happy* Benji's going home. I really am. He's made so much progress in the last few weeks. Over the last ten days, he's really started to come back to his mischievous self and has every employee wrapped around his little, wagging tail.

It just feels so overwhelming actually seeing him make the recovery of any veterinarian's dreams.

And over my dead body would I ever admit this to my dad, but I am going to miss having Benji here with us all the time.

In the last month I've spent more nights than that first one, with Adrian, sitting in his kennel at the end of a shift. Sometimes it's just me and Benji, finding comfort in each other and the silence. Other times, Adrian shows up and we'd sit together, talking about random things—anything from our favorite colors to how he and Jatin have become new friends since the haunted house.

Not to put the fate of my relationship in a dog, but it kind of feels like Benji the Beagle's a big part of what's brought Adrian and I together.

I *know* by my dad's standards—and maybe just the medical field in general—I've gotten too attached to Benji. Much like my attachment to Chispa has grown throughout her recovery.

The doors push open and Benji comes walking out. He's still a little slower than usual and has a cone on, but his excitement to be on his way home is apparent.

Polly bursts out a sob as Benji gets to her, laying at her feet ready for pets. Her reaction makes the tears I've held at bay fall over. It's just a few before I can get a handle on myself. But like he's invisibly tied to me somehow, Adrian's head turns in my direction.

As soon as it does, his face falls in affection and concern. He stands over there, holding the leash for Polly, though his gaze continues to move back to me.

It makes my heart ache—all of it. Benji the Beagle leaving, the way Adrian's looking at me, even the tears in that pain in my ass's eyes.

Finally, when my dad seems to be done talking to Polly, the two of them stand and walk to the front desk, Adrian trailing behind them. I'm doing my best to stay distracted by sending out confirmation emails and appointment reminders. Except as he moves to my side of the desk and leans his butt against the edge, I realize it's a fruitless goal.

Turning my head up to him, a soft smile already forming on my face, a worse distraction catches my attention.

When my eyes snag on the scowl that Polly's throwing in my direction, I can't look away. Squinting at her, I huff, "What?"

"That's no way to talk to a client, dear," she scolds.

Adrian hides his snort with a fake cough but I'm too annoyed to tell him not to encourage her. Instead, like a petulant child, I snark back, "Well, it's not okay to look at people like *that*, Polly."

With a quirk of her eyebrow, she asks, "You aren't going to add 'pain in your ass' to the end of that?" My mouth pops open in surprise, and even my dad and Adrian look stunned by her question.

"Excuse me?" I squeak out.

"You think I didn't know about that?" For the first time in maybe ever, there's clear amusement dropping from Polly's tone.

"What are you going to do?" I retort, sarcasm thick. "Leave another one-star review?"

"Apparently, the Google only lets you leave one review for a place." She lifts her nose in the air and that's the last straw for Adrian. He covers his mouth, his laugh slipping through his fingers anyway.

"I'm going to leave *you* a one-star review, Polly."

She flinches back, looking like someone just tried to steal the glasses off her face. "You can't *review* people."

"You can do just about anything on *the Google* these days—try me."

Squinting at me, she turns her head toward my dad and tells him, "You've raised a *horrible* child."

"I tell them that about Grady all the time," I cut in with a dramatic eye roll.

To my dad again, she adds, "Fire her."

The demand is undermined by the fact that her beagle has slipped out of her reach and tries to jump onto the desk between Adrian and me. When his cone knocks him back down, he lays on the ground, his tail wagging as he looks up at us with his signature puppy eyes.

Giving Polly a mocking smile, I lean down and pet Benji the Beagle's back.

"I'm not going to fire my daughter, Polly," my dad finally advocates for me but he's grinning in entertainment too.

Just to piss her off more, I stick my tongue out at her. With that, she huffs and goes to grab Benji's leash off the floor. Like the kind-hearted traitor that he is, Adrian gets to it before she can throw her back out or something.

She grabs it out of his hand in a dramatic manner and moves toward the door. Right as she's stepping through the threshold, she looks over her shoulder at me and throws me a quick wink.

Biting back my smile and shaking my head, I look back at my dad and Adrian. There's that familiar expression of adoration plastered on Adrian's face—the one I've grown far too accustomed to in the last few weeks. However, my dad's expression is more conflicted.

Seeming to pick up on the tension, Adrian softly knocks his knee against my leg before excusing himself. Once he's pushed through the back doors, it's just my dad and I in the lobby.

Looking up at him, I suddenly feel like a little girl again—that nostalgic cocktail of feeling like he's the best person to ever walk this earth and wanting nothing more than for him to be proud of me.

And knowing, in my gut, he wouldn't be after some of my recent decisions.

"Are you okay?" he asks. His tone is mostly paternal, caring.

"I'm okay," I promise.

He looks at me for a long moment, letting his eyes sweep across my features—an even split of his and my mom's—and try not to fidget.

He then asks, "You're sure?" I hear that rare undertone of true authority, when he completely shuts the door on *Dad Mode* and moves into *Boss Mode*.

It's not often, but it's happening now.

"I'm sure," I answer with more attitude than I intend. "I don't see you asking anyone else that."

We've never had a real fight. I've been grounded, lectured, and had the 'I'm *very* disappointed in you' guilt trips. But truthfully, I deserved all of those. He's calm and fair, and a lot more patient than me.

Right now though, I can't see those great traits of his.

Making a show of it, he looks around the room. "Don't see anyone else about to cry because a *now healthy* pet is going *home.*"

Mimicking his gesture, I sweep my gaze across the room and shrug. "Don't see anyone else here at all."

With a deep sigh, which tells me he's done with this day, he rubs his eyes for a minute before looking at me. *Really* looking at me. "I know it can be overwhelming—even when the results are good. But you have to separate yourself from the emotions. Even when you know someone as more than a client."

Pushing past the guilt, I tell him, "I don't plan on being a vet."

Nodding slowly, he seems to be thinking through his next words. He's always known that I had no desire to follow in his or my mom's professional footsteps. "Are you planning on quitting this job sometime soon?" He gestures to the seat and desk.

"What?" I ask, clearly offended. "No?"

"Good. I love having you here, honey. Even in this role, there are certain boundaries you can't cross." His eyes bounce between mine. "I don't want you to lose that heart of yours, Blake, but I also need you to hear what I'm saying."

"Okay," I insist. "I do."

After another long moment of silence, he lets out a breath and some of the tension from his shoulders leaves. I know *Dad Mode* is back on before he even opens his mouth. "I love you, honey. And I *am* so proud of you."

"I love you too, Dad."

We both can tell that the conversation is done, though he's reluctant to walk away. As soon as he's out of sight, I can't help but roll my eyes. It's annoying that he's lecturing me because I let out a few tears when Polly and Benji were officially reunited. I've seen all of his employees—and him—cry over a variety of cases, good and bad.

Except just as quickly, that annoyance is washed away and guilt bleeds into the cracks. Because maybe I wasn't out of line *this* time... but that wasn't the case with Zippy. And he was nicer than he needed to be when I came to the clinic after he asked me not to for Chispa's surgery.

Not to mention I've gotten his new favorite employee mixed into the chaos created by my inability to say no sometimes.

With a heavy weight in my stomach, I start closing down the front and cleaning up for the night. Later in bed, after talking on the phone with Adrian and texting with my friends, it lingers—more potent—to the point that I feel that nausea of anxiety taking over again.

Chapter Forty

Adrian

One hand carrying a bag of food and the other holding Luke's small hand, I lead us back to the table where Blake's currently waiting with the older two Paulson boys. We had plans to come to the Loop for dinner tonight, since we haven't had a chance all week, and it's become our thing over the last couple of months.

When she texted me earlier, trying to cancel—the boys' mom needed help so she could pick up an extra shift—I wasn't easily deterred. Not totally sure why they trust me with their kids after what happened with Zippy, Erika and Kevin have welcomed me any time I've shown up to hang out with Blake while she's babysitting.

Blake still had to call Erica to ask if it was okay that we took the boys out for dinner. She was on the phone for a while, and I could hear her from the kitchen. It didn't sound like Erica was against us taking the boys, but more like she felt guilty. Blake reassured her multiple times that they didn't need to pay us back, and Blake would cover the cost for the boys.

Mikey, Shawn, and Luke stood in shocked silence for about five seconds before they broke out in a quiet cheer at the prospect of going to The Loop for dinner. And then

I remembered Blake had mentioned the Paulsons live paycheck to paycheck, and it's a big reason she didn't wanna call her dad when Zippy got hurt.

As the boys ran off to gather their shoes and coats, I stepped into Blake's space. Wrapping an arm around her waist before placing a soft kiss against her lips, I made it clear that neither she nor the Paulsons were paying for anything tonight.

I was happy to do it. Not only did helping the community in any way—big or small—make Blake happy, I was also starting to love this town as my own. And I don't mind taking care of the three boys that were slowly becoming our sidekicks.

That's how we ended up here—the five of us at The Loop with a dish or two from each of the food trucks. Luke casually mentioned that they'd never been to The Loop. I saw the wrinkle in Blake's brow before she looked away from him, blinking quickly.

Truthfully, the three little dudes are pretty cool. It's been four weeks since Benji the Beagle went home, and thankfully, it's been pretty quiet since then.

Other than the chaos that spending time with the Paulson kids brings, I've had time to focus on the end of my first semester. Blake's been great about how busy I've been. We've spent a few nights together since Halloween, even though we haven't gone further than pleasuring each other with our mouths.

But she doesn't mind when I have to go a few nights without our evening calls. And a lot of the time, when she is at the apartment, she's quietly watching TV and working on different knitting projects. She just wants to be there with me as badly as I always want her around me. The most exciting part of the last few weeks for Blake was getting to visit Margo and Meera in New York for the week of Thanksgiving. Meera had a huge solo in the winter recital, and I guess it's rare that a freshman is granted such a major part.

Much like their visit for fall break, Blake was radiating genuine happiness for weeks after. The kind that only seems to come out when she's with the two of them.

As I set down the two stacks of waffles, I round out our selection for the evening. Birthday cake and peppermint mocha waffles, a rack of ribs and potato salad, way too many chicken tacos, a medium pepperoni pizza, and five homemade dog treats from the pet centered truck that opened a week ago. Luke was so excited when he saw it, it only felt right to get the smallest member of their family something too.

"Adrian," Blake quietly chastises, but there's a small affectionate tug to her lips. "This is way too much food."

"I wanted the boys to get a taste of everything. It's the only way for them to know which is their favorite." I wink at them. Blake made me try each one over the course of a few weeks for the same reason. She shakes her head as she starts opening the boxes. "Plus, whatever we don't finish, we can take back for Kevin and Erica."

Blake's hand slams down on the waffles lid. "Those are for dessert." Mikey rolls his eyes and goes back to his taco. I can't stop the derisive snort that slips out. Blake *always* has the waffles for dinner. Although I've seen the boys on a sugar high before, and I have to agree with her on this.

Her scolding—yet hot as fuck—look is cut short when Shawn says, "Dad *loves* ribs, but he never has time to grill. He's always sad about it."

"Let's save those for him," Mikey instructs. Even if he drives her crazy, I can see the care Blake feels for them. It's written clearly across her face, and it's reflected back by each one of the boys every time they look at her. They respect her more than she might see, but they obviously feel comfortable and safe enough with her to just be young, rambunctious boys too.

"Nah, you guys eat whatever you want. We can pick up more on the way out if we need."

All four of their smiles are so wide, but the way Blake's looking at me feels like maybe I'm *her* superhero.

And coming from Blake, that's not a small thing.

Over the course of a few weeks, she's opened up to me in such subtle yet meaningful ways. Her smiles grace her plush lips more freely, and there's less hesitation on her part when she wants to touch me—or for me to touch her.

The boys eat a little of everything, but there's still plenty to take back to their parents.

After we pack it up, Blake has the idea to walk along the shore after. Her unspoken intention is that the boys will burn off some of their energy. It's late in the afternoon, the winter days ending early. The sun is just peaking over the horizon when Mikey runs back to Blake and me, cupping something in his hands.

"I got this for you," he chimes, his voice a little too sweet to mean anything good.

As if on instinct, Blake takes a step back and squints at him. Considering he was just digging into the still wet sand from the high tide earlier, I don't blame her.

He steps forward, pushing his hands closer toward her, but she gives him a look that clearly says, *don't fuck with me.*

"Alright, bud." With a hand to his shoulder, I stop him from getting closer to her. He looks up at me with a mix of fear and slight betrayal. Chuckling, I kneel down so we're at eye level. Shawn and Luke walk up behind him, and I wait until they all can hear. "You three are *done* messing with Blake, understand me? She only stopped wrapping her ankle about two weeks ago." Gesturing toward her behind me, their eyes follow my hand and move back to me in sync.

"It was an accident," Mikey pouts.

Nodding, I squeeze his shoulder reassuringly. "I know it was, or I wouldn't come to hang out with you guys. And I definitely wouldn't be okay with Blake still babysitting you three if I thought you had actually wanted to hurt her." His shoulders relax at my words. "*But*, enough is still enough."

"Okay," Shawn agrees easily, Luke nodding behind him.

Mikey still looks unsure and as his eyes go back up to Blake, I can see him conceding before he mutters, "Yeah, okay. No more." Gently, he drops the sand crab back onto the ground.

"*Ugh*," Blake spats, and the reaction seems like a big enough victory based on Mikey's grin.

Shaking my head, I ask dumbfounded, "Where'd you even find that this time of the year?"

"I had to dig *really* far," he admitted, a little pleased with himself.

Blake's laughing at his mostly harmless failed prank when we hear a loud yelping sound and a man's distressed shout.

Even from here, we can see his dog is limping as he tries to move away from his owner's prying. The three boys and Blake all moved closer to me on instinct, as if I'm the protector in this situation.

But I don't think they need protecting... I think *he* needs help.

As if reading my thoughts, Blake looks up at me with a worried expression. "We can't just leave him."

There isn't a lot I can do for him if his dog is seriously injured, and I have a feeling this will be another incident where Blake won't want to call her dad for help. Against my better judgement, I nod. "Okay. Just stay here."

Giving Blake a look over my shoulder, one that's begging her to stay where she is, I walk toward the man who's muttering too low to make out the words, but the distress in his voice is clear. He's up on the sidewalk, under a street-light. I kneel down next to him when I see that his lab mix is bleeding from its foot—no, its toe. It's a fairly common injury in dogs, especially one that looks to be around ten years old.

"Hey, man," I greet him, looking around for what could have snagged the nail.

He turns toward me with a confused look, grief pushing through to the front anyway. "Hello," he quietly, but politely responds as I notice the deep crack in the sidewalk. It doesn't look that bad from the way the weeds have started to grow through the broken cement. If you look closer, you can see that it's a few inches deep and not very wide, making it the perfect thing to catch a nail.

"Can I try to help?" When he doesn't answer right away, I tell him honestly, "I'm not a vet but I am going to school to be one. I can stop the bleeding, and once I do, I can see how bad it is. More times than not, it can heal on its own."

"Mr. Gibson?" Blake's concerned voice rips through the air behind me. I turn, wanting to chastise her about coming up to a strange man, even if she seems to know him. "Mr. Gibson," she repeats, "I'm Blake. Your old student, Blake M—"

"Miller. Blake Miller. Yes, I remember you." More relaxed, he adds, "You were always such a good student. Just like your brother... but not like that damn Davies boy."

Her head actually falls back on a laugh as she kneels down with the boys tucked behind her. "Asher, yeah. He always gave you guys a run for your money."

"Makes a man want to retire, I'll tell you that," he jokes, his face immediately morphing into regret at his own words.

I'm not sure what's going on in his life, but Blake seems to know. She reaches out and squeezes his shoulder in a reassuring way, similar to how I was with Mikey early. "We can help." Her brows scrunch and she looks to me with pleading eyes, in addition to the three sets looking over her shoulder at me. "Right?"

"Yeah, I think I can help. Are you okay staying here while I run to the store?"

The four of them nod and settle on the grass between the sidewalk and the beach. Luke crawls into Blake's lap, like he often does when he needs comfort away from his parents. Shawn and Mikey sit sentry over the dog, petting him in a soothing manner. As I wait for a car to pass, I hear a choked sob breaking from the older man's throat as I cross the street toward the general store.

Chapter Forty-One

Blake

Once again, I'm reminded why I continue to babysit the three boys even though they're little hellions. They're also really fucking sweet when they want to be and take the community aspect of the church very seriously. Though I think it would be hard not to, being a part of a family that's relied so heavily on their neighbors.

For the last ten minutes, each one has offered Mr. Gibson words of comfort and soothing pats to his large dog, Archie. The dog has calmed down and is laying between the five of us while we wait for Adrian to get back, but his soft whimper tells us that he's still uncomfortable and the bleeding hasn't let up at all.

I let the boys fawn over Archie while I tell Mr. Gibson about the last few years of my life since I left the public school system. He's asking me all of the typical questions an old teacher would be curious about—graduation, swimming, what I'm doing now. I usually do my best to avoid these conversations. For once, I'm willing to make an exception if it means distracting him for a few more minutes.

I don't mention his wife who passed away four years ago, or what I've overheard from my mom and dad—he didn't cope well with the loss, was fired from his job and that he's been down on his luck ever since.

No, I let him pry and question my life in a way very few people are allowed. The relief is written across his face with every minute of casual conversation I let float between us.

And finally, about fifteen minutes after he left, Adrian jogs back across the street. He drops down next to me and gently rubs my back for a few seconds before turning to the task at hand.

"I'm going to need to clean it first. I don't have anything for the pain, but hopefully once we stop the bleeding, some of his discomfort should be alleviated." Mr. Gibson nods, looking concerned as Adrian pulls out saline for wounds, gauze, and cornstarch. We watch as he takes the lid off a to-go coffee cup full of water. He must have stopped at the small convenience store near here.

Adrian's eyes cut to mine—and I can see his reluctance to do this, and it tears me up inside. I'm not trying to put him in the same situation my dad was in, but I genuinely don't know how to *not* help someone who's in need.

And when I—or really, someone I'm with—can do something for this man who just needs a fucking win, I *have* to.

I try to express that guilty plea to him through my own expression, and I can tell the second he truly accepts that we're doing this.

"Okay, all we have to do after I clean it is use the cornstarch to stop the bleeding." He goes on to explain to Mr. Gibson everything he'll have to do—from the cleaning, to applying the cornstarch, to wrapping it. "Before I wrap it, I'll make sure it doesn't look worse than a broken nail. There's no real way to know without going to a clinic... but if there's nothing obvious, then you'll be able to tell by how he's acting within the next twenty-four hours."

Mr. Gibson nods earnestly, still looking concerned, albeit more hopeful than he has since we got here.

There seems to be a silent agreement between Adrian and I, that we don't often kiss each other with an audience—outside of Margo and Meera. Which I appreciate, if only because we haven't had that conversation. But without a second thought, I lean over and place a soft kiss on his jaw. "Thank you," I murmur, ignoring the giggling from three boys mocking us.

"I've always got you, Storm Cloud," he whispers only to me. "Now, let's see what we can do for Archie here." His attention goes back to the dog, and I sit back, watching as he does what he was so clearly born to do.

The hope in Mr. Gibson's eyes dimmed as soon as Adrian got the dog's paw cleaned. While Adrian gets the bleeding to stop, it's obvious, even to me, that Archie needs more than what we can provide him. The nail partially ripped off, the jagged shape appearing to poke into his skin, resulting in more bleeding. I've pulled the boys a few feet away, sitting in the grass, but not before he mentioned that he was worried about the dog's tendon.

The cornstarch has stopped the bleeding, which is why Adrian's able to make a better assessment given his limited experience.

I step up behind him, after getting the three boys to calm down when Adrian made his statement. Mikey's the only one that knows what a tendon is, but his hysterics typically cause his brothers to react the same.

Turning his head slowly, he gives me an apologetic look, and I know what he's going to say before he opens his mouth. "I *have* to call your dad... or the clinic. Whichever you prefer. But this..." He gestures to Archie, still whimpering in pain.

"I know," I admit and nod. "I'll call my dad."

He stands and steps closer. "I can do it."

"No," I insist. "It needs to be me."

He gives me a long, assessing look before he nods and steps back to Mr. Gibson. Even though I can see the reluctance in the old man's features, he never makes a fuss about having to take his dog into the vet. I'm sure he knew from the beginning this is where it would end. Maybe he was just entertaining us.

Twirling around until I'm facing the road, and can't see any of the people I'm with, I pull out my phone and scroll through my contacts.

After only two rings, my dad answers, "Hi, honey."

"Dad..." I swallow down the knowledge that I'm about to be in deep shit. "I need you to meet me at the clinic. Now."

Chapter Forty-Two

Adrian

After Blake quickly explained the situation to her dad, he confirmed it was okay if we picked up Archie and drove him to the clinic. It wasn't the easiest situation, considering we had three kids with us and had walked from their house.

Even though I can tell Blake doesn't feel great about this situation—and the inevitable conversation with her dad—she switched into crisis mode easily. We agreed that she would stay with the boys, Mr. Gibson, and Archie, while I went to get my SUV. After that, she took the boys back home to get their booster seats and brought them to the clinic in her car.

Which brings us to now—Blake and I sitting in the lobby with three very bored and anxious kids. Except the most anxious of all is Blake.

From what I heard, which is only her side of the conversation, Tim had a lot of questions. Things like what was going on, but also about how Blake found herself in this position. And even though it was a coincidence, it doesn't seem like he believes her.

He hasn't questioned me on anything. He did, however, ask me if I could 'have a chat with him' after he finished with Mr. Gibson and Archie.

It's been about forty-five minutes when a new thought pops into my overwhelmed mind. "Hey," I speak quietly, and knock my knee against hers. Her eyes move to mine and my own emotions are written across her face. "Do we need to call Erika or Kevin?"

She shakes her head. "I called Erika on the way here. She knows where the boys are, and said she'd get them as soon as she could. I told her not to rush. It's my fault anyway."

"Blake," I whisper and turn toward her. "It's not your fault that Archie got hurt."

She rolls her eyes but there's no anger behind it. "I don't mean that. I don't need my dad to tell me that I've made some irresponsible choices lately. And I shouldn't have ever asked you to help."

"I said this last time, and I'll say it again—you didn't *make* me do anything. I'm a grown man and make my own choices, okay? I was confident that Zippy was having an allergic reaction. Today, I knew Archie needed more help than I could provide. You couldn't have changed my mind."

"Promise?" she utters.

"Yes," I insist, trying to stay quiet. "I'd do just about anything for you, Blake, but I wouldn't go against my own morals."

She lets out a deep breath and nods, finally seeming to hear me on this.

A little while later, Tim walks out of the back with Mr. Gibson and Archie. The dog is walking, just sporting a new cone and a bandage around his paw. There's a small chance he had to get surgery, although from how quickly they're wrapping up, I believe that it's not too serious.

They stop near us, and Tim looks toward the older man. Seeming to give him the choice in telling us what was wrong.

"The nail cracked down the middle," Mr. Gibson says, "but Dr. Miller thinks we were able to avoid further damage by getting him here."

Mikey lets out a sigh of relief; it's exactly how we're all feeling.

Until sweet, naive Luke perks up and tells Blake and me, "Good job! You guys saved *two* pets!"

Neither of us say anything or dare to look at anyone other than the five-year-old. I can feel Dr. Miller's glare as he tries to work out what Luke means.

Mikey picks up on the tension—probably understanding very well when a parent is pissed at their kid. "*Luke*," he warns his youngest brother and shakes his head.

"What?" Luke asks innocently. "They saved Zippy and then they saved Archie."

"Stop talking," Mikey instructs and pinches his leg.

"*Ow!* Don't pinch me." Luke pinches his oldest brother back before hopping off his seat and moving to stand between mine and Blake's legs. "Tell them. Your dad will be so proud of you."

He pats Blake's cheek, and it's so sweet. So wholesome. She smiles at him but it's clearly for his own sake.

"Luke, I need you to go sit with your brothers, okay?" she softly tells him, turning him toward the other two boys. Looking at me over his shoulder, he gives me a confused look.

When he gets back to his seat, Shawn leans over and whispers something in his ear. From Luke's morphing expression, I think his brother is explaining that they've accidentally gotten Blake and me in trouble.

"How long until Erika or Kevin get here?" Dr. Miller asks Blake, and we both finally look up at him.

"I think in like thirty minutes." Blake's voice is so small I'm not sure he can hear her.

He just nods stiffly and tells us, "Stay right here and wait with the boys while I go over some things with Mr. Gibson. I want to talk to you both before either of you leave."

"Okay," Blake whispers.

"Yes, sir," I tell him, sounding more confident than I feel.

He gives us a look that's partly disappointment, but more so confusion, before walking to his office with the older man and his dog.

Chapter Forty-Three

Adrian

Sitting next to Blake in Tim's office, we're all silent for a minute. I don't want to make assumptions about what he's thinking—I'd rather know before making a baseless apology—and I don't want to accidentally get us into deeper shit than we're already in.

Finally finding his words, Tim breaks the silence. "Okay, look. I have an idea of what's going on here, but I want to give you two the chance to speak first."

Before I can form a word, Blake cuts me off. "This isn't Adrian's fault. All of it was my idea."

"Blake..." I trail off, shaking my head. She reaches over to squeeze the hand resting on my thigh but pulls away when she leans forward in her chair, addressing her dad again.

"The Paulson boys were being their typical selves and pulling pranks when I sprained my ankle."

"I knew there was more to that story than you were telling us." It's the driest I've ever heard his tone when talking to anyone, especially his daughter.

"My ankle doesn't have anything to do with Zippy—not really, I guess. They set up some Halloween decorations in the shed to scare me. They got me out there by saying Zippy was stuck." Her dad doesn't say anything as Blake gives him the short story of what happened that night. The skeleton, her falling, calling me, and Luke remembering Zippy before anyone else.

Immediately, Tim asks, "Why didn't you call me, Blake? It could have been venomous, or he could have been allergic."

Her mouth gapes open. I know she was ready for this question, so this is her stalling. She doesn't want to answer it. "I've worked here long enough to know when something is an emergency," she argues.

He shakes his head. "That's not your call to make. Why didn't you call me, Blake?" he repeats.

"Because... I—I don't know." I watch them share a long, meaningful look. Most people would think she has a good poker face, but if you know her, it's impossible for her to hide her emotions from you. There's a slight quiver to her bottom lip and her eyebrows raise the faintest bit.

Sighing, he looks at me, seeming to have forgotten I was a part of this conversation. "If you want to be a veterinarian one day, you're going to have to learn to set these bound-aries. It's not easy, but it's crucial." I nod, opening my mouth to speak again, when he asks, "What happened with Mr. Gibson's dog?"

"That was me to—"

He holds up a finger. "I'm asking Adrian."

Nodding, I answer honestly. "We took the boys to dinner at The Loop, then for a walk along the beach. We heard a commotion, which was Archie catching his nail on some-thing causing it to bleed."

"And how did you handle that?" His tone is more clinical than I've ever heard. In a way, I appreciate that. It feels like he's talking to me as my boss right now, not as a guy who's been spending too much time with his daughter.

I love working for Dr. Miller, but I'm falling in love with his daughter, too.

That distinction between employee and Blake's friend feels important.

Sitting a little straighter, I explain to him how I cleaned it and stopped the bleeding.

"Cornstarch," he slowly confirms once I'm done.

"Yes, sir. A professor mentioned it once in a course about emergency situations."

"It's a common solution to stop bleeding. I'm not saying you were wrong to do it."

He's not saying I was right either.

As if sensing that, Blake tries to interject, "What were we supposed to do?"

Looking almost hurt, he turns back to his daughter. "I'm going to ask you for the third time... why didn't you call me?"

Looking like a fish out of water for a few seconds, her protectiveness of me wins out against her consideration for her dad's feelings. As honored as I am, it's not necessary.

"You know why!" she accuses. "I couldn't put you in that position again. I overheard Mom talking to Bonnie more than once about how she was worried about you. I'm not blind to how your career affects you, Dad."

"I'm the father here," he argues in a gentle voice. "You're the kid—*my* kid. I'm the one who makes the big decisions, especially when it comes to the wellbeing of my family and my business."

"It's a lose-lose situation. If I call you, then the family would have to either pay to be told that their animal is fine, or you have to potentially lose the hard-set boundaries you've worked so hard for."

His brows set in a stern line. "That's my choice to make, Blake."

There's a hard look to her, one of pure stubbornness. "I don't like the choice you'd make. And unlike you, I can't choose to not help someone in need."

The words feel like a bomb dropping. The despair on Blake's face shows she regrets it, but there's still so much passion in her eyes, a hot flame burning through the storm. She doesn't try to take it back.

And I fucking hate that her defense of me is causing this much contention between them.

"I know it doesn't always make sense—it's a part of the career I still struggle with—*however*, there are reasons why you can't run around town playing amateur vet." His tone is losing some of its patience, but I can also tell that fighting hurts him as much as it does her. "If something worse happened—like an allergic reaction to the medicine you gave Zippy or causing more damage to Archie's paw—the consequences would've been a hell of a lot more expensive than the initial examination."

"I was *helping* them," she desperately insists.

"You were, but did Erika even consent to her dog taking Benadryl?"

"She wasn't mad about it," Blake argues. I know exactly where Dr. Miller's thoughts are headed.

"Because her dog was fine. I wouldn't put it past Erika to take something like that to a court, and I couldn't blame her if she did. Zippy means a lot to her—he's more than just a family dog."

My face scrunches in confusion as Blake's expression almost crumples. "I know that. I *know* why he means so much to her after her miscarriage. I also know that Erika and Kevin can't afford any extra expenses, considering they've never once paid me since she was laid off from the bank a couple years ago."

My eyebrows jerk up at the proclamation. I've never asked Blake how much she makes, nor expected her to pay me for choosing to hang out with the four of them. At least one night a week is spent babysitting the three tornadoes, so it's initially surprising that she's never been paid. And it makes me wonder if that's why they've lost so many other babysitters according to her.

"So don't sit here," she goes on, angrier now, "and tell me that I don't know, or care about any of that. And don't pretend I don't know that Archie isn't one of the last things Mr. Gibson hasn't lost recently."

"Blake," he starts, and I can see how painful this argument is for him.

"I—I'm done talking." Quickly standing and grabbing her small crossbody purse, she walks out the office door. I hear the front door of the lobby bang shut before I've even processed the last few seconds.

Turning back to Tim, he's looking at the door with a shocked expression. Most of the anger has dissolved from his expression. When he looks back at me, he admits, "She's never walked out on me or her mom before."

"That doesn't surprise me," I admit.

"I hope Blake has told you a bit about... her past. I'd like for her to open up to anyone other than her therapist, truthfully."

Nodding, I run my hands down my thighs. "She has."

"Good. I'm glad. Then it probably isn't surprising that Blake has always avoided making waves—and that's what clues me into how important this is to her."

"You... aren't mad?"

He leans back, blowing out a breath. "That's a loaded question. I didn't mean to get as worked up as I did while talking to her. Regardless, that's neither here nor there right now... I'm more concerned than I am angry."

The old 'I'm not mad, I'm just disappointed speech.' It's the same one my dad uses, and it's always been worse than yelling ever could be.

"I know it seems like an extreme case, Adrian, but you need to be careful with the decisions you make right now. A program—especially one as prestigious as UCAH's—will drop you if there's a scandal attached to your name. Even if they don't, it'll be nearly impossible to get a job worth anything in this field. I hope you understand that under those hypothetical circumstances, I wouldn't be able to write you a recommendation letter either."

"Yes, sir, I understand." My hands fidget in my lap, and as badly as I want to look away, I don't.

He leans forward, his elbows on the desk, and looks down at his clasped hands. "You're a long way out from graduation, I know that. I also think you're going to make a damn good veterinarian. If things stay on the right path here"—he points between us then into the air, indicating the clinic itself—"I hope you can find a happy career working here. I just need you to not *fuck up* before then."

Nodding, my throat suddenly thick with emotions, I tell him, "I'd be honored to work here as a veterinarian after I graduate. I understand that I can't change your feelings on the matter, but I hope you don't blame Blake too much. Ultimately, I knew that what I was doing was tip-toeing the line of unethical."

"Why'd you do it then?" He's genuinely curious, even so it still feels like it's a test in a way.

"I didn't know that Blake's been babysitting for the Paulson family completely for free until a few minutes ago, but I had an idea that they weren't in the most financially secure spot either. I wanted to help." I shrug, thinking about all the times I was warned about getting too involved with a client or patient.

"Has Blake ever told you about my past? With the clinic and the town?"

Scrunching my eyebrows, I shake my head. "She's made it clear that she doesn't want to put you in a position to make a hard call—like turning someone away if they can't afford the medical care."

He nods slowly and doesn't say anything for a long moment. "A few years ago—probably more like eight now—I found myself in a similar position. Except the dog was hurt much worse than any you've faced, and I was in a position to do something about it.

"I figured, 'what the hell? Just once can't hurt.' It was a family friend we had been close with for years. So, I gave them a very discounted rate when their young puppy broke his leg. In a small community like Amada Beach, there aren't a lot of secrets. So, word spread. Expectations were placed on me, and I couldn't deliver."

"She's never mentioned this, but it makes sense…" I'm talking more to myself.

"Blake was young, and it was right around the time she was starting at SPA. She has a memory like an elephant, so I'm sure that time affected her more than we've realized. I struggled a lot for months after that, but it wasn't the first time that I've dealt with depression due to the profession. Learning how to maintain boundaries is an important ethical requirement of the job. That being said, it's as much for your own mental health as anything else."

I can hear the sincerity in his voice, along with a layer of lingering pain as well.

"I hear you, sir." Stumbling over my words for a moment, I tell him, "Blake's made me realize how important therapy can be regardless of what you're going through at the moment. And I've thought about it for a couple of weeks, but I know it's something I need to do right away."

"Is that so?" His brows lift, looking interested in what I have to say.

"Yes, I do mean that. I've felt conflicted about what happened with Zippy for over two months now. It's hard to feel good about helping them when I know we went about it in the wrong way."

"I'm proud of you for realizing that." He sits back and crosses his arms. "As for Blake, my feelings on the matter are more complex, and I'll let her decide how much of our inevitable conversation she wants to tell you. However, even though we've never really fought, I didn't expect we'd go our entire lives without it either. And it's good to see Blake feel so passionately about something… and *someone*."

He gives me a meaningful look. I'm sure he's putting the clues together as quickly as he did earlier, but that's still Blake's conversation to have with her parents. Still, I admit, "I hope you still feel that way after this."

"I do, because I blame you two separately and equally." I let out a shocked laugh at his honesty, the genuinely kind smile he offers me not surprising at all. "And I trust you two won't do this again, and you'll call me if it's something that requires medical attention."

I promise him that we won't, feeling cautiously hopeful about making that oath on her behalf.

As I move to stand, knowing that I've been dismissed, Dr. Miller stops me as I'm walking out the office door.

"Adrian."

With my hand on the frame, I turn toward him. "Yes, sir?"

He clears his throat. "Moving out of boss mode... I have a question. And I don't mean to overstep. Blake mentioned that you won't be seeing your parents or godmother for Christmas?"

"Oh," I mutter, slightly shocked. Not that it's out of line, it just wasn't what I was expecting right now. "No, I won't see them for the holiday. My parents are in Maine, working until a couple days before New Year's Eve. And my godmother is taking her parents to visit family across the country."

He nods, seeming to think over his words. "Maybe I should leave the invitation to Blake—and I do think we should check with her—but Selena and I would love for you to spend the holiday with us. If you want."

My brows flick up. This definitely wasn't what I was anticipating today. Though, it does sound a hell of a lot better than eating takeout and watching a football game alone.

"I'll talk to Blake, but if she's okay with it... Yeah, yes. I'd love to spend the day with you guys."

He offers me a small, earnest smile and a quick nod. With that, I take my leave and text Blake, hoping to at least find out where she went.

Chapter Forty-Four

Adrian

It's been about five hours since Blake stormed out of the clinic. I started to worry about three hours ago, however Tim let me know she was okay. She hadn't gone home, but both of her parents had her phone's location and said she was safe.

It still didn't do anything to calm my nerves though. Not like seeing her standing at my front door, hair wet and face a blotchy red. I hate the sight of her upset, but I love seeing her here.

And a small, selfish part of me can't help noticing that she didn't go home. She came here. In the past, if she needed space, I'm not sure where she would go to get away from her parents—I don't know if she's ever needed to. With me she has a safe place to land, and it does something to my heart to know she's actually utilizing it.

"Hey, Storm Cloud," I quietly greet her.

Her throat bobs and she whispers, "Hi."

Opening one arm, she easily falls into my embrace as I shut the door with my other one.

"Sorry I just showed up," she mumbles into my chest.

"You don't have to apologize. I'll give you a key if it makes you feel better." She leans her head back, resting her chin on my chest, to look at me. "I really would."

She chuckles lightly. "I believe you."

"I called your parents," I confess. "I was worried about you."

Her face falls, washing away the short-lived amusement with guilt. "I should've texted you."

Shaking my head, I tell her, "It's okay to need space sometimes, Blake. I just worry."

"I'll tell you when I need space next time," she promises.

I lean down to place a soft kiss on her lips. It's quick and tender, and hopefully exactly what she needs right now. "You hungry?"

She nods. "I was at the gym—well, the pool. It's usually where I go when I'm feeling anxious." She slips into one of the stools at the small breakfast bar and watches as I finish getting out the ingredients for the burrito bowl I'd planned to make for dinner, and a few lunches for the week. There's chicken already in the oven, so I can at least stay closer to Blake while I finish everything else.

"That's good to know." I walk to the sink and wash my hands—using the time to think over my next words. When I turn back to the counter across from her, I take a second to fully observe her beauty—getting stuck on those god-damn lightning eyes that haunt me every moment now. "I wouldn't expect you to take me, but if you ever want to be alone, but *not* alone, I'm there. I'll work out while you swim."

She doesn't say anything for a while, so I focus on the food, not wanting her to have to wait if she's hungry. After a minute or two, Blake quietly tells me, "I like when you're there with me."

"Me too. I'll meet you next time then."

She smiles and finally looks like she's starting to relax. Her eyes are sad, and I can see that the argument with her dad is still weighing on her. I know this is something we have to talk about—and it'd be good for her— it just feels delicate.

"I know from calling them that you share your location with them, but did you let them know you wouldn't be going home tonight?" Her eyes drift up to mine, so vulnerable, yet more trusting than I've ever seen them. "Assuming you wanted to stay here," I add.

"I do," she admits, her voice cracking as her face crumples.

"Blake..." I grab a hand towel, about to move toward her when she stops me with a hand in the air.

"It'll be easier for me to talk like this... if you come over here and hold me, I probably won't stop crying."

And for some reason, that makes me feel like I've won the lottery. Like I might actually be Blake's safe place.

"Okay," I agree. Picking the knife back up and looking down at the cutting board, hoping it offers her a little more space to say what she needs.

"I've never fought with my parents—not really. I mean, I threw temper tantrums as a kid, and I've talked back to them. But I've never truly been mad at my dad... I just feel so silly and adolescent. I'm embarrassed," she admits.

"Storm Cloud, I know you think I'm like this perfectly nice guy," I tease, hoping to ease some more of the tension in her body. A small smile pulls at her lips as she rolls her eyes. *I'll take that as a win.* "Honestly I've had way worse fights with my parents and Maria, over way stupider things than wanting to help people in need."

"Really? Like what?"

"Almost everything. What time my curfew was, even though the state has a legal curfew. Being a little jerk who wanted a different first car than the one I got for free. Sneaking out and skipping class because it seemed fun. So many things that were selfish and childish."

"I guess that makes me feel a little better. What I said to my dad…" She looks away in shame. "I don't know if I'll ever get over that. I don't know if he will get over that."

"He already has, Blake," I promise.

"You don't know that," she accuses. She steamrolls on before I can tell her that I do in fact know he has. "I didn't mean it. I know he cares about people—every person he meets. Even every person he hasn't met but has heard of, or seen on TV, or listened to on the radio. That's just who my dad is. So for me to insinuate he *doesn't*? That was fucking mean, Adrian." She's working herself up, starting to breathe harder as she does her best to hold the tears back.

I set the knife back down, not moving and respecting her wishes for me to give her physical space.

"It was mean." I decide not to sugarcoat it. The shock and possible anger takes her attention temporarily away from her guilt. "But it didn't come from a place of hate or resentment. It came from a place of passion and empathy. And I know your dad understands that."

"You don—"

"I do," I cut her off. "I wanted to immediately go after you except your dad told me I should give you space. So, I stayed to talk to him."

"Was he rude? Did he say anything?" That earlier protectiveness reaches her expression. It makes me want to smile, but I know now isn't the time.

"Nah, he wasn't mean. We had a really honest conversation though, and most of it was about why I need to learn to set these boundaries now rather than later."

Her nose scrunches in a cute, but sad way. "Boundaries with me?"

"No—I mean, *kinda*, yes. I have a hard time saying no to you because I just want to make you so fucking happy. You aren't solely the reason I agreed to help in ways I wasn't fully comfortable with. I didn't feel good about leaving someone who needed help either."

"I shouldn't have asked you to help though. The whole point of asking you was to not involve my dad. And I see now that it was a really stupid plan."

"It took Tim pointing it out for me to realize the connection. You aren't fully to blame here, Blake, and I won't let you take all the responsibility. I'm a grown man, and I'm going to take care of you as much as you want to do the same for me. That's non-negotiable in this relationship."

She's quiet for a long time, like accepting this is hard for her. She isn't letting her instincts kick in to deny it, so I can offer her all the time she needs. The oven timer goes off, the only thing breaking the silence between us. It isn't until I set the pan on the counter that she says, "Okay. We both should've thought about the possible consequences."

"And he's not mad—I promise—but you will have to talk to him."

"Let me guess," she utters, although I hear a slight tone of amusement there. "He's just *really disappointed*?"

Smirking over my shoulder, I tell her, "Exactly."

She slowly stands and walks around the counter. "Can I help with something?"

I nod and assign her to cutting the avocado and tomatoes. She takes her time washing her hands, seeming to be lost in her own mind. When she settles next to me, getting set up and cutting the tomatoes first, she sighs, "I know I have to talk to him. I'm going to, tomorrow. I just need tonight to get over my embarrassment, and I'm still a little overwhelmed."

"Makes sense. You're welcome to stay as long as you need."

She looks up with more affection than I've ever seen from her. "Thanks, Adrian."

We finish the rest of dinner, mostly in silence, but there's comfortable conversation when one of us does have something to say. Despite the situation, I'm happy she's here.

We finally settle on the couch, burrito bowls in hand; chips to scoop for me, while Blake has a tortilla she rips into smaller pieces. I let her choose what to watch, and she settles on one of her god-awful reality shows, but I don't say anything. The irony that she often complains about how cheesy her mom's telenovelas are, is not lost on me.

The volume is low, so we make small talk to fill the silence. After a lull, I finally bring up something that's been weighing on me for most of the afternoon. It feels like something that has been brewing in the back of my mind for a while now, even if I wasn't fully aware of it.

"So, I was wondering if you've thought any more about college," I say, trying to tread lightly.

She side-eyes me. "I mean, no. I've told you that I'll think about it once I have any semblance of an idea of what I want to do with my life."

Shrugging a little helplessly, I tell her, "I'm not judging, pretty girl. I just had an idea."

Cautiously, she turns her body toward me. Balancing her bowl on a knee, she asks, "An idea about me and college?"

"Yeah," I nod tentatively. "I think there's an option for you to help more people in a way that benefits your dad's clinic as well."

She slowly takes a bite of her food and gives me a disbelieving look yet not shutting me down either. By the end of the conversation, she even seems excited.

Chapter Forty-Five

Blake

Lying in bed, waiting for Adrian to finish getting ready, I feel a newfound hopefulness. It's been there for the last couple of hours, since Adrian told me what he spent his afternoon looking into.

Community outreach programs.

And there are some that are run through vet clinics. They offer things I try to do already—pet insurance and basic care education, emotional support during medical procedures, and volunteer pet caretaking. There are endless possibilities of what I could do for the community with the right licenses, permits and grants.

We could hold free clinic days, offer discounted mandatory procedures like spaying or neutering, have emergency relief funds, and so much more. Those are only a few of the many opportunities Adrian mentioned.

His note taking really is impressive so when he realized I was more than interested in his idea, he brought out a notebook and his laptop. For about an hour and a half—while we waited for the cookies he ordered for me—we went over everything he's learned in the last couple of hours.

It's more than I can fully process at the moment, but the one thing I realized was, I do need to start thinking about college. Like *right now*. I don't feel overwhelmed, like I always worried I would. There are nerves but they're the excited kind.

Part of those nerves could be the fact that I'm lying in Adrian's bed in nothing besides my panties and tank top. I showered at the gym. And truthfully, I've enjoyed the time with my thoughts while he's been in the shower and doing whatever else he needs.

Only the water turned off about ten minutes ago, so I know he'll be walking out any minute now.

This isn't the first night we've spent together, but it feels different. Like we somehow took a step forward. And the longer I lay here, the clearer it becomes. The guilt over our lapses in judgement isn't building a wall between us anymore.

Maybe tonight isn't the best night to have sex, all things considered after the day's events, but I feel closer to Adrian than ever before. And that's saying something because he's easily become my person in the last few weeks.

And now, I want to share everything with him... including my body.

As if my thoughts were a beacon, he comes out of the bathroom in nothing but a towel. And God, what a marvelous fucking sight it is. Even though we haven't gone further than oral, Adrian isn't shy about his body. And he sure as hell has no reason to be.

Regardless, if we just watch movies or go straight to sleep, he's always peeling off layers of fabric, and en-couraging me to take off as much as possible. I think he just likes the skin-to-skin-contact—something I've quickly become accustomed to.

I watch as he drops the towel and grabs a pair of boxer-briefs, not trying to hide my intentions. When he looks back at me, I feel my face warm, but I let my eyes move up his body until I meet his gaze.

It's new—feeling confident in my desires and expressing those to the person I'm dating. Ever since Adrian promised that I was safe with him, he's done everything in his power to stick to his word.

His eyes shamelessly move over the curves of my body too, pausing on the cleavage that's falling out of the tank top. I'm on my side, propped up on my elbow. From this angle, and without a bra, it doesn't leave a lot to the imagination... Especially to someone as well acquainted with my body as he is now.

"So," he slowly starts and moves to get in bed next to me. Pulling the covers down for him, I wait for him to continue. He seems nervous suddenly. "Your dad mentioned something earlier, and I wanted to talk to you about it."

Pushing up until I'm sitting next to him, looking down at where he's settling against his pillow, I ask, "What did he say?" There's a slight panic in my voice—feeling like everything was too good to be true and this is the other shoe about to drop.

"Shh, pretty girl," he soothes and wraps an arm around my back. He pulls me down until my front is flush against his and holds me to him. "It's nothing bad. I promise."

Taking a breath, I nod and look at him. Waiting.

"I just don't want you to feel like I'm inviting myself into something, if you weren't ready for that." Now I'm just confused, and the way my brows scrunch must clue him into that. He sighs and shyly admits, "Your dad invited me to spend Christmas at your house."

Surprised, I sputter, "He did?"

My heart pinches at the thought of my dad ending their conversation on that note. I had mentioned to my parents at dinner a few days ago that I wasn't sure what Adrian's plans were, after my dad noticed he hadn't requested any time off.

From the look my mom gave my dad, I knew where her mind was at. But considering my dad and I haven't ever talked about what's going on between Adrian and I, I wasn't sure how he *actually* feels about everything—or having his employee over on a holiday.

This feels like a confirmation that my dad is okay with this thing unfolding between us, and a white flag that Adrian, nor I, deserve right now.

And it's exactly why I love that man so goddamn much.

"Yeah, he did."

Biting my lip, I run my fingers gently over his chest. "Do you want to spend Christmas with us?"

"Honestly," he exhales, "*yes*. You know I'd love to see my parents, but it makes the most sense to wait until New Year's Eve. And the only other place I'd want to be is with you and your family."

A smile breaks out across my face. "I want you there. I was going to ask you, after I talked to my parents about it. I just... I haven't really told my parents about us."

He nods, but there's obvious confusion mixed into his features. "What do you mean? We spend a lot of time together. You've stayed here. They must know something."

"They do," I assure. "I mean, you asked me on a date in front of my dad." My cheeks warm at the reminder; so does my heart. I love the straightforward approach he's always taken with me. And he's easily the one responsible for getting us as far as we've come.

"Olivia told me about three weeks into the job that I was doing 'a horrible job at hiding my crush on the boss's daughter.'"

That makes me laugh, and I can perfectly imagine Olivia giving him a hard time. She knows all the work gossip and is very proud of that.

"Okay, so everyone has an idea that something is going on. I just mean, I haven't been sure exactly what to tell my parents. And I wanted to figure it out first, you know?" He nods but seems to pick up on the fact that I'm working out my thoughts. "Earlier," I quietly tell him, "You said we were in a relationship."

He tilts his head, looking curious and cautious. "Aren't we?"

Scared to meet his eye, I stare at the wall behind him. "Are we?"

He grabs me by the waist and pulls closer, which causes me to lay more on top of him with my legs straddling him. "Blake," he breathes. "You aren't a dumb girl, so don't act like it."

The words are similar to the ones he told me when we went to dinner at SunRay's. That was the night I realized I wasn't imagining a second of my time with Adrian—he really was interested in me. And his intentions were made clear to anyone who asked.

"I'm not trying to play stupid," I argue. Being this close to him is a little distracting, but I cling to him anyway, still needing the contact despite it. "I can't just make assumptions here, Adrian."

He nods and grips my hip tighter, wrapping both of his arms around my lower back so I'm trapped with our bodies melded together. Leaning forward, my hair creates a thin curtain around us causing it to feel more intimate.

One arm is bent next to his head, holding me up, the other lightly moving up his arm and shoulder. I continue brushing along his neck and jaw, before making my way back down the path.

I'm comfortable with this—the nonverbal types of intimacy when our bodies do the talking for us. But I know we've gotten to the point where we need to start having some of those conversations if we want this to actually go somewhere.

And I do.

"Let me make it clear for you, so there's no confusion," he murmurs, our lips only inches from each other now. "I'm not interested in anyone else, Blake. Truthfully, I haven't been able to think about anyone other than the prettiest girl I've *ever* seen, with the lightning eyes, since that night at the grocery store."

"Really?" I breathe, wrapping my hand around the nape of his neck and pulling him closer.

"Really." The hand on my hip tightens. "I want whatever you'll give me, as long as it's just the two of us."

"I don't want anyone else. And I hate the thought of you with anyone other than me," I admit. In a lighter tone, I add, "It makes me feel *weird*."

He chuckles quietly and I can feel his warm breath against my lips. "We're in agreement on that then."

After a second, my playful smile disappears, and the intensity of the moment takes over again. "I think you're the best thing to ever happen to me," I whisper.

He shakes his head and one of his hands slides up my spine until he's cradling the back of my head. "That's what I've been thinking about you for weeks now..." He breathes a little harder and I can tell that the next words out of his mouth are about to change everything between us.

"Say it," I urge when he's quiet for a few seconds too long.

He places a light kiss on my lips before saying the most beautiful words I've ever heard. "I love you, Blake. I've been in love with you for weeks now. Maybe even months, truthfully. I thought love at first sight was a stupid, made up concept but I don't know how else to explain it."

"Adrian," I cut him off. "I love you. It's like a part of me even knew that night—I never forgot you either." He's always known that I remembered him just as well as he did me—and Margo accidentally confirmed that—but it's the first time I'm admitting it to him.

"And now you're here, and hopefully mine."

Pushing back to squint at him, I only partly joke, "I can't believe you'd still want me after everything I've put you through—emotionally and professionally."

"I'm going to tell you this for the last time, baby," he says as he flips us onto my back, and settles between my legs. "You didn't make me do anything. We made choices, together—as partners. They weren't the greatest choices, I'll admit." That signature charming grin tugs on his lips. "But they were *ours*. You're not carrying that guilt alone."

Chapter Forty-Six

Blake

The sound that claws out of his throat is deep, primal, and masculine. His forearms are resting next to my head and his hands tangle into my hair, laying more of his weight on me.

With the new position, he has full control of the moment. And there's not a single ounce of worry as he moves his hard length against my center, both of us covered. Still, the sensation is everything.

Pushing back until he's holding himself above me and looking down at where we aren't quite connected, he pumps his hips again. This time, he slides against my clit a little harder, causing me to claw at his shoulders and cry out.

"Fuck, that's it," he groans, watching the way our bodies move together. I try to look down too, but he changes speed and it's too much.

Yet somehow. *Not. Enough.*

"Adrian, God, please," I whine and slide my hands under his boxer-briefs. Grabbing onto his tight ass, I have more control to grind our pelvises at a faster, harder pace.

"Please what?" He drops down until his lips are an inch from mine and stops his movement all together. "I told you before—tell me what you need and I'll make it happen, pretty girl."

Trying to buck my hips against him, I can't find the friction I desperately need.

"You. I just need you..." whispering, I add, "inside me. Deep inside me."

"That's all I want," he breathes and kisses down my neck. "I've spent a lot of lonely nights thinking about that actually."

My nails scratch down the back of his head. "Me too."

His head pops up and the shocked expression is almost comical. It's usually me who is left speechless. "Don't lie to me about that."

Quietly laughing, I shake my head. "I'm not. I've had your fingers and mouth... of course I've thought about it."

"Fuck," he groans and pumps his hips a little faster. Moaning, I grab onto him and move my body with his. It's been a long time since I've done anything with someone else, but I don't remember dry humping ever being this erotic.

His head starts to move down south, and I quickly stop him, shaking my head frantically.

I've had that. It's not what I need now.

"Can we skip that?" I ask, a desperate note to my voice.

He looks a little confused but mostly disappointed by my suggestion. "Why?"

Laughing, I feel freer than I ever have during sex. I didn't know it could be this hot and intense and yet so... comfortable and casual. "I just told you I wanted you inside me. We can save that talented tongue for another night."

He huffs, as if it's an inconvenience to him, but it quickly turns into a groan as I lean up to pull my tank top over my head.

"You know," he teases and slides a hand up my body to pinch my nipple. "Your idea sounds fucking fantastic."

I want to laugh, but he's already building me up to the edge of an orgasm just by the squeeze of his hands and the thrust of his dick against my most sensitive area.

He leans back to slide my panties off and take his own underwear off as well. As he settles over me again, his hand cups my pussy.

"You're fucking soaked," he muses, an appreciative note to his tone as he slides a finger inside me. Even though I've been practically begging him to fuck me already, I appreciate him taking the time to get me ready.

He's big. And thick. Not so much that I'm worried about my anatomy, but definitely bigger than anyone else I've been with.

So, I lay back and leave my pleasure in Adrian's hands. Literally.

He kisses me and uses the palm of his hand to rub my clit as he works his finger into me. Eventually, sliding another finger into me... then one more.

"Oh my God," I moan.

I feel right on the line of pleasure, but know I'd take that pinch of pain if it meant having him—really having him.

On the same wavelength as me, he groans out, "Blake." It's deep and primal—and I know it's more of a plea of his own than anything else.

"I'm ready," I promise him and hitch one of my legs higher.

He nods, eyes dark. Reluctantly, he pulls his body off of me and reaches to the left side of the bed.

Watching, he pulls out the un-open box of condoms we found and makes quick work of the cardboard tab. When he drops the aluminum package onto the mattress and reaches to put the box on the nightstand, I quickly snatch it up.

I'm not sure what comes over me. I've never done this before.

I find myself reaching toward Adrian's waistline as he moves back between my legs. With a little bit of fumbling, and his instruction on how to pinch the tip of the latex, I slowly roll it down his length—enjoying every inch of him.

But nothing could prepare me for the overwhelming euphoria of having him position the crown of his cock at my entrance and slowly thrust into me. Not once—over and over.

He takes his time and seems to enjoy each tortuous moment of working himself into me.

As he seems to go slower with each whimper, and moan I let out—probably worried he's going to hurt me—I grow more impatient by the second. Until all I can think to do is slide my hands back down to his ass. On his next thrust, I lock my legs around him tighter and encourage him to close the last couple of inches between us.

"Fuck," we both cry out as he slams home, filling both my body and heart.

The stab of pain from being stretched around him quickly morphs into pleasure, so I buck my hips against him. His head drops to my shoulder as he pants against my skin. With my patience almost gone, I try to move, encouraging him to do something.

He grabs onto my hips and holds me still, with him buried to the hilt. "Blake," he pleads. "I'm going to come."

Letting out a desperate whiney sound, I tell him, "I *want* to come, Adrian."

Nodding into my neck, he slowly moves his cock inside of me. It's not what I need but to make up for that, he rubs my clit in tight, hard circles and drops his mouth to my breast. He teases me by avoiding my nipples and focuses on sucking the skin around them.

When he lifts his mouth from the first spot, I notice a light hickey forming already. It's something I've gone out of my way to avoid in the past but with Adrian, I almost wish he'd move further up and leave one on my collarbone.

The thought immediately leaves my mind as his hot tongue finally makes contact with my pinched bud. Though, it's nothing compared to the way he closes his lips around me and nibbles on the sensitive skin.

He matches the delicious sensation to the speed of his fingers and cock. The faster he moves inside of me, the faster I'm working up to my orgasm and hoping he's right there with me.

"I want to stay right here—forever. With my cock buried inside your sweet pussy and your perfect tits in my mouth or hands."

"Adrian," I whimper. It starts out as an almost inaudible mewl but with each time I repeat it, it grows louder and stronger. Mimicking the way my pleasure overtakes every inch of my body with each of his deep thrusts.

"Is that what you need, baby?" he asks, mouth still pressed against my chest. I know he's asking about the way he's playing with my clit since he's never once assumed he knows my body better than me. Instead, he always looks for confirmation that I'm enjoying this as much as he is.

I nod emphatically, to the point where words are out of reach. It's just our bodies and spirits together now.

"Me too." His voice is low and desperate as he removes his mouth from my breast and drags them up to my lips. It's a hot, possessive kiss as he pumps into me harder and faster. "I've needed you forever, I think."

"Forever," I repeat. It's both an agreement and a promise. My body tenses, almost at the precipice of it all.

But it's the feel of Adrian's body against mine—every muscle slowly starts to tighten as his hips move more erratically—that sends me over the edge.

And by the way he grabs the globes of my ass and pulls me onto his length one final time, holding me there as his body pushes him through his orgasm, I know we shared even that intimacy together for the first time.

The realization makes me smile, feeling a sense of not totally foreign hope and completeness in my chest. Adrian's panting, leaning over me. Accepting the fact I'll never have my fill of him, I wrap my arms and legs around him and pull my body flush against his, kissing him deep. After a few minutes, he slides out of me, and carries me to the bathroom, so we can clean up before bed.

Chapter Forty-Seven

Blake

This morning, I woke up feeling more anxious than at any point yesterday. It was almost paralyzing as I laid in Adrian's bed, him sleeping next to me while I tried to gain the courage to face my dad.

He woke up soon after I did and stayed there with me, laying soft kisses on my skin and offering words of encouragement, until I knew I needed to do this before any of us—my dad, Adrian, or I—saw each other at work this morning.

Now, as I stand outside of my house, I'm nervous to go inside for the first time in my life.

Biting my lip, I stand at the bottom of the steps and just stare at the door. More than anything, I'm embarrassed and a bit ashamed of the way I acted toward my dad.

I wasn't lying about why I never wanted to call my dad and not want to put him in a position that compromises his boundaries again. But the way I lashed out at him was out of line. I didn't mean any of it, and I know none of it is true. I knew it as the words were falling off my tongue, I just couldn't stop them.

Usually, my word vomit causes *me* embarrassment. Not ever harm to someone else. Especially not someone I care about.

The front door opens slowly, and my breath catches in my throat. It comes out in a whoosh when I see my mom standing in the doorway, her arms crossed and hip on the frame. But it's the soft, maternal smile painted on her lips that gives me the courage to take the first step.

When I'm only a foot in front of her, she pulls me into her arms. "Morrita," she murmurs into my hair. "I'm proud of you."

Pulling back, I look at her in disbelief. "You shouldn't be. Hasn't Dad told you?"

Running a hand down my head, hair loose and air drying from my shower this morning, she nods. "He did. And I didn't mean *that*—it's not our conversation to have. I'm proud of you for being here this morning. You're allowed to take time, but you can't avoid these hard conversations either."

Quietly, I tell her, "I know. I don't want to hide from them anymore."

Even if every hard conversation doesn't result in positive changes, it doesn't mean they aren't important. And over the last couple of months, Adrian's given me the space, and safety, to grow more confident in myself; to learn to trust the intentions of others.

With her arm wrapped around my shoulder, she guides me into the kitchen where my dad's already putting together breakfast burritos. The one he's wrapping, I know, is for me. I'm the only one in the family who likes my tortillas a little more burnt and crunchier.

When I walk into the room, he looks up and there's a soft tilt of his lips. It's sadder than the one I got from my mom.

"Hi, Dad," I greet him. Slowly, I take the seat next to my mom and watch as my dad finishes putting the burrito together and pushes the plate toward me.

"Hi, honey. Do you want coffee?" I shake my head. Adrian already made me coffee and breakfast, but this feels like an olive branch. One I don't deserve—it pinches at my heart anyway. Turning toward the cabinet, he asks, "Juice?"

My eyes suddenly fill with tears—my guilt and love for this man growing exponentially. Nodding, I mutter, "Sure."

His brows furrow, pouring me a glass of pineapple juice before he leans his hands on the island across from me. The look on his face is open, as much as it is expected.

"I'm sorry," I blurt out, the first tear sliding down my cheek. Clearing her throat, my mom grabs for her plate and moves to stand. I gently grab her wrist. "No, no. You can stay... You *should* stay."

She glances from Dad back to me and tenderly says, "I don't have to, Blake. Your dad can tell me later."

"No," I insist. With a deep breath, I meet her eye and add, "I know I messed up. And you deserve to hear this from me as well."

A proud look crosses her face as she sits back down and settles in her seat, sipping her coffee. I know this is her way of saying she's a bystander—and possibly a mediator—but isn't a participant of the conversation.

With one more meaningful look in her direction, I square my shoulders and meet my dad's gaze. I don't know how to read him at this moment because there's so many conflicting emotions flashing through his eyes.

"Dad," I start again, gathering my bearings this time, "I'm sorry. I'm sorry for going behind your back and doubting you would know how to handle these situations in a fair way. I'm sorry that I brought Adrian into this mess. I know how much you've enjoyed mentoring him. And I know he loves the relationship just as much.

"I never understood how this field could suck you in emotionally. I saw the toll it took on you, and I heard you talk openly about the challenges my entire life, but I was never able to understand past that initial empathy. I have a better idea of what you go through every single day now."

His brows flick up only there's no judgement. Just curiosity. "You do?"

Nodding, I promise, "I do." Biting my tongue—literally—I think through my next words before letting the anxiety get the best of me. "It's on a much smaller scale than what you deal with every single day, but fuck—"

"Cuida tu boca," my mom chimes in, reminding me to watch my mouth.

With a small eye roll, I side-eye her and amend, "But *freaking* A, it's hard." She just squints at me, not correcting me any further. "I thought... I thought if I just helped Erika with Zippy, it would be the same thing as helping Lela with the insurance or sitting with Polly during the surgery. Even as we made the choice, it didn't feel the same... It didn't feel *right*."

"And if Archie's nail hadn't cracked in half the way it did, would you have called me? Or would you have taken matters into your own hands again?"

For the first time during the conversation, I look away from him. Dropping my gaze to my lap, I watch as I begin to fidget—my thumb starts by tapping my pointer finger, moving through each one and back up. Without a word, my mom slides her hand into mine and interlaces them.

"I think I would've tried to fix it myself," I confess in a small voice.

From my peripheral, he nods his head, and I can see the hurt, making me double down on being too scared to meet his eye.

"Thank you for being honest." To his credit, he sounds like he means it. "Now, after this conversation, what would you do for an animal in need?"

Sighing, I lift my head and say, "I would call you—or the hospital if I knew you were off or whatever. I would do the right thing and trust that you all know the best course of action—both medically and financially."

The small smile reaches his lips again, except this time it's a little less sad. "Good. I don't know what I've done for you to not trust me—"

"It's not that," I cut in, almost desperately. "Dad, I promise. You haven't done anything wrong. I was trying to protect you. That's all."

My mom's hand squeezes around mine as my dad tells me, in a firm but affectionate voice, "It's not your responsibility to protect me. We"—he points between my mom and himself— "are meant to protect you, honey."

The sentiment is sweet, yet it causes a small bubble of anger inside of me. "But we're a *family*. Just because I'm the youngest person in it doesn't mean I have to be sheltered forever. And I know—I *know*—I didn't do it right this time, okay? *But* it's Grady too. Just because I'm three years younger than him. I'm strong enough to be there for you all as well."

"You're one of the strongest people we've ever known, Blake." My mom's hand moves from mine to smooth down my hair lovingly.

"That's not what I meant—you being incapable of handling it. I'm sorry I implied that." As fast as it came, the anger subsides, and I'm left feeling silly for my reaction again. "Only that we're your parents and you've already spent so much of your life worrying. About everything, all the time. And it's your turn to just live your life. Not worry about us, or the clients, or animals. And if this job is too much for you, then okay—let's talk about that."

Shaking my head, I bite my lip and ruefully admit, "That's not an option anymore." My parents look at each other in confusion before their heads swing simultaneously back to me. Shifting in my seat awkwardly, I tell them, "Well... I texted Mom to let her know I'd be staying with Adrian."

My dad doesn't look nearly as perturbed by the information as I expected. "I figured you would, since Margo and Meera aren't an option."

"Yeah, well, he helped me come up with a plan. For my future."

"Your future?" my mom asks gently. It's not something they've pushed offering more space than most parents probably would on the matter.

I nod once. "It's not that I haven't thought about it, I just really wasn't sure what I wanted to do. But we spent most of the evening going over it and I think... No, no. I know I want to work at the vet clinic long-term."

The surprise on my dad's face is evident since I've never shown interest in any type of medicine before. "You know there's no pressure on you and Grady to ever become a veterinarian."

"God, *no*. Not that." That makes both of my parents chuckle. "I want to open an outreach program through the clinic. Like a community health sector, for animals though."

"Morrita," my mom warmly murmurs; my eyes stay fixed on my dad now.

"I—*we*—could help more people. It would be independently funded from the clinic itself, but most importantly, it would be ethical." He opens his mouth to say something, while I steamroll on, "It wouldn't only be surgeries. We could host free clinic days and pet education courses. It's actually crazy how many options there are. So many things I've never even considered, but we could do it."

"Blake," he cuts in. "This sounds amazing—truly, honey. I'd be honored to be a part of this with you. Just don't get ahead of yourself. This isn't something we could do overnight."

"I know," I insist. "It would be at least a six-year plan. And that's if I can get into UCAH for the fall semester."

"University of California, Aurora Hills?" my mom asks, surprised. "You're that sure about this?"

Finally turning toward her, I nod emphatically. "Yeah, I am. It's the first thing that's ever made me feel *excited* for a career. I feel stupid not thinking of it myself."

"Don't say that," she chastises.

"I'm serious. It never occurred to me that I could make this into a career. I mean, obviously, I know there are charities and community programs. But you guys raised us to help when we can and taught us how to be a kind neighbor—all of that stuff. It's just something you *do*." I shrug. "I never thought about it further than that."

With a mischievous smirk, she hits my shoulder with hers. "Adrian helped you realize that, huh?"

Rolling my eyes, I huff out a breath, my cheeks warming by the second. "Yes, he did."

"I think it's a brilliant idea, honey," my dad cuts in. And that paternal pride has lit up his eyes again. "I'd love to be able to do more for the residents of Amada Beach, and Aurora Hills, but I'm at my bandwidth between medical exams, surgeries and admin tasks."

"Maybe I can start helping with that more, the smaller tasks at least, until I get more education and experience. I want to be involved, Dad. And I hope you'll give me the chance to do it right this time."

Walking around the island, he pulls me into his arms, and I hug him back, reveling in the unconditional love he has for me. "I'd love that, Blake. This was a learning experience, but that's all it can be. *Once*. Let's do this the right way, together."

Smiling up at him, I nod. "Together."

My mom taps her finger on the island, and I imagine her attempting to bite her tongue behind me. After only three taps, she poses, "Does that 'together' include Adrian too then?"

Turning in my chair toward her, I scowl, but it's playful. "I mean, he's the one most responsible for the new plan. So, I'd say yes." Though, I don't really know how involved he wants to be going forward. He was supportive and seemed excited, but he's still figuring out what part of the field he'd want to specialize in.

"And does that mean Adrian's a part of more plans than just your professional one's going forward?"

As if to encourage me to be honest, my dad squeezes my shoulder and walks back to his coffee mug.

"I—yes. I think so." *I hope so.* "It's new, like very new. But we're together."

My mom breaks out into a wide, giddy smile. She's been Adrian's biggest supporter since the beginning. "Oh, that's great. He's a good one."

"He is," I nod in agreement, while blushing, and wishing the conversation would end. Turning to my dad, I ask, "Are you okay with this?"

He gives me a weird look before nodding. "Of course I am. Adrian's proven to be everything I thought he was from the interview—*mostly* responsible, tolerant, a fast thinker, kind. I have eyes so don't think I haven't noticed how loyal he's been to you in these last few months. If you're happy, then I'm happy, Blake."

Trying to hide my smile, I quietly admit, "I am happy with him." I can't make eye contact with either of them. It's a big admission for me. And after everything this morning, I'm feeling more vulnerable than usual.

"Good," my mom chirps. "Because your father invited him to spend Christmas with us."

Laughing, I pick up my burrito, taking a small bite. "He told me. And thank you for doing that. It means a lot to him." Biting again, I shrug and swallow. "And me."

The rest of our short breakfast goes easier, with them asking about what my plans are for the fall semester and offering advice along the way. Soon after I finish my juice and set the remainder of my food down, my dad leaves for the clinic, and I promise to see him there in a couple hours.

island of misfit toys
Sun, Dec 14 at 7:47 AM

> I've figured it out.

That's all I have to say for Meera and Margo to understand.

"*You'll figure it out, Blake,*" they've told me a hundred times now.

Meera

> You mean *IT*?

> Like the big life decision IT?

Margo

> Don't keep us waiting, bitch

Meera

> I'm calling you right now

Laughing, I fall back on my bed and answer the FaceTime call from Meera. Margo's in the frame too, the sight of them makes me emotional all over. Shoving that down, I start talking as more of that weight lifts off of me.

Chapter Forty-Eight

Blake

It's *been a long day*, I think to myself before grabbing my phone to check the time. When I see it's only after four p.m., I close my eyes and take a deep breath.

Yet *nowhere near done.*

Ignoring the unanswered texts from my friends, I check for any updates from my family, or a reply from Adrian.

Margo and Meera have been reaching out to me all day, seeming to anticipate the adrenaline crash I'm facing after the last forty-eight hours. I don't mean to ignore them; I've just felt depleted of energy from the moment I woke up.

It was almost a relief when my brother called to tell us Arielle is in labor because I knew it meant my parents would be on the first plane there, and out of the house for a little bit. They were too focused on my brother to notice the first signs of my anxiety attack, or I know one of them would've sacrificed meeting their granddaughter to stay with me.

Thankfully, they didn't ask me for a ride to the airport, and I practically shoved them into Bonnie's car when she showed up to chauffeur them.

But the emotional rollercoaster I've been on for the last few hours isn't helping the deep-rooted fatigue crawling to the surface.

When that numb, dark feeling started to slither through my veins, and I had to sit on the shower floor crying for twenty minutes, I knew what I needed to do.

Call Catalina.

It's rare that I ask for an emergency session, especially months into our therapist-client relationship. We were both proud I was able to recognize my journey toward healing is not linear, and probably a lifelong one.

More than anything, I was hoping it would help me pull myself together to see Adrian.

After I quickly caught him up on my family's conversation, he declared a celebration—one for me. With my family and best friends, I'm no stranger to big birthday parties, and treating every swim meet as if it was the Olympics. But deciding on what I want to go to school for is so *mundane*.

It doesn't feel that way though, and of course, Adrian can see that.

In a lot of ways, going to talk with Catalina did help.

Like reminding me it's okay to cancel plans sometimes.

"A mental sick day is *not* the same thing as falling into old patterns. It's a necessity for everyone," she finally said as a way to convince me.

I'm not sure how she knew I was already falling down that spiral, but it's exactly where my mind was going. One of the things that worried my mom the most after I transferred out of SPA, was how little she saw Margo and Meera for a couple of months.

There's always this lingering anxiety the further I go on this healing journey. It reminds me that I know what bad looks like, and at any second it can go back to that in the blink of an eye.

So, no one's more scared of me showing symptoms again than I am.

But Catalina's words were exactly what I needed to hear today.

As soon as I got back in my car, I texted Adrian and told him I needed a raincheck. He quickly replied and asked if I decided to go to Phoenix with my parents after all. He hasn't replied since I told him I was home, but not feeling good.

He's never gotten mad about things like this, so I'm doing my best to remind myself of that. Except it's been about three hours now. He usually gets home from classes about an hour ago and doesn't typically work on Mondays.

Dropping my phone next to me on the couch, I curl into a ball and focus on my breathing. The longer I do, the more tears begin to fall. I don't fight them, knowing it will only make the drowning feeling linger.

Turning onto my back and laying like that for a few minutes, my heart begins to slow, and the tears do too.

As I make a plan for myself—order food and take a shower—I almost burst out in a fresh wave of tears when even doing *that* feels like too much. A knock on the door distracts me enough to keep those feelings temporarily at bay.

Slowly, I walk to the door and peek through the peephole. I'm not surprised when the slightly distorted sight breaks the final constraint on my emotions.

Swinging the door open, I lamely greet Adrian through tears. "Hi."

His face breaks, looking closer than I've ever seen to tears himself. With the hand not holding a bag of food, he wraps an arm around my waist and steps closer. "Hey, what's going on?"

"I—I just..." I hiccup. Embarrassment is quickly mixing with my anxiety, and it all blurts out. "I thought I'd feel happier after everything—and I *am*—I'm just so tired too. Then my brother called because he's having a *baby*. Well... *he* isn't having a baby, but you know what I mean. My brother is becoming a *dad*. There are so many 'what the fucks' in that I don't even know where to start. Plus, my friends won't stop texting me. It's all too much right now.

"And... and... *you* didn't text me back," I sputter and cover my face with my hands. "I'm sorry I cancelled on dinn—"

"Nope," he cuts in and gives me a quick peck to ensure I stop talking. "You don't apologize for that. If you need space, then you need space. It's okay, *but* you did promise to tell me next time."

My mouth falls open. "Oh, I—"

"Shut up, Blake." That does the trick. He sounds as gentle as when he calls me 'pretty girl,' though he usually coddles me more. And honestly, I kind of like that he isn't. "I'm not mad. I'm concerned that you've been feeling like this all day and haven't talked to anyone."

"I had a session with Catalina," I admit.

"Good, that's something." He sounds genuine so I chance looking up at him. "Do you want me to leave?"

I shake my head and wrap my arms around his waist. "I thought I wanted to be alone. I was feeling so overwhelmed earlier, and you wanted to celebrate."

The hand wrapped around me leaves my shoulders, and tangles it into my hair, tilting my head back so I'm looking up at him. "It's not the celebration part of it I care about. It's making you know how loved you are." I nod, biting my lip to fight more tears. His thumb gently pulls it free and rubs the raw skin. "What do you need right now?"

"I was going to take a shower," I quietly tell him. "Ordering food and taking a shower just felt like a lot."

He nods, seeming to understand even though he doesn't experience anxiety to the depth I do. Lifting the bag of food, clearly from The Loop, he states, "Already have that first part covered. Why don't you go take a shower and I'll get this ready?"

Taking a step back, I look down the hallway and nod. It feels mechanical and too fast. When I look back at Adrian, he's watching me, and I know it didn't look natural to him either.

"Go turn the water on and I'll meet you in the bathroom, okay?" He nods to the bag, letting me know he needs to do something with that first.

"Okay," I exhale. This time, when I turn in that direction, my feet actually move.

True to his word, Adrian walks into the small room less than two minutes later. He doesn't try to force me to talk or ask questions, instead rambling about his day and classes. He talks the entire time we're getting undressed and the quick shower we take together.

When we finish, I get my laptop and crawl into bed. As he brings our food to bed, I'm turning on a random episode of *New Girl.*

He takes in the room, his eyes lingering on some of the decor like the collage of photos of my friends and me, or the faint light of the glow-in-the-dark stars on the ceiling. He doesn't let himself get too caught up in that right now, choosing to come to the bed, and me.

It's the most settled I've felt since waking up in his bed yesterday, and before I know it, two hours have passed.

The only thing that pulls my attention away from the show is my buzzing phone.

"Oh my God," I gasp when I see Grady's name on the screen. With fresh, happier tears, I answer the FaceTime call.

As soon as it connects, Grady pulls the camera back to show him holding a tiny baby girl. "Hey, kid. Stella needed to meet her aunt."

"Stella?" I breathe out, taking in her small, rosy features. It was one of the names he had mentioned they liked but weren't deciding until she was born.

"Stella Brynn Miller," he confirms with a small smile, his eyes moving between my face and hers.

"Wow," I whisper. There aren't words big enough to express everything I'm feeling, though the most important pushes through. "You're going to be a great dad, Grady."

With a soft expression, he shrugs lightly. "I hope so."

Turning my head, I smile at Adrian, letting my eyes linger on him affectionately for a couple of seconds.

When I look back at the screen, Grady has a knowing smirk on his face, except he doesn't say anything. We talk for a couple more minutes, but I know it's probably hectic with our parents and Arielle's, along with the nursing staff. So, it's a quick call—one that eases more of the tension.

I hang up with my brother and instead of putting my phone down, I open the group chat to text my friends. It's a quick promise that I'm okay and will call them tomorrow. They both reply within seconds, but it's only to tell me they love me and to call whenever.

Adrian's reading the short exchange over my shoulder and whispers into my ear, "You've got a lot of people who love you."

Nodding, I throw my phone onto the bed and lay on my back.

"I love you," he adds.

A small, tired smile tugs at my lips. "I love you too."

"How are you feeling?"

Twisting my lips, I think his question over, wondering the same thing. I knew showering and eating were the first steps I needed to take, and it did help. The anxiety of waiting to hear from my brother, and the guilt of ignoring my friends have settled too.

My eyes move along Adrian's handsome features I memorized months ago. He didn't *fix* anything today, but he stood with me when my instinct was to push everyone away. And that means more than anything else.

"Better," I answer with a small, resolute nod. "Not one hundred percent, but *better*."

"It's a start." Rearranging the laptop so it's propped next to me and his body is curled around mine, he starts the next episode. "And tomorrow's a new day."

Looking over my shoulder at him, I revel in the fact this man not only noticed me, he is so openly devoted to me. I never thought I'd be this lucky, but I fight my nature to question it, choosing to enjoy it instead.

Chapter Forty-Nine

Blake

My mom and I are in the kitchen, making sugar cookies while she quietly sings along to the Christmas music playing in the background. It's a tradition we've had for almost a decade now.

Every Christmas Eve morning, we make *biscochitos*. It's something she's been doing with her mom since she was a little girl. But one year, Calypso Davies asked if we could try making decorated sugar cookies too.

Calypso, her little sister Vivi, and I used to spend all evening with our moms just like this. They'd be drinking sangria and singing along to Last Christmas, while we ate way too much sugar, and made more cookies than our families could eat. We'd go pass them out around town the day after Christmas.

It's been a few years since our families spent Christmas together—at least since I was fourteen and before Grady went off to college. But even by then, we'd all started to grow up and grow apart.

As we started spending the holidays as individual families, my mom and I never fell out of our Christmas Eve tradition.

The butterflies in my stomach are new though and have been fluttering around since I woke up this morning. I thought after we had sex, there wasn't going to be a lot of big firsts anymore. But I was wrong.

Because spending Christmas together for the first time feels monumental. And I hope it really is just the first of many.

Fingers crossed.

The doorbell rings as I'm just starting to knead the next batch of dough. My head whips up at the sound, only now realizing how late in the afternoon it is. It's one of those activities that makes time fly.

"I'll get it, morrita," my mom tells me and gently rubs my back. I smile at her over my shoulder and try to get my nerves in check.

It's almost five p.m. when Adrian gets here; it's still earlier than I expected since he worked today. My dad isn't home yet, but he typically stays until everyone, minus the overnight staff, has already left on holidays. So, I don't really expect him back until closer to seven when we sit down to eat.

The soft sounds of my mom and Adrian talking flitter into the kitchen, except I can't make out the words until they've rounded the corner.

"Oh, you didn't have to do that, mijo," my mom practically coos. "It's enough of a gift to have you here with us, but I do appreciate it."

She leans over to pat him on the cheek before taking the gifts out of his hands and moves to put them under the tree. I'm still at the counter with my hands sticky with cookie dough so, when his eyes move to me, I just offer him a small, sweet smile.

"Hi," I murmur as he walks over to me. There was a bit of doubt he'd actually wear pajamas when he showed up for Christmas Eve dinner. I shouldn't have questioned him for a second. It's not nearly as festive as my gingerbread print set, but the dark green flannel bottoms and plain tee check the box in my opinion.

It's a tradition around here.

"Hey, Storm Cloud." His eyes glance to my mom, who seems to be distracting herself in the living room. I figure she's doing it to offer us a private moment to greet each other—and I appreciate it.

"I'm glad you're here," I admit quietly.

"Me too." Before the words are even out of his mouth, his lips are already on mine. It's not a quick kiss, but it is chaste and tender. Pulling away, he moves toward the sink and asks, "How can I help?"

Seeming to hear his question, my mom makes her way back toward us and re-washes her hands as well. "Oh, do you like baking? Blake mentioned you enjoy cooking and trying different types of food."

He nods and moves to stand next to me, examining some of the cookie cutters that are piled nearby. "I love to cook—got into the hobby from my dad. I've never experimented with baking much, but I'd love to help, if that's okay."

His eyes move from my mom to me, then back again.

I gently nudge him with my shoulder. "Of course it's okay."

"Blake's almost done with the next batch of dough, so she can show you how to cut and lay them out. I'll get the frosting ready, and we can start on the ones cooling next."

"Sounds good to me," he easily agrees, and waits for me to give him his next instructions.

This isn't the hardest part of the process, but it helps that Adrian listens and takes instructions well. He's also not scared to ask questions rather than assume he can figure it out. It makes sense why my dad enjoys having him as an employee so much.

The conversation between my mom, him and I flows easily. We talk about my friends, and Adrian's parents, and how my parents usually pop over to see their best friend Bonnie's family before bed. I don't go, though I always spend the day after Christmas with Bonnie for lunch and for presents.

My dad gets home earlier than expected. By seven-thirty p.m., we're done with dinner, and drinking hot chocolate with only a few more cookies to decorate.

"This is really good, by the way," Adrian tells me. "I like peppermint, I just never think to add it."

I roll my eyes and admit, "It's my brother's recipe actually. He spent a couple winters perfecting it." My dad chuckles at the memory of a young Grady making little Vivi *very* sick one year.

At the same moment, my phone starts to vibrate on the counter.

"Speak of the devil," I say as I accept the FaceTime call.

Grady's looking down at his infant daughter, who's currently perched against his chest as he uses his free hand to hold her little nose up like a Who from The Grinch. His head snaps up when he hears me.

"Excuse me, you're one to talk."

Laughing, I shake my head. "We were just talking about your hot chocolate. And will you leave the poor girl alone?"

At that, my mom jumps out of her seat to look into the screen. Her eyes squint, relaxing as soon as she realizes her granddaughter isn't in any real danger. Only at the expense of my brother's boredom.

"Oh, pollito," she muses when she sees the two of them cuddling. I can't help but snort when she uses that childhood nickname for him. Depending on the context, morrita just means *little girl*. Sometime during Grady's toddler years, he was given the nickname of *little chicken*.

And considering the fact he was scared of the dark until middle school, it easily stuck.

He rolls his eyes at her, but it's affectionate. "Hi, Mom. Where's Dad?"

Grabbing the phone out of my hand, she rounds the island to put my dad in frame. "He's here."

"Hi, Grady."

"Hey, Dad. How was the cl—"

Before he can finish the question, my mom is walking around the other side of the island, toward Adrian.

"We have a guest with us tonight."

"Oh?" Grady asks cautiously. And I don't blame him. You never know what my meddling mother has up her sleeve.

"This is Adrian—Blake's boyfriend and your dad's employee."

"Oh," Adrian mutters as she forces the phone in front of his face. "Uh, hey, man."

It's the most awkward I've ever seen Adrian act—which does make me snicker a little—I'm sure this isn't how he expected to meet my brother. It isn't out of the question for it to be on a FaceTime call, but I don't think anyone thought my mom would do the honor of introductions.

"Hey," Grady greets, seeming to recover from the weirdness. He's much more used to our mother. "Nice to kind of meet you."

"Yeah, you too."

"I'll be right back to talk to you more. Can someone hand me to Blake for a second?"

Snatching my phone back, I tell Grady, "Sorry—"

Interrupting me instead, he adds to the moment by saying, "Boyfriend?" There's surprise in his tone, but it's mostly just happiness and even a bit of pride. There was definitely a fifty percent chance I was still going to chicken out of pursuing things with Adrian the last time I talked to him about it.

"Oh my God, you're on speaker, you know."

His smile is mischievous because he does, in fact, know that. "It's adorable, kid."

"Thanks, bye," I tell him with a fake smile, and hand my phone back to my mom.

I can hear Grady's laugh as she takes the phone and spends another fifteen minutes talking to him about God knows what. Before he hangs up though, I take the phone and Adrian to the couch.

The three of us sit and talk for a while—mostly about Stella, but a little about their college courses.

During a lull, Adrian tells him, "Blake's thinking about sending in a late application for the fall."

I wasn't really planning on telling a lot of people until I figured out if I was starting in the fall or spring. So it's not that I was hiding it from my brother, but we hardly talk anyway. There's so much warmth and pride in Adrian's voice, I'm not mad at him for doing the honors.

"Really?" Grady asks. He tries to sit up straighter, though Stella whines a little until he settles back again.

"Yeah," I admit as my cheeks warm. "It all kind of came together after we got in trouble with Dad recently."

"*You?* In trouble with Dad? Yeah, right."

"No, he was pissed… then I was pissed." I quickly fill him in on what happened and where we went wrong in trying to be helpful.

Grady blows out a breath as I finish. "Yeah, that wasn't your best plan. But your heart was in the right place. Both of yours," he adds with a nod in Adrian's direction.

Nodding, I tell him, "It was. Dad knows that even though it was still wrong. Because of that, and with Adrian's help"—I glance up at him quickly—"I've realized I want to create something that allows me to help in a way that's ethical and beneficial."

"That sounds amazing, Blake." He smiles gently at me, and I remember the night I told Grady I didn't want to go to college yet.

He was in town on a break, and my parents didn't know yet. He was the one who convinced me they'd understand—which they did, with some conditions, like working at the clinic, and continuing therapy. But he also told me he wasn't worried. He knew I'd figure it out when the time was right for me, and when I did, 'it would be *amazing*.'

With more gusto, I tell him everything. "I don't know if it's too late to get into UCAH for the fall. So, that's why I hadn't mentioned it. I'm thinking I want to major in nonprofit management, with a minor in business administration. It seems to make the most sense?"

It ends with a question, and I glance between Grady and Adrian.

Adrian wryly shakes his head, not saying anything. We've talked about this a lot, and he agrees it seems like the best route. Even so, I have an appointment with an advisor in January to make sure.

"Sounds like a great plan to me," Grady confirms. He assesses me for a moment, seeming to take in all the small differences from the last time we saw each other. "It actually seems like the most perfect career I could think of for you."

I grin at him, and before I can say anything, my dad's voice comes from behind me. "I agree." Leaning over the back of the couch, he puts his face in frame. "I'm proud of both my kids."

"Excuse me—I'm creating a program that could change thousands of lives, and he lost his chance at the MLB, and got his girlfriend pregnant at twenty-one. How can you even compare us?"

Grady laughs, knowing I'm joking. There was still a chance he could've had an athletic career after his injury, but I think the ACL tear and Stella's conception happening so close together, flipped his world upside down.

And being a father suits him in a way baseball never did.

Ignoring me, my dad continues, "I came to say bye and that we'll call you tomorrow. We're going to head over to Bonnie's for a while."

As if she's already in tune with her dad, Stella lets out a startled cry at the mention of the Davies family. Grady and

I both can't help but burst out laughing at the coincidence. My dad rolls his eyes and walks away.

"On that note," Grady says and sits up now that she's awake. "She's probably hungry, and Arielle is with her mom in the back."

"Okay, Grady. Thanks for calling."

"Love you, kid." His tone is giddy with affection and pride, and it almost feels like a gift of its own. "Adrian, it was nice meeting you. Can't wait to do it in person."

"You too," Adrian nods. "See ya."

After a quick goodbye, I hang up and turn toward Adrian. "Sooo, what should we do?"

One of his brows flicks up and he glances toward the back door before tilting his head in a way that suggests he has a few ideas.

Chapter Fifty

Adrian

Grabbing my bag off the floor with my free hand, I follow Blake down the hallway until we stop in front of a partially closed door.

When I stayed the night with her about a week and a half ago, I was too focused on her to really pay attention to any of the details in the low-lit room and unfortunately couldn't linger in the morning because of classes.

The space isn't cluttered and is pretty minimal with a queen size bed covered with too many pillows and a few soft blankets, a simple desk, a full length mirror, and chair set up nearby. There are some lights pinned to her roof along with the glow-in-the-dark stars. I noticed them the last time and remembered thinking that I hadn't seen them since I was a kid.

She has a few shelves and prints on her walls, but the most noticeable is a collage. It caught my eye the other night, though I didn't get to look at it. Before I even step up to it, I know what I'll find—years' worth of memories of Blake, Margo, and Meera. It ranges from when they met at twelve, and goes to Thanksgiving in New York City, with new ones added from the last few months.

"Margo and Meera helped me set that up," Blake explains and wraps her arms around me from behind, peeking her head around my side to look with me. "And then I helped them put one in the apartment they share in New York."

There's a wistful tone to her comment, so I can't help but ask, "Do you wish you had moved with them?"

I'm not sure why it comes out. She's never given me the impression that's what she wants, but now that she has a plan for college, I can't help wondering if maybe that's where she'd want to apply for a program.

Immediately, she puts any potential anxieties to rest when she shakes her head with certainty. "No. I miss them like crazy, and I wish they could reach their goals from San Diego, but I've honestly never had much of a desire to leave Amada Beach," she admits. "I don't know what that says about me."

Turning in her arms so I can wrap my own around her, I assure her, "It means you care about your community and want to create a life near your family. It's one of the things I love about you."

Her grin grows, and fuck, it's beautiful. The novelty of hearing those three words from each other hasn't faded yet, and truthfully, I hope it never does.

"And it's a good thing," I continue. "I'm not saying you couldn't create a program in a city like New York—but here, you have your family's support as well as the town's." Running my hand down the back of her head and settling it on the nape of her neck, I add, "And me. You have my unconditional support as long as you want it, Blake."

She stands on her tip-toes and wraps her hands around my neck, pulling us closer. "Good. Because I was kind of hoping I'd have you to build this thing with."

Her lips meet mine, and I fall into the kiss for a while. It's hard not to let myself get too lost in the moment, but I pull back, too focused on her words.

"Do you mean that? You want me to be a part of this next chapter in your life?" It sends a thrilling spark through me to think about being Blake's partner in this.

She said she liked that word—*partner*. I'm still figuring out what that means in the context of us. And I would never have assumed that Blake would want me to be involved in this going forward.

However, if she's asking, my answer is 'fuck *yes*.'

She bites her lip and looks up at me. "Yeah, I do," she whispers. "I mean, you helped me get here... for better or worse," she teasingly adds.

"Then I'm in this with you. Every step of the way."

That seems to be enough for her for now because she just grabs my jaw and practically climbs up my body. I grip her thighs, hoist her up to my waist and walk us to the bed. It's a short walk, but her lips don't leave mine once.

Dropping onto the edge of the bed, I hold her in my lap and guide her hips as she grinds against me. Her kisses mingle with the raspy moans she doesn't try to hide from me.

My hands squeeze her ass harder, and she throws her head back, letting out one of the most erotic sounds I've ever heard. As she continues to ride my lap, I move my mouth down her neck and unbutton the pajama top she's wearing.

Almost missing it from being too caught up in my desire for her, I pull back and take her in. She's wearing a red lace bra that contrasts her soft, milky skin fucking beautifully. It's sheer and gives me the perfect view of her peaked nipples. One of my hands glides up her side and cups her tit, my thumb running against the bud.

"You buy this for me, pretty girl?" She nods, looking at me through her lashes. There's a coy energy to her now, but I get the feeling it's more of an act than anything.

And I know for a fact I've never been harder than I am right now. I desperately need to be buried in her tight pussy immediately.

"I'm one lucky fucking man." She smashes our mouths together again, sliding her hot, little tongue against mine. Against her lips, I ask, "Is it a matching set?"

Instead of answering, she climbs off of me and bites her lip. Leaning back onto my elbows, I watch as she slides the matching pajama shorts down and reveals a tiny scrap of red fabric. It barely covers the short, dark curls between her thighs, but it's my favorite wet dream come to life.

"Come here. Right now," I tell her. And she obediently crawls up my body and settles herself over my hard cock. Knowing that it's better we don't waste too much time, we make quick work of my shirt and pants, taking off my underwear and pajama pants in one go.

She leans down to kiss me again, and I realize something important. "Wait," I grab her shoulders and gently push her back. "Fuck. I didn't bring any condoms... I didn't think we'd do this tonight."

"Oh," she murmurs and crawls off my body. Immediately, I regret my words even though I know it's the responsible choice for both of us.

As I watch her crawl to one of her nightstands and open the drawer, I realize that she's grabbing something.

Then her hand pops out with a strip of four condoms. She falls on her stomach and looks at me over her shoulder.

I grab the aluminum packets from her and tease, "Wow, only four left? *Red flag.*"

She rolls her eyes, shyness creeping out. "I stole them from your nightstand a few nights ago. I *did* prepare for this."

"And thank fuck you did." Lightly, I slap her ass. It isn't hard enough to even be considered spanking, just enough to watch the way it jiggles from the contact. "Pretty and smart," I muse.

Laughing, she moves to turn onto her back, but I grab one of the round globes to stop her. "I want you like this." To punctuate my point, I tap the side of her ass again.

She lets out a deep breath that has a hint of a whimper mixed in and nods. "Yes, yes." Pressing her head into the mattress as I massage her bottom more, she quietly demands, "Fuck me."

I'm already tearing open one of the packets as she spreads her legs wider and lifts her hips a couple inches off the bed.

"Even with this on"—I snap the string of fabric between her ass cheeks—"I can see how wet you are, baby."

"I want you so bad," she whines.

Rolling the condom on, I tilt my head and take in the beautiful sight in front of me. Blake laid out in front of me—at my mercy and with her trust in my hands—her arousal already soaking through her panties. And I haven't even really touched her yet.

"I love seeing how desperate you are for my cock," I smirk while sliding the thin scrap of fabric to the side and working two fingers into her. Her hips are already bucking against the mattress and she's clawing at the sheets, looking for a fullness I'll soon give her.

"I love when you're buried deep inside me. I need it." She cries out when I remove my fingers from her.

"You do, huh?" Aligning the tip of my cock to her tight, wet entrance, I slide home in one, long thrust. "Like this, baby? This is what you need?"

"Yes, yes, yes," she chants, those words turning into my name, as I start to thrust into her at a rigorous pace.

And hearing the way she gasps for air while I'm stretching her around my cock, is easily my favorite sound in the world now.

"I could stay here all fucking night, pretty girl, but we don't have that time right now." Positioning myself better behind her, I reach around her body—one hand gripping her breast and pinching her nipple through the fabric, the other finds her clit and starts to work the sensitive bundle of nerves. "You're going to come for me quick and hard—then the next time you're home with me, I'll spend hours worshipping your perfect fucking body the way you deserve. Understand?"

"Yes, Adrian," she cries out. "I understand. Make me come."

Something catches my eye and when I turn to the left, I realize that we're almost aligned with the tall mirror propped next to the bed. Making a quick decision, I pull out of her, ignoring her soft whine, and wrap my arm around her torso.

"What—oh," she cuts off when I position our bodies directly in front of the mirror. Blake falls forward, catching herself on her elbows and arching her back.

Sliding my cock back into her, I don't stop until I'm fully sheathed in her wet heat. After a second, I pull out to the tip and drive into her again, gaining speed with every thrust. I'm never rough with her but she does love when I give it to her hard and fast. "Look at us," I command in a low voice.

"What?" she asks, not seeming to process my words right away. Her head turns and those hooded eyes widen at the sight. I watch her take in how she looks while overcome by her pleasure.

It's a beautiful sight—and one that belongs solely to me now.

From the way her walls grip me even tighter, I know she loves it just as much as I do.

Pumping my hips faster, I focus on her pleasure and do my best to ignore the building tension in my own body. Either Blake realizes how limited our time is, or this view is the hottest fucking thing she's ever seen, but it doesn't take long for her body to tense undermine and her wet heat strangles my cock.

I keep pounding my hips into her until she falls limply on the bed. Knowing she's pleased and exhausted now, I grip onto her hips and pistol into her relentlessly, reveling in the way her pussy twitches around me in aftershocks.

"Yes, Adrian, yes," she quietly whimpers, and tries to move her hips in time with mine despite her fatigue.

It's enough to send me over the edge and I drown in my pleasure—coming inside of her, almost wishing there wasn't the barrier there.

Dropping down to my forearms, I hold my weight over her, not pulling out yet. Instead, I let us both catch our breath and kiss along her shoulders and spine.

After a few minutes, she turns her head enough to give me a long, carnal kiss before saying, "Let's get ready for bed."

Nodding against her neck, I ask, "Where am I sleeping?"

"Uhm? *Here*? Where else would you sleep?"

Leaning back, I pull out of her and try to ignore the breathy whimper that escapes her. "Are you sure that's okay?"

She turns on her back and untangles her legs from me. She lays them open around my legs, and even though she's still in the red lingerie set, I can see every inch of her.

"Of course it's okay. Plus, they can't really catch us doing anything if we already did it," she jokes. I smile, but don't speak. She leans up onto her elbows and tells me point blank, "I want you here, Adrian. With me in my bed."

And that's all it takes.

Because when I told Blake that I would give her anything she asks for, I meant it. So I grab a towel from her closet, and clean both of us off. I watch as she changes out of the lingerie, putting her cute Christmas pajamas back on. While she's in the bathroom, I get dressed and clean up any evidence.

When I come back from getting ready for bed, I find Blake waiting for me with the covers folded down. Leaving her bedroom door open, I slide into the spot next to her, and she wraps her body around mine, quickly falling asleep in my arms.

And for the hundredth time tonight, I can't help but think about how great all my Christmases could be if they're spent together.

Chapter Fifty-One

Adrian

Christmas morning with the Millers is something out of a Hallmark movie. All that's missing is snow outside, but it's unnecessary with the warmth that surrounds me inside. The lingering scent of banana pancakes and vanilla coffee in the air, Christmas Songs by Frank Sinatra playing on a low volume in the background, and the easy chatter of the three people who have quickly, and seamlessly, taken me into their family is all I need.

I'm sitting on the floor, leaning back onto the couch while Blake sits cross-legged next to me. When I woke up before her and had to pee really fucking bad, I was nervous about running into one of her parents in the hallway. We both had crashed out before either had gotten back from their friend's house, so I wasn't sure how they felt about us sharing a room in their home.

When I was trying to sneak out of the bathroom back to Blake's bedroom, Selena walked around the corner with two cups of coffee in her hand. Noticing me, she just smiled warmly and asked if I wanted to help her with breakfast. She met me in the kitchen after taking Tim his mug, and we spent the next couple of hours making a full breakfast spread.

Blake didn't come out until we were halfway through, and even then, she sat at the island with her dad keeping us company. It was different from last night when I was included in her traditions. This morning felt like I was creating some of my own with her family.

So, to say I'm one giddy son-of-a-bitch would be an understatement.

But nothing prepares my heart—and body—for the moment Blake coyly lifts onto her knees to grab a present, and crawls back toward me with a wrapped box in her hands. "This is for you," she mumbles as she plops down in front of me.

Smiling softly at her, I lean forward and brush my thumb along her cheek. "Thanks, Storm Cloud." I nod toward the tree, pretending it's a private moment between us; that her parents aren't mere feet away. To Tim's credit, he's taking his sweet time unwrapping the box from Blake. Selena is blatantly watching us with her coffee mug paused midair, a knowing smirk gracing her face. "There's something for you, too."

She perks up and looks over her shoulder. "Really?"

"Of course. It's the snowman wrapping paper," I add with a smug lift of my lips. "It was the easiest gift I've ever bought."

Rolling her eyes, she leans over to grab the small box, but insists I open mine first. She seems excited—nervous, but mostly excited—so I go with it.

The wrapping is pretty and simple. Brown paper with green, red, and white dots on it, and ribbon in all the same colors she expertly tied and twirled. I almost feel bad to ruin it, but of course my curiosity wins out.

Inside, I find a few folded sweatshirts and a pair of sweats.

The first one is a vintage Seattle Supersonic t-shirt. It instantly brings a smile to my face, remembering one of the nights we went to grab dinner at The Loop. I told her how my dad took me to a game once, before they rebranded to the Oklahoma City Thunder. It was one of the first times we moved for their job, and it's my favorite memory with him.

Next, I pull out two crewnecks. One with an old school *Looney Tunes* print, but the last one is something I'd recognize anywhere. It's the exact Nike crewneck I showed her at work a week or so ago. Half button with green, gray, and blue color blocks and a large NIKE on the left pec. It's from a super limited run in the early nineties—in fact, I'm positive all of this is authentic merch from at least two decades ago—and I've spent about two years trying to find this for less than a hundred bucks. I didn't even know there were matching sweats to it.

And now, I'm holding both of them.

"I don't know where you found these," I look up at her with what I'm sure is a goofy smile, "but Blake, these are dope. Thank you so much."

The smile she's been anxiously holding back breaks out into one of the most beautiful sights I've ever seen. "I'm so happy you like them," she quietly gushes, reaching over to squeeze my knee. I grab her hand before she can pull away. "I found the Supersonics tee and *Looney Tunes* crew a couple weeks ago, but I was so worried the Nike one wouldn't get here in time."

"How did you get it?"

"Well," she wryly tilts her head and looks to the side. "My brother may not play baseball anymore, he does however, still know people in some high up places." Blake isn't one to brag about herself, but she loves to talk about her brother and friends' accomplishments. "I don't know the specifics. He somehow pulled it off for me so I could do this for you."

The familiar warmth that comes with being loved by the Miller's floods my chest again. Not only because Blake cared enough to mention something that was important to me, but because her brother—who I only kind of met last night—went out of his way to help her do this for me too. It only confirms what I've suspected for a while... This family is one I want to be a part of. A family I'd want to raise my own in.

With a tight chest, I nod toward the small box in Blake's hands. "Open your gift, pretty girl."

Her eyes glance at her parents the same second the light pink color crawls up her neck and cheeks.

She gently takes the small bow off and sets it next to her. Next, she slowly turns the box over and works her pinky between the flaps of paper that are taped together. She moves toward one of the ends and does the same thing.

"Blake, you can tear it."

"She's done this her entire life," Selena rolls her eyes, smiling as she watches Blake, curiosity of what's in the box clear in her eyes. "Tim's almost as bad, but not quite."

I look over at my boss, who is chuckling good-naturedly. I really thought he was trying to give us a sense of privacy, not that he was overtly careful with wrapping paper. Though, Blake's a little less shocking.

"There we go," Blake happily sighs, pulling my attention back to her. With just as much care, she opens the lid and stares down at the contents for what feels like forever, only seconds really. She looks up to me with so much affection—almost as much as I feel for her, but not quite. "Adrian. This is... beautiful."

"Yeah? You like it?" I gesture for the box, taking the dainty silver chain out when she hands it to me. It's the twin to the one she mentioned is her favorite of mine, except this one's thinner and a little shorter. It'll hang on her collarbone whereas mine goes down to the top of my chest.

The other difference is, I love the simple, minimalist look of the bare chain. On me. Her's has a small silver cloud that hangs down.

I reach around her neck and clasp it into place. Beaming as she runs her fingers along the cold metal, she turns toward her mom to show her.

Selena smiles and nods approvingly. "That's gorgeous."

"It's perfect," Blake confirms with a soft smile.

"I knew I had to get it as soon as I saw it."

"That's how I felt when I saw the Supersonic t-shirt. Though, it feels silly in comparison now."

"Nah, it's just as perfect."

With my mom's help, I bought Tim and Selena one of those electronic picture frames. It connects through an app that Blake already sent Grady the link to. So now, he can update it as Stella grows and they can feel like they're missing a little less of that time. Selena starts crying—happy tears Blake confirms—and Tim thanks me on their behalf before handing me a present. It's a large gift bag with a new Adidas gym bag. It's no secret that my old Under Armor one has seen better days. It's one of those things I don't want to splurge on, but the fact he noticed despite the amount of responsibilities he has means a lot.

From there, the day plays out quietly and comfortably. Grady FaceTimes the family again, and this time I get a peek of his girlfriend Arielle throughout the conversation. We watch Elf and Home Alone, tucked into the couches with knitted blankets and hot chocolate. For lunch, Selena heats up some of the tamales she made a few nights ago, and I learn that she *only* cooks them during the holiday, adding to why it's Blake's favorite time of the year.

And even though I don't stay another night—wanting to give them some time alone as well—my heart is full, and I don't feel lonely like I had expected.

Chapter Fifty-Two

Blake

"That's the one," Margo declares from my bed.

In the mirror, I can see Meera nodding next to her eagerly.

Taking in my reflection again, it truthfully takes a lot of mental focus to not think about what this mirror was used for only a week ago. Other than Christmas Day, we've spent every night together since. He really did give me a spare key a few days ago—he slipped it on my keychain when I was leaving work last week and asked me to 'meet him at home' because he was working later than me.

So, I did. After grabbing an overnight bag from home and letting my mom know where I'd be, I went to his apartment and waited for him. Killing time by taking a shower and making us dinner, I didn't feel uncomfortable, or out of place, at any point.

It felt right, especially when he opened the door and found me standing at the stove in nothing but a pair of boyshort panties, and the *Looney Tunes* crewneck I had just bought for him.

And... that was that. Much like dinners at The Loop, and him watching the Paulson boys with me, it became another one of our routines.

Focusing back on the moment, I take in my reflection. I'm in a mini sequin dress with long sleeves and an open back. It's different from what I'd usually wear, but I don't dislike it either. The midnight blue compliments my dark hair and gray eyes really well, and the thin shimmery tights Margo insisted I try on with it, are a nice touch.

"Are you sure?" I ask anyway, feeling silly to dress up for a party in my parents' living room. They always host a little gathering for New Year's Eve, though usually I'm off with Margo, Meera, and her brothers, doing something else.

This year, they decided to spend the night here and even convinced their parents to break their usual traditions to come as well.

But more than just feeling silly, Adrian is going to be here tonight. With his parents and Maria. I almost wish he hadn't told me and instead had gone with the surprise approach like when he took me to SunRay's, and I met his Grammy.

The anxiety of meeting them for the first time has been brewing for three days now, ever since Adrian and I agreed that we wanted to spend the night together. Our relationship is new but is at the forefront of my life as we move into the new year, so it felt right.

And I want to meet Camille, Will, and Maria. They are the three people responsible for making Adrian into the man I've fallen in love with. That's also why I'm so worried that something will go wrong.

"Absolutely yes," Margo insists, looking so authentically herself and comfortable in that version. Her long blonde hair is curled and styled with little bows. It's the short, black dress with bell sleeves, paired with sparkly fishnet tights and combat boots, that really ties the whole look together.

Meera, on the other hand, is in a gray midi silk skirt, styled with a pretty updo, a black mesh top with a bralette underneath, and heels that add at least four inches to her height. Looking me over, she agrees with Margo for the fifth time. "You look beautiful, Blake. Promise."

"Couldn't agree more." Adrian's deep voice comes from the doorway and our heads whip in that direction. "I like them," he nods toward my friends. "They haven't been wrong since I met them."

"Hell yeah, we're always right," Margo agrees from behind me and I hear her share a high five with Meera.

Rolling my eyes, I smile at Adrian and ignore the peanut gallery sitting on my bed. As soon as I saw him leaning against the door frame, I felt this cosmic force to be closer to him. Without overthinking it, I close the gap separating us, and he pulls me into his embrace before I can reach for him.

As my arms wrap around his waist, he gently cups the back of my neck with one hand and my jaw with the other. "Hey, Storm Cloud. You really are fucking gorgeous." He drops his lips to mine and takes his time greeting me, already used to the audience we have anytime they're in town.

A little thing I've noticed about Adrian is he typically uses compliments that are broader than the current moment. Like now—I don't *look* gorgeous, I just *am*. I wouldn't turn down any types of affirmation from him, but I love these ones a little extra.

"Thanks. You look really great as well." I take a step back to take in his black pants and the dark blue satin button down he has on. It's short sleeved with a monochrome floral print to it, still I can't help but notice—

"Oh my God, they match," Meera squeals from the bed. I'm sure she's trying to be quiet except she fails miserably. And Margo's snort clues her in because she whispers, "Sorry."

Shaking my head, I walk over to the small jewelry holder pinned to my wall, picking out some earrings before I put on the necklace Adrian gave me.

"Okay," Margo singsongs. "We'll meet you out there."

From the corner of my eye, I watch as they both stop to give Adrian a quick hug in greeting, before making their way to the backyard. In the middle of putting my second earring in, I turn toward him as he softly shuts the door.

"I'm almost done. I don't want to keep your parents waiting."

"It's okay. I introduced them to your parents already and got to meet Bonnie. She's nice." I nod and finish clasping the back of the earring. "Are you feeling okay about tonight? I don't want you to be nervous, but I know you better than that."

Letting out a deep breath, I decide to just be honest because he'd know if I lied to spare his feelings. "Of course I'm nervous. My parents already liked you before we started to hang out because you're their employee. They weren't basing their judgement only on the fact that you're my boyfriend."

Stepping up to me, he reaches behind me and grabs the necklace. Just like on Christmas morning, he puts it on for me and gently cups the back of my neck. "I mean, the circumstances are different. I can't deny that. But my parents know you're a whole person outside of our re-lationship—and that's who they're excited to meet. The woman who cares so deeply for her entire community, who offers her free time to families in need without a second of doubt, who is one of the most resilient, and brilliant, people they'll ever meet. The woman that their son is lucky enough to call his girl—and hopefully one day, so much more."

"Adrian," I murmur. "That's just how you see me."

"No, baby. That's exactly who you are, and part of why I'm in love with you. And my parents already like you from everything I've told them about you."

"Oh God, I forgot you talked about me with them," I grumble.

He laughs and grabs my jaw, angling me for another kiss. "The only reason they don't love you yet, is because they haven't met you. So, let's go."

I'm not totally sure if it's a blessing or curse when we find my friends standing with my parents, Bonnie, and who I can only assume is Adrian's parents and godmother. They'd never mean to embarrass me, but Margo really lacks a filter most days. And the last thing I need is Meera squealing through our introductions.

Adrian doesn't seem deterred by my friends though. He interlaces our fingers and pulls me toward the group.

"Oh, there you two are," my mom smiles when she notices us walking over.

When Adrian's parents turn, I can't help but notice the wide, genuine grin his mom is sporting compared to the smaller, though equally as warm, smile his dad is offering us. Right off the bat, it calms some of my nerves from how similar it is to my own parents. Glancing up at Adrian, I wonder if that's why it's been so easy for him to integrate himself into my family.

"Hi, doll," Adrian's mom, Camille, greets me first. She doesn't look that much like Adrian, despite that, she's as beautiful as you'd expect for the woman who gave him life. She's a couple inches shorter than me with shoulder-length coils that frame her soft jaw. The warm gold of her modest jumpsuit complements her full curves and rich ebony skin. It's the way in which she's smiling that overtakes her entire being, making the resemblance between the two of them unmistakable. "You must be Blake."

Swallowing nervously, I nod and try to smile in spite of the butterflies thrashing my stomach. "Hi, yes. It's great to meet you."

Sticking out my hand, I'm momentarily surprised when Camille uses that to pull me into a hug. Subtly I gather my wits and tentatively offer the gesture back.

"Please, call me Cami."

"Cami—got it." When we pull apart, she grabs her husband's hand, and he steps forward. Thankfully offering me a hand rather than another embrace, I take it. "It's nice to meet you," I tell him.

"You as well, Blake. I'm Will. And thank you for inviting us over tonight." On the other hand, Adrian looks almost exactly like his father. They have the same deep mahogany complexion and dimples, but Will's hair is longer on the sides. Adrian's mentioned that he's a bit taller than his father, although it can't be by much.

Smiling, my eyes move to the last woman I haven't met. She's a younger version of her mother with warm olive skin and dark green eyes. Her chestnut brown hair that's styled in a short, messy bob and the black pants suit is the opposite of the eccentric older woman.

"Maria," she confirms, as she grabs my hand in a more tender, warm grasp than the handshake I shared with Adrian's dad. "My mom hasn't stopped talking about you for weeks now."

Laughing awkwardly, I shrug and admit, "I loved her. Adrian and I are planning on spending a whole day with them soon. I didn't get to meet your dad yet."

"Oh, I know. It was all she talked about on the plane to Florida last week."

This time, the chuckle is genuine, and I feel the anxiety starting to drift from my body.

Throughout this whole conversation, my friends have been standing silently near my parents. As much as I appreciate it, I can't help but glance suspiciously toward them.

Will pulls my attention back. "Adrian's told us so much about you."

"So I've heard," I quietly mutter, not meaning to blurt out the words.

My eyes go wide, hoping I didn't offend anyone, but Cami laughs easily. "He had no choice. I'd been hoping he'd run into the cute girl from the grocery store again."

She winks as my cheeks grow warmer, realizing that night really was somehow monumental in the grand scheme of things.

"The grocery store?" my dad cuts in for the first time.

Ruefully, I turn toward my parents, not missing the chaotic smile starting to tug on Margo's lips. Meera just looks like she needs a container of popcorn.

To his credit, my dad doesn't look mad. More so confused. "Did you know each other before Adrian got the job?"

"No," we say at the same time. Continuing, I tell my parents, "We ran into each other at the grocery store—literally."

"It was a real-life meet cute," Meera pipes in, making my parents laugh. They've been around her long enough to know she's a romantic, much like my father.

"I'll give you the story, Timmy," Margo says. The two of them are the only people to *ever* call him that as far as I'm aware. It's no surprise which of the two came up with it. "Meera and I saw the whole thing play out in real time."

Leaning into Adrian's chest, he wraps an arm around my shoulders, and we listen as my best friend, and his mother, give the detailed account of the night we saw each other for the first time.

Chapter Fifty-Three

Blake

Adrian and I spent the first couple of hours with our parents, talking on the back porch and getting to know each other. My friends gave us some privacy after the impromptu story time and the conversations flowed easily.

Bonnie and Maria floated in and out too, allowing mine and Adrian's parents, to gct to know each other as well.

Eventually Dev and Jatin got here, meeting the rest of their family at the party. After Cami fussed over Adrian's new friend Jatin, to her son's embarrassment, we broke off to the kitchen.

The six of us are easily the youngest people here by at least a decade, and everyone else has stayed outside near the heaters, or in the living room where the music and drinks are.

Meera pulled out the game Taboo about thirty minutes ago, and we've been playing ever since—boys versus girls. I'd never guess Adrian was as competitive as he's proven to be either.

With about five minutes left to midnight, we agree to regroup after the ball drops. Our friends make their way into the living room with the rest of the guests, but a really crazy, horribly reckless idea starts to take form. And once it does, I can't stop from grabbing onto some of that newfound courage and turning toward Adrian.

"There's only a few minutes left, Storm Cloud. I don't want to miss our first New Year's Eve kiss," Adrian murmurs when he grabs my waist and pulls me into him.

I loop my hands around his neck and tug him down. Brushing my lips against his, I whisper, "I have something else in mind... hopefully something better than a kiss."

That gets his attention and compliance. With a saucy grin, he lets me lead him toward the pantry. It's a large walk-in style, except there's no light. Not that I need one for what I have in mind.

Knowing that I have extremely limited time and about thirty-plus possibilities that someone will walk in on us, I quickly shut the door and push Adrian until his back meets the shelves.

"Blake," his voice is low and gravelly, "what are you doing, baby?"

"Instead of a kiss, what about a different tradition?" Leaning into him, I lightly trail my fingers over the already growing bulge in his pants.

"I know you love those," he breathes out when my palm flattens against him.

Nodding against his neck, I place kisses and agree. "I do."

"Do you have a condom?" The tone in his voice is desperate, and I can't help but chuckle.

"No," I tell him before lowering to my knees.

Groaning, he tangles a hand in my hair. He's mimicked the gesture the few times I've done this. More often than not, he'd rather be inside of me if it's a possibility. I'm not going to argue with him on that.

But I like doing this for him.

The semi-public setting is a brand new thing for me though. So far, I can't say I hate it.

"Can I?" I grab onto his belt buckle and look up at him through the dark.

Neither of us can see the other, but I can feel his eyes in my direction too.

"Fuck. Yes."

Not wanting to waste any time, I unfasten his belt and get his pants down to his thighs.

Running my hands up his legs, I feel my way to his length. My hands wrap around him and it's easier to orient myself in the dark.

He lets out a low, throaty sound as my hands start to stroke his cock and my tongue flicks out, swiping across his tip. His natural musky scent is strong and so fucking delicious.

Moving one hand down to cup his sac, I lightly suck at the base of his hardness and lick up, reveling in the salty taste of his pre-cum.

"We're running out of time, baby." Gripping onto the back of my hair, he pulls my head back, so I'm looking up in his direction again. "You wanted to suck my cock? Fucking do it then."

Releasing me enough to position myself a little more comfortably on my knees, I smile at his demand. He's not exactly bossy in bed and is willing to let me have control like right now, though he can be impatient as hell.

Knowing he's right about time, I open wide and slide him to the back of my throat. His hips push forward until I gag, and the murmured *fuck* he lets out is so hot.

Encouraged, I start bobbing my head faster and use both of my hands to pleasure him alongside my mouth. I close my lips around his thickness and suck harder, loving the flavor of him on my tongue. And when he leans off the shelves a little to better thrust into me, I can't hold back the desperate moan and I grab onto the back of his thighs, holding him closer and deeper.

"Ten... nine... eight..."

The countdown from the living room starts.

"Oh. *Fuck*! Fuck, Blake," he quietly starts to chant and moves faster. At this point, my mouth is open, and my hands are assisting in the pump of his hips, as he takes back control of the situation.

When the muffled cheers start, he's closer but not quite there.

"You're so fucking sexy," he tells me and takes a small step forward. The movement pushes me onto my heels and Adrian is almost right above me. I imagine him with one hand on the wall behind me, while he holds my head in place, as he pushes deeper. "You suck my cock like you were made for me, pretty girl."

Moaning, I open wider and silently curse myself for turning down the idea of him fucking me in here instead.

The new position seems to be what Adrian needed. His frantic, unorganized thrusts slow into deep, shaky pumps as he releases on my tongue.

Not stopping until he's still, and gently pulling my hair back, I'm already thinking about everything else that will follow when we get back to his apartment later.

As soon as I stand, I hear the sound of his belt buckle closing before his hands are on my waist. He pulls me into his chest and kisses me deep, moaning at the taste of him mixed on my tongue.

Leaning back, the reality of what we just did starts to weigh on me. There's a good chance that someone will be in the kitchen when we walk out of here, and I hope to God it's neither of our parents.

"We should go," I tell him.

He steps around me and says, "I'll peek my head out and chec—" but his voice cuts off as soon as he gets a view of the room. Quietly, he tries to close the door and step back into the pantry.

A small, surprised squeal pops out of my mouth and Adrian turns around, shaking his head.

"I might not have birthed you, Adrian Ray, but don't think God didn't bless me with eyes on the back of my head too. He knew your mother was going to need help when he gave you a face too pretty for your own good."

Adrian cringes, turning toward his godmother and opens the door more. Only enough for him to lean halfway out of it so she can't see me. But I'm positive she knows.

"Funny seeing you here." I can picture the easy grin on his face, and I truly don't know how he does it.

To my horror, the next person to speak is a familiar voice. One that belongs to the woman who is the equivalent to my godmother, without the title. "Blake, honey, we know you're in there. Just come out."

Reluctantly, I push the door open further and give Bonnie a small wave. She has a mischievous smirk I've seen a million times in my life.

"We're all in agreement about you two," Bonnie looks at Maria for confirmation and she nods. "But I think even Tim might have some hesitations about what you do to his daughter in their pantry."

Her eyes move from Adrian to me. Before I can stop myself, I blurt out, "Excuse me, Bonnie, I pulled him in there. There was no being defiled on my end."

My face is burning up, but I couldn't stop myself from digging that hole.

Bonnie snickers, a devilish contradiction to her smooth lilt and angelic face. "Atta girl. It won't give your father any more peace of mind though."

Crossing my arms, I double down on my stubbornness despite my embarrassment. "It's a good thing he isn't going to find out, right?"

Bonnie shakes her head, neither in confirmation nor denial, but I know she'll be cool about it unless she was truly worried for me.

Maria watches the scene quietly, not looking disappointed or put off either. Interlocking her arm with Bonnie's, she tilts her head and takes in her strawberry blonde hair, and heart-shaped face for a second. "Let's leave these two alone. I'd love to see the small garden you mentioned earlier."

Bonnie's eyes are trained on the small physical contact between them for a few seconds too long to be casual, before looking up and nodding at Maria with a smile. "Your secrets are always safe with me," she tells me with a wink and turns out of the room to take Maria to her backyard behind ours.

Chapter Fifty-Four

Blake

It's Adrian's twenty-third birthday, and we're at our typical table at The Loop with a full spread of food in front of us.

He insisted he didn't want anything special. Which is typical of him, but he had made my birthday almost a week-long affair. Last month, we went on a trip to Joshua Tree for the weekend, a small shopping spree at Michael's for new yarn, and dinner at SunRay's. It was the most perfect birthday I've had yet.

So, I couldn't do *nothing* for him.

Instead, we had dinner at my parents' last night with both of our families, even Grady, Arielle, and five-month-old Stella. It was his second time meeting them. Last weekend, I took him on a staycation in La Jolla. It's not much, but he seems more than happy with how the week's going.

However tonight, we have three little guys who wanted to spend Adrian's birthday with him.

We help with the Paulson boys as much as we can, but I know that time is going to be cut when I start at UCAH in the fall. There's a lot of things in my life I realized I took for granted in my year off from school. Like the amount of time I had to spend with Mikey, Shawn, and Luke. Or how my days didn't have a lot of routine, outside of work and therapy.

As the days fade into the next, I grow more and more excited to start this journey. My entire family is excited for me, and proud of the career path I've found, yet it's brought my dad and I even closer.

He's working on a budget to bring in another veterinarian and technicians, who have experience working in the community medicine sector within the next couple of years. Olivia's been one of my biggest supporters, and we've grown closer since I told her the news.

So much over the last few months has changed for Adrian and me; all for the better.

In late March, everyone's spring break fell on the same week again, so the six of us—Adrian, Margo, Meera, Jatin, Dev, and me—took a trip to Sedona. We spent the days hiking, exploring, and trying as many restaurants as we could in the short time. Other than the physical distance, I haven't noticed much of a change in my friendships with Margo and Meera, but I can't wait to have them home for the summer.

Adrian and Jatin have fallen into an easy friendship. They study together a few nights a week. He even accompanies us to the gym, and The Loop, every once in a while. The more time we spend with him, the more I realize Adrian was right. Jatin doesn't treat me like his little sister's best friend. He even asks about Margo at least once every time I see him.

The best news we've gotten recently was at the beginning of April, exactly a month ago and two days before Easter. I'm not religious, neither is Adrian, but it felt like a miracle to learn that Chispa is officially in remission and radiation was never a necessity. She'll continue coming in more often than just her annual exams, in case the tumors come back, and we have a chance to catch them early again. But since her surgeries in October, she's been recovering greatly.

Polly's still a pain in my ass, but Benji the Beagle has also recovered from his surgery and is now seeing a trainer to avoid any other avoidable complications, like eating cat poop and branches.

"What else did you do for your birthday?" Luke asks, pulling me from my thoughts. He's insisted on knowing every single detail of Adrian's week.

Chuckling, he takes a bite of his brisket sandwich. "That's it, I promise. We spent last weekend in La Jolla and had dinner with our families last night."

Not looking fully convinced, Luke huffs out a breath and looks back down to the coloring sheet one of the food trucks was offering to kids.

With all three of the boys occupied, I lean closer to Adrian's side and quietly ask, "How *did* you feel about dinner with everyone?"

It was both of our parents, my brother's family, and Maria. Bonnie couldn't make it, though I'm not fully convinced she had a valid reason.

Tilting his head, he gives me a curious look and soft smile. "I thought it was great. My parents love spending time with you guys." His eyes search mine. "How do you think dinner went last night?"

"Oh, good. *Really good*," I promise. "I know it wasn't a surprise necessarily, but I didn't ask if you would want to spend the evening with your parents and my family too."

He shakes his head, a little confused. "I'm happy with whatever time I get with my parents, and I don't know. I guess I'm hoping that it won't always be *my* family or *your* family. It'll be *our* family."

The declaration takes me by surprise a little bit. Adrian and I talk about our future a lot, even marriage in an abstract way. We've planned on moving in together officially when his lease ends next month. I'm there almost every night anyway. He tells me he loves me every day in more ways than with his words. But this somehow feels more concrete than those other times.

Making sure the boys are distracted, I lean closer and breathe out, "Really?"

He moves a few inches closer to me and wraps an arm low around my waist. "Really, Storm Cloud." With his lips near my ear, he promises, "I want an entire life with you. Careers and marriage and babies—all of it. I'm just waiting for you to catch up."

When I look up at him, he's smirking down, the affection and commitment he feels for me—for *us*—is evident.

It's on the tip of my tongue to tell him how badly I want those things too. That I think about what our future is going to look like more often than I'd like to admit.

So much of my life has been spent waiting for better days and feeling like I'm surviving. Adrian makes me feel like I'm alive though.

I've never doubted that I was whole by myself; the concept of soulmates always being whimsical and ridiculous. But he changes all of that. He makes me feel hopeful—like I can actually believe in all the good things to come in life.

As Adrian starts a game of tic-tac-toe with Mikey, I'm looking at their sweet interaction in a new light. And maybe things between us are moving fast, but I'm certain I want this forever.

Chapter Fifty-Five

Blake

Once I got in my car to come talk to Adrian's parents, the nausea hit me suddenly. But I couldn't get myself to turn back. I didn't want to.

Since his birthday six weeks ago, I haven't been able to get our conversation out of my head. And the more I thought about it, the more it felt stupid to wait. Especially if his only excuse was he's waiting for me to catch up. I'm five steps ahead of him now.

Part of those nerves were due to the fact he's spent significantly more time with my family than I have with his, and even my parents were a little apprehensive. Maybe rightfully so.

It's only been around seven months since we've officially been together, though actually closer to a year since the first time we saw each other in the grocery store.

Weirdly, it didn't feel insane until after I got my parents approval—which makes no fucking sense. I should've felt better. Except it seemed too easy. So I'm positive that Cami and Will are going to say 'hell *no*.'

I texted Cami earlier this morning, asking if it'd be okay if I went to see them for lunch. I didn't think she'd get back to me as quickly as she did. Without asking any questions—like why Adrian wouldn't be with me and why she couldn't let him know—she said she was excited to see me and would make waffles. I guess Adrian mentioned that I love them to her once.

It's the first time I've ever been alone with his parents, and I've been worried about how it would feel to be here.

As soon as I park my car, the front door is flung open to reveal a beautiful, smiling Cami leaning against the door, waiting for me. The stance is so similar to the one I've seen Adrian hold a hundred times over by now.

So much of Adrian's personality comes from his mom. Their easy charm, the way they're both quick to laugh and can make anyone feel right at home. Will, on the other hand, is more timid. He seems comfortable to let his wife take the reins of life. Like right then, I could see him peeking his head around the corner from inside, as I walked closer. He offered a swift wave before disappearing again.

"Look at you," she gushes with her arms wide and waiting. I step into the embrace, already familiar with her open affection. "Gosh, you're gorgeous. I can't get over it. I'm sure my son can't either," she teases as she tucks me under her arm and guides me inside.

I've been to the Jones's home three times now, the other two with Adrian. Still, it's not a completely foreign place to me.

It's different from my own parents' home. Cami leans more modern and neutral, with pops of color rather than bright and slightly cluttered. At the same time, there's a level of comfort that only a loving mother and father could create.

Guiding me to the island, she takes a seat in the stool next to me. "So how have you been, Blake? It was such a great surprise to hear from you this morning."

My cheeks warm. "Sorry I didn't bring Adri—"

She waves her hand and lifts her coffee mug. "You're welcome to visit whenever, with or without our son."

"Well, thank you. I actually wanted to—"

"Coffee?" Will cuts in, sliding a fresh mug my way and two different types of creamer. With a small smile I take the sugary cinnamon roll creamer and mix it in with a quiet thank you. "How was the traffic? It's not usually too bad at this time of day, despite all that construction they're doing; it's unbearable sometimes."

"It wasn't bad," I reassure. "Plus, I wanted to talk to you in person about thi—"

"Blake," Camila cuts me off this time with a soft smile and a warm hand over my own. "We're not in a rush if you aren't." I want to tell her that I kind of am in a rush—the longer I have to wait, the more I want to find Adrian and start our life together *right now*—but Adrian isn't going anywhere and truthfully, it was a great reassurance that they both are so happy to have me at their home. "My son can wait—Lord knows he's gotten more than enough attention in his lifetime. I want to hear about you, doll."

I can't help preening a little, even if tears are burning my eyes all the same. "Oh?" I ask, trying to gather my senses.

"How are you feeling about classes starting soon? There's a lot of big changes coming up." She gives me a knowing smile, but there's no way she's guessed why I'm here. It must be about the apartment we're moving into at the end of the month.

Sipping my coffee and trying to relax, I answer her questions and throw in a few of mine as well—like how she's enjoying the local hospital and flight nursing, or how Will's summer courses are going.

Standing across from us, Will prepares the banana and strawberry waffles. Offering me a paternal smile when he catches my eye, as his wife throws her head back and laughs at something I said. Truthfully, it wasn't nearly as funny as she lets me pretend it to be.

It's not until about an hour later, after our food has been eaten, and our mugs of coffee sit cold next to us, that

Cami finally folds her arms and assesses me. "I've held you hostage long enough." I chuckle and shake my head, but I'm suddenly at a loss for words. "Is something going on with Adrian? Is that why he isn't here?"

There is an undertone of concern to her voice, though she doesn't look like a mother worried or anxious. If anything, she looks concerned about the relationship—like it might very well break her heart if I told her I drove all the way out there because of problems with her son.

"Adrian is okay. He's working today," I add quickly. I'm not sure if they know Adrian's schedule, especially since he's working more during the summer. "That's partly why he isn't here..." I trail off.

"Only part of it?" Will asks with an easy pull of his lips. His expression is mildly curious—as if he's not sitting there guessing what I am there for but waiting to see if he is right.

I glance between them one more time before squaring my shoulders and trying to say in a strong, even voice, "I want to ask your son to marry me."

After a couple beats of silence, Cami throws her head back and laughs. A full-belly, happy sound. Looking back to Will, he's just sitting there shaking his head with a smile that spoke of just as much elation as his wife's response.

"I told you this was why she texted us," he playfully ribs his wife.

"Oh shhh," Cami tells him. "I'll take the fifty out of your wallet, you know."

My brows furrow. "Wait... you guys bet on this?"

Camila turns back to me with so much affection and surety in her gaze. "We bet on who would get impatient first, yes. We never made a bet on if your love for each other is true and real."

"We're in perfect agreement on that," Will added.

"So..." I start, not totally sure how to read this conversation, "you both are okay with me proposing to him? Today?"

"Today?!" Cami exclaimed, laughing again. "I guess I underestimated how impatient you are, doll."

"We're more than okay with this, Blake," Will amends. "We trust both of you to make your own decisions. And we'd be honored to not only have you as a daughter-in-law, but to know our son is loved by you."

Reaching across the table, Cami lays her hand flat and open, an invitation for me to take it. Tentatively, I slip mine into hers and she offers me a gentle squeeze. "I don't care much for traditions. I only care that Adrian's with someone who loves him so much they would throw their entire life off course just to be with him." She looks over her shoulder at her husband and adds, "I know that's the love that means the most in this life—the one we didn't know we wanted but comes when we need it most. Adrian needed you."

Tears are falling silently, yet heavily down my cheeks. "No, I needed him. And now... I just want him with me so badly. Every day."

"He has no idea that today is about to be the start of his life," she muses.

<u>island of misfit toys</u>
Wed, June 17 at 2:34 PM

Margo

Are you REALLY going to do it?

Meera

Of course she is

They're SOULmates why shouldn't she??

Margo

I didn't say she shouldn't!

I'm just questioning if our baby Blake has the guts to propose to arguably the second hottest guy on this planet

Meera

Ew

I'd argue he's THE hottest guy on this planet

But yes I'm leaving Cami and Will's now

Meera

OH MY GOD YOU'RE GOING TO DO IT

Margo

I'm proud of you and I know he's going to say yes

Meera

We'll celebrate this weekend

Margo

Yeah if they're done celebrating by then

if he even says yes

Meera

He will! He has to!

Margo

I like him but not enough to spare his balls if he breaks your heart

Thanks, psychos

I'm driving now I'll try to text you later

Meera

If you don't we'll assume it went as planned

LOVE YA

Margo

Love you drive safe

Love you two more than you'll ever know

Chapter Fifty-Six

Blake

It was Cami's last sentiment that kept me sure and decisive the entire drive to the vet clinic—all three hours. And now that I'm sitting outside of the familiar sight, waiting for Adrian to walk out, I don't know what I'm doing.

At all.

It feels rash now.

Why would I do it here? Today?

There's no significance to the day other than I was feeling impatient. And in my mind, the clinic seemed... I don't know, romantic and nostalgic. It's the place we officially met and have spent so much of our time together. So many moments have happened in that building for us, both big and small.

But to propose here? God, it seems so silly now.

Adrian would've done something... more. Something better. I can't even begin to imagine how he'd make it a true grand gesture.

Although he also took me to a little hole in the wall diner for our first date. And I'd never change that for anything in the world, not after knowing how special SunRay's, and his grandparents, are to him.

So maybe this is perfect. And if anyone could see that, it's Adrian.

As if my spiraling thoughts summoned him, a light tapping on my window pulls my attention to him, standing outside my car with a soft and loving, albeit curious quirk to his lips. My heart beats faster just at the sight of him—partly because I'm freaking out inside, and partly because that's just what looking at Adrian does to me. It sends sparks through my blood while simultaneously calming my nervous system. He makes me feel alive yet safe.

"Storm Cloud?" he asks with the tilt of his head.

A little reluctantly, I get out of the car and stand in front of him. I open my mouth to say something, except no words come out. I'm speechless like a damn schoolgirl in front of her crush.

"Blake?" he asks slowly and tentatively now. "Are you okay? Are we okay?"

"Yes," I breathe out quickly, finding my voice if only so I can banish all of his fears and anxieties, like he tries to do for me every day. "I just got back from your parents," I start, and keep going before he can stop me. "Well, I talked to my parents first. Last night. Before I went to your apartment like usual. Then I texted your mom first thing this morning and asked if they'd have time to see me. She said yes."

"Of course she did," he adds quickly and surely.

"Yeah, she's great. So is your dad. And apparently they think I'm great. Just like my parents think you're great. So just a whole lot of greatness around here…" I trail off but as soon as he opens his mouth, so does my big fat one. "So I think we should just like, continue this greatness. Forever. Because I know I won't want anyone else ever, and I don't want to wait when it's all so inevitable anyway."

A hopeful smile blooms across his face. "Blake, prettiest girl in the whole world, are you… are you asking me to…?"

I nod, shallowly but quickly. "Yes, Adrian. I'm asking you to marry me. Not very well, but *yeah*. Because I love you so much. So much more than I ever even thought possible outside of movies and my own parents. Except you're real, and mine, and I want to be with you forever."

"Blake," he starts, and even though I can see the smile on his lips, I worry what his answer will be.

"It probably seems crazy. I know that. Trust me, I *know*. And I mean, it doesn't have to be forever if you don't want it to be. Divorce is a thing, you know? So if you ever change your mind, you aren't stuck with me. I want to be with you... Which I already said. But it's true."

Stepping into my space, he gently wraps a hand around the nape of my neck. "Are you seriously offering me a divorce at the same time you're proposing to me?"

Shaking my head, I whisper, "No, I'm not *offering* it. I'm reminding you that you have options."

With a small smile, he leans down until our lips are almost brushing. "I don't want options. I want you to be stuck with me forever. So, don't expect me to be as selfless as you."

"Really?" I murmur against his lips. "You don't think I'm crazy?"

"No, I don't. I think you're perfect." Closing the small distance, our lips press together, and he kisses me like it's the first time.

Clumsily I take a small box out of the waistband of my tennis skirt, where I quickly hid it. I open it to show a simple white gold band. "It was on sale," I admit with a rueful wince, "but I'll get you something better in the future."

Finally looking up at him, I see tears brimming, but the brightest, happiest smile I've ever seen too—and that's saying something for Adrian, the man who smiles easily, and freely, and genuinely. "Nah, pretty girl, I'm going to buy *you* the best ring ever."

Quickly, I place one hand on his chest and ask, "Are you mad that I proposed to you?"

"How could I be mad knowing my girl loves me just as much as I love her? I was gonna give you a year before I tied you to me forever." He pulls the ring closer and looks at me like, *what are you gonna do with it?*

I gently pull it out and place it on his finger. "A year would've been way too long."

"Thank God you're less patient than me. You've been my girl for a while now, and as great as fiancée sounds, I don't really want to wait for you to be my wife," he shrugs, a little shyly.

"Let's not wait then." I sound super fucking eager because I am. "I don't need anything fancy... as long as our families can be there, I don't need anything else."

"You tell me how soon Grady can get out here, and I'll make it happen."

My hands slide up his chest and cling to his neck. I'm giddy as a kid in a candy store and getting worse by the second. "Yeah?"

"Yeah, Blake. We can go down to the courthouse with our families and call it a fucking wedding," he teases, granted it's laced in sincerity.

"The best fucking wedding," I beam up at him, the beautiful surreal feeling warming every inch of my body.

"Pretty girl," he muses as he tilts my head back again and kisses me with passion. When we pull apart, we stand there for a second taking each other in as if we've never seen the other before.

After a few seconds, two monarch butterflies land on Adrian's shoulder. Slowly, Adrian turns his head just enough to grin down at the sight.

"What other confirmation do we need that this is right?" he quietly asks and looks back toward me.

Smiling, all I can do is nod in agreement. I've always believed monarch butterflies would lead me on the right path, and it's as clear of a sign as any I could hope for.

With a tilt of his head, he gives me a slow, indecent once over. "Let's go home and celebrate."

Standing on my toes, I pull him in for one more kiss before gently pushing him away. With a suggestive look over my shoulder, I turn away and slip into my car, excited for what's to come—both tonight and in our lives.

Chapter Fifty-Seven

Blake

Getting back into the swing of courses and assignments has been easier than I expected it would be. According to my *husband*, he never doubted me for a second.

Even after three months of being married—almost to the day since we went to the courthouse with our families—the word makes me giddy. I never imagined what my wedding would look like, or daydreamed about what dress I would wear, or who'd be standing next to me.

I respect other people's decision to declare their love for each other in whatever way is right for them, but it makes me want to break out in hives. Personally.

Sharing vows in front of the most important people in our lives, and having dinner at my parents' afterward, felt like the right decision for us. And I made sure Adrian agreed. I would've sucked it up if it was what he needed, however he genuinely didn't seem thrilled about the idea of a large party either.

I think we both just wanted to start our life together, so we did. In a weird way, it's changed everything, while absolutely nothing at the same time.

The sound of doors opening as students flood out of the building pulls my attention to the lecture hall Adrian should be coming out of anytime now.

Even though we live and work together, we don't see each other as much as I thought we would. He's pulled back his hours at the clinic due to the labs and clinicals he's taking, plus the undergrad class he's a TA for. Since I applied so late into the spring, my schedule is kind of all over the place this semester with classes ranging from seven a.m. some days to eight p.m. others. It leaves me with limited spare time.

Because of that, we spend any overlapping break to-gether—whether it's just doing our individual workouts and grabbing lunch or studying in the library with a coffee. Today, it's the former.

The butterflies that still accompany the sight of him hit me as soon as he takes his first step out of the building and the autumn sun reaches his deep mahogany skin.

His brows are drawn as he listens to the girl next to him and that's when my stomach drops. Most days, I feel so far past any trust issues I have and none of them have ever involved Adrian. So, my dread doesn't have anything to do with him, or his actions.

It has everything to do with the tall, blonde woman who's walking next with him and talking animatedly. By most people's standards, she's objectively beautiful. But the sight of her Disney Princess face will always make me want to vomit.

I don't. Though that adrenaline-filled shaking in my legs starts—the one that's telling me to run far, far away from this situation.

Standing, I clumsily grab my bag and start moving. Only I'm not going away from the scene. I'm walking right to them as I watch her grubby little hands reach out to squeeze my husband's bicep. The same one I held onto while he made love to be me, in our bed, this morning.

Sliding up to his side, I open my mouth to say something, but any words shrivel in my throat as soon as recognition crosses her features.

"Hey," Adrian says affectionately, not yet picking up on the tension.

Trying to smile up at him, knowing it's a dead giveaway that somethings wrong, I quietly respond, "Hi."

Clearly not reading the room, Morgan cuts in, "Uh, I was talking to my TA, *Blake*." She spats my name like it's a slur.

I feel Adrian look down at me, and I know he's smart enough to realize that this random girl from the lecture he's a teacher's assistant in, is one of three girls who—for almost half of it—made my life hell.

I don't know if it's the fact that I don't want Adrian to see her still bullying me, or that she doesn't have a group of minions to push me into the nearest pool. More than anything, I think I'm just so fucking over this. And her.

"Last I checked, class was over, and office hours are tomorrow." She scoffs, ready to rip into me, but her mouth just hangs open when she sees the ring on my left hand, as I slide it around his bicep. "I'm meeting my husband for lunch."

Slipping his arm out of my hold, only to wrap it around my shoulders and pull me in closer, he gives Morgan a neutral look. And from Adrian? That's practically a death wish. "It's probably best if you take any further questions to Dr. Phillips or one of the other TAs."

Leaving *her* in embarrassment and shame for once, Adrian and I turn away, easily falling into step with each other. I hold it together long enough to round a corner out of the main walkway, before the adrenaline crashes, and the tears start.

"Come here, baby," Adrian murmurs and pulls me under a staircase. He usually only calls me baby during sex, though sometimes it slips out, in the moments I need the deepest comfort.

Falling into his embrace, I let the tears fall and focus on my breath. After a couple of minutes, Adrian uses the hand at the base of my neck to turn my eyes up to his. "What do you need?"

Closing my eyes, it pushes the last lingering tears over as Adrian gently wipes each one. "I don't know why I'm crying," I rasp in a small voice. Not sure why I say it. I *know* the exact reason.

Adrian does too because he tells me, "It's the adrenaline. That's all."

Nodding, I take a deep breath and try to articulate how I'm feeling. "Yeah, no. I know. I'm not even upset... I mean, it sucks to be reminded of those years." The word vomit starts, but Adrian just softly cups my neck and lets me work out my thoughts. "I think... for the first time, I understand what Catalina has been trying to help me see."

"What's that?" he quietly asks, leaning his forehead against mine.

"My life is going to be so much bigger than those years. Even just the last three months with you has made it feel almost unimportant. I'll always be who I am because of those years..." I trail off, scrunching my eyebrows and feeling like I'm not making sense.

"I want you to be who you are, and whoever that is tomorrow, and the next day."

Letting out a sigh of relief, I get to the point. "I'm not upset. I'm just tired. I'm ready to move on and really leave that part of my life behind."

A soft, proud gleam reaches his eyes. "You're going to make yourself the happiest girl in the world, and I'm here to love you through every second of it."

Smiling up at him, tears reach my eyes again, happy ones this time. "You'll have to change it to 'Sunshine soon.'"

"Nah," he disagrees and drops his hand to the silver charm I've worn every day since last December. He repeats the words he said to me the first afternoon we spent together, a little over a year ago now, "I've always liked rain more."

Epilogue

Adrian

Two years and six months later...

Stepping outside behind my dad and Tim, I breathe in the evening air. When I moved to Amada Beach four years ago, I never expected to love the town as much as I do. Nor did I expect for my life to play out the way it has.

But as I settle against the porch railing, I can't pull my eyes away from Blake. She's still inside, though I have a clear view of her in the living room. Our eighteen-month-old daughter Millie is rattling a toy and talking incoherently to her mom and her grandmothers. All of them look enthralled by the moment, especially Blake as she rubs her swollen belly.

She's eight months pregnant with our second child. A boy. Leo Michael Jones.

Truthfully, we haven't been as careful with protection since we got married. It's not that we *never* use it, but sometimes we're desperate, or crave that connection. So, neither of us are all that surprised that we're having our second child by the time I'm graduating with my Doctor of Veterinary Medicine degree. Blake has another year before she finishes her bachelor's in Community Health with a minor in Business Administration.

Both times we learned she was pregnant we had long conversations about what we wanted to do—what Blake wanted to do.

There was more consideration with the first pregnancy, but ultimately Blake was sure that she wanted to start our family. And even though I was terrified for a million reasons, there hasn't been a second of doubt since Blake and I got together. The blessing and support of our parents made a world of difference.

Her education was one of the biggest reasons I wanted to make sure that Blake understood I would support any decision we made, and we were partners in this like everything else. Although when Blake puts her mind to something, she dedicates everything she has to that. With a lot of help, a few summer courses, and a couple of half-semester ones, we made it work.

This time around, we'll have even more help. My mom has moved into an administrative role that allows her to work from home, and the online courses my dad instructs have always allowed him a lot of freedom to work from wherever. It's not permanent, but they have signed onto a six-month rental in a townhouse a couple blocks away from our small home.

There's been some hard moments throughout it, like Blake having to adjust to a new medication that she can take while she's pregnant, and my busier schedule recently. But I wouldn't change a minute of our lives together, and she swears by the same thought.

"How are you feeling?" Tim asks, pulling me from my thoughts and my attention from my wife.

I figured this is why they brought me out here, even if I don't know how to articulate everything that I'm feeling. "Overwhelmed, but in a good way." Glancing back through the window, I catch Blake's eye, and she offers me a small, proud smile. "Recently, a lot of the big milestones have been about Blake and me, together—getting married, moving in together, having two babies. And fuck, I love every second of it. But... but today is *my* accomplishment. Something I've been working on for years before I knew Blake, and the only other thing I feel dedicated to outside of my family. Maybe it's selfish, but it's a different feeling of accomplishment."

Clapping my shoulder, my dad says in a thick voice, "You should be proud, Adrian. Your mother and I are so very proud you're our son. You're building a beautiful life in Amada Beach, yet your individual accomplishments matter just as much. Don't forget that."

Nodding, I swallow the lump of emotions clogging my throat and try to find the words to thank him for everything he's done for me in my life. I'm not blind to the fact that he and my mother worked their asses off to build a life where I didn't have to worry about money. I've been blessed to have their emotional, and financial, support throughout every step in my life. And regardless of the small inheritance Blake has, she's aware of everything my parents have offered us.

And all I can do is work to create the same life for my kids—one of stability, love, and comfort.

His eyes brim with tears and I know that there aren't any more words we need to share. I take after my mom's personality, though I've never needed my father's words to know how much he cares about me. He shows it to my mom, and me, in a hundred other ways.

Clearing his throat, Tim takes a tentative step forward, seeming to not want to interrupt the moment. But my dad steps to my side and opens space for him.

Over the years, Tim and I have grown closer. Both as family, and also professionally. Even when I had to quit my vet assistant position in the last two years of my program, he supported me, offering advice all the same.

And we haven't talked about it recently, still I have an idea of what he's going to bring up.

"I'm also proud, Adrian," Tim starts. "To have you as a son-in-law and to watch the exceptional veterinarian you're going to become. And I agree with Will. Be proud of your accomplishments because I promise that your family is."

"Thank you, Tim. For everything over the last four years." Taking in his features—so similar to Blake's in a lot of ways—I note the paternal affection in his eyes that goes deeper than me being married to his daughter. "You changed my life when you offered me that job. I had no idea how much at the time."

He shakes his head, though it's more in a speechless way than disagreement. "You changed ours too, Adrian. Especially my daughter's."

Smiling, that brings a new spark of life to my heart. Blake's bloomed in the last few years, but I don't want to take any credit for that.

"I know your exam is coming up soon, and I have all the faith in you to pass it."

"Thanks." The word comes out thick and full of emotion. I've never craved the approval of another man before—outside of my father and grandfathers. From my first day of training under Tim, that changed. I wanted him to see me as a competent employee with a lot of potential. As time has gone on, I've looked for his approval in more ways than just professionally.

And I think I have it from him.

With an almost shy smile, he rubs a hand down the back of his neck. "I know we've talked about you working at the vet clinic as soon as you graduated but..." My brows furrow and my heart drops. It doesn't make sense for him to rescind his job offer, especially when Blake and I have plans for the outreach program starting in the next couple of years.

"But," he continues, "I want you to know you have options. You aren't on a time limit, and that position will always be available for you. This is a really exciting and new time for you, Adrian. I encourage you to consider an internship and residency if you feel so inclined."

"Oh," I breathe out. In the last year, I had started to think more about a surgical residency. Tim is an amazing veterinarian, and focuses primarily on patients who need intensive surgeries, leaving the less complicated procedures to some of the other veterinarians. However, we both know he can't offer me that.

"Look, Adrian," he lowers his voice in that way he does when he wants you to *hear* what he's saying. "I know you and Blake have amazing plans for the outreach program, and I'm so proud to be a part of that with you two. Blake's goals don't have to be your only goals.

"So, if there's something you want to explore or study, do it now. Blake has the support she needs to get things in order after she graduates. I've hired staff in the last couple of years with her future needs in mind, and Olivia's really stepped up to help Blake, as you know. We will always be waiting with open arms, and a white coat for you, son, so chase *your* dreams first. Hear me?"

It's not the first time Tim's called me son, but it's rare, nonetheless. Glancing at my dad, I note the appreciative smile he offers Tim before turning to look at me. I've mentioned the idea of a residency to Blake a couple of times, and of course she's been supportive—encouraging me to do this for myself.

Honestly, it's my dad who I've opened up to about this the most. He knows my fears—missing my opportunity to work under Tim—and where my guilt lies—taking on another educational pursuit when we're expecting our second child. But the small nod he gives reminds me of everything else we've talked about.

How much help Blake and I have from our families. How I can't lose myself in being a husband, or father, because Adrian Jones the man, is just as important as those roles.

How being the best version of myself is the best thing I can be for my family.

Clearing my throat, I glance at the living room window again. Blake's eyes are on me still. She tilts her head in a silent question, and I offer her a small, tentative smile. Her lightning eyes move from my father to hers and back to me. After years together, she can practically read my mind by now. So, the nod she gives me is enough, before turning back to the conversation around her, giving us privacy out here.

"Actually..." I turn toward Tim and square my shoulders. "I've been thinking about that for a while. And I wasn't sure, because everything you, Blake and I have planned means so much to me. But I think—no, I *know* I want to join a residency program. One of the doctors I worked under during clinicals works at the animal hospital in Aurora Hills, and they have a great surgical program."

Tim grins. "That's an amazing facility, and the few people I know there are great at what they do."

"I've heard. So, I'm planning on applying for that after I finish my exams." Most of the time, an internship is a requirement for a residency. After briefly speaking with Dr. Forrester at Aurora Hills Animal Hospital, and with my advisor extensively, I should have gained enough experience to bypass that year. But even if I need that additional year, I'll still be done with my residency a year before Blake is set to launch the program. And I want to be right there with her for that.

His lips tug even further up, matching the energy of my dad next to me. Pulling me into a hug, Tim tells me, "Let me know when you need a letter of recommendation."

Smiling and nodding at him, a weight lifts off my chest, and I know I've made the right choice. More than that, I know Blake and I will get everything we want from life with the people we're lucky enough to know.

After another couple of minutes of talking, I find a lull in conversation and slip back inside. As soon as the sliding door opens, Blake and Millie's heads turn in my direction from the kitchen island.

Everyone inside has moved to the kitchen now. Selena and my mom are getting another glass of wine and preparing dessert—berry cheesecake with chocolate sauce, Blake's favorite. Sweets in general aren't my favorite, though I find myself eating them a lot more since I met Blake. Millie's taking after her mom in that way though.

Walking up behind her, I wrap my arms around Blake's shoulders and place a soft kiss on her head. Millie's sitting on the counter in front of her, playing with an edible slime Selena makes for her sometimes. She does well at not eating it, yet she stays entertained for hours.

Maria and Bonnie walk back inside at the same time our dads do. They had gone to Bonnie's for a couple minutes, having bonded over gardening and become good friends in the last few years. By this point, everyone knows Maria's a lesbian. She was dating a woman for about two years until they recently broke up. Not that I'd ever ask, I'm not sure how interested Bonnie is in Maria. I can't help but notice there are hints of something *more*.

Taking a look around, almost everyone that we care about is here, celebrating my graduation.

Grady couldn't make it, but he's been more distant lately. It hurts Blake. Though outside of Catalina and me, she doesn't talk about it much.

Over the years, Jatin and I have stayed close. It's been nice having a friend to go through the program with. He's planning on moving to New York City to be with his siblings. I'm not worried about our friendship. Blake's still best friends with Margo and Meera. The former is on a family vacation in Europe, and the latter is celebrating her brother's graduation with their family. We have plans to celebrate over dinner when Margo gets back into town. It'll be our typical group of friends—Jatin, Dev, his fiancée Lina, Meera, her boyfriend of about a year Zane, Margo, Blake, and me.

For a while, Blake was worried about Margo feeling left out, or rejected by Jatin, with everyone else paired up. But after our winter trip to Durango, she's starting to see what I always did. Jatin's growing interest in Margo and the real chance she has.

It's been a good few years.

Blake's hands grab onto my forearms, pulling me closer to her back. Her familiar fresh melon scent envelopes me as I get lost in the chatter of our family, and the sight of my daughter giggling in excitement. One of my hands drops to Blake's belly the same moment our son kicks, causing her to slightly flinch, but smiling up at me all the same.

And I know it'll be an even better life.

Blake

Four more years later...

Standing next to my brother, I take in the sight before me, tears in my eyes.

It's been about seven and a half years since Adrian, and I first talked about the possibility of opening this program to help pet owners and animals in the area. From that day in his old apartment, it feels like time has sped up. More than my professional future changed that day—like my relationship with Adrian, which has brought us seven years of marriage and three children. Our youngest and last child, Kayson, is a little over a year and a half now.

He wraps an arm around my shoulder and asks, "So, how are you feeling?"

Looking up at him, a peace settles over me. It's been about three weeks since Grady moved back to Amada Beach with his two daughters. He and Arielle separated when their youngest daughter Daisy was three. I know he has mixed feelings on the situation, even if he won't talk about it. He's lighter in some ways, and the happiness of being back in our hometown is apparent. But I see the way he looks at our parents, or Adrian and me.

It makes me feel a little guilty to be so happy that he's permanently back in town. Though it doesn't change the fact that I am. Our kids get to grow up together. They get the same sense of camaraderie we had with the Davies siblings, despite our mostly estranged relationships with them now.

All five of the kids—my three and Grady's two—are with my mom and Cami today. Adrian's dad and Maria are volunteering in the registration tent, along with our friends. Jatin included since he isn't licensed in California. But now that Margo has had him wrapped around her finger for about two years, I know he prefers being with her when it's possible. He's the oldest of the Iyer siblings, and the last to get married, though everyone's parents are very excited about their families joining in the future.

"I'm overwhelmed," I admit. "What if it fails? What if it ruins our dad's business? What if—"

Shaking his head, he turns toward me and grabs me by the shoulders. He's less than half a foot taller than me, but he leans down to look me in the eye all the same.

"No, kid." The last time he called me that was when I gave birth to Millie. In a lot of ways, I appreciated that he dropped the nickname. It felt like he was starting to see me as more than someone he has to take care of. But at this moment, it's a comfort I didn't know I needed.

"You've put too much into this," he continues. "You have every ounce of Dad's support in this. You have an amazing team who has dedicated the last three years to this and so much family that loves you. Not to mention, a husband who would never let you not reach your dreams. But more than anything, you have the heart, and the brains, for this."

Feeling like a young girl afraid of rejection and disappointment again, I quietly ask, "Do you mean that?"

"Yes, with everything I have. I believe in you, Blake."

Stepping back, he sweeps an arm out to the side. My eyes follow the movement and take in the large tents that cover the clinic's parking lot. Part of them will be used for check-in, and the other half will be used for routine exams and vaccinations. The scheduled surgeries we have for the day, including room for limited walk-ins, will be handled inside as usual. We have the full staff volunteering, as well as staff from Aurora Hills Animal Hospital and another clinic in San Diego.

And with the budget we've worked out through grants, donations, and fundraising, it's more than I ever could've dreamed that night on Adrian's old leather couch.

"This is just the beginning," Grady promises.

Smiling, I look at him from the corner of my eye.

I don't see Catalina anymore. It depends on what I need at different times, but I'm still on my medication and I've started to see another therapist. A couple of years ago, she suggested it was time. That we'd gotten to a point in our professional relationship that had sort of met its peak. It took me a while to understand that without feeling rejected or dismissed, and I've talked about it with my new therapist.

But Grady's sentiment reminds me of her, sending a wave of comfort through me.

Catalina promised that my life was just beginning, that there was so much *good* to come, and that I had no idea.

And... she was right. I'm confident in saying she'd be proud of me today.

"You're right," I tell my brother.

Nodding toward one of the registration tables, he takes a step in that direction. "I'm going to talk to Olivia and see where she wants me to help up here. However, in case you didn't get the memo, I'm proud of you, Blake."

Rolling my eyes, I turn to walk inside, instead coming face to face with Adrian.

He's a few feet away, leaning against the front door's frame with his hands in his pockets, and that goddamn perfect grin of his.

He's as handsome as ever. Maybe more so since time has only been in his favor. Some of his boyish features have faded. His round face has sharpened slightly into a more defined jaw and cheekbones. But his deep dimples and affectionate gaze are the same as seven years ago.

Taking a step in his direction, I watch how he takes in my body every second of the way. When he runs a hand over his buzzed hair, and down the back of his neck, it never fails to send a thrill through me. He has this ability to make me feel like I'm getting more beautiful by the day too.

"Hey, pretty girl," he greets in a low voice and wraps an arm around my waist.

Leaning on my toes, I press our lips together, knowing we're going to be busy for the rest of the day. "Hey, love you."

Pulling me in for one more long, but chaste kiss, he murmurs against my lips, "Love you. And I'm so fucking proud of you."

Falling on my heels, I tilt my head and let my gaze move affectionately over him. "Don't fight me on it, but I couldn't have done this without you."

He squints his eyes and shakes his head as he smiles and doesn't argue with me.

I mean it though. Deep in my soul, I know it's true and he does too. Maybe our lives would've been happy, but it wouldn't be *this* life.

And I wouldn't want any other alternative because it couldn't be better than ours.

Bonus Chapter:
Starting Their Family

Blake

One year and a month after the wedding...

Leaning back in the hospital bed, I hold my breath and wait for the first cry out of our baby's mouth. Adrian's arm is gently wrapped around my shoulders as his hand brushes sweat slick hair off my forehead, exactly as he has been since I went into labor twelve hours ago, not including the time I was pushing.

Everything and everyone is moving so quickly around me. It's probably only been about five seconds since the doctor passed her off—beautiful regardless of the blood and everything else on her—to check on me but it feels like an eternity while one nurse works on wiping off her nose and mouth as the other clamps the umbilical cord. I watch as the nurse takes the little rag to her nose and at the same second, the most precious high pitched wail breaks out of our baby.

Immediately, before I can even process what all is going on, I turn my head into Adrian's chest and start to sob. His arms tighten around me—not too much, he's still aware of what my body just went through—and whispers, "You did so good, Storm Cloud." Pulling away to hold my cheeks and look me in the eyes, he tells me with a voice thick of love and appreciation, "Thank you for starting our family, Blake.

You've given me so much already but *her*, our child—that's the best gift I've ever received. Especially knowing she comes from the strongest, most beautiful momma a girl could ever want."

"I love you," I declare quietly, pulling him in for a soft kiss by his shirt until Nurse Pam walks over with an already calmed down, cleaned off baby girl and asks if we want to do skin on skin contact first. Nodding, I open my arms and let Pam settle her on my chest, reveling in the feeling of her soft, slightly still gooey skin and the small but mighty rise and fall of her body with each passing breath. By this point, words are beyond me so I just stare down at her with tears in my eyes and a heart so full of love, I don't know how it won't burst.

"I didn't know I could love anything this much... this *fiercely*," I whisper just for her, even though Adrian can hear every word from my side. "You've already made my life so much brighter, I can only hope to fill yours with a lifetime of happiness and love, mi ciela." *My darling.*

We lay there for about ten minutes, Adrian hovering protectively over us, running his fingers along her tiny features while his other stays on the base of my neck. Looking up at him, I ask, "Do you want to hold her?"

"I will, but I know this part was important to you, storm cloud."

Before I can open my mouth, Pam is walking back into the room after letting our waiting families know that we both are well and healthy. I considered letting my mom in the room while I gave birth but I wanted this moment for Adrian and I, and our now growing family.

"It's good to do skin on skin with the father as well," Pam tells us with a soft tilt of her lips. "It helps with their immune systems and neural development, but also, mom's just love to watch."

"It does sound pretty adorable," I lovingly tease but Adrian's already pulling his t-shirt off and dragging a chair closer to the bed. I let my eyes fall down his chest and torso, taking in the hard, toned muscles leading down to the small patch of hair above the waistband of his pants. He flashes me a quick smile—one full of love *and* desire—with a wink as he falls into the seat next to me.

Helping Adrian get settled so I don't have to move too much, Pam tells us that she told my parents to give us thirty minutes to ourselves but they're already getting antsy. I chuckle and thank her, but my eyes are glued on my husband and the beautiful girl curled up on his chest.

Pam was right, I fucking love the sight before me.

She isn't sleeping, just making little smacking noises with her lips that are nearly inaudible in the now quiet room. Her eyes are flitting around but keep landing on Adrian's face. Maybe it's only because it's the closest thing to her and her eyesight will develop over time but I like to think it's because she knows who he is—her dad, her protector, the best man to have in your corner. And I can say that last part with all the confidence in the world.

"It's only the beginning for us, pretty girl," Adrian murmurs when he places a light kiss on her soft head but his gaze is on me. It's the same sentiment he shared with me—whispered against my lips as a promise just for me—after he kissed me in the courthouse and we were stepping into the next chapter of our lives together.

About an hour later, our families make their way into the room. It's a small gathering—just my parents, Adrian's parents, and Grady with Stella. Arielle stayed back in Phoenix. Despite the small progress we've made in the last two years,

I'm not that upset that she isn't here. It feels right with the seven people who are now crowding around us.

"Morrita," my mom sighs at the sight of me, coming straight to hug me and plant a kiss on my forehead. "How did it all go? You're okay? No complications?" She sprouts off questions too quickly to even answer. With a gentle hand around her waist, my dad pulls her back to his chest and grabs my hand.

"You're a very strong, young woman, Blake," my dad tells me, his voice cracking with emotions.

"She really is," Cami agrees from over Adrian's shoulder, a tear sliding down her cheek.

"Dios mio," my mom gasps when her eyes finally move from her baby girl to mine, happily nestled in her dad's arms. Adrian carefully stands and rounds the bed to gently set her in my mom's arms before going to his parents, wrapping their arms around him, watching from the other side of the bed.

My brother comes to the space Adrian left and places a hand on my head, gently tipping it back to look into his warm brown eyes—the same shade of golden brown as our dad but every other feature of his is reminiscent of our mothers, with his light golden brown skin and short mocha curls. "You're going to be the best mom there ever was, kid."

My lip starts to tremble as I let his words fall over me. "I hope so," I whisper to him like a secret, one I wouldn't admit to most people, but I will with him. I'm *scared*.

"I know so." He gives a soft nod of resolution before shifting Stella who is slowly waking from a nap on his shoulder. Her head shyly peaks around the room until she sees me.

"Aunnie," she perks up and reaches for me. She only knows about five words so far but the fact that '*auntie*' is one of them always sends a wave of affection right through me.

"Hi, little lady," I murmur and reach up to run my hand along her head. "You'll always be my first girl." I wink at her, causing her to giggle as if she understands my words. In her heart and soul, maybe she does.

"Aunnie!" She yells, trying to crawl out of Grady's arms to get to me. He pulls her back and whispers in her ear, probably trying to get her to settle but she just looks at me with big pleading eyes. "*Aunnie*," she whimpers with tears in her eyes.

Grady and I look at each other, a rueful smile tugging on his lips.

"Come sit with me, Stell." I scoot over, giving her some room, and Adrian's immediately at my side again, helping me to get rearranged before Grady sets his daughter on the bed next to me.

The baby has made her way around the room, everyone having held her except for Grady, so far. At this second, she's in my dad's arms and I watch him as he watches her, gently rocking her in a similar fashion I can faintly remember from when I was just a little girl and those very arms were the safest place I could've ever imagined to be.

His brown eyes meet my gray ones—and just like Grady getting all of his features from my mom, mine mostly came from my dad with the one stormy exception. But my ivory skin that burns way too easily and my raven black hair that creates a stark contrast are all him. Maybe some little girls don't want to be their dad's twin, but I've always loved it.

And the little girl cuddling up with him very well may be a little copy of her own father as well. With her thin layer of dark brown almost black hair that already lays in waves and slight curls atop her head and her warm brown complexion. I hope she loves it just as much as I do—those physical traits that tie us both to the very men who have sworn a sacred oath to love us through every day of our lives.

"We picked a name," I tell the room but really I'm only talking to my father. His lips tilt up, but he patiently waits for the big reveal. Adrian already told his parents, so it won't be a surprise to them. "Her name is Millie. Millie Rae Jones."

Her middle and last name will always tie her to Adrian's family, to our home, to half the people who love her with their entire beings. But her first name? *That* will always tie her to him, to them—my parents and brother. To me and where I came from, not only where I'm going.

Grady wraps an arm around my mom, who for once in her life is actually speechless, and guides her a foot or so to the side, giving this moment to our dad and me.

With Millie in one arm, his other hand falls to my head in a loving fashion similar to what Grady did. His eyes are brimming with tears, but I swallow the lump in my own throat and tell him, "I've spent my entire life being so proud of being a Miller. And I just want her to have an ounce of that with her throughout her life."

"It's perfect, honey," he whispers and lays a kiss on my head. "I'm so proud of you and the woman you've become. I can't take credit for that."

"You can, though," I rasp.

He shakes his head. "We've guided and raised you—but who you are, at your core, Blake, that's all you. And it's been one of the greatest gifts of my life to watch it. I can't wait to do it all over."

A sob breaks through but it's one of love and happiness. And even some of that pesky, contagious hope I've gotten from Adrian over the last year and a half.

Adrian

One year later...

Lazily, I lean back in bed and scroll through emails on my phone. Blake went to take a shower while I put Millie down for bed. My precious girl was tired after a day at the aquarium. She already loves animals, like me. And even though she doesn't love water like Blake, she has started to associate it with her mom after countless afternoons where I take her to watch Blake teach beginning swim classes.

She's only been doing it for about five months, since she ran into her coach—the one from before she went to SPA. Denise was leaving the gym when Blake was getting there, and after a few minutes of talking, she told Blake that she's looking for an assistant. She wasn't sure about taking on another responsibility, but I could see how much she wanted to connect with this side of her again, in a whole new way.

Of course, my pretty girl is taking it in stride like she does everything else.

Speaking of the beautiful angel of my life, she comes out of the bathroom—her raven black hair is wet and loose down her back, her face make-up free, and she's in one of the short little spaghetti strap sleep dresses she's taken a liking to since she was about seven months pregnant with Millie. If anything took a hit during her pregnancy, it was the capacity of her bladder. She'd always been a simple pair of panties and t-shirt kinda girl, but this was easier when she was getting up more throughout the night.

Can't say I mind as she walks to me, easily settling her weight on my legs and straddles me—especially because I know she's taken a liking to not wearing panties to bed even if she doesn't need the restroom nearly as often.

"Hi, pretty girl," I murmur as I lean forward and place a kiss on her collarbone, my hands instinctively finding their place on her thighs. It doesn't go unnoticed that even though she's on top of me, she isn't *touching* me. After her initial insecurities, she's become as needy for my touch as I am for hers.

Now that I notice it, her hands are behind her back. Given the fact that neither of us are into bondage or anything similar, I'm not sure what she's doing—or hiding. Meeting her gaze, she looks nervous though.

After the nearly perfect day we had as a family, I can't imagine what's wrong. I say nearly perfect because she was feeling nauseous for part of the day. It's happened a few times in the last week or so, now that I think about it...

"Adrian," she starts, pulling me from my thoughts. The dots are starting to connect but from the quiet excitement in her eyes, I have an idea what she's going to say.

"Blake," I answer cautiously, not wanting to get my hopes up for an assumption.

She bites her lips and twists her hands behind her back. "I have something to tell you."

My heart rate picks up, and I'm not sure if it's excitement or fear. Maybe a mix of both—just like last time. "Whatever it is, you know I've got you."

She smiles, and the sincerity of it calms some of my nerves. Looking at me with vulnerability, she moves her arms from behind her back but doesn't say anything. Based on the long, thin shape, I know exactly what it is before she unwraps the toilet paper.

Once she does, there it is. A positive pregnancy test.

Staring for a few seconds, I slowly look up at her. For once, I'm unsure how to read her expression. There's clearly excitement but it's tampered down by some sort of uncertainty.

We've never talked about having more kids in absolutes or with a concrete plan. However, that doesn't mean we don't talk about it.

We actually do—often. It hasn't always been easy, considering we're both going to school and working part-time. Having financial help from my parents, plus child-care help from Blake's parents and half of Amada Beach, does make a difference though. We both know we're lucky in a way that most people our age aren't, and neither of us take that for granted.

Just like Millie's conception, this isn't something we planned. Though we weren't nearly as careful as we could have been in the months following. We haven't used a condom since we found out she was pregnant a little over two years ago, though we do our best to track her period. It's not foolproof, and we both know that. It's one of those conversations that have been avoided in the grand scheme of life.

And, we both enjoy the intimacy of not having a barrier between us.

"I'm pregnant," she finally says. The obviousness of her statement makes me smile.

Nodding toward the test, I quietly tell her, "I can see that." Sliding my hands to the back of her thighs, squeezing where her knee bends, I ask, "How are you feeling about that?"

She bites her lip for half a second, before answering, "*Happy*. Excited. But scared you aren't feeling that."

Letting my hands run up her legs to the crease of her thighs, I shake my head at a loss for words. "All I want is to continue building our life and family together. I don't care what that timeline looks like, or if it isn't the most traditional route. That's never been out pace."

"That's true." She smiles and runs a finger across my chest in light patterns. "I want this, if you do."

"Storm Cloud," I murmur, gently pushing her chin up until she's looking at me, "the biggest factor here is if *you* want to do this again."

"You know I do," she insists.

"Sure, eventually," I remind her. "Millie's an angel, but she's still an infant." One who can't seem to sleep through the night—she is the lightest sleeper known to man. We have offered to pay people to stay right where they are if she falls asleep in their arms. No one has agreed to take the money, probably from our sheer desperation. But it's why I want to make sure that Blake doesn't have any doubts.

"Honestly, I've been thinking about what I want to do for the last week." My brows scrunch in confusion, wondering why she wouldn't tell me for so long, but she quickly adds, "I didn't take a test, I promise. There were signs though... I've been nauseous for the last two weeks, plus my boobs have been so sensitive."

That I've noticed. She came from me playing with her nipples two nights ago, and that's extremely uncommon for Blake. I just can't believe I didn't notice there was more going on.

"I'm not supposed to start my period for a few more days, but I figured I should make sure now."

Running my hand down her wet hair and settling it on her lower back, I admit, "I'm glad you did, and that you aren't hiding it from me."

She smiles softly. "I never would. It's just, I wasn't sure how I felt about it at first. But as the week went on, I got more excited at the thought of having another child, especially while Millie's so young." That doesn't surprise me. Blake loved being pregnant, and once she managed her new medication, it was relatively easy nine months. Her doctor jokes that it's in large part due to all the time she spends in the water.

"What if I decide to join a residency program?" Nothing has been decided but it's something I consider often, talking to Blake and my dad about it multiple times a month. "It doesn't change my mind at all, but I want our expectations to be realistic."

Nodding, she runs her fingers in soft patterns along my skin. "I agree, and that was my biggest hesitation as well. But the timeline seems pretty perfect, all things considered. He'd be born after you graduate, so I'd have the summer off, and a program wouldn't start immediately." There's also a licensure exam I have to pass but we both know that, so I don't mention it. "And between my mom and Bonnie's help, and the discounted child-care through the university, I can't think of any reason why we shouldn't do this. Unless you aren't ready for us to have another baby."

"Pretty girl," I murmur, "You don't have to convince me."

She nods her head and quietly tells me, "It's my body, but *our* family. I know you'd respect any decision I make, but it's important to me that you know I respect and hear you too."

"Never doubted that, but I appreciate the reminder." Grinning down at her, I can't help but admire her natural, ethereal beauty. Her lightning-silver eyes still captivate me as much as they did the first night at the grocery store. Needing her closer, always, my hands smooth down her silky nightdress and slip underneath. The surprised gasp turns into an appreciative moan when I grab her by the ass and pull her further up my body.

Catching herself with her hands on my shoulders, she leans back with a mischievous glint in her eye. Her pussy's perfectly positioned over my covered cock. Not only can I feel her wetness through my briefs, but her pajamas slide up over her hips when she spread her legs to fit our new position. I hold her still for a second, needing to make my stance on this clear.

"You and Millie are the best things to ever happen to me, why wouldn't I think this baby would be too?" Her smile grows from lust to affection. "We're having this baby."

She leans forward and kisses me passionately, wasting no time by slipping her tongue into my mouth. One hand slides from her ass to her inner thigh, lifting her weight enough to quickly push my boxer-briefs down. Breaking the kiss to look down, Blake wraps her small, soft hand around my length and gives it one firm tug—just the way I like it.

"I love you, Adrian," she whispers against my lips. "And I love our family."

"Me too, baby. It's only the start," I promise, knowing we both ideally want four kids.

My free hand lightly traces the contours of her arm and shoulder, before slipping one of the thin straps off of her shoulder. Her breathing grows more labored, and she positions the tip of my cock at her slit, rocking her hips to tease me with her wet heat. I watch as she bites her lip and gently pushes the other side down, letting the dress fall around her waist.

Our eyes lock for short moment before I grip her hip and push her down onto my cock. Only a couple of inches, knowing she'll prefer time to adjust since we didn't have any foreplay. Her head falls back on a low, needy moan and I take the opportunity to lean forward and suck one of her nipples into my mouth.

"Oh my God," she whimpers, pulling me closer by the nape of my neck. I'm more gentle than usual, not wanting to pleasure to turn into any sort of uncomfortableness. Lowering herself further and rocking her hips, she breathes out, "Just like that, baby."

Groaning in confirmation, I kiss across the valley between her breasts and take the opposite rosy bud into my mouth.

Outside of the obvious excitement, there are a few things that I'm selfishly looking forward to. Like getting to come inside my wife anytime I want, without having to worry or plan in advance. Never thought I had a breeding kink until I got Blake pregnant the first time—it unlocked something primal in me that I've only ever felt with her.

"Take all of me, pretty girl," I demand against her skin. "I know you can."

With a quick nod, she lets her head fall back and she slides down my cock, stopping once I'm fully seated inside her tight pussy. Groaning at the same time, she tries to catch her breath while she adjusts to my thickness. Before she can, I grab the globes of her ass and pull her to the tip, letting her take every inch of me again.

"If you're going to be on top, baby," I tease, swiping my fingers throw her wetness before using them to toy with her sensitive nipples again. "You're going to have to do some of the work."

She gives me a scowl that's short-lived as she starts to rock her hips. The most she tries to take control of the situation, the more I play with her rosy buds, eventually bringing my other hand to tease her clit. It's not fair, knowing how sensitive she is, but I really don't give a fuck.

I don't want Blake's focus to be on pleasuring me tonight, not when she's given me some of the best news of my life for a second time.

When her body tenses up and she digs her fingers into my pecs, an orgasm building, I quickly pull her weight off of me and flip us around.

"Adrian, what the *fuck*?" She cries out. Not fighting my chuckle, I lean down to place a soft kiss on her lips before I pull back to realign myself with her.

But the sight of her pretty, pink pussy—so wet and needy from the orgasm I took away from her—makes me want a taste of her. Without another thought, I roughly settle her legs over my shoulders and bend down to meet her arousal. My tongue laps at her wetness, focusing on the warm, tight slit rather than her clit. I'm feeling greedy enough right now to want her pleasure mixed with mine when we come.

Edging isn't something we do often, but it's more fun when she's this sensitive to every little touch and sensation.

"Mmm, *Adrian*," she whimpers while thrusting her hips off the bed, trying to push them further toward me. This time when she calls out my name, it's full of desire and affection.

Enjoying the sweet, musky flavor of her for a few more minutes, I reluctantly pull myself away. It's only enjoyable for Blake up to a certain point, and I'm aware of that.

And the quiet, desperation in her voice when she tells me, "I need you," as I'm lining my tip up with her entrance, clues me in to where she's at. Without wasting more time, I push into her in one, slow thrust and keep that rhythm for a few seconds. Her legs, still hanging over my shoulders, shake with each long pump of my cock and I know there's no fighting her orgasm anymore.

Leaning forward—basically folding her in half and knowing this is one position we won't be doing soon—I move my hips faster and take her mouth in a deep, raw kiss. One of her hands moves to the back of my neck, and she holds me there as she sucks the taste of herself off my tongue. The sensation is overwhelming, pushing me right into my own pleasure.

My thrusts grow a little rougher, a little more frantic, while the heat shoots through my body and my sac begins to tighten. "Fuck, baby, I'm going to come."

She opens her mouth to say something, but the words are caught in her throat, turning into a loud moan that she quickly covers with her free hand. The sound alone is enough for me to know she's right there with me, but it's the way her pussy tightens around me, making it almost impossible to pump my hips, which does me in.

"Fuck, *fuck*, Blake," I let out in a gravelly tone as I fill her up, making sure every last drop is spent inside her. "Fuck. I love you," I breathe out, dropping some of my weight onto her.

Easily, she untangles her legs and loosely wraps them around my waist, not ready to break the connection yet. She places a few kiss along my neck and jaw, murmuring, "I love you," in between each one.

We stay just like that for about five minutes before I gently pull out of her and lay her back down when she tries to follow me to the bathroom. "Stay there," I softly demand. "I'll be right back."

She silently smiles and falls onto her back, her body still limp and satiated from a few minutes ago. It takes me only a minute to warm up the water and get a cloth to clean us both up. It doesn't matter how many times Blake and I have had sex, or that I've given her after care. It always feels like a sacred experience we share together. After I'm done wiping the mess between her thighs, she rolls up to sit before I can stop her.

"We need to change the sheets," she admits with a laugh.

Glancing down, I realize she's right at the same second Millie starts crying. Our heads swing toward each other, and I nod in the direction of our daughter. "Why don't you go get her while I change the sheets? She can lay with us for a while."

Smiling, Blake hops off the bed, stopping to place a kiss on my jaw before grabbing her dress, and leaves the room. Watching the spot she just disappeared, I rub a hand on my chest and let the giddy grin finally take over my features.

I can't wait to do this again with her.

Blake

Three years and five months later...

Waddling down the long hallway, I make my way from the master bedroom to the room closest to the living room. I can hear soft giggles and Adrian quietly murmuring warnings to not make too much noise so I can rest.

Except I'm so fucking tired of resting. I've been put on bedrest for the last two and a half months, and it's been miserable. Millie and Leo have done their best to understand why I can't play and do as much for them as usual. But it's never easy for a five-year-old and almost three-year-old to understand big changes, especially when it's all mixed into a really exciting one—like having a new little brother.

My doctors were worried about my blood-pressure when I was pregnant with Leo a few years ago, but other than a C-section, I got lucky with how smoothly the birth went. Both he and I were healthy, even if the hormone changes hit me even harder that time around. Thankfully, we were able to buy our house about six months into that pregnancy, so

Cami is planning on staying a few weeks after I give birth to help. Last time, they rented a house in Amada Beach for a few months, but they aren't ready to officially sell their home in Bakersfield either. Truthfully, I don't think Adrian's excited by the idea either.

He's stepped up to juggle more of the responsibilities in the home, even while he was finishing his residency. Between his parents, the small inheritance from my paternal grandparents, and our even smaller saving account, we were able to get by with only me working part-time, after a few months of maternal leave. It wasn't always easy, but we made it work how we always had—a lot of open conversations and understanding what we were able to realistically give each other during that time.

There hasn't been a day that passed where I'm not thankful for Adrian, or where I'm not falling more in love with him.

He's everything I could've dreamed of in a partner, and more than that, in the father of my children. But his unwavering love and support during every chapter of our lives so far is something I will never take for granted.

This time around, Adrian is working as a licensed veterinarian at the clinic, after finishing the surgical residency at Aurora Hills Animal Hospital a couple of months ago. So, we're extremely lucky that he has more flexibility right now than anyone else would have in this field and some of the best health insurance.

As long as I can manage my blood-pressure and stress for the next couple of weeks, the doctors aren't worried. The fact we've gotten to thirty-six weeks without any major complications is the important thing to focus on, or so everyone tries to tell me. It's not easy to remind myself of that when I'm growing a baby inside of me, and my anxiety naturally causes me to spiral at any little hiccup. My doctor probably expected me to call less often with questions and concerns after Millie was born, but if anything, it's gotten worse with each one.

Truthfully, I'm torn on how I feel. Part of me is ready to get this baby out of there, so I can meet him and love him and just hold him after everything we've already been through together. But another, very large, part of me knows that this will be the last time I can carry pregnancy.

Adrian and I *always* talked about having four kids. I don't know why, but six felt like the right number for us. We've talked about the reality of our situation, and sure, blood pressure can be managed. I'm lucky that it hasn't developed into anything more serious, like preeclampsia, but it's not worth the risk going forward, especially when I have the most loving husband and two—soon to be three—perfect little munchkins who all depend on me. Nothing is worth risking that, and I know he feels the same way.

Finally making it to the open door, I quietly push it further and lean against the door frame. Adrian will insist that I sit down once he notices me standing here and Leo will want to crawl right in my lap while Millie shows me all the ways she's being the helpful big sister. But for a few seconds, I just want to watch them—my whole world and heart—as they get Kayson's nursery together.

With so much going on, we've pushed it off until the last minute, but we've always used a small crib in our room for the first few months too, just to make the adjustment easier. So we have time.

And Adrian hasn't been in a rush. Instead he's taken on the project at a snail's pace, if only so he can include Millie and Leo in every step of the process. They chose a jungle theme for Kayson—we landed on the name about a month ago. So Adrian and I went with light wooden furniture, green walls, a wall decorated with cartoon animal prints and an oversized leaf-print armchair that has enough room for Millie and Leo to snuggle in around me or Adrian.

Even with just the armchair in the middle, the crib half assembled in a corner and one wall still unpainted, it feels cozy and inviting somehow. And it's not too far off from Millie's flower power themed room, or Leo's prehistoric vibes.

A quiet grunt rips out of me when a sharp pain stabs my lower back, pulling all three of their attentions my way.

"Mama!" Leo shouts and runs to me with arms opened wide. Before he can crash into me, Adrian takes a couple quick strides and lifts him off the ground. Leo's giggling in his arms but cries out again, "Mama!"

"Your mama's gotta sit down before she can hold you, remember, lil guy?" Leo huffs in impatience but nods in understanding anyway. "And no crawling on her, okay? Gentle touches only."

Leo bobs his head again, but I can't help the laugh that flits out of me. Trying to explain to a toddler that his mom isn't his own personal jungle gym hasn't been the easiest feat, to say the least.

Slowly, I lower myself onto the big chair, smiling at Millie when she pushes the ottoman closer so I can settle my legs on it. "Gracias, mi ciela," I tell her. "Do you want to come sit with us?"

"No, I'm helping Dad." She says it so matter-of-factly you'd almost forget that she's only five. She takes her role as an older sister very seriously though, wanting to shower both of her brothers in affection and gifts whenever she can. "He says we should be done painting today! Then I can help him put all the furniture together."

"Mama! I sit with you," Leo grumbles as he pulls himself up on the chair next to me. I can't offer much help right now but at almost three, he's a little daredevil so he wouldn't want it anyway. But still, Adrian stays nearby until he's turned around and snuggled under my arm. He lets out a big yawn and immediately starts to tear up, fighting his own sleepiness. He has the opposite problem of Millie, who still struggles to sleep through the night. This little guy could take five naps a day and still get a sold nine hours of sleep. He hates missing out on anything though.

"Shhh, cariño. Todos estamos aqui contigo," I reassure him. *Shhh, dear. We're all here with you.*

He's picking up the language easier than Millie—half of his first words have been in Spanish so far.

Letting out another moody huff that ends in a yawn, he lays his head on my rounded tummy, hoping to feel the baby move. It's one of his and Millie's favorite things, especially when they're lying down for a nap or to watch a movie on the couch together.

When Kayson gives a little kick, Leo gently rubs over the bump and tiredly whispers, "Shh, hermano. Aqui, aqui." *Shh, brother. Here, here.*

He repeats my own words back to the baby as best he can. It sounds more like 'her-man-oh' and 'ack-ee, ack-ee.' But it brings happy tears to my eyes anyway.

Lifting my gaze, I make contact with Adrian's dark, warm eyes as he lifts Millie onto his shoulders so she can help paint the top of the wall. "I love you, pretty girl."

I open my mouth to return the sentiment, but Millie cuts in with a sweet, "Mommy is the prettiest, isn't she, daddy?"

"She sure is," Adrian agrees, placing a soft kiss on the shin he catches when she kicks it into the air, but his eyes stay on me. "You're a lucky little bunch to have her as your mom, you know that?"

Millie nods emphatically, messily swiping the paint brush along the wall as Adrian follows her path with a roller to even it out. I sit back, watching them paint and talk quietly, while running my hand down Leo's back. And I can't help but think that I'm the luckiest one in this room—though, Adrian would argue it's him.

Acknowledgements

If you've gotten this far in the book, the first person I want to thank is you, dear reader. I often joke that writing *Always Been Yours* felt like a fever dream—I had this idea, and there was no choice but to sit down and get it out of my head. It felt like the story practically wrote itself. That was not the case with *Between Us*. I pushed through multiple drafts and outlines, tears and frustrations, and that pesky imposter syndrome. Now, I can truthfully say it was worth it. I hope you loved Blake and Adrian as much as I do, and I hope you continue to visit Amada Beach with each book.

First, I want to throw so much praise to my sweet friend, Alaina. From the vet clinic to Blake's character, you truly inspired so much of this story. Thank you for educating me on the realities of working in the veterinary field, and pushing me to include those aspects in the story. Not only did it add so much to the book, but I learned so much through you while writing this. You are one of the greatest friends and biggest supporters I could ever ask for.

I could never forget my editor and friend, Christana. You sat through so many FaceTime calls with me when I just wasn't sure of what to do or where to go next. You encouraged me to push through the insecurities, and to rest when the burnout became too much. Thank you for all the time, and love, you pour into each one of these stories.

And my line editor and friend, Aaliyah. Your friendship is one of the best things to come from the craziness of self-publishing. I'm so grateful for your friendship, help, and support. It feels a lot less lonely having you to go on this journey with.

Thank you to all of my alpha, beta, and sensitivity readers. Hillary, Lyra, Melissa, Paola, Tabby, Jas, Adriana, and Kai. This book really took a village, and I am so fucking lucky to have all of you in mine. Your friendships mean so much to me, and are some of the absolute best things books have brought into my life. Thank you. I love you.

And to Lorah, for being such a dear friend and helping me with my character development. The natal and synastry charts started as a fun, random idea, but have grown into such an important part of my process. And I love having you be a part of this journey with me.

Kyle, you're my biggest cheerleader, fiercest believer, and my best friend. There are simultaneously too many words, and not enough, to express everything that you are to me. But I hope you know, always. Thank you, and I love you.

Finally, to my parents for always letting me believe that I could do anything I wanted. You've never made me feel like my dreams were out of reach, and it's that encouragement that has gotten me this far.

Until next time. <3

About the Author

Ashtyn Kiana is a Latina indie romance author whose stories feature flawed but endearing characters, hot and swoony relationships, female friendships, and blended families. Her corporate day job doesn't leave a lot of room for creativity, so she started writing her first novel as a way to express that side of herself. When she's not writing, she's probably walking her dogs, making candles, or picking up a new hobby.

Instagram: @ashtynkiana.author
TikTok: @ashtynkiana.author